This Bloody Country

A satire about the
United Kingdom of Great Britain
and Northern Ireland

Mark E. Wilson

www.intrepidwilson.com

First published in 2022 via Kindle Direct Publishing

Paperback ISBN 9798839006706
Hardback ISBN 9798839143081

To Joyce, our family, and all other influences.

Talent is what they say
you have after the novel
is published and favorably
reviewed. Beforehand what
you have is a tedious
delusion, a hobby like knitting.

- *from 'For the Young Who Want To'*
  by Marge Piercy

Chapter 1 – Sunday 1st May 2016

The front door to the flats was ajar again. It was entirely Ollie's friend Mayhew's fault. Another boozy night out and, in their rush to eat their recently purchased saveloys and chips, Ollie's Territorial Army buddies, a group of individuals not renowned for their patience and forethought, decided to kick the door open rather than wait to be let in. Everything had been 'kind of' repaired; new glass 'kind of' put in, an electric or magnetic dongle thingy to 'kind of' buzz it open, when it worked, and Mayhew's snapped fibula put in a cast so now he 'kind of' walked straight. After all, they were too impatient to realise that the door opened outwards. The hinges were still faulty and Mayhew – since promoted, by the way – got a lot of traction retelling the story of how he got his limp.

Through that communal entrance were the stairs, where Chelsea and I had once shared an awkward, post-pub snog before Ollie came into the picture. The faded, musty carpet could tell a hundred stories just like ours, could it talk. If it could talk, of course, the carpet would probably have a distinct, husky, cancerous voice, like Joe Cocker in a pool hall, if the fag burns and indistinct stains were anything to go by.

The flat itself, on the first floor, was, according to the investigating officer, an absolutely ideal target for thieves. Fortunately, the intruder only made off with a bike and a couple of old phones. Easy to carry, less likely to be noticed, and easy to sell, she'd said, without any hint of reassurance. I used the key, of course, although it would only have taken a moderate Van Damme-style front kick to lift the pine and MDF door off of its frame, which seemed to be precisely how the burglar had got in.

What were the chances of both of our doors being broken? Actually, in this part of town, high. Clicking it shut ('kind of') behind me, I dumped a carrier bag full of shopping on the kitchen counter and unpacked it. Tins of soup. Microwave noodles. Tea bags. Nothing to suggest a life of luxury. I couldn't help but notice Chelsea's cupboard, the door unable to close, with the range of opulent teas, the aromatic array of spices, and her fashionable, Belgian chocolates. That's what family money can buy you. Nothing like the more modest wages I collected from Scintilla.

"You don't know how lucky you've got it," my mother's voice would replay at times like this. "Your *Papá* and I came here with less than fifty pounds and we made a life for all of us. We had saved up every penny for so long that we thought, when we'd get here, there would be a welcoming party for us!" I used to comment sarcastically about that being enough money to buy a house back in the fifties which was met with a barrage of colourful language delivered in her mother tongue with all the grace of a JCB dumping gravel on a convertible. Apparently, she could make fun of their situation but not me.

I dumped a second carrier on the work surface, closely followed by my phone, wallet, and keys. The jingle must have given me away.

"That you, Frankie?" Chelsea had called an emergency flatmate meeting this evening so it made sense that she would tell Ollie first – and then be fashionably late for her own soiree.

"Yeah. Got supplies."

"Beers?"

"Yeah." Inevitably, it would be a boozy night. As I unpacked the carrier bags, I worried about Ollie; he would have too many drinks, as usual, and then start an argument about politics. In truth, he couldn't have cared less about ethics, elections, MPs, etc; he just did it because Chelsea cared and I got drawn into it. When we first moved in, the arguments got pretty angry but that was before I realised Ollie was only being controversial to get reactions from Chelsea and me. It didn't matter if it was electoral reform, funding for schools, or what day the bins went out. They'd end up rowing until both sides committed to a de-escalation of hostilities - or were physically separated because Chelsea would dramatically sigh and sulk away to their bedroom, eventually texting Ollie, who would still be sat in front of the TV, when she was ready to accept him into their bed. We were friends as well as flatmates but it probably seemed like a strange relationship to outsiders. The rowing and needling; I'm sure their make up sex made up for it all but because I would end up feeling compelled to intervene in the debate, I definitely felt like I was getting the short straw as there was no reward afterwards for me. I had nobody to make up with so, well, so there it is.

"You haven't got a clue!" Chelsea would bawl at him. "There are innocent children washing up on the beach… dead!"

"How do you expect anyone to police a border that's thousands of miles long?" Ollie knew just when to respond with facts and statistics – whether they were credible, relevant, or not – and when to throw in a dismissive comment that made him out to be an educated expert deigning to scrap in the slums with his intellectual inferiors. He wasn't though; not in the academic sense. He didn't want to go to Uni after college so he joined the army. 'School of Hard Knocks' he called it. I wonder how many of those were to the head?

"So the parents should be charged with manslaughter, right? We live in a democratic society so, if they want to live here, they should follow our rules. That, of course, means they get a roof over their heads in prison…" Chelsea used to be the first to take the bait.

"But that's not what we're saying… we're saying…"

"I know – you're telling me that Europe should just welcome as many people as possible…" He and I knew just where this was headed but it was like watching the opening scenes from an episode of Casualty. First up, a phone zombie on a zebra crossing texting 'B their L8r - love u'; then the camera takes you to the interior of the flashy sports car with the driver fiddling with the radio; then the guy on their phone; then back to the car, where he's still trying to find the right station; the car's still coming and you see the pedestrian just gazing into the LCD abyss take that fatal step off the kerb…

"No, no, I'm not saying that…"

"Okay, so you think there should be some way to count or limit refugee numbers? Or do you just think these people don't have to obey the law? I'm not clear."

"It's not black and white," she would contest. "You're simplifying everything!"

"Well simplify it for me, if I'm not smart enough to understand you academic types." The arguments would continue like that for over an hour. Hopefully, tonight would be different but, having lived together for eighteen months, that seemed unlikely. The clunk of the front door signalled Chelsea's arrival.

We had met at one of last year's Freshers' events. She approached me, of course – not to say that I'm self-centred enough to think I warrant an approach from an attractive stranger but I mean to say that she approached me because she's that type. You know, forward, confident, bordering on oblivious, innocent perhaps, but someone who's never been slapped in the face at 2am in a sticky-floored nightclub. Initially at least, I had thought she was interested in me beyond my hunky good looks and blistering intellect - sarcasm doesn't work so well when it's written, by the way, but that doesn't mean I won't be giving it a try. Her advance was to canvas support for one of her single-issue groups, the objective of which I can't quite remember, now I think about it. I closed the cupboard door on the last of my food, which needed to last the week, maybe longer.

"Chels?" came Ollie's voice from the bedroom.

"The one and only!" she replied with her characteristic upbeat demeanour. The three of us got busy getting comfortable; changing, washing her face, tying up her hair, and tidying up after Ollie in Chelsea's case. Slipping on some jogging bottoms and cracking open a beer in Ollie's. I, on the other hand, went into my bedroom before emerging in an old t-shirt, shorts, and flip flops a good half an hour later. I don't think they knew I noticed but whenever I spent more than five minutes away from them, I sensed the occasional weird look. Sure, I have secrets, don't we all, but I don't think it's normal to be so obsessed by what goes on behind someone's locked bedroom door. It does seem suspicious to me that they appear so concerned by it but don't have the compulsion to actually ask me, not that I would necessarily tell them of course. My personal life is personal.

Settled into our usual seats, Chelsea clinked her wine glass with a fingernail adorned with chipped purple varnish. Ollie rubbed a hand through his dirty blonde hair and made satisfied noises as he slurped back his first lager.

"I formally declare this House Board Meeting open." Everyone took a solemn drink, switching eye contact to one another whilst drinking to signal their deeply held respect for the process. "We are now quorate so, as Chair, I call this meeting to order." Ollie usually rolled his eyes, affectionately, at her excessive efforts at playful formality but strangely not tonight. He once commented that she needed a white wig, to which she said that was only for judges. He then suggested a black square of material would be more appropriate as she was boring him to death but she abstained from responding.

"Frankie, C's already told me what this is about."

"Yes – don't hurry me, Ollie – Frankie, the landlord called me and has told me that he's had to make some significant financial sacrifices, his words, of course, but now has no choice but to increase the monthly rent."

"How much by?"

"Thirty quid a week," she said, before pre-empting our responses. "Each."

"Fucking hell." I did not need this right now. "I've been paying down my debts with my money from Scintilla but this will only make it worse." My flatmates nervously drank some of their drinks. It wasn't out of solidarity.

"You can always get more shifts," recommended Ollie.

"Why not think about extending your overdraft?" endorsed Chelsea.

"I've picked up a couple of extra shifts but I'll need more." Chelsea looked at Ollie for another suggestion but he wordlessly urged her to say something. They could see I was annoyed and both of them knew that I didn't have the resources they did, with my parents no longer around. "I've still got to fit in studying around them too…"

"I can lend you some money, if you need it," offered Chelsea, eager to help. Or rather, eager to help by offering to put her parents' money at my disposal. She was sincere but, deep down, she knew that I'd never accept. I can't spend money that's not my own, it makes me feel sort of itchy, being indebted to someone else; a bad business brain, according to Ollie, but then he couldn't talk as most of the money he spent was Chelsea's anyway. I needed a moment to think so I drank my beer and got up to put the can in the recycling.

"Did he say what sacrifices he's made?" I ventured, over the breakfast bar.

"Pardon?"

"Did the landlord tell you what significant financial sacrifices he's had to make?" Chelsea didn't like to be questioned and, especially when it related to money, she often looked for a way to deflect any enquiries. I didn't like to stick my head above the parapet and ask these kinds of questions, but my back was against the wall when it came to money.

"No, not specifically. I didn't like to ask." She nibbled her bottom lip, child-like, and flicked the hair away from her forehead.

"Can we not tell him we can't afford it and see if he can bring it down a bit?" My suggestion was met with a bemused look from Chelsea and a poor imitation of consideration by Ollie. "I can get a few extra shifts this month, maybe not next month though, but I don't know what it will be like after that. How can I find the money before the Summer holidays?"

"Look, rents in Birmingham have been going up about 10% every year. Some of the lads at the Museum are paying nearly a grand a month. We've been lucky until now, so I think we just have to take it on the chin." You can afford to, I thought, knowing that Chelsea's family were unwittingly bank-rolling Ollie's lifestyle as much as their daughter's. "Property is still a good investment, don't let anyone tell you otherwise."

"I'm in no position to invest in anything…" I murmured.

"Ollie's right, but so's Frankie." Chelsea revelled in the role of adjudicator, attempting to moderate a pending dispute. She might make a good diplomat someday, mainly because she loved to talk so much. "Perhaps we should ask him to bring the rent down, maybe only increase it by twenty pounds a month."

"Each…" I added.

12

"After all, we are just poor students and it's not fair that the wealthy can increase their wealth off of the labours of the poor like us." Poor students whose rent is paid for by mummy and daddy and whose kitchen cupboard is too full to close.

"Chels, are you saying, you don't want to be wealthy? Do you think the wealthy need to make life easier for the rest of us?" As her face turned red, both Ollie and I knew that there was about to be another one of their 'debates', which would turn to an argument and then noisy, ungainly sex in the room next to mine. It wasn't clear which Ollie anticipated more – if he was even aware of the potential outcome. This engineered argument was just one of the ways in which Ollie didn't seem to be much of a friend but more of a catalyst for less than friendly moments.

I considered wrestling the topic of the discussion back to the rent and how we might argue against an increase but the two of them had already started their argument and Chelsea was reaching for the bottle of pinot noir, which was a bad sign.

Disappointed, I decided against getting another drink and opened the door to my bedroom, where I hoped to find seclusion, refuge, and neither of my flatmates.

Chapter 2 – Tuesday 3rd May 2016

At the bar, with one brogue indifferently laid upon the brass footrest, stood an athletic young man with the body language of a regular. Unaware that I was watching him, he beamed at the staff, waiting for his turn. The black-shirted servers moved methodically, separated from the customers by an old, thick, oak counter, topped with beer towels, puddles of spilt liquids, and an array of menus, containing promotional offers and reminders to book tables for Christmas and New Year. The literature swept to one side by a thick-knuckled paw, the man waited as best he could. The subtle tap of the corner of his card on the counter was his only tell.

"'Scuse me," muttered the builder, or darts players, or union rep at the sprockets factory, whatever he was; all descriptions that darted, I assumed, prejudiciously through Ollie Driver's mind whilst he tapped a little faster. Drips of beer slopped from the lugged pint glasses onto the floor and the toe of his well-polished shoe. Ollie grimaced.

"No drama," he sneered and squirmed his body so he was squared up against the bar. He put both feet on the brass roll, raising his height up to, in his belief, increase his chances of being served ahead of his position in the barmaid's pecking order. He liked that barmaid at The Dog especially; he didn't have to tell me for me to know - I was a single guy too, I understood the body language of attraction. Not real infatuation, but the scent of an idea that someone might want to sleep with you because of their job, or their tattoos, or dyed-hair, or whatever it was that triggered an impression in us both that a member of the opposite sex might be readily persuaded to abandon all of their preconceptions or

14

standards for the opportunity for an inevitably
disappointing and brief tumble in the broom closet.
Chelsea, Ollie's girlfriend, idly scrolled on her phone.

The barmaid had a sweet, pale complexion with
a brunette bob that framed her face. That was the first
thing I had noticed before her slender waist and legs but
now Ollie wanted to know all of her. She scooped up two
pint glasses and tugged at the tall, white, ale pump.
Sudden spurts of warm beer filled the first glass but she
reset the arm and pulled until she was finished and rapidly
moved on to the next one. Another satisfied customer and
yet Ollie still fantasised of being served by her.

Two platters of sizzling gammon – one with a
fried egg on top, the other with a glistening pineapple ring
– made their way to table 66, conveyed expertly by a red-
cheeked waitress; her toothy smile there to attract tips
rather than express her joy at her current employer's
generosity. An artless chime from the fruit machine,
followed by the rhythmic tumble of coins, turned heads
throughout the pub. The clattering of dropped dishes from
the kitchen was met with an ironic but good-natured cheer
from those in earshot.

The Dog, or more formally, The Dog's Dinner,
had once been a fire station run by the West Midlands
Fire service but, now, it was a far more profitable
building for Aston Brewery, a subsidiary of a larger,
foreign, conglomerated, brewing corporation. They
retained the high-beamed ceilings and exposed red
brickwork. Sirens, bells, buckets, and other alarms were
now part of the intentionally eclectic decoration, with the
addition of sepia-tinted photographs of fire crews posing
in front of their engines or station houses, poised to
respond to the next emergency. There was no evidence
that any of these images were, in fact, of the brigade that

once sped from the three-storeyed, terraced building that now drew people in rather than shot them out. The appropriation of the building's original purpose had been so mangled over time that The Dog's signage now included an illustrated Dalmatian, a breed comprehensively not associated with British fire fighters. Rumour had it that the original fireman's pole had been cut in two and sold to Bottoms Up and Cheetahs in the Chinese Quarter. Not that either of us had made it our mission to visit those establishments just to check the veracity of the claim, of course; we just went to ogle the girls and spend £7 on flat lager.

"You next, mate?" The grizzled landlord glared through Ollie.

Ollie had sarcastically nicknamed the pub The Dog's Bollocks when it reopened after the refurbishment but, a year on, only he still called it that. The sardonic intent seemed undermined by the frequency of which he visited it. It was hard for me to be too mocking when I was often closely in tow.

"Yeah, cheers. One pint of cider, one pint of lager, and a gin and tonic, please. No straw." The landlord nodded and stomped away. Either side of Ollie, more punters squeezed in, like racehorses in the traps, shouldering arms onto the bar, wallets, cards, or neatly folded notes extended, signalling their desperate desire for urgent service. The larger notes, the AmEx black cards, the arms adorned with the shinier watches, seemed to attract the speediest response. Ollie caught his reflection in the beautifully etched mirror that ran along the length of the bar, behind the rows of bottles with gaily coloured labels that were always out of reach. Giving himself a knowing pout, he arched an eyebrow, turned faux-sexily, running through his limited emotional range before noticing Chelsea and I, sat several feet behind him, laughing and shaking our heads.

Spinning around to stare straight at me, he gave it the full Zoolander pose. We both laughed, I shook my head, and Ollie shrugged. Whilst he waited, I replayed the conversation that preceded his bar-based flirtation.

"What were you saying before?"

I drank a thoughtful gulp and slid a beermat under my glass. Ollie sat back, the tension leaving his body.

"I don't really want to dwell on it, you know."

"You've started now."

"You're the one who convinced me I should get a job so who started what now? I just need to earn a bit more cash, don't I? I've been told, informally of course, that I've passed my probation."

"Nice one. You happy about that?" We gulped our drinks again, in harmony. The enchanting smell of chips mingled with the raised, jovial voices all around them.

"Yeah, I suppose. It's not exactly what I want to do with my life. I'm not the most passionate about coffee." I don't mind admitting that I stated the fact with some pride to have been offered a position after one interview but, back then, I was still so indecisive. Scintilla's was a short walk from The Dog's Dinner. It was a popular but over-priced coffee shop, sited on the corner of Lower Temple Street and New Street – a stone's throw from the Museum and Art Gallery.

"Decent. Do you get a pay rise?"

"Yeah, I guess," I sipped my drink, this time pausing without letting Ollie back into the conversation yet. He had a habit of turning any conversation quickly back to him, so I had learned how to manage him at times and I really wanted to brag about my new source of much-needed income. "£6.70 an hour now. Plus, I'll get about fifteen to twenty hours a week now, so I can just about fit it around lectures. But, yeah, you know, it's okay pay."

"Not bad. You can buy the next round then!" Ollie crossed his arms and grinned. "Anyway, we can both be working men of the world together. I finally got my DAOR paperwork and my IPPD training finished and I get officially discharged at the end of the week. Now I'm going to be a civvie, I needed a job and one of the lads in the Company put me in touch with a security firm and they have a position for me at the museum."

It's not really important to my story that I explain what all that means because it only affected Ollie in passing but it might make some sense to elucidate because of how important Ollie's training would be in the incident which resulted in my slide into criminality.

Ollie was in the Army but, after his discharge, joined the Territorial Army – the TA – and was a 'weekend warrior'. That meant he didn't actually get to do anything that the real army should do, like fighting jihadis or distributing aid to victims of natural disasters, but he did still get to play with machine guns and drive armoured vehicles for a few hours every Saturday. Like anyone indoctrinated into their hobby, the use of acronyms became a bad habit that intentionally alienated the uninitiated from those who made their passion part of their identity. DAOR was shorthand for his discharge papers. I had no idea what IPPD meant and I knew, if asked, Ollie would take the conversation down a route I was really not all that interested in.

"Doing what?" I replied, skipping over the jargon, used to Ollie's assumptions about how much 'normal' people – i.e. people other than me – knew about the military.

"Security guard. I'll be standing around watching a load of dusty old crap. How hard can it be?"

"Anything valuable?"

"In Birmingham? Are you mad?" Both of us laughed, "Come on, your round."

"Hi!" chirped a familiar voice.

"Hi!" replied Ollie as I stood up.

"No need to get up on my account, *señor*," Chelsea said. "I thought you were just having a swift half?" Chelsea often made these poor attempts at internationalism and leaned in for a hug. She pecked me on either cheek, not in the half-committed, desperate celebrity way but a clumsier, politer manner, as if we had once been close but were estranged for too long a time to remain physically confident with one another. I obliged, of course, but I did not return the attempt at overly affectionate bonding, although I was appreciative of her effort.

19

"Sorry, babe," said Ollie, looming between us. He got the full treatment; a bear-crusher embrace followed by a forceful, grateful jam together of lips.

Ollie pulled up a chair from another table. He wordlessly gave the neighbouring table dwellers an exaggerated side-nod towards the chair with a textbook double-lift of the eyebrows, placing a hand on the back of the seat. In reply, the self-elected 'alpha' of the group – the first to respond, appointing himself to the role since he was not mid-anecdote or sipping his drink when Ollie approached – made eye contact, waved an upturned palm at the article in question, whilst making an unperturbed shrug-pout expression. A well-practised exchange duplicated across the nation every evening, uniting drinkers of all abilities and experiences and definitely something we could expect to see as part of a BBC Two documentary voiced by David Attenborough or Stephen Fry.

"I was just getting a round in, actually. Gin and tonic, C?"

"*Si, gracias, con limon, sin…* um... straw thanks." I strode off to the bar, leaving them to their own conversation, and soon returned with the order, without too much fuss.

"Frankie was just telling me the good news, weren't you?" said Ollie, once I had sat back down.

"Yes, but Ollie's got good news too."

"Well, what's your good news, Ollie?" asked Chelsea.

"Ah, no, let him say his first. I'll tell you mine after." Waiting his customary pause, Ollie saw off the dregs in his glass before starting the fresh one. A conversational fisherman baiting his line.

"Well..?"

"I've passed my probation at Scintilla. Should pick up a few more shifts too, so the rent increase should be covered," I proclaimed.

"And me too!" interjected Ollie. "I'm working security at the museum. I start next week."

"That's amazing, darling." Chelsea beamed. "And what about you, Francesco?"

"They've offered to train me up to be a fully qualified barista now and I can start my training next Saturday. The pay should go up and they'll let me fit shifts around lectures, so seems pretty good, but I'm not sure, I could do with some advice..."

"And I'll be on just over a tenner an hour. Not much to do, to be honest but mope about and chase off the rough sleepers, I reckon."

"*Muy buena,* you two! Sounds ideal – but you know Scintilla sells products with palm oil in, right? We all really have to do something about that sort of thing, don't we?" Ollie thumped down his half-finished lager and rolled his eyes melodramatically.

"Here we go again... wasn't it dripping water taps or non-Free Trade coffee beans or ground-up horsemeat in the sandwiches last week?" He leaned over the table, looking for support, staring at both Chelsea and

I in turn, his jaw widened under tension as if expecting to swallow up any of our objections. Chelsea sighed, mocking Ollie's attempt to bait her.

"Each one of which you know are valid issues we should be justifiably concerned by. There's a protest planned outside of Scintilla for next week anyway, so Francesco might want to show his solidarity for our case by speaking to the manager."

"Let's see," I muttered democratically before raising my glass to prevent any need for further elaboration. I've never been one for the relentless boozing that happens throughout Britain but it seems like the only way people know how to socialise – and, in any case, my flatmates made up for any shortfalls on my part in the average per capita alcohol consumption. At that thought, I noticed that Ollie had already seen off his drink and Chelsea was half through hers whilst I was still cradling mine.

"What're you having next?"

"I don't mind. Anything." As I said it, I regretted it, half anticipating a tequila shot or something highly flammable that might have been designed to clean paintbrushes. That came from experience not imagination.

"You always say that. Frankie, you have got to be more decisive. If you can't make a choice for yourself, I will. Lager it is."

"Here you go mate," interrupted the barman. Three glasses, two full to the brim, the other with two plastic straws bobbing to the liquid motion, almost attempting an escape from their confines, landed in front of Ollie. He turned back. His gaze was held by the condensation gliding down the outside of the lager, the light playing teasingly through the golden memory. The promise of its consumption was loaded with uncalled for honesty and the appropriate apologies, with playfulness, with lust turned to action, and with so much more than the simple four disparate ingredients united by the ambitions of some vast brewing organisation and transported to the heart of the city, where men like Ollie and Frankie can drink as many as they desire – or can afford – until that promise of lightness and freedom was fulfilled or denied.

"Mate." Firmer now. The landlord was not one who spoke excessively. Perhaps he slept a dreamless sleep and lived without unfulfilled ambitions, Ollie thought.

"Card okay?"

"Just a sec." The intimate customers wriggled into position at the bar, once they saw Ollie was paying. Just a little further, they willed. Their eyes followed the all of the servers at once, hoping they would look their way, to be ensnared by their desperate facial acrobatics.

The landlord passed the card reader to Ollie, who looked up at the proprietor's unflinching face. They'd be served in *his* good time, he thought. Ollie took the machine in one hand, making a half turn to conceal his PIN. With a disdainful snort, the landlord rolled his eyes and turned to take another shouted order, two or three people further down the bar. Arms extended onto – but never over – the wooden barrier between thirsty hope and joy-dispensing service. They could see the finish line.

Ollie's black library card slid effortlessly between the base of the card reader and his palm. His right thumb mimed the oft practised sequence as he leant one elbow nonchalantly on the bar and turned. All it took was a little manoeuvre, the faintest adjustment, and the credit card waved like a hitchhiker's thumb by Ollie's expectant and distracted fellow customer registered the transaction. A quick movement and a simple ''Scuse, mate' as he held out the scanner and nobody was any the wiser.

The library card, long since expired, slid back into his pocket and with a well-rehearsed line running through his head, should he ever get caught, Ollie scooped up his drinks and strode to the table where we were sat, Chelsea scrolling through her timeline and me, pretending to do the same as I attempted to hide my surprise, having seen his subterfuge played out so brazenly. I hardly knew what to say.

"That was quick," I said, looking up from the blank screen of my phone.

"I know a few tricks," Ollie retorted, clinking his lager on the edge of my unexpected and revolting cider. It seemed like a typical night in The Dog, but I couldn't have known how things would quickly unravel.

Chapter 3 – Saturday 21st May 2016

"The second agenda item is cashing up," Freya said whilst adjusting her glasses, to show she was being serious. "It's down again for the second time in a week. This time by £19.80. It's more frustrating because this is the third briefing this quarter I've had to speak about it. Please be accurate as any further discrepancies will result in sterner measures."

The staff shuffled awkwardly, all and none accepting responsibility. Huddled around the communal table, the six assembled employees were so close together, it was impossible to maintain eye contact for too long.

"My penultimate item is to congratulate Francesco on passing his probation period. It's been great to have you on board and to see how you've developed so quickly. So, I finally have your new uniform here." Freya rustled around under her black plastic chair and pulled out a clear bag containing two new tops. Having impressed Freya, and the shift managers, I could exchange my khaki-coloured t-shirts, which gave away the fact that I was just a trainee, for chocolate brown polo shirts. The difference between the two tones seemed to me to be barely noticeable. Other than a short-lived sense of personal accomplishment for me, I didn't think it truly mattered to anyone else what kind of shirt I wore – least of all, the customers. They just saw me as another faceless, nameless staff member; and I preferred it that way, to be honest. Drawing attention to myself was not something I liked to do; keeping my head down and getting on with it was my *modus operandi*, my motto, and it served me well at Scintilla, it seemed. Even with Ollie and Chelsea, I might share a flat and the odd night at the pub, but I didn't share much else.

"Thanks Freya." She handed them over with a handshake and the ceremony was followed by a modest, self-conscious round of applause. A ripple of politeness without the sense of triumph or envy that might come with a genuine accomplishment.

"Lastly, we have been asked by Head Office to be the pilot branch, sorry, 'commune', for a new cultural engagement initiative." Lucy beamed with anticipation and Rob theatrically slumped into his chair. I was still comparatively new but I got the impression that not everybody was enamoured with Head Office's love of new initiatives and acronyms; they recently got rid of sales-based targets and replaced them with Meaningful Feedback Stories. There were no more secret shoppers but new Knowledge Valuation Directors, who would still just show up unannounced to collect information from the store and staff surreptitiously. Even the change from calling it a store or a branch to a 'commune'; as if the people working there were somehow a ready-made society, striving to better each other's lives. I kept my opinions to myself but even I couldn't help smirking at this method of trying to soften the reality of corporate life for us, the delicately sensitive employees. In fact, most of us just worked there to make some extra cash – even if we were on Service Opportunity Entitlements, no longer called zero-hour contracts.

"As you will know, Birmingham is a very cosmopolitan city and we get lots of customers from around the world, many of them even tourists." Everybody nodded in agreement. After all, some of the customers from around the world ended up working here. "To help customers who don't always have the best grasp

26

of English, we're going to wear these yellow badges."
She rooted around in her backpack again and revealed a
pair of rectangular margarine-coloured name badges, to
demonstrate what our own badges would look like. "Your
name will go here," she pointed, "and below will be a
series of cute little flags. They will tell customers which
languages you speak or where you originate from."

"Is there going to be an English flag? Some of
the dickheads we get from round here need help speaking
their own language." Rob was trying to be funny, again,
but it fell on deaf ears.

"I'll have a little Swedish flag but you can
choose what you have. I'll give you each two badges and,
if you can fill out this slip, we can order up the right flags
for you all." Freya handed out the badges and slips. Rob
jokingly bit the corner of his first badge. Lucy pulled out
a pen and began eagerly and neatly completing her form.
The rest began filling in their forms or storing away the
badges in pockets or bags.

"Freya, what if you don't have another
language?" I asked.

"You speak Spanish, don't you? We could do
with a Spanish speaker."

"Oh, right." I hadn't spoken Spanish for a few
years now, only perhaps to Chelsea to humour her
appalling efforts at being worldly, before that it had been
over the phone to my parents, when they were able to
talk. "My mum taught me when I was a kid but we mostly
spoke English at home. By the time I went to school,
that's all I really spoke."

"What about at school?"

"In Selly Oak?"

"Didn't you put on your resumé that you got a Spanish GCSE?"

"I didn't have to study for it though. I used to be able to pass for a native speaker, so I just did the exam in year 10. I've forgotten most of it now."

"That's good enough! Put down 'Spanish' under 'Languages' and, where it says 'Heritage', put Venezuela."

"Val Verde."

"Sorry, of course, Val Verde." It was a common mistake and not one I usually troubled to correct.

"But I was born at St. Andrew's Hospital – I've only been to Escalón once. I don't really know it…"

"That's okay. Listen," Freya moved closer. "I'm putting down Norway even though I've only had a stopover in Oslo once and did a night class in Norwegian for a couple of weeks. Most of the Head Office don't know the difference between Sweden and Norway anyway. They probably couldn't differentiate a macchiato from a madeleine so I wouldn't stress if I were you." She smiled. Her chestnut brown hair slid across her forehead and she removed it with a flick of her neck. "I think you've got a future here. If you want to get a foot on the ladder in this company, sometimes you have to jump through some hoops." The mixed metaphor clanged like a piano falling down a lift shaft, but I did what I was told.

Slips were slid back to Freya and, when she had them all, she cleared her throat to conclude the meeting, or Service Team Briefing as it was now defined.

"Just before we all go, I forgot to mention one more important thing. Now that those noisy protesters in the square have dispersed, I can tell you that the Democracy Coffee CEO is going to be visiting us very soon. He wants to see how the new initiatives are being implemented by staff and received by customers. Please make sure you are wearing your brown shirts and yellow badges; you'll get new ones when the decals have been attached. There will be extra shifts for that day so check the whiteboard on Sunday. Okay, that's everything. Thank you everyone."

With the meeting concluded, most of those in attendance would be going home or off to another job where, perhaps, they would have to go through just another meeting like the one they had just sat through. Lucy had lectures, I think. Rob was off to the Amazon fulfilment centre for a shift there. Others across the city. For me, it was the end of the meeting but the start of my shift.

"Frankie," Lucy asked, she touched my arm too, to grab my attention, which was a bit uncomfortable as I didn't know her that well and had certainly not developed the kind of professional relationship where we were accustomed to physical contact. "Do you want any more hours this week?"

"Um, okay, sure."

"Only I've got exams coming up." She continued. "PPE. Politics. I'm well into my third year now so they're making us sit some mid-semester mocks all next week. You're on the same course, aren't you?"

"No, I'm doing Philosophy. It's interesting, I suppose. Second year." Considering the size of the University it was not unusual not to have met her there and, as we had only met a fortnight ago, it was hardly surprising that she didn't remember what I was studying. The thought that she didn't know me made this conversation a little more palatable.

"Maybe I can give you some pointers for next year?"

"Sure, yeah, thanks." I doubted either of us would follow through.

"What do you think about the visit from the big cheese?" She simpered.

"Huh?"

"I think it's going to be so cool! You'll get to be in the same space as Noah Wright. *The* Noah Wright! What an opportunity. He's so inspirational, isn't he?" Lucy was often overly passionate, from my limited experience working alongside her but, when it came to business, economics, or other subjects like these, all of which I found it difficult to hold a conversation about, she found a way to be even more enthusiastic. Good for her.

All of the stories Dad had told me about life back in his home country made me wary of politicians – and businessmen – and those who venerated them. There had been tales of simple protests, like the ones Chelsea had attended in Victoria Square. These often included some kind of march, which frequently ended up passing right outside Scintilla, but in my father's stories, these had quickly escalated because one group preferred one minor thing over another group's equally minor thing. An inconsiderate word. An incensed retort. A controlled push. A wild haymaker. A gas canister. A rubber bullet. An unquenchable riot. Hundreds arrested; a handful vanished. All spiralling away from the original objective of an easier life, a few hours less, or a few dollars more.

Despite Chelsea begging me, I've managed to keep away from whatever the latest issue was that she might have hitched her wagon to and I decided against talking to Freya about Fair Trade coffee. It all seemed a little desperate, somehow needy, as though fighting for those campaigns validated a directionless period in a life or filled an existence devoid of other activity. I didn't want to get involved and I didn't want to get into a conflict with Chelsea over it, so I just told her that I'd spoken to 'management' and they would think about it. I was sure she would move on to another cause the week after anyway.

As for businessmen, like Wright, well, Dad would tell me they were the worst of all. The people were taxed to pay for the police and police simply protected private property. If there was a burglary, it wasn't a crime against a person but a crime against wealth. If there was arson, it wasn't a family who had been burned, it was a building or a business. And even murder, he railed, was only a crime because the Government couldn't afford to lose another taxpayer. And when the costs of living increased for everyone, tax breaks helped businessmen pay their shareholders or buy off politicians with lobbyists. He was glad to have come to Britain where that kind of exploitation didn't happen.

31

"Yeah, definitely. Inspirational." I struggled to picture the Democracy Coffee CEO in my mind's eye. All that formed were red-framed magazine covers with faceless, suited men or television interviews with glassy-surfaced boardrooms where the voice was distant and impersonal and the face pixelated into a thousand other, similar faces that had performed countless interviews on countless channels for all time. I thought then that I should really pay more attention if the Democracy Coffee CEO was actually visiting our 'commune' – I'd hate to be the one person who asked the customer's order and name to write on their cup when it turned out to be Noah Wright. The oh-so polite laughter from that blurry-faced, grey-suited human shape, the click of cameras through the trailing media circus. Inevitably followed by the hand on the shoulder selfie by the man – was he a man? – himself before a curt whisper to Freya on the way out through the door, and an insincere thumbs up to the crowded, adoring staff, paired with his manager's downward glance. The P45 would be in my courier bag before the CEO's limousine had disappeared. Then I would have to move out of the flat because I couldn't pay the bills. Then I would have to drop out of university. Then I would become a homeless drifter, forced to selling half-finished cigarettes from the pavement to afford half a meal a day… Yeah, that's not what I want to be doing with my life, not that the alternative is all that clear.

But then I must know who the CEO would be because he'd be the one followed by the personal assistant, PR people, and press pack. So, after all my worrying, I've probably got nothing to worry about with this visit. My father's lyrical voice and gripping tales of crushed rebellions, evil dictators, drug barons, spirited freedom fighters, ruthless guerrillas, and vindictive policemen faded – to be recalled later – and the worry about remaining in this job and the awful, imaginary error which would bring about my ultimate downfall faded too.

Lucy had left. Rob was already attempting to start his motorcycle outside of the store window, and Freya was taking charge of the routine of opening up for customers – or was it 'Comrades' now, no, that was the new word for colleagues.

I took a moment to appreciate the sweetest time of the day, the most peaceful and under-valued moments before we opened for business. When the floor, tables, and all are the cleanest they would be for another twenty-four hours. The paper cups, china mugs, cutlery, cakes, and every object for consumption was in its proper place. The chalk signs seemed sharper and fresher viewed without the heat of human bodies and steam gushing from the huge gleaming, Spazzatura coffee maker. All seemed to be as it should be. Napkins were folded perfectly and crisply beneath a ripe muffin, bronzed and glistening. Taking a deep breath, as if steeling myself for an adventure, I then exhaled with a sense of personal satisfaction before joining with Freya to prepare to undo all of our hard work.

Chapter 4 – Tuesday 24th May (30 days to go)

As I was only a child and had been spared the trauma by being born in the UK, I had no memory of the soldiers beating on the front door of our family home. Terrified, I listened as my father would explain to me what had taken place and I tried to comprehend the emotions and sensations which his father never quite got around to mentioning. I couldn't say for sure if those shared memories had any effect on me at all.

"You'll never have to go through what we went through," he pledged. "You will have a simpler, easier life here now. We will see to that."

Each time I heard these legends, I would pull my knees close to my chest and scooch forward a little, excited but afraid, as Dad would recount so vividly what life had been like for them. Had I pushed the stories so deep into my psyche that the recollections were now no longer stored?

Listening ever more intently for some hint at my father's bravery or compassion, I used to wonder how my parents could possibly ensure my life would be any better than theirs when they had been unable to prevent their living room from being turned upside down. Back then, on the shattered glass carpet and amidst the inside out cushions, it must have seemed as if their entire lives were being roughly broken and left by the side of the road, not just their possessions. Father always painted a graphic picture of what happened, even though I knew they had been subject to worse physical punishment than he might have included in his family-friendly accounts.

In the plain yellow kitchen with cream tiles, some featuring sketches of flowers I did not recognise at the time, a sea of symmetry above the level, long work surface at which they sat, the destination he described seemed alien at times. My world was the four walls around us. The peaceful, possibly mundane, life of a Birmingham schoolboy jarred with the heroic legends that my parents portrayed of their resistance to a most cruel and iron-handed government. A part of me admired, and would always admire, their dynamism and passion, but another, louder, more persuasive, voice within my conscience pleaded for drab, colourless, normality, which I felt pervaded the lives of my classmates, whose stories of derring-do were often related to staying out after dark or riding their BMXs the wrong way up the road to town.

"Oh, do stop boring him" Mum would say, in jest, of course, on most occasions.

"Some people say I am quite the storyteller, you know." That would burst the magical balloon that has transported us back to the homeland and tossed us back into the here and now – or there and then, I suppose. Calmness. In vivid contrast to the tales of passion, violence, revolt, and momentarily grasped victories that, like in all tragedies, would be tugged a finger's grip out of reach by an unseen hand. Mainly, I looked forward to our next adventure in that present that now I recalled – a train journey to some unusually named, parochial village, preceded by Middle, Lesser, or Upper, and an afternoon of strolling down streets sparsely populated but always welcoming. Those were the memories I cherish the most, the memories we had both truly lived through.

Unlike the stories Dad told. For instance, I remember sitting on the seafront at Eastbourne, the wind blowing hard and straight, while I peeked from beneath a plastic, blue hood to tentatively lick the only ice cream the tea shop had sold that day. That memory was so powerful and so cherished because it was mine. And ours, all at once. And it was my memory where me and my parents were safe. Wet, cold, and huddled under a wooden bus shelter as two scoops of vanilla melted onto my lap but safe, nonetheless.

"Okay, story time is over for another day." As certain as that ice cream would be melted by the rain, Dad would clap his thick hands together, pick me up, give me a big squeeze, plant me standing on the ground again, give his wife a kiss, and step out of the back door for a smoke. Wondrous chromatic, ribbon-like fumes of tobacco and clouds of his hot breath entranced me – it was like magic to me, conceiving memories now of the trains, billowing steam from their chimneys and launching us, headlong, at moderate speed, to our next adventure – until I was old enough to know what was happening inside him. I wondered if he had finally quit, as he had promised. I appreciated that moment again much later, just as I savoured the idea of the coldness of the wet wind on my cheeks and the stories in my memory more now than the time they were first felt. Time flies and I always worried that I could not hold tightly to these moments forever. I always fancied the idea of recording them in some way, some written record of his stories – and mine, I suppose – so that others might cherish them, as I did. I worried a little more each time my mind wandered back to them that that might be the last time that thought was remembered. Was that to be his legacy? Stories eventually forgotten by an old and frail son? I had supposed I should write them down but I always worried that I didn't have the ability to properly convey the feelings they aroused in me through just words...

My recollections were interrupted by an unexpected and authoritative whump against the fragile door to the flat. It had to be Ollie, I assumed; that idiot must have forgotten his keys again. Carefully, I rose from my swivel chair and, precariously and methodically, placed delicate items on top of the chest of drawers, then gymnastically squeezed myself to the doorway, turned the handle silently, and extended a foot into the living room, with my body cautiously following just behind. Just across the lounge and behind the door frame, I presumed, would be a sheepish looking flatmate back from working at the museum with a self-deprecating, idiotic expression. Because he can't be trusted or given responsibility, because he's careless, because he's a clown, I mentally moaned. He will ruin everything in his life, and Chelsea's, and mine. But he's a good friend so what am I supposed to do? Because he gives me space and because he thinks about me, at times, I'd just give him his keys and not berate him like I should. Whump. Whump. Whump.

"I'm coming," People didn't have to be so impatient; we have plenty of time. The corridor outside sounded ready to explode; I noticed an energy, a feeling, that something was not right. It was as if there was a pressure building from beyond that rickety door that threatened to finally destroy the belligerently, resistant hinge apart, exposing the flat to the elements.

"We're from the Home Office. We'd like to talk to you. Can you open the door, please."

I froze. The created vision of forced entry crisply manifested. The crunch of locks bursting forward, hinges shrieking. Splintered wood reflected on shards of glass. A feminine gasp joined with a whirling summer dress.

Hypermasculine green uniforms waving second-hand rifles. Shouted orders that invited no questions.

All constructed memories from his father's experiences but not mine.

"Just a sec," There was a knack to opening the door from the inside, so I put my hip under the handle, turned the latch and propped open the front door with little effort. The busted door swung inwards pitifully, like a piss-soaked drunk, embarrassed and apologetic. Stranger looking than I expected were two individuals – one a thickset cube of a man with a bland, inattentive expression, the other a woman with a well-trained, enquiring face, her eyes close together like a bird of prey, and bereft of the make-up necessary to give her a façade of warmth, with her warrant card extended – looking like reluctant models from a long out-of-date catalogue. The impression of what a normal person *should* look like. All washed-out colours and blurred edges. Fastest to react, the woman stepped narrowly inside the threshold, her flat shoe over the redundant draught excluder in an instant.

"Goode," she said. "Officer Goode. This is my colleague, Officer Kean." No ice breakers or pleasantries. "We were wondering when you might be home. We popped over just the other day, didn't we." Kean nodded.

"It was right cold, bitterly cold day, most unseasonable." Was this what passed for the pleasantries – a typical moan about the weather? Typically British but their demeanour had none of the stereotypical over-politeness or deference. The recollection of my father's experiences gushed into view all at once. "Tough doing our job, sir." Kean noted. "Crying out for a bit of warmth when we're walking the streets, sir." With that, Kean stepped forward, ostensibly to engage in conversation but his movement made Goode move forward and her move forward made me step back, which meant that both of them could now walk into the flat. There wasn't an invitation and there wasn't a demand; it just, sort of, happened.

"Right you are, Officer," asserted Goode. I recognised the English mannerism of not simply asking for what you want outright but hinting and hoping.

"Sorry, what's this about?"

"Just a house call, sir, hoping you can help us with some enquiries." I hoped they couldn't see the dread rising. I wracked my brain to think of something to say, something to do, something that might conceal my unease and buy me some space to consider what was going on.

"Sure, sure. Could I get you a cup of coffee?"

"Smashing, sir. That would be lovely."

"We won't take up much of your time," Goode assured. "Have you ever had a meeting with the Home Office before?"

"Of course not," I regretted saying that as I was sure it made me seem instinctively defensive. Maybe that was all they might need to be suspicious of me, but for what, I couldn't imagine. "I mean, why would I?" The two agents sat themselves beside one another on the living room sofa while I went to the kitchen, watching them as closely as I could, without seeming like I was nervous of them or, worse, suspicious of them. They did say it wouldn't take up much of my time, but then they did appear to be making themselves pretty comfortable on the sofa.

"We had a tip that there might be a foreign national dwelling illegally in these premises, sir." To make matters worse, I'd forgotten to buy any instant coffee.

"Tea alright?"

"Thank you, sir. White with two sugars for me."

"Same." Goode watched me intently, I knew they must be analysing my every move. Bag in first? Good. Milk in before the kettle has boiled? Make a note of that, officer. If I'd left the teabag in when I added the milk, the zip ties would have been round my wrists and ankles before you could say Darjeeling.

"Yes, there's evidence to suggest that a non-British national has been dwelling in these premises nearly beyond the terms of their visa and so we are required to commence our investigation into the said national. Would you be the sole occupant of the residence?" I jumped as she turned her tone from matter-of-fact to a question directed at me; this seemed to be scripted and, therefore, well prepared.

"No, no, there's three of us here." I spooned the sugar into the mugs and a little tumbled onto the work surface. The spoon clattered loudly against the ceramic. "Sorry, but what is this all about? I'm really not following you."

"You are..." Goode examined her notepad. "Francesco Cualquiera, correct?" I froze. Her pronunciation was better than Chelsea's. They knew my name. How? I put the mugs down noisily on the coffee table but remained standing.

"Er, yeah."

"You are *the* Francesco Cualquiera, currently enrolled at Birmingham University, currently studying Philosophy." I couldn't tell if it was a question or a statement but I could tell by the way she said 'philosophy' that she would not have been impressed if I had added that I had hopes to complete the course with a first with honours.

"Yes..." Sitting now felt like the right thing to do, as if I was being encouraged, no, pressured into sitting by nothing more than body language and hundreds of years of social evolution, so I sat facing them both on Ollie's comfy chair. After all, there was nowhere else to sit. As soon as I sat, the startling urge to stand up again increased but it was too late, I'd made my choice now and to change position again might seem weird, suspicious even, in their eyes.

"Well, that being confirmed, sir," Kean took up the lead now. "Your student visa is going to expire in exactly four weeks and we have no record of you having submitted an application for indefinite leave to remain or an extension of said visa." I stared blankly at both of them as they sipped their coffee in punctuating harmony.

"I'm sorry, you're going to have to say that again." He repeated himself verbatim. I stared back at them both with little clue as to what I was expected to say. I led with the truth.

"I'm from Birmingham. I was born in Druids Heath."

"That's not the information we have on record." If ever there was a phrase to kill a conversation dead, that

41

was it. The three of us simply sat – the officers sipped their beverages again, in unison – and paused, anticipating that the other might speak first. It felt longer than it must have truly lasted. A nascent, heavy waiting. A surfer watching the breakers build, paddling softly out from shore, before the realisation that it wasn't a normal curl to ride but a tsunami, created to destroy. Almost inevitably, it was me who felt most compelled to breach the silence.

"I went to school at The Oaks... Do you know it..?" My interviewers remained silent. They waited, hoping I'd say more. Something incriminating to make their lives easier. I hoped they'd just go away. That lengthy pause made me more anxious. Of course they don't know it, why would you say something so stupid.

"Yes, we can see that."

"Then I must not need a student visa or any kind of visa..."

"Not according to our records."

The intransigence. The pure bloody-mindedness. It was these things I dreaded most from his father's stories. Not the physicality or brutality. Bullies got tired and there is always a way to fight back, to be tougher or smarter. It was the relentless, plodding, stubbornness to never compromise or question that scared me. It's hard to resist monotony.

I trusted my intellect, what there is of it. I couldn't resist them but I could make them doubt the authenticity of their information, perhaps. I had to think philosophically and try to challenge their arguments. The idea emboldened me.

"What records? You don't even know who else lives here, do you? Or you wouldn't have asked, would you?"

"That's a different department, sir, and the other residents of this abode are not currently being investigated by our department."

"Okay." He seemed determined but I wouldn't be put off so quickly. "But what records?"

"We have files on all suspected illegal immigrants, refugees, and asylum seekers. The Home Office recently invested a great deal of money in a brand-new IT system to give us real-time data on each individual – you might have seen it in the news." I was sure I must have but couldn't get the faint picture of a cowering MP hunched beneath the glare of a bench of enquiring peers and that weird word 'cronyism' out of my head.

"Well, I know my rights." I didn't, of course - who does - but I had to try and stand up for myself now. Every fibre of me wanted just to curl up and wait for this all to go away but they had come into my home and made blatantly false accusations about me. "I demand to know what's on my record. You… I'll submit a… what's it called… Freedom…"

"A Freedom of Information Request, sir. We have your record here, sir, for just such an eventuality." Rather than a tablet, from his battered laptop bag, Kean brought out an altogether more traditional, manila folder, enclosing several different coloured papers.

"That's it, yes." I really hoped they would just back down in the face of my outburst. They hadn't, of course. The female agent continued by pulling out a bulky-looking tablet device from her bag and, thumbing it, unlocked it.

"Francisco David Cualquiera. Says here you were born in Escalón, Val Verde, on June the 19th 1995. Your correspondence address is this flat. Your academic details have been confirmed. That's all we require, along with your visa details..."

"But I don't have a visa!"

Goode looked up in stern conviction and then met Kean's gaze before turning her attention back to Mr. Cualquiera.

"I mean, I don't need one – I was born here, not in Val Verde." Her questioning, patient look did not abate. "My parents were – are – from Val Verde but they moved here and had me." Kean glanced at Goode, but it seemed her façade was unchanged by my explanation.

"Not according to our records. Says here, you came together in 1996."

"What records? Where did you get this information from?" Kean placed his half empty mug down on the coffee table and leaned forward, ominously, his hands clasped together and elbows perched on his knees, presumably for effect. Whatever the effect he was going for was lost when he remembered his manners and slid a coaster under the mug in haste.

"The thing is, sir, we have a number of relationships with a number of agencies here in the UK and overseas."

"What records?" I couldn't come across as being a helpless victim, even though I was, I was the one being inconvenienced and now accused of being an illegal immigrant. I had to challenge them but I felt so, so guilty. I wonder if my parents felt this way when they fought back? Had they fought back? Maybe they were all stories and maybe The Cualquiera Way was to just sit down and take the beating?

"In this instance, sir," Kean hesitated, "The Student Loans Company. They sent information you require to an address in Digbeth but, when they received no response and the Post Office returned the paperwork six months later, they discovered that the property was unoccupied. They spoke to the University who passed on your current details, including an overseas contact address, and, within that information, there was no record of a visa or that you have the right to remain in this country. That prompted an investigation by our department and that is how we find ourselves here, sir." Having listened to every word they had said, I looked from one unfeeling officer to the other and back again. They looked back and we all just waited again.

"This can't be happening," I thought that but couldn't help blurting it out loud. It immediately made me feel worse. "That's probably my parents' old address. The one in Digbeth. We lived there for ages but they... left... must be four years ago now. What's the overseas address?" At this point, Goode, the more senior of the two, by her mannerisms at least, I assumed, took over.

"The overseas contact address is the British Consulate in Escalón, Val Verde. It seems that your parents and you may have been evacuated during one of the periods of civil unrest that your nation periodically experiences."

"*My* nation? What are you saying? I am a British citizen."

"The emergency contact address left on your University application was the British Consulate in Escalón and, through our connections there, we can see you and your parents didn't apply for a visa." The information I was hearing seemed unreal, ethereal even, as if it was being floated down from another realm to a Frankie I was watching have this conversation in another dimension, yet we were both being asked to accept this new reality.

"I'm from Druids Heath..." I muttered.

"*Señor* Cualquiera," she continued, and now it was her turn to clasp her palms together and loom forwards in her seat. "What happened to your parents?"

"They..." Oh God, what should I say? What could I say? Whatever I tell them would have to be true, at least to me, in this reality. But whatever I say, though it would undoubtedly be the truth, might sound like lies to them. "They came here in 1995, to get away from the arrests of protestors. The British Government offered them asylum." I had to look up for the first time in perhaps a minute or two, to meet their gaze. Both were leant forward, hands together, as if pleading with me, begging, but I knew they didn't want anything from me other than confirmation of what they thought they knew. For some reason, neither of them had picked up their notepads and pens from the coffee table. I carried on; "Esperanza and his regime was finished and the new Communist government was rounding up protestors like my parents so they were told they had to leave. I think some people went to the US, elsewhere in South America maybe, but they came here. They were given asylum

46

because it was too dangerous to, you know, be there. Now the Communists are out and the Fascists have gone, they wanted to go back, but I heard rumours that the new Government isn't happy about protestors coming back so they are threatening to arrest anyone if they go back, so my parents hid. I don't know where they are, I don't know if they're safe. I haven't spoken to them for over a year. I miss them…"

I stopped myself. This wasn't the right moment to show too much emotion. I could not share that side of me with them, that *weakness*, that could give them a means of manipulating me or bending the truth to suit their own motives.

"So, they did go back, sir?"

"I don't know," I composed myself quickly and tried to concentrate only on the facts I knew. That helped me hold back the desire to scream. "Yes, I guess so. They wanted to but knew they could be arrested if they did so they decided not to. But the Government, our Government, the British Government, *wanted* them to go back and ordered them to go. We would have fought it in the courts, if we could have afforded to. We did everything… so they… they left me here." The officers made conciliatory faces but their body language was unchanged. "They haven't been able to see what I've made here, it's been me, on my own, just getting on with everything..."

The emotion and the worry bubbled up so suddenly that I had to stop myself from talking because the talking made it all worse, like a sneeze that won't come out.

"We understand your situation, sir." I'd heard that tone before, in the shopping centre, when Ollie was caught shoplifting and doing his best to blag his way out of it. For him, it had worked but the comparison might stop there; he wasn't me. Their words were mollifying but the delivery had the opposite effect. "I'm afraid that there's nothing we can do now that our investigation has started."

"What do you mean? I thought you were making enquiries – asking me a few questions?"

"We were," the cool Goode interrupted. "Now we have heard answers to those questions from you and we have confirmed your identity then we have now officially commenced our investigation."

"Should you wish to clarify your situation further, sir, you may ring this number." He gave me a crisp, black and white business card. "Or you may wish to take this up with the University or the Students' Loan Company. Your University provided the Students' Loan Company with your information, so if you believe this is incorrect you should discuss your case with them, sir..."

"My case?"

"...and we subsequently obtained said information from the University. So, as you see, the proper checks have been carried out by ourselves and you do have the right to appeal any final decision."

"What happens now?" I heard my voice croak a little.

"In a weeks' time, we will come back to update you on your case. We can discuss matters then but, in the meantime, it would be prudent for you to discuss your situation with the University. Thank you for your time, *señor Cualquiera*." Goode stood.

"And for the teas. *Es muy bueno*." Kean grinned excessively in what I assumed was an attempt to establish familiarity. Without another word, they stood up and left. I stood instinctively and politely, mumbled soundlessly 'Thanks' and slumped back down again. The dirty mugs and business cards brought to mind the terrible wreckage of a plane crash.

The one word that flashed in a pink neon tube that ran around a dressing room mirror inside my brain was 'Impotent', as if an advert for erectile dysfunction. 'Impotent'. Emblazoned furiously without a light switch and without the ability to close my eyes and not see it. It followed me as I swept up the mugs and passionlessly washed them with a thick, feathery lather in the sink and ceremonially stacked them back in their normal places, as if anything could be so normal again. The word followed me back to my bedroom, where I squeezed into the tiny space, and settled onto the office chair once again. It only faded after a couple of hours of focus on something totally unrelated to this very real and pressing dilemma I now found myself in. But finding oneself was part of the problem, it seemed – what they told me and what I knew differed at key points; the location of my birth, even if the date was correct; the arrival of my parents; my educational history; right up to the point of the visa.

I could not recall ever having one or needing one or even thinking about it. Had I lost it? Had I lost myself, who I really was, because this did not feel real. This was something that happened to other people. Those 'Go

49

Home' vans that Chelsea was so irate about; I hadn't seen them so could only take her word for how they portrayed immigrants as criminals. The scroungers that Ollie moaned about sneaking into the country in the backs of lorries. I wasn't a criminal and I wasn't a scrounger so why were the Home Office coming to see me if there were criminals and scroungers out there in the rest of the world? After an hour or so of tossing the idea around in my head like a red-hot cricket ball, all it felt like was a moment that had passed and would not come back again and, because of that, I shouldn't dwell on it. It would be some kind of clerical error or mix-up with the forms. All I could tell myself was to focus on what kept my mind busy, what kept me from going mad. But as soon as I stopped, or closed my eyes, rubbing them and my temples with my tired, paint-spattered hands, the word flashed up before me relentlessly; 'Impotent'.

Chapter 5 – Tuesday 24th May (still) (30 days to go)

It had been just over three weeks since my first day at Scintilla but the three of us had only spent a few evenings all at home together. Chelsea was attending meetings most nights with various different socially conscious groups, each with a more pressing issue to take on than the last. Ollie picked up a few more evening shifts to help cover the increase in rent, meaning he actually ended up spending a larger proportion of his pay packet in the pub for post-work pints. I was the exception. I spent most evenings at home, either sanctuaried in my room behind the comfort of a locked door or at the kitchen table tapping away at my laptop in an ineffectual effort to keep up with the demands of my University course.

"There's another parcel for you," Ollie said, when he came home, shoving the nondescript brown cardboard box towards me. Chelsea glanced up from the TV but looked away again when she realised it was for me. I knew what it was so just placed the parcel on the worktop and went back to cooking.

"What's that weird smell?" Ollie kicked his boots off at the door and stomped into the main bedroom before returning shortly afterwards in a faded pair of tracksuit bottoms and matching sweatshirt. Chelsea was engrossed in her documentary, wordlessly making notes in her Smythson cahier notebook, punctuating her elegant script with the occasional gasp or 'Gosh!' or knowing 'Hmm'.

I was busy stirring the rice and red pinto beans together with the onion, green chilli, and garlic. In a pan in the oven, the tilapia – or *yojoa*, as Mum called it – I bought from the Holte Ethnic Market was roasting. It was one of the few things I could actually cook well, and it reminded him of her, which was the comforting familiarity I really needed right now, although sharing that with Chelsea and Ollie just felt like a bit much. That soothing memory of cooking dinner together, even if she could not be there to salve me was mine, not ours. Neither the contents of the oven or the contents of the pan had a particularly strong or noticeable odour; rice, vegetables, and fish – pretty basic. But Ollie was getting on my nerves. I didn't know if he was looking for an argument from me or not, but I didn't want to take that chance and give him the satisfaction or risk going to bed angry. I stirred more forcefully and did not make eye contact for several minutes.

"When are you going to be finished, mate?"

"Just five more minutes, I reckon."

"Good, 'cause that fish stuff stinks." Ollie took a lager from the fridge, cracked it with bravado, and slumped down next to Chelsea. "What's this rubbish?" Chelsea sighed.

"Would you like me to change it, Oliver? Is the plight of the south London white squirrel too difficult for you to comprehend?"

"White squirrels? Lovely between two slices of toast!" He snorted at his own joke and took a hearty swig from the can. Before the two of them started trying to wind each other up, I decided I had to intervene.

"Guys, can you just listen to me for a minute please?" I stood behind the unoccupied sofa that served as a simple barrier between the 'corridor' and 'lounge'. The flat wasn't big enough to have such well-defined spaces but there were zones that we all understood.

"What's up?"

"I had a visit today from the Home Office. They said that they're looking into me and whether I should be allowed to stay in the UK." Chelsea looked shocked. Ollie seemed angrily confused.

"I don't understand," he blurted. "You're from England, aren't you?"

"Yes, but my parents aren't."

"But you were born here?"

"Yes. Surely that's adequate," stated Chelsea decisively. "You should just show them your passport or your birth certificate." She half-turned back to the squirrels, somehow assured that her calm and forthright demeanour had managed to save the day again.

"It's more complicated than that. I just wanted to let you know." I really didn't feel like explaining much more to either of them right now. I wasn't sure how they would react; would they be supportive, would they be angry, like me, or would they try and kick me out? I doubted the latter, but it was obviously something that formed in my mind, an amoeba at first but soon a fully blown organism of an idea. That's what happens when you over analyse things, I knew from experience. Your brain becomes a primordial swamp of creatures that develop from the slightest cell division. Some of those ideas go extinct, some plod along like domesticated animals finding shelter in your mind, and others, well, only a few, they become the lions, and tigers, and bears that eat the other ideas for breakfast.

What else could I explain? I wasn't sure I quite understood it all myself just yet. I had hoped they would be more sympathetic, no, that's not quite right, maybe enraged about it and keen to fight for me, just as Chelsea fought for her other causes. I wanted them to get upset on my behalf and, maybe, to step up and do something, to solve this all for me.

"Mate, what were they like? Did they give you a hard time?"

"Oh, no... not really. They seemed sort of normal but they just wouldn't listen to me. They told me what they were going to do and that in a week they'll give me an update. But they wouldn't listen to reason. It's like they had been told to ignore everything I said."

"Typical," huffed Chelsea, who had never met anyone from the Home Office in her life. "These small-minded jobsworths are positively ruining our country. Surely they have the common sense and decency to treat you like an individual. You should complain to their superiors."

"You're right, love. Don't worry about it, mate. They were just doing their job. I bet they'll come back and tell you it's all fine. You can't waste time getting upset over nothing." Ollie turned his back and dug deep into a family pack of crisps, before wrapping his spare arm around Chelsea, who modestly nuzzled towards him.

"Absolutely. I always say 'Don't sweat the small stuff'. Show them your birth certificate and I'm sure they will be fine with that." Chelsea smiled purposefully and turned her attention back to the squirrels. I looked at them both for a dumbstruck moment and then went back to the kitchen.

Perhaps it was my pervasive silence or body language but a moment later, Chelsea placed the remote on the coffee table, stood up, patted her dress flat, and strode into the kitchen and flung her arms around me. Before she let go, I reminisced about the first time we had met, but, now, those seemed like immature fantasies and she wasn't the same person – neither was I, perhaps. The spell was broken when she let go.

"Ignore him," she consoled. "He's in one of his moods tonight." I could hardly tell recently. She leaned gracefully against the cupboard and toyed with her enviously long hair. "What are you cooking anyway?"

"It's pinto – rice, veg, beans – with some fish. My mum taught me how to prepare it, stuff it, and cook it."

"That's nice. I do love smoked salmon or king prawns myself. But they have to be ethically sourced, don't they?" She paused. "What kind of fish is that?" I opened the tin foil package, spooning the slick, herby juice that collected around the bottom of the sizzling fish on top of the whole tilapia. On contact, it crackled perfectly and my hunger returned in a rush, replacing all else at the forefront of my consideration.

"It's a snapper but in South America they call in *yojoa*."

"Oh. So, where's it from?" Chelsea tilted her head in a way that I recognised.

"The Indian place on the corner..."

"Ha ha." I wasn't joking. "No, I mean before that? Where was it caught?"

"...The sea..." When Chelsea's head bobbed to the other shoulder, I knew I'd said something inappropriate or that she didn't approve of.

"You know that we're overfishing the North Atlantic right now and fish stocks of cod and bluefin tuna are diminishing all the time, don't you?"

"This is red snapper."

"And we all need to be more conscientious about the provenance of things we put inside ourselves, especially the sustainability of the food we eat so that there will be enough for generations to come after us."

"I think it's from the Gulf of Mexico..."

"And if we don't reduce the amount of commercially caught fish, especially those species caught with drift nets, then we run the risk of never being able to eat fish again and, if the fish runs out, what will other sea creatures eat? Can you imagine the devastating impact on the fragile, global ecosystem if we carried on thoughtlessly just eating whichever fish we wanted without any comprehension of the dire consequences?"

"Yeah, I mean, yes, yes, totally, of course." All I could do was to punctuate her diatribe whilst carefully plating my dinner.

"So I hope, next time, Francesco, you will give a little more thought towards what you eat. Maybe you'll consider going vegan. Like me." She smiled condescendingly, as if she had given a particularly thought-provoking TED Talk, and skipped back to the sofa to resume her silent sitting with Ollie. I looked at his plate and found my hunger wavering. From the cupboard below, I took out a tray, put my plate on it and headed for my room again. I wasn't in the mood to sit in with them.

Using my elbow to turn the handle, I cautiously sidled into the room, navigating around some of my things inside. I had to quickly return to take in the parcel, and I noticed Ollie cradling a sleeping Chelsea with one arm whilst drinking a second beer with the other. The football was on the TV now and there was no point in returning until the morning.

Chapter 6 – Thursday 26th May
(28 days to go)

My hand slammed the espresso hopper to the steamer and gave it a sharp twist. The motion was smooth and practiced. With another twist, steam was forced through the grounds and into the tray below, splashing my trousers and apron.

"Shit."

"Come on, mate, I'm in a hurry."

"Sorry." I had to start again, but this time with a cup. More grounds, More steam. A double espresso handed over to an impatient customer. Not impatient; just pissed off.

"What's the matter?" Freya pried.

"Nothing," I blurted. "Just lots on my mind, sorry."

"Wait," Freya grabbed my elbow. "You need these for Noah Wright's visit. Don't lose them." She handed me a new pair of yellow rectangular badges. On the back of both was a bar safety pin and on the front of both was my name, 'Francesco' – I was relieved they hadn't put 'Francesca', which was what my first trainee badge had on it – and beside it were two convex, glossy flags; one, the familiar red and yellow flag of Spain, and, beside it, a tricolour of black, green, and red, with an encircled representation of Mount Belmonte in the middle. A twinge of pride sparked inside; this might be the first time Democracy Coffee had ever had to make a Val Verdean flag for one of their staff badges, I might be making history, but then they might have outsourced it, but, anyway, I could still feel a rare sense of patriotism that was unusual for me.

The rest of the day drifted into a blur. I found the simple acts – any acts – of serving customers took my thoughts away from the more serious, pressing worries and my annoying flatmates – were they good people? The more I thought about how they behaved after the Home Office visit, the more I thought that perhaps they were not.

With the rent going up, it just put into perspective things for me. I came to the realisation that Ollie and Chelsea were not the friends I thought they would become and it seemed like the perfect solution would be to move out. But we had two years of living together and I had hardly developed any other friends beyond them. Sure, there were friends, but only those who were introduced via Ollie and Chelsea, so, if I wasn't part of that group, would they even be friends with me? How does someone go from a standing start to having a friendship group? How do you even do that? 'Making' friends is not something you can just do. Who or what qualifies as a 'friend' anyway, and who decided? Was Ollie my friend? If he was, he sometimes had a strange way of showing it. When I needed someone to talk to, to confide in, he had been there for me but he could also become evasive, or maybe retreat to a distance where his rugged determination to be aloof became more noticeable. All this time I thought I was self-reliant, independent, free. In fact, I think I might have been wrong. Perhaps they were just comforting descriptions for what was really loneliness, isolation, awkwardness. And even having one person, one romantic relationship, seemed elusive. After Chelsea and I hadn't worked out, I'd been on dates but sometimes was the one who never followed up and, in most cases, was the one who waited for the other person to get in touch. Invariably, they didn't and by the time I wondered whether I should reach out, my emotions were clouded by self-doubt; if they wanted to see me again, they would have been in touch. Maybe they were waiting for me? Should I reconnect? Is it too late now, too desperate? This indecision left me in the same limbo-like situation. No friends. No money. Nobody to spend time with, not that I could afford to spend money on them even if I wanted to. By the time my shift was winding down, around 4pm, with the last few office workers, I was in a deep state of despondency. And that was all before I even got started on the risk of deportation.

"Can I help you?" The false cheeriness was more forced than ever and I did my best to hide the slumping body posture.

"Worse things happen at sea." Great advice. Up there with 'Smile – it might never happen' for useless comments. We're not *at* sea. It is *already* happening. Go take a long walk off a short pier. How's that for some advice?

"Hot drink? Pastry, sir?"

"Sir? Well, I do feel special!" I knew enough not to engage in excessive chit chat. Not because it was against Democracy Coffee policy, and they had binders and binders of policies covering everything from sick leave to dealing with the discovery of a dead body in the toilet. I didn't want to engage because I knew I might say something to pick myself out to be a 'chatter', to whom the customer might try to form a bond with. I felt uncomfortable enough knowing a customer's name and their regular order, as if it was somehow too personal to repeat it without feeling slightly awkward, like knowing a stranger's email password. There was power in it, in a small way. So, I simply waited. Saying nothing felt safe.

"Okay. I think I'll have a *grande* Americano with a scone. I do like your English scones." The pronoun and the slight accent gave him away immediately as a tourist. As I prepared the man's drink, it felt as though I was being watched. Of course, I considered, everyone watches me make their order to some extent as customers don't know me so they don't trust me and, after all, whatever I prep, they're putting in their stomachs. I would watch anyone who made my food too, if I could. Maybe that's why restaurant kitchens are hidden away. You couldn't concentrate if sixty tables of starving diners were scrutinising your every move.

"There you go, sir." I placed the cup, plate, knife and spoon on the tray on top of the counter, noticing a tell-tale wince. His reaction gave me a moment to observe him; shorter than average, tanned in a natural way, as opposed to the spray on stuff, thick, black hair, cut in a 1960s movie-star sweep, and the most bright white eyes with emerald green irises I had ever seen. Attractive, self-assured, dignified, and a genuinely unusual type of man to encounter in a bog-standard coffee shop in central Birmingham.

"I'm sorry, I should have said 'to go' shouldn't I?"

"It's no problem. I can put it…"

"No, no, it's my fault. You know what, I'll have it here anyway. It's better for the environment, isn't it?" He looked around, as if deciding where to sit, but Scintilla was almost empty now. "The paradox of choice. I could sit anywhere, yet I choose nowhere." He turned with a

61

smile and a glint in his eye. "Do you ever experience that? The inability to choose something when you have the opportunity to pick anything you want?"

"Yes, often." This brief, personal admission tumbled from my lips like an autumn leaf falling.

"How much?"

"Er, well, maybe twice a week. Three times on weekends..." I had started now and found the steady, reassuring charisma of the customer made me feel quite at ease with him. First impressions really do matter.

"I'm sorry, I meant the coffee and the scone." We both laughed politely. Together.

"Four sixty-five, please." The man pulled a neatly creased, five-pound note from his wallet and handed it over in a manner that was deliberate and precise yet effortless. A money magician, the conjurer of cash, the pound sterling *prestidigitateur*.

"I would say something witty normally like 'cheap at twice the price' but I really do think it is overpriced." My hesitation to engage returned, so I offered a weak smile and rang through the purchase.

"Your change." The man had turned his back on the empty seats and tables, having already noticed Lucy sweeping up and tidying the chairs heavily, in a way that implied she was eager to get home, even though they still had an hour and a half before our shift was over. There was something familiar about the man, but I couldn't place it, which, perhaps was why I noticed the small details about him. His authority without conventional height. The crisp lines that defined his grey stubble.

"What we all need but none of us desire." He chuckled at his private joke, which reminded me of the memory of a distant uncle at a rare family gathering reciting an over-told witticism, then he pocketed the coins, and took a swig of his Americano.

"Nice badge. *¿De dondé eres en Val Verde?*" Instinctively, I looked down at the yellow Cultural Engagement Initiative badge that now adorned my chest and bore the Val Verdean flag.

"Oh, *lo siento*, I don't speak much Spanish."

"*Qué lastima.* That means that it is a shame. So, you aren't from Val Verde then?" Normally cautious of too much conversation with customers, I hesitated. This habit of not quite rudeness but abrupt and controlled pleasantry that I had been encouraged to cultivate was simply good business. If staff avoided lengthy interactions with customers – some of whom might have mental health issues, be former inmates, or come from a broken home, Rob had helpfully added – means that whilst that one customer has had a pleasant experience, three or four behind them, who could be rushing to get somewhere – like picking up their seven kids from school or getting home before their cheating husband does, Rob, again, obligingly contributed – will be late or put out and we don't want to have disgruntled customers. Disgruntled; my overactive brain cogitated. You only hear that word in the context of customers. People don't talk about how they were 'disgruntled' by the late goal that upset their accumulator or 'disgruntled' when the storm brought that big fir tree crashing into the guest bedroom. But this customer would not be 'disgruntled' and there were no others waiting in line that I could disgrunt by sharing brief pleasantries. Perhaps an act of gruntling someone – surely the opposite of disgruntling, so intentionally being pleasant or kind perhaps – would be good practice for when an opportunity came to make friends. Maybe it was a risk-free endeavour, so I decided to give gruntling a go.

"Actually, my parents came here from Val Verde in the Nineties. How about you?" It wasn't hard; an answer followed by a related question. Perhaps this is what I should have done more on the dates Ollie kept setting me up with. I don't know why this romantic connection appeared out of the blue but the comparison seemed logical.

"My family runs a large chicken farm in the north, close to the border. It's an honest living, I respect them, but it's not for me. I have grander plans!" No question to answer, which gave me pause. Would one be forthcoming or was that the conversation ended already? The man blew over the rim of the coffee, took a large sip and, a moment later, a bite of his scone. I was transfixed by him, like nobody had ever affected me before. His movements were so orderly and smooth that he appeared otherworldly.

"What plans?" Needing to fill the silence, the next part of the conversation happened more easily than thinking about it.

"Mm, I lead a group, we meet nearby. It's a kind of think tank, I suppose you'd call it. We host speakers, we organise social events, fundraisers, and discuss all kinds of things, like culture, politics, that kind of thing. Many of my friendships have been built through it as we welcome all kinds of people."

"What kind of friends?" The promise of friendships sounded appealing.

"South and Central Americans living over here." My attention was snared. "Like you."

"Me?"

"Yes, we welcome anyone with a connection to their homeland." Doubting whether I would be accepted, I chose to clarify.

"I was born up the road so Val Verde's hardly my home." I turned away, silently wishing for this stranger to pull me back, if only to authenticate my initial, unspoken interest. I wanted that validation.

"But what if you could build a connection to your past? Your family?"

"I don't understand."

"We have members from all countries – first generation to third – and they get to understand more about where they've come from. You can't accurately plan for where you are going in life without having any clue about where you've been."

"Is there anyone from Val Verde?"

"Aside from me? Yes, a few. Marcos, one or two others. You'd like them – Marcos is about your age, slightly older, very passionate. Eva is about your age too, but she's from Venezuela. She is my right-hand woman. I couldn't run the group without her."

"When do you meet?" This felt like one of those bad dates. One person asking all the questions and the other simply answering them, more like a job interview than a date, only this time I was asking the questions and was genuinely interested in hearing the answers.

"Fridays from 7pm in the Hotel Trianon, mostly. Why don't you pop in to our next meeting tomorrow night? There's no charge and I can introduce you to people so you won't feel like a stranger. Maybe I can make some introductions." It all seemed settled and easily coordinated.

"Great. That's great. Thank you. Uh, what was your name?"

"Ernesto. And it still is! Ernesto Benemerito. Nice to meet you..?"

"Francesco Cualquiera." We shook hands, me slightly more awkwardly than Ernesto. Ernesto quickly finished off his coffee and Ernesto turned to walk out of the front door. I used his name in my inner monologue to be sure I wouldn't forget it. Ernesto Benemerito.

"And I'd love to hear more about your family and how they ended up here." Ernesto waved briskly and left the store in a moment, which seemed to pass more fleetingly than I would have liked. I could already say that I was delighted by the prospect of getting in touch with my roots and possibly even meeting some new people. And my fascination with this unusual man had been piqued; I was compelled to find out more about him.

It was just words, for now, but Ernesto's final comment gave me an unexplained chill.

Chapter 7 – Friday 27th May
(27 days to go)

I had to do something but I didn't know what to do. Lazing in bed was no way to get out of this situation but I did it anyway. It was reassuring to lie in a safe space, without any need to get out from under my cosy duvet, aside from the guilt tapping away at me from inside my own head. I ran through what I would say and what I would do when I eventually got to the campus.

'I demand to speak to the Vice-Chancellor at once.'

'No, I don't have an appointment but he will live to regret it if he doesn't see me immediately.'

'Now, look here, there's something amiss with my records and this oversight needs to be rectified post haste.'

'Why, yes, I will have a brandy, thank you…'

Rolling out from under the covers, my body responded to my brain's whining and I got ready to leave. The walk to the University wasn't far but I took my time; it was mid-morning so I didn't feel like there was any need to rush. My feet reluctantly leading me through the city centre, where there were the most distractions and opportunities to bump into someone I might recognise. No such luck.

At the main entrance, I was made to wait whilst three other people were dealt with. I sat patiently on one of the economically upholstered seats until it was my turn.

"Good morning. How can we help you today?"

"Er, I'm not sure, really. I need to speak to someone about a student visa, I think."

"Of course. I believe you need to speak to the Home Office for student visa applications."

"No, no, they told me to come here and speak to you. You see, I don't have one, I don't think, and they said I should but I'm not an overseas student, so, yeah, so I need to check with someone here about what I'm supposed to do."

"Right…" The receptionist hesitated. I wasn't sure if she was just thinking about everything I'd said or was waiting for more. "I see." She didn't, of course.

"Yeah, so I need to talk to someone but I don't know who."

"No, I understand… Let me speak to someone in the Students' Union…"

"Sorry but I don't think they can help, can they?" Didn't they just run the bar or had that been sub-contracted further out of the university's responsibility, I wondered.

"Hmmm," She ran her forefinger down the computer screen, the contents of which were concealed from my view. "I don't know then…" She frowned, for show, and then picked up the receiver of the desk telephone and tapped in a short number. "Hello?" I heard another voice, muffled and slow. "Hello." It replied but I couldn't make it out. Conscious that she might think I was eavesdropping, I took a hesitant step backwards. "I've got

68

a student here who needs some help with his student visa … Yes, I've told him that but, according to him, they've sent him here … Right … Okay … Student Records Department, yes? … If not, Overseas Student Support … Lovely, thank you … Yes, you too … Bye." With the click of the receiver, I stepped forward again, already fairly sure what information would be imparted to me.

"So, you need to see the Student Records Department on the third floor. Now, if they can't help, you need to visit Overseas Student Support in the basement, alright?" I nodded and looked around at the vast rotunda, in which the ornate reception desk sat, like the cherry on a Bakewell tart. The room was elaborately decorated with ancient marble tiles and aged wainscoting that appeared to have borne witness to thousands of students and graduates alike passing through this revered lobby. The room, not quite round but more hexagonal, was adorned with several plaques and alarming portraits of serious men of academia, hands firmly crossed on laps, dark gowns draped over shoulders, hooded grey eyes peering from behind a long, white nose. Yet no signs directed me to the third floor or Student Records Department so I returned to the desk.

"Excuse me…"

"You'll have to wait, there's two people before you."

"But, I just…"

"Wait your turn, please." I looked at the frumpily-dressed Indian girl who looked like all the Scooby Doo characters tossed into one – cravat, short skirt, thick, round glasses, baggy sweatshirt with biscuit crumbs down the front - and the lanky goth, paleness accentuated by black, stretched out like a wet towel. Both had pretended not to notice me and I shuffled into place behind them both.

"How can we help you today?" She was still the only person at the desk.

"You just told me to go to the Student Records Department on the third floor but I don't know how to get there, there's no signs."

"I thought you were a student here?"

"I am but I've not been here before."

"The main reception? Come on, you must have, what about when you first visited on the open day?"

"That was a while ago, I don't really remember…"

"What about when you picked up your ID? Did you not come here?"

"I mean, yeah, maybe, possibly, look, I just need to know how to get to the third floor."

"Oh, it's very easy. Just walk past the desk here, then go right through the double doors and turn back on yourself and the stairs are there. It's about four flights up so it's not on the third floor but the floor marked three as there's a mezzanine level for the refectory."

"A what?"

"It's like another floor but not a floor – halfway between a floor."

"No, no, the other thing, the rectory?"

"Refectory. You don't know what a refectory is? It's like an indoor auditorium, for lectures and events."

"Right, right, I see. Through the double doors and right…"

"No, no, no, the double doors are on the left…

"But you said…"

"…and you go right through them before you turn back on yourself."

"Double doors on the left. Turn back on myself – is that right or left?"

"Right."

"Right."

"Yes."

"Okay. And, just so I know, is there a room number?"

"8C.08"

"I thought it was on the third floor, sorry, floor three?"

"Yes, it's an old building but the older building behind this one has floors one and two so we are technically on floor four now, the basement is floor three, and Student Records are on floor eight. It was confusing so we've had to change the signage, so floor eight in this block is signposted as floor three." I had so many things I could have said but I was getting my head around this warren and didn't want to forget what I already understood. I smiled as politely as I could at this guardian of the labyrinth.

"Right…" I walked to the left, past another stiff-moustachioed head, this time cast in bronze on a chest high plinth. I pushed open the double doors and went right through. I looked to my right and saw another door leading to a hallway at the bottom of a staircase. I shouldn't have but I couldn't help it; I looked to my left. There was another corridor that, theoretically at least, could have had another staircase further down it. Trusting what the riddler at the reception desk had told me, I went to my right, passed along the thin corridor and turned, to my left, to ascend the steps. Just as she said, there was a sign for the refectory, and a 1/2 sign below it. Up the next flight of stairs and there was a 2/3 sign. I hesitated before figuring that, well, if I went up one more flight, I would only have to go downstairs if I was wrong, which would be less tiring. Arising, the floor, just like the one below, spread away from the stairs to the left, the right, and straight ahead. I sucked in the angry air through my bottom teeth and let it out calmly through pursed lips.

It took me a good ten minutes to work out that dead ahead were rooms 8A.01 to 8A.12, before I had to return to the stairs because the corridor ended, and the rooms to the right were 8B.01 to 8B.09 – with an 8B.06d and 8B.06e thrown in for good measure. I thought of enquiring as to why the rooms were numbered like this and laid out in such an illogical manner but realised that I didn't care. What would I do with the information if someone explained it to me?

Walking along what was the left-hand corridor once you walked up – or down – the stairway, the door signs suggested I was on the right track – 8C.01 was the first on the left but 8C.18 was on the right. Getting to the end of the passage, I saw 8C.08 at the end; a long, hazy, horizontal window, through which I could see an old, oak-style reception desk and several banks of similarly wooden desks, three at a time, laid out very orderly yet cluttered with papers and stationery. I pushed the door but it wouldn't budge and the seated attendant behind the dark main desk pointed fervently at something in my direction. I looked around and found a buzzer that looked like an old bell push – with the word 'Press' on it – which, having pressed it, enabled the staff member to unlock the electronic bolt and let me in.

"Do you have an appointment?"

"With who?"

"I'll take it that's a 'no' then."

"I need to speak to someone about my Student Visa."

"You must speak with the Home Office."

"No, they said to come here, and… look, the woman at reception…"

"Which reception?"

"Main reception. The woman at reception…"

"Which woman?"

"Does it matt… I don't know," I felt myself getting frustrated but I knew I couldn't let it show. I didn't want to give anyone any reason to make this all the more difficult. My parents came to mind and I momentarily had to justify myself to them; 'No, I'm not telling truth to power, no, I'm not organising a boycott, I just want what's right for me and I can't lose control.' "She had grey hair. A cardigan." The grey-haired man emotionlessly looked back at me through his spectacles. "A blue one."

"Barbara."

"Okay, sure, Barbara. She said I should come here. She rang up and spoke to someone a couple of minutes ago."

"How many minutes ago?" Don't lose control.

"About three or four."

"Take a seat." I did as I was told. Another frugally cushioned seat to wait on. The receptionist got up and walked over to what I assumed was a colleague at one of the desks before returning to his seat and, without even acknowledging me, carried on impassively with whatever it was on his computer screen that clearly was no more mildly diverting than a plain cheese sandwich on white unbuttered bread with the crusts cut off. I was hungry, food was on my mind, and my stomach reminded me of the fact. Even the dullest of foods – white rice, potatoes, lettuce – would do right now. In my haste, I'd neglected breakfast again. I really hoped that this wouldn't take too long.

Above the lead-decorated window opposite, which was covered by a wholly out-of-place vertical blind, was an ancient sepia-faced clock. I watched its hands turn languidly but I also watched the man the receptionist had spoken to. He didn't look particularly urgent. I continued to pretend to watch the clock as if it were some elaborate dance that I was entertained and allured by; I still eyed the man, he adjusted his leather office chair, he moved his mouse, he wrote something down on a yellow pad. Of course, I knew when every minute went by. Two and then three, I didn't mind. Four, five, and six, I felt my legs pulling me forward, demanding I take action, but I couldn't do it. The chair squeaked a little beneath me. The emotionless golem still gazed at his screen at the main desk and the man he spoke to scratched his chin. Seven. He stood and the energy in my legs increased. Of course, he went to his tweed jacket pocket. Don't lose it, Frankie, I warned myself. I didn't want to end up like them. Eight. Here he comes, at last.

"Good morning. How can we help you today?"

"I need to speak to someone about my student visa," I began, continuing without hesitation as the man's mouth opened before his brain kicked in, to say, I was sure, something about the Home Office. "The Home Office sent me here because they said that you have some information which they used to determine that I need a student visa, when in fact I don't. I don't have a visa and I've never had one. I was born in Birmingham, I used to live in Druid's Heath, I've been studying here all of this year and last year..." I stopped as I couldn't risk getting over-excited and giving anyone a reason to think of me as hysterical and, therefore, wrong about everything.

"I see, okay, well, why don't you come over here and take a seat and I will take a look at your file. What's your name?" I told him. "I see, okay, mine's Holding, Mr. Holding, but you can call me Paul. I'm one of the Student Information Administrators here. Just give me a minute and I'll be right with you." I'd already given him nine but a few more couldn't hurt. Taking a seat beside his desk, I already felt calmed. The office was nothing like my room

– light, compact, tidy but hard – it was dark, aside from the desks closest to the window, musty, and soft, in a way. Blurred edges and dust hanging in the tight strips of daylight that invaded through the vertical blinds, the only hint at modernisation aside from the computers.

Paul calmly tapped my details into his terminal and my profile appeared, although he turned the screen slightly away from me. I looked away, as if somehow interested in the wood-lined walls or the green floral carpet. He quietly read, letting out a breathy whisper as he did.

"Everything seems fine to me." I felt my shoulders relax. "Oh… Hold on, here… It seems as though we have a little bit of an issue…" He tapped away then folded one arm, resting one hand on his inner elbow and tugging his underlip with his other hand. He slapped the return key decisively, as if it was an old typewriter, and turned his swivel chair to face me. "It seems like it could be something serious or it could be nothing. We've got your address – your home address – from when you enrolled, which was in Digbeth, correct?" I nodded, although, in hindsight perhaps it wasn't a question. "But you moved to a flat in…Selly Oak and changed your contact details with us." This all seemed pretty straight forward so I continued to listen, not really seeing where this was going. "For your student loan details, we needed to send your change of home address to the Students' Loan Company." I nodded again, both in agreement but also to urge him to continue as it seemed he was just about to reveal the reason why the Home Office were threatening to deport me. We looked at each other. "There's your issue."

"What's my issue?" I stared back at him compelling him, silently, with what I hoped he could see was a desperate, enraged stare but which, again, on reflection, might have seemed to him to have been simply my face.

"We needed to send your change of address. But you didn't give us your permission."

"I didn't know I needed to give you permission."

"Oh, well, it's all that red tape we have to deal with now. We're not allowed to send out your personal information willy-nilly, we have to seek permission first."

"Did you? Seek permission?"

"I'm afraid I don't know... I don't think we keep records of whether we tried or not..."

"How can I fix this then? I just want to get back to how things were, before all this."

"It's the Students' Loan Company's responsibility now. They've got your information too – well, not your new address, I wouldn't imagine – so they might know what your issue is and even how to remedy it. Possibly." He stood and stuck his hand out to shake mine, which I accepted instinctively. "You should probably speak to them to get to the bottom of your issue."

Now standing, awkwardly, I asked "But don't you have any information about my visa?"

"Oh yes, yes, of course we do."

"What does your system say?"

"Your file shows us that you need a visa."

"Well, how are the Students' Loan Company going to help?" He seemed puzzled by this, as if making Bolognese was as simple as giving someone a shopping list and expecting them to put those ingredients together in the correct way without a recipe.

"They told us that you need a visa and we simply updated your information. We handle all of the information for all students and staff here." I nodded, feeling like we had already had this conversation. "Well, they could have some inaccurate details for you but we've worked with them for many years and we have no complaints about them. Only one or two minor snafus."

"But that still doesn't tell me how *your* system says I need a visa." Hold it together, I thought, you do not want to cause a scene.

"Ah, well, the Students' Loans Company have some of the most sophisticated IT systems in the country – far better than our old contraptions." He chuckled. "They manage money, you see, whilst we handle information. There's money to be made in money!" He chortled at his own joke which fell flat with me. His arm jabbed out from the elbow, iron-stiff, indicating the door back into the corridor, as if his pun was the end of a thoroughly top-class dinner party but now, I'm sorry to say, it was time to turn in, thanks for coming, we must have you over again some time. I wasn't going to stand for it! I wasn't going to be told to leave, when I hadn't got what I had come for. I wouldn't have it, I would… and there I was standing outside, in the corridor.

Holding had turned back to his bureau and his armchair and the receptionist was still glued to the screen in front of him. My finger hovered over the word 'Press' and I stared ahead, my jaw set. The light blue glow from the computer monitor faded and the receptionist began tidying away; my eyes focused on the gold leaf paint on the glass between us which read 'Office Hours; Monday-Wednesday 10:00-12:30 & 14:00-15:30, Thursday Closed, Friday 10:30-12:30' and, without glancing at my phone, I could have guessed the time.

I was in no mood to speak to anyone at the Overseas Students whatever, even if they were still open. I suspected I would be exhausted if I had to recount my situation to another University stiff again and, in any case, it seemed like my next move was to speak to the Students' Loans Company and see what they could do.

The walk home felt like it took twice as long as the walk there.

Chapter 8 – Friday 27th May (27 days to go)

With the desperate need for cash, I took on more shifts. With the urgent desire to pass my course, I went to every lecture and every seminar. With the disbelief and self-denial that any of this was real or that deportation was a realistic outcome, I spent the whole week putting off going to the Students' Loan Company. A smarter version of me would have identified that I was simply in a stage of denial and I should have moved past this quickly or else I would have wasted opportunities to tackle the problem I faced. I wasn't that person then and I steadfastly clung to lie-ins and distractions to keep myself active. It was just one of those distractions that I found myself going to with a little more than three weeks before I might have been evicted from the country of my birth - and yet, it did not play on my mind as much as it should as I still barely believed it might happen to me.

Inside the hotel foyer, past the brass decorated doors and into the marble-floored hallway, there was a modest Reception desk.

"Sir?" I knew that 'Sir' tone; where the listener is not *really* being referred to in a reverent way but more accusatory. I'd used the same tone when I had to knock on the disabled toilet when it was my turn to eject the serial masturbator who used to frequent the coffee shop. "Can I help you?" asked the concierge.

"Yes, I'm here for a meeting. The South American one." The custodian of the reception desk grinned and gesticulated towards a door to the side of the staircase, in front of which there was a free-standing brass sign, before returning to whatever else it was that concierges did.

The sign showed guests all of the different private events taking place, at once directing visitors to where they needed to be whilst showing off all of the secretive and devious summits going on behind closed doors. Just what the Womens' Institute and local secondary school PTA were up to, I couldn't guess; perhaps they were just a front for the true meetings of the Freemasons and Illuminati and their mysterious financiers… Or perhaps, it was just a convenient venue for local groups to meet and discuss fundraising ideas to pay for more of these meetings… I shouldn't be so cynical, perhaps it was all innocent, I had doubts and these were now manifesting into groundless pessimism. I had promised myself on the way here that I would go into this with an open mind. The sign told me that the Embassy Room was where the group would meet – that it was listed as WMSCACE, which stood for the West Midlands South & Central American Cultural Exchange.

I pushed through the doors behind the sign and into a corridor. The Embassy room was signposted as being right at the end.

Yes, I had made the effort to attend but I really didn't want to stand out. The new guy, the outsider, I'd been both before and it didn't suit my personality. With all of the stories from my father and their desperation to always fight for what they saw as right, it felt like my only choice was to leap into life with both feet first and be the accurate representation of the saying 'the apple doesn't fall far from the tree'. But that would have come with risk, commitment, a certain immutability, just like Chelsea had, in one way, in her unwavering dedication to the *raison du jour*. I did admire her for that but it wasn't for me.

I made the other choice, which was unflinching detachment, from the inane sense of not wanting to suffer the violence and the persecution my parents had faced. Chased out of Val Verde and into the arms of a welcoming Great Britain. Having made a life in their new homeland, once the political landscape had changed, they were shepherded home, against their will. But not into the nation they hoped a change in Government would bring but a nation desperate to bury the conflicts of the past – and that meant disappearing those who had spoken out most vocally about the Fascist Esperanza government or the Communist San Marcos government. And they'd spoken out against both. And I could not bear the idea of them putting themselves in the crosshairs again.

As long as I didn't get the spotlight shone on me tonight, I would be fine. Approaching the heavy double doors, I gave one a push but it wouldn't budge. It seemed to be locked or barricaded by something. Another try, but nothing. I may as well go home then, was the initial, pessimistic thought, but the hope of finding something or someone beyond those doors that could help make some sense of this aimless life nagged hard. I looked closely at the handles but there were no keyholes to peek through or, I suppose, to lock, so the doors should be open, in theory. Then I noticed the steel panel on the side, on the corridor wall, for disabled access. I tried pushing that. It depressed but nothing happened. Okay, one more go, but I was already feeling that nagging sense of failure that compelled me to turn around and go home. With an audible groan, the two doors heaved themselves insistently outwards, towards me. Beyond, revealed were row upon row of conference chairs, all facing the lectern to the left, half of which were empty, but on which sat an army of blank faces, accusatorily staring at me. It felt like I was interrupting something important at just the wrong time. Maybe it was an Illuminati cover-up...

"Francesco! Welcome!" The words boomed from the public address system. Ernesto, partially concealed by the wooden plinth behind which it appeared he was addressing the small crowd, called out and was picked up on the microphone that jutted out before him. Most of the initially irate expressions softened somewhat as the doors reached their apex and juddered to an automated halt. "Take a seat, wait, come down the front here... next to Marcos." Ernesto gesticulated surely at a vacant seat as close to him as it could be possible without raising questions about impropriety. I kept my head down and stepped forward, avoiding the gazes of those who were still watching me, which was everyone of course. Other attendees on the front row, even though the indicated seat was free, shuffled in their seats as if creating additional space, not that it was needed. Ernesto stepped aside at the podium, sitting in a plastic chair, and a younger woman took his place.

"Good evening everyone. Firstly, thanks to Luis and Carlos for sorting last weekend's bake sale – after all, we need to cover the cost of these meetings. Thank you if you contributed too, there were a lot of happy faces and full stomachs, even though the weather wasn't so great. Broad Street was a good location but I'm going to try and get a pitch nearer to a public building for our next event, celebrating the Argentinian Gauchos in June, so we can make the most of the increased footfall. Now, next on the agenda, is the election to the position of Treasurer. Since I've not had any nominations, I will retain this position until we get someone who is willing to take responsibility..." Her speech continued in this manner for around ten minutes; seamlessly hopping from one topic to another, all positivity and encouragement, and it was mildly interesting, but not exactly enthralling. The names and events meant nothing yet, not that I expected everything to be explained for my benefit, so it did make me feel like an outsider again. I looked for Ernesto, who remained on a chair just behind the speaker, and who was either thoroughly interested at everything that was spoken or doing a very good job of appearing so.

When the speaker had finished, she briskly tidied her papers and sat at the empty chair next to Ernesto's. He stood as she sat and instigated a brief ripple of applause, yielding a curt nod from his colleague. The clapping died down before Ernesto consented to step up to the microphone.

"Thank you, Eva. A wonderful update. *Gracias. Obrigado*. I wanted to welcome all of you to our June meeting and especially to a handful of new faces." Instinctively, I turned and looked around the room, trying to see who it was who was new like me. There were two guys and one girl who looked more positive or hopeful than the rest of the crowd and I assumed that Ernesto must be talking about them. "Thank you for joining us and I hope you enjoy this meeting and will continue to support our causes." Ernesto had an air of dignity about him that made me sit straight in my chair when he spoke and furrow my brow, as if my own seriousness would add extra meaning to Ernesto's words. Or Ernesto words compelled me to concentrate hard on exactly what was being said; as though each word and stress had some deeper, ancient bearing which I simply must cogitate on at length to gain the full meaning. I was also pretty knackered after a long day at Scintilla so frowning and shifting position helped me to stay awake. If I fell asleep, sat on the front row, at my first meeting, I thought I would rather the world would open up and swallow me whole rather than suffer that embarrassment. I mean, what would these new strangers think of me?

"Friends," he lingered, "We live in unpredictable times. We must all cope with the changing nature of our lives, mustn't we?" His gaze met all the attendees at once and yet felt, to each one, like a personally ascribed question. "We have a new Brazilian President. Poor Álvaro has had to relocate his family after the earthquake in Ecuador. We see ongoing protests on the streets of Caracas, Managua, and Quito. Ewerson had his car stolen outside of his own home and we all know about Fernando's health problems but, God willing, he is getting better and told me that he wished he could be here tonight. Even here, in our home, the voters of Britain are being asked to decide whether they will stay safe and secure within the European Union or forge their own destiny outside it." My neighbour, presumably the Marcos Ernesto had referred to earlier, fidgeted and I felt him eyeing me up from a very acute angle.

"Volatility is part of life. We either get a thrill from not knowing what might happen next or we panic about the lack of foresight and are forced to do something about it. My address this month is about change and the opportunities that change presents us with…" I didn't feel like the centre of attention anymore, I even grew a little more comfortable in these unfamiliar surroundings. The chairs might not be the most relaxing but all of the reproving stares were changed into admiring gazes directed towards Ernesto. As he spoke, not a rustle, not a cough was heard. Like the rest of the audience, I leaned forward the more Ernesto spoke, drawn towards him by his oratory.

He began by posing a simple question; "What have you really got to look forward to?" I felt the innate tug of someone who understood what I was thinking. I knew there was something about him that was mesmerising and I don't think I blinked once for the next twenty minutes.

Once he had finished, after a pause that felt as if the air had been sucked out of the room, each person in attendance unleashed an impassioned round of applause, with a couple of wolf whistles thrown in for good measure. Marcos – I was sure now that he must be who Ernesto had referred to – stood promptly and slapped Ernesto on the back, grinning plainly, and Eva, the previous speaker, smiled and nodded curtly to him. Other members of the congregation stepped forward savouring the glory he brought to them. I cautiously eyed two of the newcomers, who stood but remained by their seats, too awe-struck by the power of Ernesto's speech to venture closer. The woman dabbed a handkerchief to her eyes. Ernesto himself was a totem of beatification, consenting to shake hands and thank each and every person who came forth to show gratitude to him.

All round me was a sense of calm confidence, an unfamiliar feeling of peace. It was as if I had just had a hot shower, in an empty flat, on a Saturday morning. I felt pure and tranquil. Strangely, I had some trouble quite recalling precisely *what* Ernesto had said, but I did know *how* he had said it. With composure, surety, and a statesmanlike command over the podium, room, and even the people within it, who had, without interruption, listened as intently to him as a cat eyes a canary through the bars of a cage. I had honestly never seen anything like it and I had an impression that this was one of those epiphanic moments I would look back on as a divergence between who I was before and what I might become afterwards. There were no lectures like this, even in Philosophy, which some might have considered to be one of the more 'rock 'n' roll' subjects. Still, no *specific* words or phrases that Ernesto had said could be brought to mind at that moment but they would probably come back to me with the right stimulus.

"Ernesto, that was amazing," I was awkwardly gushing.

"Thank you, Francesco, thank you. I really appreciate it. Your opinion matters to me," he stepped closer, "perhaps more than the rest of the group because you haven't heard me prattle on before." He smirked and the infection spread, and I smirked back at the joy of that shared secret which both praised me and self-deprecated Ernesto.

"I really felt... er..." I couldn't get my teeth around the right word, and I didn't want Ernesto to step in and stop me from finishing without getting across the exact meaning of my words or to cut in with a suggestion, but the older man simply held his gaze and listened. "...moved... I felt moved by your speech. I've not felt like that before. I didn't know words could do that. But, I was wondering, could you just explain what you said when..."

"Come on, you are too kind. Now, I want you to meet my assistant," Ernesto said, leading me to where there were three other group members waiting. The audience had begun to gather in small groups, gravitating towards the coffee and teas which the hotel had laid on beside the double doors for them to pick up as they left. "Marcos, Eva, this is Francesco."

Marcos, who had definitely been studying me for much of the evening, was no longer grinning but extended his hand courteously. As I accepted the handshake, Marcos' head turned away, towards Ernesto, and he murmured something, before swiftly withdrawing his hand mid-shake and walking away, having not even made eye contact with me. Who does that? I felt irked by this rudeness but it was too late to do anything, and I worried about what I would say anyway. Maybe he had a condition. As Ernesto engaged in conversation with other group members, Eva stepped forward and took her turn to welcome me to WMSCACE.

"Hi, I'm Eva," she said, but her words were unheard as I took in her face. Sophisticated and built upon round, high cheeks, she had playful eyes separated by an elegant nose, that bordered on being too large for her face, and a prominent neck that held her upright with poise.

"Hi. Frankie, I mean, Francesco. Ernesto invited me." I tugged my hand away from hers, afraid of maintaining contact for too long and, therefore, creating an awkwardness between us that, ironically, was established anyway by my rapid shake and withdrawal of her hand.

"Right. Where did he find you?"

"What do you mean?"

"Birmingham's not exactly crawling with south Americans, is it? Where did Ernesto find you."

"In the coffee shop, a coffee shop," I corrected myself, conscious of being precise for her benefit. "Scintillas, you know the one? Near New Street station?.."

"Right." Her face didn't give away any particular emotion. She took my answer in and digested it without seeking any flavour.

"How did Ernesto find you?"

"Oh no, I found WMSCACE. I have always been interested in taking an active part in my community. I volunteered to help and met Ernesto at one of these events."

"Right."

"Nice to meet you. I hope you decide to come back next time."

"Yes, yeah, of course. You're welcome." Oh no. I immediately wished I could take those last words back. She softly frowned at me, dissecting my being with a beautiful but cruel sneer and a single, arched eyebrow. Speaking to the empty space she had occupied, I could simply, inaudibly mumble 'Nice to meet you too…'

A paw-like hand planted upon my shoulder and the comforting presence of Ernesto appeared beside me.

"How was your first visit to our little gathering?"

"Yeah, good, thanks."

"You met my colleagues too, I see – they are so important to what we do here. They are truly making a difference to all of the people in our family, Francesco. I'm getting on a bit now, of course, I need young, spirited people like Eva and Marcos to help me but, most important of all, to help all of you." Ernesto was staring squarely at me now, pulling me in with his gaze.

I questioned what the group actually did for its members. That is to say, I didn't question Ernesto, I didn't think I was brave enough to do that yet, but I mulled it over. I was sure they had explained it, either Eva or Ernesto, or perhaps I had imagined it. Either way, if there was something I could get behind, that might give me a chance to make some new friends, perhaps even move out of the flat, I might be interested in attending more often. Maybe that was me over-thinking again and imaging the future before taking care of the present but I can't change who I am. Little did I know, it would be something bigger and more powerful than I had ever been a part of before.

"You wanted to ask me a question earlier, didn't you?" The question broke my trance. With Ernesto standing right in front of me, my fears evaporated and I felt free to ask him anything, with no concerns that he would think any less of me.

"Yeah, I just wanted to know what you do here. I feel like I should know and I feel embarrassed just asking, you definitely told me, I'm sure, but I'm maybe not one hundred percent clear." An expectant mood became one of doubt; would this uncertainty prevent him from asking me back? If I couldn't join, I might not have the chance to make any new friends, besides the staff at Scintilla's but they were all a bit weird and I didn't really know how to socialise with other students, they all seemed to switched on and achingly fashionable compared to me, and then any chance of finding someone to move in with might be blown. My mind often waffled like this, whilst I waited for Ernesto.

"We help people. People like you. People with south or central American heritage. Don't worry about what we *do* – ask yourself what you *want*. Then, we'll find a way to help you make that happen." Ernesto shook my hand and indicated the way out. Was that an answer or just another question for me to dwell on?

"I want you to have an answer next time; what is it that you *want*, Francesco? *Qué tenga una buena noche.*" I watched him walk over to Eva, pick up his things, and stride out together through the side door indicated by the Fire Exit sign, leaving me alone in the conference room feeling confused but intrigued, hesitant yet desperate to be part of this mysterious man's organisation. What did he want? No, what did *I* want, that was the question that needed answering.

But the most pressing matter was the Home Office meeting. I had just three weeks to try and piece together an appeal and my first port of call would be the University. Maybe trying to avoid being deported for now would be an acceptable answer to Ernesto's question.

Chapter 9 – Saturday 28th May (26 days to go)

On that stroll home, I had tried not to think about the University or the Students' Loan Company or the Home Office, any of that, as I knew it would just get me down. I tried to focus on what I could do now, to take my mind off of it. There was some work to be done from my last lecture, a little bit of research on fallacies and rhetoric, but it wasn't urgent. There had been discussion about logical fallacies and how the opposite position could be argued should a point of view be expressed with a logical fallacy. For instance, if a flat-earther argued that we should all help save the environment, would the preposterousness of the person making the argument invalidate it? Or even, if someone in authority said something nonsensical, would that validate the nonsense? Someone from the Home Office, for example... Damn! Okay, think about the work, not the deportation. Would I even bother doing it? It wasn't a huge amount of work, maybe 1'500 words. But, I mean, if I got deported, there'd be no point. Agh! I knew it.

Now it was the weekend, when I might be able to do something that could help me to get away from any distractions and become swamped in my own thoughts, but everything I tried to think about dragged me back to my present problem.

I had to find something to divert me – either that or solve the problem for good – but I couldn't do that now, the SLC would be closed anyway. Maybe Ollie or Chelsea could help? It's worth asking them; Ollie always manages to get his own way through a mix of relentlessness and manipulation, whilst Chelsea loves a cause – maybe she could be my champion? I read *Refugee*

Boy in school, the kid in that – Alan? – he got his friends to rally round him, didn't he? It was a while ago so I don't really remember what happened next.

Inside the flat, I was met by a surprisingly industrious Ollie, hunched over the coffee table with paperwork sprawled across it, bearing an instantly recognisable logo and almost unavoidable images of smiling faces.

"What are you up to?"

"Doing a bit of campaigning, aren't I," he said as if I should have known.

"What for?" For some reason, I assumed it must have had to do with Chelsea but then dismissed the thought, considering the materials he had in front of him.

"Brexit," he said, without looking up. "Mayhew and the lads asked if I could help out. They're dropping some leaflets around and I said I could do our flats if they wanted." It seemed strange somehow – I could imagine Chelsea volunteering to promote a political movement but not Ollie. But there he was, his nose stuck in the pamphlets and, when he paused from reading, he would start folding another pile. I could see a stack of envelopes in an A4 paper box under the table that were either filled or about to be stuffed.

"That's not like you," I commented, whilst taking off my coat and bag. I didn't want to seem too accusatory.

"I've got a system – don't you worry. I only stick the flap down on every third envelope. Saves me bloody hours!"

"I mean politics."

"Oh, yeah, I know, but it sounds like a really good idea. Just think about it. We elect MPs but their ideas and policies get overridden by Europe. It doesn't make sense! You know, why do we even have a democracy anyway if we can't use it? Millions of people died to give us the right to vote but what was that sacrifice all for if voting for our MPs doesn't make a difference?"

"I s'pose so," I replied. "What does C think?" Ollie dropped the pamphlet. He quickly turned to look at me. I sensed I'd hit a nerve.

"You cannot tell her, I mean it, mate, you cannot tell her. She's got a bee in her bonnet about Brexit and has already said she wants to vote Remain – and wants me to do the same." His voice was hushed and there was a look in his eyes, almost desperate. I think, maybe for the first time, I got an impression that he loved her. Or maybe he was a little bit afraid of her.

"Mate, she's not going to dump you…"

"Don't tempt fate!"

"…She loves you, doesn't she?"

"You know what she's like with causes, Frankie," I did. "She'll try and get you to support whatever protest she's on, or sign a petition, or whatever, and before you know it, you're getting weekly emails about some mouthy kid who's banged up in Afghanistan for shitting in a church or God knows what and you're paying a tenner a month to some charity about starving, disabled guinea pigs!" At least he's still got his sense of humour, dark as it is, I thought. "Just, keep it between us, yeah? Let me tell her. If I have to."

"No worries, I can keep a secret." Ollie turned back to his folding.

"Where have you been all day? Uni?"

"Sort of. I went to talk to them about my visa situation."

"Sorted?" He didn't look up.

"No, not really." When he didn't immediately respond, I started to reconsider asking him to help. What could he do anyway? A cup of tea would sort me out and then, perhaps, I might ask him. After all, he's even started to do something for someone else. That seemed unusual for him.

Walking into the kitchen brought colliding images sharply into clarity.

A speckled Formica countertop stained and overused, on which the young Frankie perched. The kitchen table and chairs taken over by his parents and their friends, who would occasionally stop by. Like Ollie and Chelsea, their conversations could get heated and, lying in bed past midnight, Frankie could hear the laughter and chatter turn to heated shouts and slammed fists on surfaces. On the table were several long batons of wood and large sheets of plain card – his junior painting set requisitioned and the paint slapped on the card liberally. It was exciting to watch them all, buzzing around one another, reaching across to grab something else to decorate these huge signs; there was even an old bedsheet with thick, black paint swathed across it, in a language Frankie did not recognise yet.

His parents moved like ice skaters, gliding gleefully around one another with surreptitious pulls on each other's fingers or waists, circling the table, darting away to get some vital component, pausing to make something to eat for the group or, in my Dad's case, pacing outside for a cigarette and a joke with his closest mates. I sat and watched, sharing the odd smile when someone looked my way and drawing back when Mum tried to pinch my cheek. I loved the playful atmosphere and the fact that I could watch it all and enjoy it without commitment. All anyone needed me to do was sit there and, if they started singing one of their rhythmic and antagonistic songs, to sing along as heartily as they did, even if I had no idea what the words were I was singing, just the sounds, nor what the songs really meant. My bare knees swung side to side, my thighs pressed tight against shorts I was growing out of, and white socks pulled up over the ankle.

Even now, I know those memories were some of the best I had. They were more comforting than any cuddly animal or pet. But the romanticism was ruined when I was thirteen. I was old enough to be left at home alone during the day when their friends would come over to collect them and my parents would leave the house with all the signs they had made on the kitchen table. Dressed like beggars, I would tease. I could have the house to myself and would make myself whatever I wanted to eat. It was fantastic and I felt like the times without them made the times with them all the better because I had two sides to my life and I cherished them both equally.

They were late. I had been told that they'd only be out until six but it was already eight o'clock. I had my Dad's old 3310 and it rang from a withheld number. The unfamiliar voice on the line asked if I was Francesco and then explained that my parents would be on their way home soon, they were just in the hospital, no, no, nothing serious, just a couple of bumps and bruises but they wanted me to know and your Mum's a bit emotional so she wanted me to talk to you, okay? I'd worried about them for about an hour before the call and I continued to worry more and more for another three hours until they came home. By this time, I'd turned off the TV, had eaten a fish finger sandwich and was sitting at the foot of the stairs, unsure whether to stay up until they got home or go straight to bed. I wouldn't have been able to sleep but it felt like what I ought to have done.

When they walked through the door, I saw mum's eyes were red and she had her arm round Dad, not supporting him totally but not letting him move under his own steam. He cracked a grin, a boy again, but it wasn't the same. One side of his smile was crooked, inflamed, and he had a thick wedge of bandage pressed to the front of his head by gauze binding. Beneath, his right eye was bloodshot and signs of a fresh, yellow bruise loomed like shadows.

Rather than ask the questions rising inside me, I fled upstairs at the sight of them both and lay like a corpse in my bed, unfocused on the glow-in-the-dark stars glued to my dark blue ceiling.

By the next morning, I had slept for a couple of hours perhaps but my dreams were violent and colourful. I dreaded what would await me downstairs, the visions of scythes and blood spatter clanging like bells behind my eyes. But it was sedate. My father, the protective dressing forming a white helmet and two fingers on his left hand shackled together with plasters and a splint, from my view had his back to the kitchen and was engrossed in the newspaper and his toast. My mother, with no sign of distress or pain, poured the kettle and hummed what sounded like one of their chants.

I sat at the table, as usual, and waited for an explanation.

"*Hola, cariño*," said Mum.

"Hey, *hijo*," Dad tried to say, but it came out as a murmur.

"Are you going to tell me what happened?" I demanded.

"Thish?" Dad replied.

"Your *papá* got a little over excited again. He'll be okay."

"You should have sheen your *mamá*! Ha! Thee knowth how to thwing a bat!" He tried to laugh but I saw the twinge of pain.

"It's not funny. You got hurt." He wasn't the only one.

"Baby, no, it's okay, he's fine. You know, your *papá* got into much worse situations back home." Their lack of care for themselves made me so angry. He might have been bashed about this time but what about next time? How far would they go before they went too far? I ate my breakfast in silence and just nodded and grunted when they tried to spark a conversation. I wanted old, harmless memories back but now, this one, was the one that almost erased those happy ones.

My reminiscing was interrupted when Chelsea came home, earlier than expected.

"Hi boys!" she trilled.

Ollie's eyes darted to the door but it was too late. His expression couldn't let him act cool and there was no way to make clearing the coffee table with one sweeping arm motion seem anything other than suspicious.

"What are you two up to?"

"Frankie was just telling me how he got his visa thing sorted."

"Sort of, well, I have to speak to someone else now, it's complicated…" I tried to position myself between her and the coffee table but her long legs had conquered the space from the front door more quickly than I should have anticipated.

"Great. And what's all this paperwork, Ollie…?" Her expression changed from curiosity to what seemed like her often deployed weapon of condescending disappointment but she went past that point and on to shock. "What… why have you got all this… this… *propaganda* in our flat?"

"Aren't all of your leaflets and posters propaganda too?" Ollie reacted.

"Don't fucking change the subject." I hadn't heard her swear until then. She didn't come across as the sort - maybe with a few gins in her and with an elaborate hat askew as she sportingly cheered on a horse at the races but I'd never heard her drop the F-bomb before. I didn't know where to look so I sort of looked at my shoes and defocused my eyes, hoping not to be drawn into this. "What is all this shit and why is it on my fucking coffee table?" Ollie also looked away, afraid to engage either of us.

"I said I'd help the guys out with it. I'm just going to put a few leaflets through letterboxes and post some letters."

"I can't believe you would do this to me," she raged. "Do you think this is one of your silly games? This is our lives, Ollie, our futures. You can't possibly believe in the lies that are printed in that crap." I desperately tried to think of a good reason to be somewhere else without making the situation worse. I couldn't remember a time when I'd seen Chelsea this furious – not the protester, false ire, rowdy kind of angry but nostrils flared, fists clenched, about to snap incensed.

"Chelsea, love, listen, you have your causes and I've found one too, I thought you might be happy…" he paused as he saw her about to say something that they might both regret and then hold back. "…or proud of me, for doing something for someone else. You always ask me to think of other people, don't you?" She carelessly shrugged off her rucksack with a punctuated whump and stepped closer to him.

"Not this, though, Jesus, it's bullshit. Unelected EU officials – you know we voted in the European elections two years ago, don't you? Take back control –

control of what? We have a Parliamentary veto on any rules from the EU and our elected MEPs come up with the policies in the first place!" I could see Ollie's face going red, he was annoyed and I knew he could only defend himself by going on the front foot.

"You're smarter than that, C, you know our MEPs are outnumbered. The EU tells us to jump and we say how high. And how many people actually voted in the European election anyway? It was only about 30% - how is that democracy?"

"I didn't hear you moaning about it then! You've been brainwashed by all this shit, Ollie…"

"And you can't accept that someone with a different opinion to you might actually be right!" He stood up and my eyes refocused. I had seen things get confrontational after a few drinks but this was on another level. Ollie had switched it up a gear now and I contemplated whether that was the right tack. "What have you got against me doing this anyway?"

"It's not *you*, it's the cause. They're fucking deluded…

"That's not how you persuade someone to change their mind, is it?" She recoiled, her own criticisms coming back to haunt her. But then Ollie over-reached. "They've got a point and you find it uncomfortable."

"They only make one point and it's bullshit!"

"And what's that then?" They were only a foot apart now, eyes wide and shoulders back. I thought one of them was going to hit the other, but I couldn't guess who.

"Immigrants ruining the country! What absolute crap!"

"And you're telling me there's no negative effects of hundreds of thousands of people coming to the UK?"

"Bollocks."

"They're driving down wages, they're using public services…"

"That's not the EU's fault is it?" she countered.

"Isn't it? So, where the hell are they all coming from?"

"I don't see you blaming Frankie for ruining the country!"

Both of them suddenly fell silent. They turned to look at me and, if I'm honest, when I think back, I don't remember feeling anything.

"Oh God, I'm sorry, Frankie, I didn't mean it."

I remember the confusion and then the words she had said registered and I comprehended what she meant. When you hear something but you aren't listening, you don't truly *hear* it, it just washes over you. When those sounds then coagulate into meaning and that meaning is deciphered, initially, it's still meaningless until you remember who is speaking. The caring, ultra-liberal, privileged, generous, pretty, self-centred, flatmate, ex-girlfriend.

"Oh, mate, she didn't mean it…"

Ollie tried to patch up the wound but it was too late. I couldn't look at either of them, or rather I couldn't focus. My vision began to blur and I just walked away, to my room, where I sat on my own and, between my fingers, ripped and tore at the quaint, private, artwork I had spent so long crafting.

Chapter 10 – Tuesday 31st May (23 days to go)

After a tedious lecture on composition and division, a fairly unproductive seminar, and a shift at Scintilla, which dragged interminably, the last thing I wanted to do was to have to go back into the campus and speak to the Students' Loan Company people but I had no choice. At least I could look forward to that evenings WMSCACE social that I'd been invited to, which might take my mind off of Chelsea and Ollie.

Fortunately, they had a presence in the University building which, I hoped, would save me the hassle of having to wait on the phone for hours until a real human being answered. As exhausted as I was, I still had an optimistic view that a one-to-one conversation could rectify the mistakes that had led to the Home Office visit by agents Kean and Goode. The Students' Union was a glass-fronted cube with a far more modern feel to the university reception I had been to previously.

The doors swished open and a sparse lobby welcomed me with a cheery 'hello', literally sculpted into the curved, white pine-fronted entrance desk, and called out by the bright-eyed and convivial attendant.

"How are you doing today?" I got the impression he was genuinely interested in my answer.

"Yeah, great. I need to speak to someone at the Students' Loan Company." He nodded curtly and tapped swiftly into a digital display.

"No problem. Their workspace is on the first floor. Walk up the stairs -" he indicated them with a sharp extension of his hand; the sleek arcing staircase started beside the desk and swept up to a mezzanine level "- and there is a signpost in front of you. Follow the arrows, through the doors, and you'll find their office pretty easily as it's the first on the right."

"That's it?"

"Yep, that's it!"

"Does the office have a number...?" He frowned.

"No, but there is a sign on the door that says 'Students' Loan Company'," he smiled at his humour, innocent of the confusion I had already been through at the main University building. I thanked him, to which he thanked me, and then I went up the stairs to the mezzanine, through the doors, and straight to the first office on the right that did indeed have a sign on the outside stating 'Students' Loan Company'. I looked for a buzzer or a sign with their opening hours but there were neither so I pushed the door and simply walked in.

Before me, laid out in precise order, were four crisp, perfect desks, with Apple Macs on each, operated by four neatly dressed, fresh-faced staff members in grey trousers, black shoes, and light blue roll necks. They appeared composed rather than morose and active rather than half asleep. I considered this a good sign.

"Good afternoon, my name's Ali, how can I help?" He shook my hand formally and indicated a spotless table and chairs. We sat and he produced an iPad and logged in.

"Hi Ali, I'm Frankie. Basically, the University have some incorrect information and it's caused some…

issues... and that information came from the Students' Loan Company so I need to sort it out with you."

"No problem, Frankie. Lovely to meet you." Ali smiled at me and put his iPad on the table between us so I could see the screen. "Why don't you just type your full name in here and we'll bring up all of your data." A few simple tamps later and I slid the tablet back to Ali and he scanned over my details. The office, Ali, his demeanour at least, and everything about the Students' Loan Company seemed a stark contrast to the University's archives office. His eyebrows arched and then he looked up.

"Is everything okay?" I queried.

"Yes, I've just never met someone from Val Verde before, That's really cool." He gave me a beguiling smile, which spread to me unexpectedly and, rather than my initial compulsion to deny that I was from some little-known Central American nation and to explain that I was born and raised a matter of miles away, I smiled in a self-assured way, feeling that little bit prouder of where my parents came from.

"Thanks, Ali."

"No problem, Frankie," he focused back on the tablet screen, gave it a few swipes and set it down between us. "Okay, so, you have had your loan from us for coming up to eighteen months now, haven't you?"

"That's right."

"And you've not missed a payment from your current account overdraft on any of your other bills." He looked up at me, briefly. "That's good."

"Thanks." I didn't wonder how they knew that; I supposed all financial bodies talked to one another.

"Don't worry – we have insight into the accounts linked with your loan. There's really nothing to worry about, Frankie. You've got a good credit score for a student, too, in case you ever wanted to get a credit card."

"Oh, great, thanks for telling me." Ali was *really* helpful. Not like the old duffer at the main building.

"I can see that there's a red flag on your residency status though. That could make it trickier to get a mortgage, though," he smiled at me again and, for the first time, I felt like this issue I had was somehow minor. Inconsequential. And, honestly, I shouldn't have got so wound up about it. I noticed the soft twinkling tones of mood music which I hadn't heard before. "I'm going to speak to my colleague but can I get you a glass of water first? We have still, iced, or sparkling?"

"Iced, thank you." I had no plans for a mortgage so, if that was what worried Ali the most, I felt reassured. When Ali goose-stepped back from his conversation with the iPad under one arm and two glasses of revitalising, crisp water, he had plenty to ask me.

"Can I check that your home address is the one we have in Digbeth?"

"It was when I applied for the loan. That's where my family live, lived, I mean. I now live in a flat in Selly Oak."

"Did you inform us of a change of address via letter?"

"Yes, I think so." I sipped the water and it was like I had never truly tasted water before. "Wow. What's in this?"

"I think it's kiwi. Good, isn't it?" We shared a nod and a smile and Ali continued. "Great, you did, thank you for that, Frankie. I just needed to confirm that with you, for security reasons."

"How does that affect my residency status then?"

"SLC is a major financial operation so we are extremely careful with your data. We wouldn't want it getting in the wrong hands, would we? As you should be aware, the amount which we can lend you is dependent upon your parents' household income. When you changed your home address, it is our policy to send an automated letter to your parents' address to cross-reference the information you provide us and to see if their financial circumstances have changed. If they were earning less, for example, you could be entitled to an increased loan amount." I knew they were both earning less now, if they were earning anything, so perhaps this meant I could get a bit more money. I wouldn't have to pay it back for a few years yet anyway. This might turn out alright after all.

"That makes sense."

"You can't be too careful with identity theft and online scams, can you?" He looked back down at the iPad and carried on. "We sent a letter to your address in, let me see, Sedgley but it was returned to sender. We phoned the homeowner and they gave us another address in Digbeth. We then sent the communication to that address via the Royal Mail's Signed delivery service but the letter was returned as it has to be signed for. We then resent it via the Tracked delivery service. This enables us to see, if there is a forwarding address, where the letter ends up. It's a very efficient way to automatically update you or your parents' information."

"That is smart, Ali." I took a long drink of the delicious water and crossed my legs to emphasise my sense of being impressed but I don't think Ali noticed. He didn't even respond.

"Your updated records show that your parents' new contact address is the Val Verde Embassy in London. Typically, if we see that a forwarding address is a Government building, we would follow up as it could be that parents' have died, are employed by the state and have been relocated, or that they have been deported." He looked up now.

"I see." I didn't understand but the silence and the pause made me feel uncomfortable and I instinctively said something for the sake of filling the void.

"Our system records all of the call notes and allows staff to input audio files of any telephone conversations or copy the system into any outbound emails, so they are all stored in our data cloud. We are aspiring to be a paperless organisation, as you can see." I hadn't noticed before but there was a now-noticeable absence of filing cabinets, printers, faxes, even notepads. "One of my colleagues spoke to the Embassy and they said that your parents – the Cualquieras, am I saying that correctly?"

"Yes, thanks…"

"The Cualquieras had been returned home. Once we input that information into the system, it automatically cross-references the Home Office database and, if there is no visa status for the individual – in this case, that's you – then it updates our records to show that you do not have Indefinite Leave to Remain status or a student visa."

"But, Ali, I'm British. I was born here. I don't need either of those things."

"Not according to the information in the system, Mr. Cualquiera." Not 'Frankie' now. "It says you were born in Val Verde in June 1995. Is that incorrect?" Oh God, I dreaded this now. If I told them it was wrong, would that make matters worse? Would two uniformed goons jump me and drag me off into the back of a van? But if I said it was true – which it wasn't – would I get found out later on and the same thing happen?

"No, no, Ali, I was born in Druid's Heath. Your records are.." I gulped. "…wrong."

"I don't think so. We have some of the most sophisticated database management technology in the country."

"Why didn't you call me and talk to me? You have my contact phone number, don't you?"

"Does your number end 24783?"

"Yes."

"That's the correct number. I just needed to confirm that with you, for security reasons. We are not allowed to contact you in these circumstances without written authorisation from your parents. It's GDPR; data protection."

"I'm here now. Can you update your records?"

"We can update your records, yes. Do you have a passport or driving licence?"

"No, but I can... I can give you my student ID card. Or a mobile phone bill."

"I'm sorry but we need Government issued documentation."

"I can get a new passport, but it might take a while." He smiled and I felt like, perhaps, I had said the right combination of words to make this problem go away.

"That's excellent. As soon as you have your passport, come and see me, and I will update all of your information here."

"Brilliant. And that will mean all of your records are correct..."

"Absolutely."

"...and the whole visa issue would be sorted?"

"I'm afraid not, Mr. Cualquiera."

"Why not?" I shifted uncomfortably in the hard-plastic chair, which now felt as though it wasn't as ergonomically designed as my initial assessment inferred.

"Our automated system routinely coordinates with the Home Office database in accordance with anti-extremism laws that were brought in as part of the Government's 2011 Prevent strategy"

"But I'm not a *terrorist*!" Amidst the tranquility one of the other SLC staff members allowed themselves to peer over the top of their monitor before seeing that nobody else was looking and sliding their gaze back to the task at hand.

"Please, sir, remain calm." That's what I would have told myself, had this situation not been so idiotic.

"This can't be real…" I resented that frozen water now; it was just two chemicals covalently bonded together. If it was the same chemicals comprised differently it would not be recognisable, or even edible, possibly. "You got a returned letter and, instead of talking to me, you spoke to the Val Verdean Embassy and now *I'm* getting deported! Do you see how ridiculous this is?"

"Sir, I need you to relax or I will have to request that you leave the office."

"I am relaxed, but I just want you to understand how crazy this is. Do you understand?"

"I understand your predicament. Unfortunately, I am unable to help."

"You can change the data in the system. You can update it and then it will update the Home Office system, right?" He seemed confused, as if nobody had ever suggested such a thing before. "Look, I'll do it for you." I reached for the iPad but Ali's hand shot out and he slid it back and out of my reach.

"You are not permitted to touch SLC property. You are acting hysterically. I am now asking that you leave, sir."

"I only want to get this all sorted, I don't want to make a scene."

"Please, sir." That was it then. I picked up my coat, looked back at the office, hoping for someone to step up and say something in my defence, but they all looked at their screens, choosing to ignore me. *Me*. The lunatic that was apparently acting hysterically. They wouldn't know hysteria if it jumped up and punched them in the eye.

That evening, I went to WMSCACE reluctantly. When Ernesto had invited me, I had put the event in my phone, and I had an indefinable urge to go and waited for the time to come with anticipation. Even when other minor things get to me – a difficult customer, bumping into Chelsea the morning after her argument with Ollie when she couldn't look me in the eye – the knowledge that I had something else to look forward to buoyed my mood. Now I was angry. The University – *my* university – couldn't help, the Students' Loan Company wouldn't help, the Home Office agents were just jobsworths, doing as they were told without thinking or even, perhaps, considering me as a human being just like them.

This time we were meeting upstairs at The Gallivanting Gendarme pub – or 'Wandering Wanker', as Ollie preferred to call it. It was opposite The Mint & Chips, which went bust a few weeks ago, and the football was on at the Head in Clouds, which was a stopping off point for Blues fans, so the Gendarme was significantly more busy than usual. The entrance was a steel-framed arch, with worn wooden planters, no doubt harking back to a simpler, more industrial age, when people didn't worry about deportation – they worried about diphtheria. The thought wasn't especially consoling.

Through the crush of conviviality, I found the rear staircase and ascended to the meeting room. It was all exposed brickwork and bare floorboards, so drinks were, more often than not, either elaborately floral, designer gin and tonics, small batch pale ales, or something unrecognisable served in jam jars.

I noticed, through the traffic, that the group were huddled around a table at the back of the bar. Confused, as this was a very different setting to the first meeting I had attended, I walked over, unsure of what the protocol was and hoping not to cause as much disruption as last time.

"Francesco!" Ernesto called out; despite the fact I clearly knew where he was. I gave them a discreet wave and took a chair. "Welcome! Glad you could make it."

"Hi everyone." There was Marcos, who barely acknowledged me, Eva, who smiled before taking a sip of her drink, and two others I didn't know, but who I recognised from the hotel.

"*Dale una copa al chico, no tú?*" Ernesto whispered sharply at Marcos, who shot him a glare back, but Ernesto responded similarly, appearing to communicate just with his eyebrows, and Marcos grudgingly stood up.

"*¿Quieres una cerveza?*" He loomed over me, giving me that look I gave gherkins in Big Macs.

"*Si, si por favor.*" He stomped off, leaving me with a sense of having set something regrettable in motion by my actions, or lack of actions, or just by generally existing. "Ernesto, why are we meeting here?"

"Cosy, no? It's a bit more personal than the hotel."

"How are you, Francesco?"

"Fine thanks, Eva. You?" We used each others' names the way you do when you really don't want to forget it.

"*Bien, gracias.* How are your studies? Ernesto says you are studying at the university."

"Ah, pretty good, you know, not brilliant, but, uh, alright yeah…" Marcos nearly dropped a pint glass full to the brim on the table in front of me with a clunk, spilling a little. "Is that lager? *¿Es esa servir?*" I thought he grunted but I couldn't tell. Eva chuckled and Ernesto leaned into Marcos and began talking rapidly with him.

"So, you're not originally from the Americas?"

"No, I'm from the Midlands. How can you tell?"

"Your pronunciation, of course, and the words you use, and what you wear…"

"Okay, alright," I laughed, even though it slighted. "Like what?"

"*Servir* means serving, but *cerveza* means beer."

"What's the difference?"

"You don't hear it?" She smiled. I felt suddenly self-conscious and a little embarrassed.

"What about you, are you working or studying? Or something?"

"Yes, I study too. Law. It's good, I mean, very Anglo-centric, of course, but I enjoy it anyway." At that, we both drank, buying ourselves time. Ernesto and Marcos had stopped and turned to address us. Our other two guests had met a mutual friend, it seemed, and begun a conversation of their own, the man's head flinging back, the way that some people laughed in a very affected way, or so I thought.

"Francesco, how are you doing?"

"Good, yeah, you know," I wasn't sure what to say because I felt as if Ernesto didn't really want to know but was trying to open up a conversation.

"No, no, please, I would like to know what you do. I know you work in the coffee shop, and study, but what else do you do?" I wasn't quite sure how to answer as I was reluctant to talk about my private life, what there was of it. I had little that I wanted to share when it came to hobbies and even less to talk about when it came to friends. Now, at least. Perhaps, though, I could alleviate the anger I was feeling towards my flatmates by talking about them; after all, a problem shared was a problem halved, wasn't it?

"I had a bit of a fight with my flatmates, so I'm not feeling too chatty, if you know what I mean."

"*¿Acerca de?* What about? Was it serious?"

"I mean, nothing serious, they…" No, no, my subconscious interrupted, no, it *was* serious, it did make me feel angry. I should talk about it. "They called me an outsider, I thought they were my friends…"

"That sounds pretty serious to me. Why did they say that?"

"I.. I.. can't really put my finger on it. They were arguing about Brexit and it just got out of hand…" It was the truth but it didn't get to the root of the issue and I wasn't sure how to verbalise my true feelings. "I feel betrayed by them, as if they got angry about something that doesn't even involve me and… and their ranting spilled over and pulled me into their row. Does that make sense?"

"Yes, *claro*. I understand but it seems like you have been affected very deeply by this. Are they more than flatmates?" I nodded but had shared enough. What did I expect Ernesto to be able to do?

"Yeah, I thought so." I hesitated. "I trusted them as friends but, now, I don't think I can." I thought that Ernesto understood but he took the opportunity to change the subject, for my benefit.

"How much do you know about Val Verde, Francesco?"

"A bit."

"I'm sure you know all about the politics, don't you? The situation there is so changeable and has been for decades." I nodded along. "We, I mean, WMSCACE, are always keen to help our members stay close to what is happening back home or find out more about their homeland, in your situation." Eva and Marcos watched me, closely. Their faces edged closer – except Marcos; he leaned back nonchalantly, draping one arm across the window ledge behind him.

"Okay."

"Would you like to find out more about your homeland?"

"It's more my parents' homeland than mine…" It didn't feel as if that was the response they were looking for, nor the direction I wanted to take the conversation, having only met them all together once before. "Yeah, sure, why not."

"Fantastic. Do you know who's in power now, Francesco?"

"Calderon, is it? Isn't it?" Marcos snorted and Eva looked at Ernesto, measuring his response.

"Yes, that's right!" I felt a riffle of satisfaction. "He's been in power for a few years now but there's an election coming up soon, I've heard."

"The centre-right government have been imprisoning anyone who speaks out against them. But also anyone who spoke up about their predecessors too." Eva added, sharing the news like a whispered secret. "Calderon doesn't want *anyone* who he thinks might upset the balance of power he has enjoyed for so long." I leaned in, almost close enough to feel their breath. Here we were; co-conspirators, talking about the politics of Val Verde, like we were the Resistance in wartime France, cloistered in the cobwebbed wine cellar of an ancient monastery rather than a fashionable wine bar in central Birmingham. I felt a little ridiculous but let the novelty of the occasion take me.

"Marcos is from Val Verde," Ernesto added. They glanced at him but he just scowled back, straining his jaw. "He knows all about Calderon's methods." The phrase hung there between us. Despite his frosty demeanour, I momentarily felt a pang of sympathy for the seething brute. "But we want to do something together, Francesco. We want to do something incredible. We want to bring to Calderon the one thing he truly fears; change." I nodded subconsciously. "Change from the queues for bread, change from the brutality and armed police, change from the poverty, squalor, and inequality." Ernesto was doing it again – speaking so powerfully, in a way that compelled me to obey, yet *saying* almost nothing. At least there was nothing he was saying that I would ordinarily disagree with – surely nobody could defend destitution or starvation? – and yet I was compelled to heed all he said attentively.

"Calderon must know that a reckoning is coming. He is doing all he can to ensure his brutal reign continues unchecked." Ernesto broke off to whet his palate.

"Why are you bringing this up?" At my questioning, Marcos lunged towards Ernesto to compel him with some spoken direction, married with a firm, angular hand motion. Ernesto responded by talking over him in a lower, muted voice, with gestures of his own.

"We are hoping that you would be interested in joining a working group within WMSCACE. We are putting a small group of like-minded individuals together to, er, to discuss how we can influence the outcome of the election. To improve the state of the nation." Marcos watched him closely.

That was the moment when Ernesto gripped my attention like a boa constrictor. I can remember it all clearly now but not so clearly as I could when I was alone, walking home, and really thinking about what it was Ernesto had asked of me.

"Yeah, sure," I sipped my beer, to give me a chance to watch their reactions. Why were they acting so secretively over such an innocent question?

"You have to attend another meeting a week next Tuesday. Are you free in the evening?" Eva asked. I nodded but made a mental note to check my rota at Scintilla. I was hoping for something more exciting to come out of this meeting, something to take my mind off of my impending reacquaintance with the Home Office.

The rest of the evening was fairly relaxed. I learned that the two, now three, other members of the party were José, Marta, and Luis, but, in the end, they didn't play as big a part in what happened next as Ernesto and Marcos. This little get together was just the preamble for what was to come – which was all together more dangerous – and I was oblivious to what I had signed up to.

Ernesto nodded and then, with his forefinger, tapped on the table in between us to emphasise the importance of his next question.

"What else have you really got to look forward to, Francesco?" He may have intended it to be rhetorical but it was the same question he had asked me the last time we met. I still didn't have an answer and two more beers didn't help me to find one.

Chapter 11 – Wednesday 1st June
(22 days to go)

I didn't used to dream of things that have actually happened. Less often do I remember what I dreamed about by the time I awoke. Most nights, I got up with only a sense or a vague emotion that related back to what I had imagined. With what you must know of me, you probably think I dream of train journeys to countryside villages or watching heated debates between the world's great philosophical minds - inspired by my studies rather than Ollie and Chelsea's blazing arguments, I can assure you. This night though I dreamt so vividly and clearly that if it wasn't a memory of an event that had already taken place I might have been forgiven for thinking it was a supernatural premonition of something yet to pass.

There seemed to be no reason for this particular memory to rise to the surface of my consciousness like tea leaves stewing in the pot. Perhaps, in a way it was a foreshadowing of future events, or at least similar events that I will explain later on.

My parents had been preparing for this particular demo for weeks. They had arranged with a bunch of friends to hire a minibus that would pick us up outside Snow Hill station and take the group of us down to London, where the Val Verdean Embassy was based. The plan was to get up at 5am and get ready, leave the house at 6am and walk to the train station, with a stop to get some breakfast on the way, where the minibus would collect us all at 7:15am. We'd be driven down to the Royal Albert Hall, getting in at 10ish, if the traffic was good and we didn't have to make too many pit stops. They chose the venue more known for classical musical performances than chants to overthrow the bourgeoisie because there was always coach parking available close by and they could drop us all off and park up elsewhere if it was too busy. From that famous concert hall, we would march to Belgrave Square, home of several embassies and consulates, including that of Val Verde. We were intending to stage a protest outside the pale Neoclassical terraces, which would involve uniting with my parents' country folk at the embassy, loudly playing a range of traditional musical styles, handing out flyers and a selection of *cachitos* and *pastelitos*, warmed up over a Calor gas grill one of the organisers from London was bringing, along with cans of soft drink. Papá wanted to bring a cooler full of beers but, upon consulting some of the others in the group, he was voted down because of the risk that it could attract additional police attention or could invalidate the permit they had acquired to stage the protest in the first place. He settled for a couple of Red Stripes in the minibus on the way down.

I wasn't yet fully awake when I heard banging on the bathroom door.

"*¡Muévete!* Don't use up all the hot water!" It was too warm and too steamy to leave just yet. I took my time towelling dry, brushing my teeth twice before breakfast, and contemplating which colour of blue socks I should wear for my first trip to the capital.

"Come on, we'll be late!" I sighed and spooned another mouthful of Coco Pops, sucking the chocolatey milk before meticulously chewing the soggy hoops. Papá ferried painted banners and a small cool box - "To sit on…" - to the front door, beaming from ear to ear. Mamá had a pile of cling film wrapped Tupperware right up to her chin and she stacked them up in wide open carrier bags before deciding that the best way to keep everyone happy was to put the carrier bags into the cool box.

Papá's smile faded when he realised that he would have to carry it to the station.

"Aren't you ready yet?" she asked.

"Do I have to come?"

I got the frown.

This was going to be my first trip on a demonstration but I hadn't paid attention to what we were protesting. Sitting on the bottom step, I listlessly tied and retied my trainers. I watched the two of them exchanging crisp words with steady glares and Mamá's jabbed finger at Papá's chin.

"Come on, let's go," he said, tossing a rucksack over both shoulders and securing the cool box between his bear-like hands. Mamá held the keys in her hand, jangling them. I huffed and stood up, wishing to be almost anywhere else but here.

"What's the matter with you?"

"Nothing." She encouraged me away from the doorstep so she could lock the door. "Alright.." I muttered. She grunted. Papá made a comment about hoping that we wouldn't be like this for the coach ride down.

The upside of living in a Council-owned home was that it was possible to be in a city centre location, or at least really close to it, without the expense of renting privately. Yet there was nothing particular to recall about walking to the train station as Birmingham was my home and, like anywhere you've grown up in, much of it becomes

123

background noise - a regular drumbeat below the rising and falling vocal sounds that punctuated life, the gaps between stations where the world passes by in running watercolours. That day and that journey was one such terminus that my subconscious deemed relevant and necessary to me at this moment and herded to the foreground, giving me the chance to relive all of the reticence, impatience, excitement, and betrayal I experienced all over again. Despite that, Snow Hill was not a particularly eye-catching station and once we arrived, we waited outside the ticket hall, Papá glad of the rest and testing out the structural integrity of his well-packed cooler-chair.

The greyness enveloped me and I wished I could have been swallowed up by my duvet and avoided this journey and all the crap that would go with it. Perched on scratchy seats in a battered old Transit. Listening to unfamiliar voices speak half understood words. Hours of monotonous roads and then standing in the street watching my parents and their stupid friends waving their banners and shouting out who knows what. What I wouldn't do to be left at home to entertain myself. Saturday morning TV, eating what I want when I want, I'd drag my duvet onto the sofa and probably not get up all day. Bliss.

When the coach did arrive, late, as I thought it would, it took ages to get on board. Everyone piled out and they all started hugging each other and kissing their cheeks and all that, as if they hadn't seen each other in forever. If I had to be here, couldn't we hurry it up a bit? We were the last to be collected so didn't have much choice about the seats. From what I gathered, the organisers knew my parents were coming but weren't sure about me, so there were two seats together for them and I got squished in a spare seat at the back, beside one of the three other kids. None of them seemed particularly excited to be there and my neighbour - Julia, I think - had a hot pink Nintendo DS and wore a pair of headphones. I don't think she looked up from playing until we reached the services at Oxford.

I had been right about the itchy material that upholstered the seats. Even through my jeans, it felt uncomfortable and the humid atmosphere only made things worse. But, as I sat there seething at the situation I could not get out of, what I did notice was that everyone else, with the exception of the fixated Julia, was smiling. Whether they were in trios or on their own, there were drinks (soft only, sorry Dad) and snacks passed around and there seemed to be much more giving than taking.

Nobody else appeared to have noticed the material on the seats. Nobody else seemed to mind that the suspension was hard and the steering not quite erratic but certainly absent-minded, with jerked turns at almost the last possible moment. Julia rocked silently from one side to the other, oblivious to the flurry of curses lobbed at the driver like rotten tomatoes. They all seemed to care very little for the fact that from when we hit the M6 up until the M4 Interchange, all you saw was grey tarmac and other vehicles.

What was it that made them behave like this? Did they not realise we could all be at home curled up under the covers eating crisp sandwiches? Maybe they'd never eaten cheese and onion in between two slices of Kingsmill.

"Your first time?" One of the other boys leaned on his elbows over the back of the seat in front of me.

"No, I mean, yeah."

"I was scared my first time too."

"I'm not scared!"

"Sure."

"I'm not," I persisted. "I'm bored. I don't want to be here, that's all. I'd rather be at home." He shrugged.

"You never know, you might enjoy yourself." Satisfied that I was neither a threat nor a friend, he sat back down and closed his eyes.

There were around twenty of us on the minibus and we looked no larger than a family outing when we disembarked in London. Around the Albert Memorial were huge crowds of Japanese tourists, following a tall, ash blonde woman with a decisive voice and a wry smile. Her leadership skills were demonstrated with an effortless wave of her umbrella, which she held aloft for the group to follow. I would have happily followed that group and wandered off into the unknown but for my parents and their hare-brained protest.

It was another endless walk from the drop off to Belgrave Square but this time, we were hindered by slow walkers, dawdlers, amblers, and strollers that all happened to be in the way. How could anyone enjoy coming here? My frustration and boredom were only prevented from overspilling by the need for constant alertness to navigate the capital's pavements. At the square, I was unimpressed - another strip of tarmac, parking bays packed full, more pedestrians selfishly taking up too much space and time, and a load of identical, tall, terrace buildings smooshed together in front of a dark green garden sealed off with a black metal railing topped with spikes. For a bunch of buildings that contained organisations whose purpose, I thought, was to aid and protect their nations' citizens, the setting was anything but cordial.

It didn't take long for our cadre to huddle together, unprotected from the suddenly bleak weather by the heater on the bus. We sheltered on the park side of the street, which ran all around the island of foliage. Most pulled out plastic macs and wrapped themselves in them, looking like sausages wrapped in cling film, squeezed together in the fridge cabinets. Some, like my Dad, had a sweatshirt, which he took from the top of his backpack and gave to Mamá without a thought. He tried to hide his discomfort by starting up a song, and he was joined by a few lusty voices to start with. They soon faded away.

For almost an hour, the group stood, dishevelled and cold, as if they had been plucked out of the Channel and dragged ashore, and the rain sprayed them for that whole time. Mum had an umbrella that she shared with another lady but, by the time it got to half eleven, all the snacks for the journey back had been eaten and some of the kids, with the exception of Julia, were already eyeing up the contents of the cool box.

"*Mamá*, can I go for a walk?" She looked over me, my slumped shoulders and reclining rubber neck telling her everything she needed to know.

"Sure, but don't go too far. It's all about to start. Soon." I wasn't convinced.

"Be back before 1 o'clock," prompted Papá.

There's little point describing the dull white buildings that formed the palisades of the square, I've not got the eye for architecture. I knew they were ornate and Georgian but I couldn't tell you which George or what made them so. Lots of carvings and columns and stairs up to broad, gloss doors. I was looking for adventure; if that was even possible.

I was never the sort of child that, if I had nothing to do, would turn to destruction or attention-seeking. Happy in my own little world, as a child to an adult, I was able to find my own entertainment. I was proud of not needing the distraction of computer games like Julia - although, I would have loved to have been able to immerse myself in a puzzle game for the whole journey back, if I could. My instincts told me to go in one direction so I did and I kept the gardens to my left and meandered along the pavement, testing my knowledge of the flags that limply hung from the front of the buildings opposite.

Austria, Brunei, Germany, Spain.

I wasn't walking quickly and I stopped to look at a statue, set back from the road but exposed to it. Columbus or Colón, depending on who you believe, and which is apt as he really was a total shit. Claiming to have discovered a route to India when you couldn't accept that you got lost. Instigating genocide. Raping a native woman. Cutting the hands off of indigenous people. My Dad made sure I knew all of this as soon as we started studying History. His blemishless, holy face gazing off into the middle distance, holding a map aloft in front of him, like a toddler with his first finger painting, begging his parents to stick it to the front of the fridge. That's what Colón was. If I was braver, I would have spat on him - Dad would have approved but not Mum.

Norway. Serbia. Qatar.

At the end of the square, roads split off invitingly but I decided to heed my parents desire for me to join them for the protest, not that I'd seen much of that so far. The weather seemed to have put paid to their hopes for a big turnout.

I recalled standing square up to the Great Liberator, Simón Bolívar. His pose invited a decision - one hand held up, bent at the elbow, as if offering a choice; his left hand held a scroll or manuscript. From his expression, I imagined him saying 'You can have option A or take a look at the parchment to see what option B is but, let me tell you, you don't want to know what option B is...' Unlike Colón, Papá held Bolívar in high regard as he saw him as a diplomat who would not be pushed around. Despite being from a Spanish family, he recognised that the Empire of Spain, technically the nation of his birth, were in the wrong and needed to be overthrown. I thought of it as ingratitude at the time but, now, I wonder what gratitude governments deserve.

I must admit that I was moved by the legend of Bolívar. His proud chest. His resolute expression. Along with all I had been told, a little spark of patriotism arose in me. Sure, he had not had any involvement with Val Verde but his accomplishments were no less impressive.

Before I turned to go, lighter from having glimpsed something truly enlightening, I read the inscription on the plinth; 'I am convinced that England alone is capable of protecting the world's rights as she is great, glorious and wise.'

What the hell? The guy liberates six countries and doesn't have a memorable quote about one of them?

Any why England - why not France or Italy or India? I bet the other foreign diplomats, especially those from the South and Central American countries where *el Libertador* is so revered are ashamed to see what has been carved. If England was so great and glorious and wise, why were we having to protest out the front of the Val Verdean embassy? Couldn't England greatly, wisely, and gloriously make sure that the people of Val Verde were not being mistreated and oppressed?

Any remaining lightness left me and I trudged on, paying no more attention to the flags which glimmered and swayed as the sun broke through the cloud. I failed to be moved by Don Jose de San Martin and I never even realised that there was a statue of Leonardo da Vinci's Vitruvian Man. The street bent around and I drearily followed. I was lost in my thoughts and only broke free when I realised that I had walked straight instead of bending left and rather than seeing what I thought would be the Ghanaian embassy, as I had noticed it when we arrived, it was the Romanian one instead. I turned on my heel and tried to work out where I had gone wrong. Fortunately, I wasn't far of course, and I could turn back and bear right and end up back to my parents and, oh wow, it was nearly one.

There was one last statue that I felt compelled to examine. Flanked by two obedient, bronze dogs and looking every inch like a man with a plan, was Sir Robert Grosvenor, so one of the many plaques read. He had an embossed and very grand coat of arms and beneath it read;

'When we build, let us think we build for ever'.

I didn't bother reading the other plaques as I had found a message, a sign. Why wasn't that on Bolívar's pedestal? The phrase hit home so cleanly, I felt as if someone had told me a truth about myself that swept aside any fog, any confusion. When we build, let us think we build for ever. It wasn't just a platitude but a command, assuming that the person reading this was a builder by nature, or a creator, or designer, it didn't matter as they all could fall into the category of 'builder'. This man might have been English but so was I and we had that in common, just as much in common, more so, than I did with Bolívar. I started to consider what it was that I built or what was I building towards. Did I have something I wanted to last for ever? I had so much to contemplate but I had to get back. This thought rang inside my head for days after that trip to London and, up until I dreamed about that journey, I had almost forgotten it. Perhaps, there was a reason why it resurfaced at this very moment.

I jogged back to the square and around the corner.

Kuwait, Portugal, Ghana.

The main body of our group had swelled now that the London Val Verdeans had arrived. Typical of them to be late to their own event. Mamá and Papá caught my eye and I made a beeline for them. Under the glowing skies, they wore their smiles softly and the cool box had finally been cracked open. One of the local guys had managed to get a small grill fired up and was heating through the provisions stuffed into backpacks and coolers. The addition of more people raised the mood, in tandem with the weather, and the arrival of the sound system raised it further. The banners flapped more merrily. Passers-by more often gave a little wave and took one of the black and white flyers being handed out. Even Julia managed to glimpse the rest of the world before returning

131

to her games. Perhaps the kid on the bus had been right - I might enjoy this after all.

We ate *empanadas* and drank some of the own brand lemonade. Papá snuck off with a couple of the local guys and they popped cans of Red Stripe in the garden, much to the annoyance of some of the diplomats on their lunch break and local retirees walking their dogs. His arms got wilder as he drank more, but it was only ever expressions, not aggression.

The joyous celebration was mobilised for the cause and pounding beats from the huge speaker sparked chanting, in Spanish, in a dialect I did not recognise. Mamá joined in straight away and, after extinguishing his cigarette on the wrought ironwork gate, Papá joined in too, with his buddies. Before long, all the adults and a couple of the children were chanting and singing, mostly in the direction of the embassy. It only took the faintest twitch of a net curtain on the first floor for the whole group - now numbering over fifty - to cheer in unison. The message was getting through.

The banner fluttered more fiercely, the people's passion grew, the sweet smell of the grill spread, and, before long, those pedestrians who had ignored us before, now joined in with dancing and singing. Like me, they could only pick out a few words but there was joy in making the noises. We sang like dogs howling around the dinner table, trying their best to be part of the pack - but what I didn't realise was that those pedestrians were sympathetic enough but could not have got embroiled in what happened to the rest of us. For we were still outsiders and they were English, in both appearance and citizenship. To them, we were the other.

I was not witness to how it started. In the arguments that rang out sporadically on the bus back home, it sounded as if one of our group had told the pedestrians that they didn't know what they were singing so why were they singing it? There had been a row. They were trying to have a bit of fun but we were trying to do something serious. We were being rude; they were being insensitive. An unkind word. An angry response. A playful shove. A surreptitious phone call to the police as they slunk off.

Before we knew it, there were two police vans - one a Ford Transit and the other a 'paddy wagon', as they used to call it - rolling up with twelve men in all black piling out. I watched the next moments unravel at a funereal pace. The first one out of the van looked hawklike and pinched. He immediately lunged towards the London Val Verdean manning the barbecue.

"You. Where's your Street Trading Licence?" Behind him, the others formed up, with the van as a barricade between us and the embassy. Before a response could be formed, the grill was flipped over and the food ruined. "That's a Health and Safety violation." Other stepped in to right the grill and clear the food but two other officers waded in, raising their truncheons. Papá couldn't hold back, he stepped forward, flanked by two more. Then three of the London group came forward, the leader trying to explain over the gasps and shouts. He had his hands out in front of him and, almost immediately, a pair of cuffs was on him and three of the group had bundled him around the back of the van. That was when I ran. I shouldn't know at that age but I had an idea of what was about to happen and I didn't want to be a part of it. I darted through the open gate into the gardens.

Over my shoulder, I heard the shouts as the clashes grew in intensity and I wanted to be anywhere else again, I wanted to be back under my duvet but it was too late for that now. I looked for somewhere safe to go but the centre of the park was exposed, with a tennis court surrounded by a chain link fence cage. In the line of trees, within the cold shadows, I could duck away until it was all over, but what about my parents. I panicked and hid, scrabbling into the soil and shrubs. Torn by indecision, my only option seemed to be to go to them and hope that because I was a child, I would be safe.

A loud crack of metal on metal reverberated through a garden party atmosphere. I watched as one protestor, of the same mind as me, made for the tennis court, attempting to climb the fence to get away. He was clawed down and pinned to the floor whilst he swore and wriggled. I dug deeper into the undergrowth and recollections of my father, battered and bloodied, stumbling through the front door under Mamá's shoulder, forced me to reconsider revealing myself.

Black gloved hands pierced the bushes and felt desperately for me. I batted them away and screamed, shouted. What I don't recall, but I tried all I could instinctively call upon to force them to back away. The fingers found purchase and hoisted me, by bicep and elbow out of the bush and thumped down on the lawn.

"Stop, stop, it's okay, it's okay!" The officer had both of his hands up in front of me. "It's okay, don't worry, okay, I'm here to help." I could make a sudden move and then change directions but he was so close, right up to me, that there was no way I could break free. "What's your name? I'm Officer Wells. Now you."

"Frankie," I panted.

"Okay, Frankie, nice to meet you." I felt suddenly thirsty and my eyes stang with tears. "Frankie, I'm going to ask who you came here with? Was it your mum and dad?" I nodded.

"They're over there," and I pointed, aware that had I done that earlier, there was an opportunity to escape whilst Officer Wells followed my extended finger.

"Can you get up? Are you hurt?" I heaved a breath like granite out of me, wetness on my cheeks, and pushed my untouched arm against the ground to stand. I shook my head, unable to form words in my warm, unresponsive mouth.

"Shall we go and take a look?" I led and he followed. I longed for them; I wanted nothing more than to see both of them, Mamá and Papá, unhurt and ready to take us home. But as we exited the park, they weren't there. The grill was righted, the prison van had gone, two paramedics dealt with one woman who was struggling to breathe, a torn banner violated the pavement, and the cool box, it's lid ungainly detached, was toppled and empty.

"They're not here…"

"Okay, let me see if they're in the van." He spoke to another officer but he shook his head. Had they been hurt? Had they ran? Wells talked to one of the medics. "Looks like they're not here," he said, disappointment in his tone. "Why don't you sit tight - I'm sure they'll be back."

I was alone. But this time I wasn't on my own because I was trying to hide but because I had been abandoned. How could they do this? My mind lurched from explanation to explanation, each landing on a sense of neglect. I was a child; I had to run. They were adults; they had to protect. This didn't make any sense. I stood, then sat, then stood again. Wells hopped from one uniformed person to another asking them all on my behalf but without luck. I doubted they could differentiate between individuals when all they had done was see a mob.

How would I get home? What about the keys - I couldn't even get into the house? Maybe I would have to stay a night in the police cells. Would that mean I would have a criminal record? There's no way I could get a job with that kind of blemish. This was the end.

"*Cariño!*" Mamá called out and I knew it was her. But how could she have left me? Left with the police, who had battered our friends, who had broken the only reason we were here in the first place. I stood but made no movement to suggest relief or joy. She ran and crushed me in her arms. Papá enveloped her and kissed my head. I stood still, ungrateful and irate beyond childish explanation. Behind their embrace, I saw Julia dragged away by her mother, crying out, her console bent in her hand.

I awoke with a false feeling of betrayal, as if the one thing I remembered from that entire episode was my immature feelings towards my parents, as though, at the time, nothing could possibly make me feel so lonely and helpless. But also betrayal by the police, who, at the time, symbolised for me a sense of right and wrong and justice for victims of crime, not the perpetrators of violence that I saw then. There has always been something uniquely 'British' about the police, their uniform, their demeanour, but now it seemed they were no better than the khaki

thugs in my father's stories. And the thoughts that
dissipated as I gained consciousness were two contrasting
ones; what am I building that will last for ever and where
are my parents now when I need them the most?

Chapter 12 – Thursday 2nd June
(21 days to go)

Days can slide by without you noticing them. One minute it's Monday then suddenly it's October. The repetition of lectures contributed to that sensation, but I've purposefully not mentioned in detail in this account of what happened to me in 2016 due to the fact that my need for the content of those professors' and lecturers' brains has not been of any immediate benefit to my present situation. My second-year exams were weeks away but, had I cared as much for them as I did my ability to remain in the country of my birth, I may have approached them with a greater sense of gravity. The more urgent deadlines were those I thought about in terms of days. Today was the scheduled return of the Home Office agents and I felt criminally underprepared.

My unproductive meeting at the University had led me to the Students' Loan Company, which had been, it appeared, a dead end. What else was there to do?

All I had gained was an understanding about *how* the Home Office now believed I was in the country illegally and it all seemed too ludicrous to be real. It seemed so minor to me; a letter sent to an out-of-date address had triggered an existential crisis in me and a heavy-handed intervention from the authorities. I wondered if anything so apparently insignificant had ever caused such a seemingly disproportionate outcome?

Following on from the first meeting, I had received a text from the Home Office asking me to rate their service on a scale of one to ten. I had ignored it. The subsequent text that confirmed the second visitation of the officers for today had arrived so swiftly I had felt guilty at not giving them feedback, as if it was somehow connected. These, it turns out, are normal feelings, believing that a tiny decision could influence something far more powerful. It took me a few minutes of fretting to come to the conclusion that the senders of these texts were probably not even in the same building, let alone looking at the same scruffy manila folder that contained my personal details.

At Scintilla, it seemed that all was as it usually was. A sense of urgency pervading the area close to the counter but artificially constructed tranquility where the customers – or should that be 'comrades'? – sipped, nibbled, and quaintly went about their days oblivious to the stresses and troubles of anyone else. On the way to start my shift, walking across the square from the direction of the flat, before I was able to discern the members of the crowd close to the coffee shop, I saw Chelsea.

We never talked about what she had said and she had tried to mumble an apology the morning after, which I had nodded acquiescence to but had not engaged with. Neither of us were truly satisfied and possibly wouldn't be until we had a chance to clear the air.

I can't say I'd ever really been a victim of xenophobia or racism. In school, there were people with all kinds of backgrounds, Bangladeshi, Pakistani, Indian, Jamaican, Irish. The 'white' kids didn't really come with 'backgrounds'. Nobody ever asked them where they were 'from'? Or, if they gave a reply, their answers were never challenged with a 'Nah, but really…?' I saw and heard plenty of racism between different groups – in most occasions, the kids involved hated each other but in some cases they were best mates and could brush it off. It never occurred to me at the time that some of the things they said or did to each other were motivated by anything more complex than liking or not liking someone for who they were in that moment. I wasn't part of any group myself which, I imagine, may have made it harder for me to empathise; I caught flack off of everyone. I suppose that because I didn't really lean towards one group or another I was isolated by this fact and so I was mostly accommodated and never got into any serious trouble.

The mad thing is there is loads of white 'history', the stuff we learned about, the maps, the politics, but no 'background'. My situation was much like theirs, in that I knew my parents were South American but I was British and that was that. It didn't need any discussion really because nobody else cared that much to ask. When I told them where they were from, they didn't know where that was so carried on in ignorance, which suited me fine. But whilst the white kids and I didn't have the burden of being judged by our heritage, we didn't have any of the connections – in my teen years, it became a bit of a joke that I used to think was funny.

A Jamaican walks into a bar. Sat on a stool, he sees another black guy with dreadlocks and a rasta cap. The Jamaican says 'Wah gwaan, bredrin?' The other says 'Mi deh yah. Yuh irie?' and they strike up a conversation, buy each other a drink, and have a laugh and go their separate ways. Two white guys and best mates walk in the same bar. The first one says 'Alright, mate.' The second replies 'Yeah, alright' and they proceed to drink six pints each in silence for the rest of the night.

It stops being funny anymore when the jokes begin to resemble reality.

Maybe I wished for the ability to make connections with people like me, but they didn't exist at

140

that moment, so it was easier to make light of what people had, not what they didn't have. The white guys in that joke might not have had the ability to make lifelong friendships with strangers because of how a shared appearance could invite an unsolicited approach but then they didn't have to worry about driving home late at night and getting stopped five times.

I wasn't sure which of those two extremes I would prefer to associate myself with.

Chelsea made eye contact and half-waved – non-committal, waiting to see if I would respond – and tilted her head to speak to one of the crowd of people close by to her. I made what I would call a conciliatory expression and half-waved back. There was nothing for it but to face the whole awkward situation head on now.

She walked purposefully but slowly and I met her with as docile body language as I knew how to. For the first time in a while, my mind was almost totally blank – I had no idea what she would say or how I would react, which startled me and distracted my train of thought away from that moment and to a reflection on when the last time was my thoughts had been so blank, so vacant, and I couldn't remember a time before.

"Hola, Frankie," she uttered with a soft tone.

"Hola, C. What are you doing here?"

"We're staging a small protest about the hairdresser's policy on trans rights." She paused, I think, to see how I would react. I'd begun to notice it now that people who have a cause to champion often want to do it in spite of popular apathy or antagonism, not because of it. "They force customers to make a choice about whether they have a male or female hairdresser. Well, what if their staff don't want to define themselves in such archaic ways?" She maintained her appearance of composed grace, although we both knew she would normally have got riled up about the issue in a bid to compel me to support her cause (her opinion) or to contest the view that she was a privileged, spoilt, stuck-up, condescending bitch (my opinion – and, boy, did *that* come out of nowhere…) Now my mind was absolutely not empty of thought.

"Right."

"Listen, I'm glad I caught you. Frankie, I'm so sad about what happened the other night. It shouldn't have got out of hand like it did and we never meant to upset you."

"Yeah."

"You know how Ollie and I can get. When we start debating, it does sometimes, sort of, overflow into other topics. We really need to be more thoughtful about the language we use, as it would break my heart if you were ever offended by anything Ollie or I might have said."

"Uh-huh."

"I hope we can put this all behind us. After all, we are living together and there's nothing worse than an uncomfortable atmosphere in such a condensed space, is there? Can you find a way to accept my apology?"

I paused intentionally before I replied. "What apology?"

"What?"

"What. Apology."

"I don't… I'm trying to find the words to say I'm sorry, Frankie."

"But those *are* the words. You just didn't use them." The waterfall of thoughts had to be channelled.

"What do you mean?"

"You are trying to say sorry. Correct?"

"Yes, exactly." She beamed.

"Then say it. Say 'sorry'."

"Sorry." Her smile faded to an actress' attempt at contrition.

"Sorry what?"

"Sorry about what happened the other night."

"No. Try again."

There was a power I'd not felt before. This sense of things being correct. The things I said and how I said it could not be questioned or challenged. I knew I was in the right and I deserved a real apology. My body language slipped from placating to confronting, not because I wanted to start a fight but because I wanted to stand my ground. I was in the right, she was in the wrong, I deserved an authentic apology, and I would be damned if I didn't get one from her.

"Sorry about the things we said…"

"No, try again."

"Why are you being like this, Francesco?"

"Say what you mean, Chelsea. What do you really want to say to me?"

"I'm sorry for what I said to you the other night. I didn't think about how it would affect you and I had no intention to hurt you or blame you like that."

"That's it, thank you." My gratitude was for effect, like her facial expression. "Don't be sorry for the other night, don't be sorry for Ollie, don't be sorry on my behalf. You should be apologising to me for what *you* did, nobody else. *You*." I didn't feel it was fair to hammer the point home, after all, we did date once or twice, and she was only human, but that other voice inside me disagreed; if we dated, she should care more for me than this and who cares if she's female – so was Boudicca, Thatcher, Ranavalona, Cleopatra, Perón, and I doubt I would have felt like they deserved to be treated with kid gloves. So, I let her have it. "*You* made me feel like an outsider. *You* made me feel unwanted. *You* need to own it."

Until that point, I'd never seen someone who I would describe as being dumb-struck but Chelsea might never have been spoken to with real honesty before. She appeared, automatically, offended at first, then straightened herself out, smartening her body language to avoid seemingly like the victim.

"Okay," she started, "I see. Like I said, I'm sorry, Francesco for what we, I mean, what *I* said. Okay? I wasn't thinking clearly and you didn't, you don't, deserve to be thought of as... as an... an outsider. I should see the similarities between us, not the differences."

My two conscientious voices became one again and agreed that this was an acceptable response, given the location in which we were now publicly repairing our friendship. Any further criticism could wait and I decided that, whilst the power was in my hands, I should extend the hand of conciliation and really mix those metaphors while I was at it.

"I'm happy to bury the hatchet if you are."

"Yes, absolutely. I won't let you down," she shook my hand and then her head as she realised how odd she sounded. "I won't let myself down, I mean." To me, that sounded weirder, but I let her have it and said goodbye so we could both get back to the real reasons we were here; her protest for the transgender people of Birmingham and my interminable shift at Scintilla's that I was desperate to complete so I could get home and desperate for it to last forever so I would not have to go home and face the Home Office again.

I could not resist the inevitable passage of time and so I entered the flat around mid-afternoon, knowing that the next knock on the door could be the last one I heard in the flat or, perhaps, even as a British citizen. The only thing I could do to stop myself worrying incessantly about what the Home Office might say was the thought of going to the following week's WMSCACE meeting and seeing Eva again.

My first impressions of her coldness seemed to be misplaced. She was cautious, intelligent, weighing me up. That might have made me nervous but the exchange with Chelsea had given me a bit of a buzz. Was it wrong to think that? Should I feel guilty for telling her off and then trying to hammer it into her? I knew I was overthinking things again. Eva didn't have to know all of that, I would just be myself and we'll see where things end up.

Until then, rather than sit around waiting, I went into my room and carried on with my project. I've never wanted to share with anyone else what it is that I do on my own in my bedroom late at night. I feel I can freely admit it now, without shame, that I avidly play with myself. Alright, let me explain before you start jumping to lewd conclusions.

Inside the packet that had arrived a few days ago was a small, red rectangular box, swaddled in bubble wrap. I recognised it immediately from the trademark domed top and 18-panel glazed sides. It was a K2, designed in 1924 by Sir Giles Gilbert Scott. Originally built in cast iron, this version was a superb facsimile. Not like the cheap, plastic Hornby Skaledale K6, this was a German-made, Brawa 5437 with an interior bulb that actually lit the kiosk up properly.

I carefully slid it out from the box, avoiding putting any pressure on the door, in case the hinges were a little basic. Peeling away the wrapping, I could finally admire my purchase. The battery was wrapped separately but I hastily ripped away the packaging, popped the panel, and slotted it in, and tested out the switch. The dome and interior emitted a warm, soothing glow, and I couldn't stop myself from smiling.

This would be the first of two – maybe three, I couldn't decide – three telephone boxes that I would add to my miniature railway terrain. Lyonesse-on-Lethe, I called it, recalling the sounds, if not the words, I associated with the quaint villages we used to visit.

Sprawling from the window sill at one end of my bedroom, resting its weight on my desk, which I had to pull out from the rear wall slightly, and protruding two-thirds into the entire length of the room, Lyonesse-on-Lethe had left me with my single bed, now turned to run alongside the left-hand wall, rather than protrude out at right angles as it had when I first moved in, and a double wardrobe which was at the foot of the bed, the end closest the window, but from which I could only access one side, as the other door would not open fully because of all the craft materials I had stacked up in front of it. It was my *magnum opus*, my masterpiece to model railways, I write about it now with a deep-seated sense of accomplishment and pride.

There were still torn fragments of my furious response to Chelsea and Ollie's unfeeling insults speckled on the flock meadow, which separated the modest car park entrance to the mainline station from the fringes of the town, which were still taking shape. The anger that had overtaken my normal calmness still shocked me now; nobody would have described me as having a destructive side before - and they wouldn't know as I would not let anyone see what I had done. It was almost embarrassing to have been driven to externalise my rage in such a petty way. The urge overtook me and my hands moved whilst, and I don't mind admitting this, I sobbed, tearing and rending at the model station signage I had painstakingly constructed and hand painted. Maybe my unconscious was telling me that if I had made it, I could destroy it and that was an acceptable, manageable, way to vent my feelings at the time.

Having berated Chelsea, perhaps I would not have to resort to this childishness but could find another way.

I gently brushed away the peeled paint flecks, snapped balsa, and card with a large, dry brush and considered where I would place my new addition first. Would it be outside the ticket office or would it be close to the bus stop?

I see this juvenile, innocent hobby for what it was now. I can't only see myself playing with the model scenery and judging myself from afar but I still feel now what I felt then. The power of choice, of control. This was my world where the decisions I made were my own and no one else's and I dealt with the consequences myself. If I wanted to make a change, I could, without worrying that something out of my control might undo or undermine my decisions. Even if that meant tearing up miniature foliage or ripping up hills like some Classical Greek giant just to satisfy my inability to handle conflict. But it was a comfort too; a reminder of nostalgic times with my family, when we did things on the spur of the moment.

Yet I kept it secret.

I was worried that Ollie and Chelsea would judge me for it. People who play with train sets as adults don't always attract a positive response – you don't see many model railway enthusiasts on the front cover of magazines. Silly, now, to worry what others think or thought about me then. As though I would have been branded by my hobby, despite everything else I have done since.

The rapping startled me, even though I had expected it. Checking the time every five minutes was exhausting and, after a couple of hours, I'd stopped and had resigned myself to the visit being delayed until tomorrow or perhaps never, in hope at least.

I didn't waste my time with pleasantries or offers of drinks – what was the point? They sat in the same spaces as their previous visit. I did too. They attempted to engage in small talk. I did not. Kean began by recapping what they 'knew' about me. I glazed over, having heard it all already. I felt only two people could really tell me something new that I might be genuinely interested in; Ernesto and Eva. Kean's diatribe tailed off and I was back in the room.

"And so that brings us up to date, sir."

"Right…"

"We understand that you have spoken to the University and the Students' Loan Company."

"How did you know that?" I feigned as if an answer would be helpful.

"As we explained before, the SLC systems plug into the Home Office systems."

"But not the other way around..?" Goode and Kean glanced at each other. "Ali, the man I spoke to at the Students' Loan Company, he said that if they changed my details in the SLC system it would not update the Home Office system."

"Ah, hmm, yes, that's correct, sir, we likely have read-only access."

"Yeah, but it was their letter to my old home address that caused this whole thing, isn't it?" Standing up to Chelsea had made me feel confident that if I could put her in her place, why not these two? They stared back at me. "Why don't you look in your folder?"

Kean pulled the manila file out from his bag and quickly thumbed through the various printed pages. "This is it…"

"I'm sorry," interjected Goode, without sounding sorry at all. "We can't share this file with you due to General Data Protection Regulation 2016/679 which forbids us from releasing personally identifiable information…" She used the words like a drunk leaning against a bar.

"It's my information."

"You must submit a written request to the Home Office for us to share this information with you."

"Who came up with this regulation?" I pressed.

"It was very recent, so…"

"Who came up with this regulation?"

"I believe it was agreed at a European level."

"Do I need to write to the EU then?"

"You have to write to the Home Office."

"Can you tell me if the reason I am being threatened with deportation is because the SLC sent a letter to my parent's old address?" My voice loudly broke at the words, I kept it together, or so I thought, but I felt the tingle behind my eyes and a redness warming the bridge of my nose like mustard. It felt just like it did with Chelsea, as though something inside had broken, a tectonic rift with magma surging forth. "It's a yes or no question."

"Yes," stammered Kean, "I'm sorry." Goode didn't look at him, as I thought she might, or me, but her eyes sank to the floor. God, it was awkward. I squirm at the memory of it but I was falling apart. First the rent, then the incident with Chelsea and Ollie, now deportation. That's not even taking into account the lack of friends, parents, or, well, a life. That neon tinted word appeared like ice cobwebbing on a windowpane; 'Impotent'.

Goode spoke up, taking the attention away from her colleague. "In the interim, we would advise you to seek legal representation."

"I'm a student. From Druids Heath. With what money?"

"The Citizens Advice office is on Corporation Street. You could speak to them."

"You know I shouldn't have to, don't you? You can see how this is unfair."

"We don't want to take up any more of your time, Mr. Cualquiera, I'm sure you have other things you would rather be doing than talking to us. Let me just remind you that now the investigation is ongoing, you will only be hearing from us once a decision is made, which we will inform you of via telephone, and you should know that the time between this follow-up meeting and enforcement is often between two to three weeks." She stood and Kean followed.

"What about flying to Val Verde and getting a visa there, I mean, that might cost less than a solicitor..." Kean suggested.

"I've got exams coming up." That seemed like such a reasonable excuse back then. Goode remained detached and flattened her trousers and stepped through the threshold, out to the corridor. Kean extended his hand; "Best of luck with it." I shook it, clammy and paw-like, and believed he truly meant what he said. Goode's expression suggested that this was not appropriate procedure for a Home Office agent.

When Ollie got home, he found me slumped on the sofa channel-hopping. We shared a nod and he went into the kitchenette with a bag full of takeaway. I couldn't concentrate and wasn't in the mood to have a row with anyone anymore.

He dumped himself a cushion apart from me on the couch and slid across a plastic dinner tray laid out with cutlery, plate, and pint glasses of Coke and tore open the plastic bag that he'd put on the coffee table. Silver ingots spilled out, steaming and delicious, and he peeled off the card tops, putting the containers in a semi-circle of colours, golden rice, glistening red sweet and sour chicken, dark purple plum sauce slathered over pork ribs, khaki and bronze saag aloo, waves of snow white prawn crackers, a criss-cross of chips like stacked pallets.

"Sorry about being a dick the other night."

We didn't speak again until all the food was finished, or we were stuffed, but it meant something to me. It made me think about whether I'd been harsh on

Chelsea or not mean enough to reject Ollie's food and tell him what I told her. But then I thought more as I ate more and decided that, perhaps, they both got what they needed from it. I don't think Chelsea had ever been told off before and Ollie had never felt guilt that deeply before – or at least that's the impression he gave me.

I wonder whether it was double-standards, whether my reaction was down to the fact that she was an ex-girlfriend and he was a flatmate, so perhaps I didn't care for him like I cared for her, but, in the end, it was probably because I had let loose on Chelsea and had to handle Goode and Kean that I didn't have the energy or the emotion to berate Ollie that night. He got lucky, I suppose, as he always did. I needed him as a true friend, it would transpire, more than I ever thought I would.

Chapter 13 – Friday 3rd June (20 days to go)

"I wondered when I might run in to you."

I never expected to bump into Eva, even though I hoped I would. A small pile of books was cradled between her hip and her elbow.

"Morning – nice to see you…" Oh man, what was I saying? Please, please, don't let me get tongue-tied again.

"You too. Just had a lecture?"

"Yep, yep, it was... good. How about you?" She flicked her head towards the building behind her. "Get anything… good?"

"I wouldn't say *good* but definitely interesting." Spots of rain bloomed on the grey concrete slabs and we instinctively looked for cloud. "Great timing – I'm not running for a bus in this. Want to grab a coffee?"

"You're asking the guy who works in Scintilla?" I snorted. She looked blankly back at me. "I mean, yes, sure, but I'll have a tea, if that's okay with you…" Too many words tumbled out before I could control them. I hoped she didn't notice.

"Come on." She turned on a heel and led me inside. The café was on the first floor of the library and was exposed to the high, glass atrium which half-reflected, half-lightened the rainclouds that greyed out the sky. I fretted about ordering the tea – and being seen as a predictable man of my word – or getting something else – and being considered spontaneous but indecisive. I worried my teaspoon made too much noise when I stirred. But when we sat and Eva spoke in her measured tone, I only thought about her words.

"…and that's it really, now I'm here, thank goodness."

"And what do you want to do with your degree?"

"I'd like to practice Criminal Law back in Venezuela, but we'll see, I might stay here. I have to complete my volunteer work in a legal practice to gain experience. I've been there a month or so now. But I'd prefer to be back home." Her easy demeanour was in contrast to when we first met, when I thought she was professional or aloof. Perhaps it was all about the context.

"Anywhere in particular? Caracas?"

"Maracaibo. My home." I couldn't say I'd heard of it and had only guessed at Caracas.

"What's it like?" She smiled, setting me at ease.

"You've never seen lightning like it. We call it *catatumbo* and it can turn the sky indigo purple in an instant. Before I went to school in the city, I lived on the south side of the lake, down in Lagunetas, in *palafitos*, you know, the houses on stilts." Her nimble fingers made a spindly, fragile gesture to show me what her home was like. "My family were fishers for as long as I knew and we went out on the water at night, when the lightning would be strongest. Imagine the total blackness of the sky suddenly cracked open by bright white and the shadow it cast was like a lilac silk sheet. We would listen for the roll of thunder that would set off the howler monkeys, they would go crazy, it was all you could hear a little way off, back to shore, until they calmed down for a little while. My Dad, his friend's family, my brothers, and me, we would just drift in the peace, on two boats roped together. I loved it so much, I'd go back home some weekends, even though it was an eight-, nine-hour journey, just on the off chance it would happen when I was there."

I listened intently as she told me more about her youth in Lagunetas and I thought to myself how my interest in her stories was so similar to the speeches of Ernesto. Was it because we shared something genetic or cultural? Was it their rhythms of speech or accents that drew me in?

"The only legal careers are for the oil companies and I can't bring myself to work for those assholes. Every time I go back, I worry that the lake is just another accident away from being ruined."

"But you sound proud of where you're from? Isn't that because of the money the oil companies invest?"

"Huh, no, despite them. It is so corrupt, I want to do something about it, maybe, prosecute them for the damage they're doing, if I can."

We ordered another tea, unaware that the clouds had long since passed. She told me about this unique and rebellious city of Maracaibo, that seemed almost fantastical. Her description, filled with knowledge; the Caribs and Arawaks and other indigenous people, whose names I could not pronounce with her skill, who fought the Spanish, the Dutch, and the Germans; the pirate legends that torched towns and plundered warships; how Maracaibo defied Venezuelan independence, at first, with

156

Marabinos long-since plotting their own republic; the people's love of literature, *gaita* music, and art; and their staunch loyalty to the state of Zulia, the nation within a nation, that fuels Venezuela's economy from the low banks of the vast lake. It was clear that she was proud of how city leaders stood up for them against the rest of the country, how Maracaibo is a sanctuary for left-field thinkers and rebels, who are passionate about a cause and fight for a shared vision of a better life for everyone, and how she hoped that she could be as immune to corruption and unafraid to stand alone against a powerful majority when the need arose, just like them.

"It sounds like you're not really Venezuelan at all. You're, what, Zulian?"

"I prefer *gaiteros*. But who here knows where Zulia is?"

I shrugged. "I have the same problem, don't I?"

"What about you? What do you want to do after Uni?" I didn't know and I told her as much before talking about philosophy for a little while but, like I said – wrote? – before, there's no point in detailing what I know about my subject as it would turn out that I would have little use for it.

"Do you know where your parents are now?"

"I don't know." There was no point making up a story. "All I know is that they were told to return to Val Verde in 2012, when I was seventeen."

"Oh, wow, what happened to you then?"

"I was taken into care, by the Council, they placed me with a family in Sedgley, about an hour away by bus. It was fine, I saw a social worker once a fortnight. All I wanted was to leave though and have my independence."

"But could you not have left with your parents or could they not have stayed, if you had Indefinite Leave to Remain?" I'd almost forgotten that she was training to be a lawyer and might use some of the bureaucratic jargon I had begun to understand with confidence; I had just been enjoying her company.

"I don't want to talk about it," had been my stock answer if anyone ever tried to get too close. Four years felt like a long time but the scars were fresh. I thought I was quite a mature child, and my parents felt the same, but I couldn't put on a grown-up's easy façade when they told me the decision they had made.

"You're abandoning me here! Don't pretend!" I had never screamed at my Mamá before, not like this. Maybe as a baby but that was for hunger or tiredness; this was hatred.

"*Cariño*, it's not like that," she started. "It's for your own good…"

"I've heard that before – you're lying!"

"Hey, cut that out! Your *mamá* loves you, I love you, we only want the best for you…"

"Then why are you abandoning me!" The feeling of fury, even all these years later, still stirs and this was one of the moments when I felt out of control.

"That's just what we have to say, for the, what are they called, the… authorities. Why are we going over this again?" He pushed himself away from the kitchen table and through the back door, the cigarette and lighter in his hand before the door had slammed shut behind him. Just as it did, he yelled out "We're playing the system! If we can't change it, we'll use it to help you!"

"Francesco, listen, you know we have to go so that can't change and we can either take you with us, back to God knows what will happen under that *carajo* Calderon, or you can stay here where it is safe and you can get a great education. Isn't that better? For you?" She reached for my hand but I wouldn't let her hold me.

"You are abandoning me, you and Dad, you don't care! You would rather go and fight your fight and go to your protests than even think about me."

"It's the law. We have to abandon you so you can stay. If you come with us, who knows what might happen to you. If you stay, you are safe and will be taken care of."

"By who?"

"The Government."

"The same ones who are forcing you to leave?"

"No, no, it's different… They're not the same…"

I could only understand their perspective now, at a distance, but not without a sense of betrayal, and whilst we had fought bitterly for three months, on the day we separated, accompanied by the Home Office agents and police, the wall I had built up to isolate myself from them had gradually started to crack. But any fractures in my hatred were temporarily healed and every time I thought about them it deepened the foundations of that wall. Living with the family in Sedgley was a year of stability but it was never my home and I looked forward to its end without appreciating what they were sacrificing for me. I don't mind admitting I am ashamed about how ungrateful I was and I haven't kept in touch with them for that reason.

This time was different though. An urge to share what had happened to me rose in my throat for the first time. My explanations were not judged. I avoided placing the blame solely on them or painting myself out to be too much of a victim. Eva listened and asked one or two questions as I spoke and we seemed to share that lack of urgency when you don't have to go somewhere or do something.

"You've been so brave," she said once I had finished, without a hint of condescension. "I don't know if I would have managed like you did."

"Maybe I could have managed better if I had you there."

She blushed and I panicked.

"To fight my corner, you know, as a solicitor."

She nodded quickly.

"I want to be able to fight someone's corner someday. I have the Marabino soul; we love fighting for the underdog. It sounds like your parents meant well but I see now why you don't talk very much. Normally!"

I was suddenly self-aware of just how much I had shared with her and how much time we had been talking. I had shared my life story, which felt like the shedding of a burden, but she took it on without complaint, whilst she shared her attitudes and principles, which were more noble and impressive than I could hope to be. It made me think that my rage had been almost juvenile, in contrast to her patience at hearing about it.

"I wish I had your bravery." She frowned softly at my words. "You seem so decided, you know, you want to do something to help the powerless. I feel like I'm the underdog right now, maybe I'm the one trapped in prison, not my parents."

"You think that's what happened to them?"

"I haven't heard anything for almost two years, so maybe. They didn't have the money to pay their way out of it."

"I don't get the impression that they were those kind of people though."

"No, I suppose not."

"How do you feel trapped?"

"Life! Isn't it? The rent goes up but my pay cheque doesn't. I've been living on the edge of my overdraft limit since I've started at Uni. My flatmates, ah, well, they aren't exactly the same people I thought they were when I moved in but what can I do? I can't afford to move my stuff, so I just have to stay and figure something out. I feel powerless to do anything right now..." The compulsion to share my life with her crept up on me again and I hesitated just long enough for her to shift uncomfortably. That motion triggered in me an impulse to clam up and stop my depressing moaning or to blurt out what was really taking up much of my thoughts.

"And I'm probably getting deported too."

"What!? Why?"

"There was a mix-up with my student loan and now the Home Office have given me only a couple of weeks to sort something out or they are sending me to Val Verde."

"What can I do to help?"

"Nothing. I can't afford to pay for a solicitor to fight *my* corner. I didn't even know I needed a visa or leave to remain until a couple of weeks ago."

"Maybe I could speak to someone who might be able to do some *pro bono* work for you."

"That would be great, but I don't have much time."

"Ernesto must know someone who can help – let me speak to him this afternoon and then we can talk to him together next week. You are coming, right?" I had been in two minds about going but, in the face of her insistence, I sharpened my mind to it. Perhaps he could help; surely he must have encountered similar situations like this?

"What time is it again?"

"Seven thirty."

I instinctively checked my watch. "Oh crap! I've got a shift to get to! I'm sorry, I talked too much."

"Don't be silly," she soothed. "I'll see you at the meeting, okay? I'll talk to Ernesto for you – I'm sure he can do something for you." Despite craving the intimacy of a hug goodbye, maybe even a peck on the cheek, the desire of keeping my job and not letting Freya or the rest of the staff down forced me to grab my bag and run, leaving Eva with just a sorry wave of my hand.

I was out of breath by the time I reached Scintilla but managed to get there five minutes before my shift started.

"Thank goodness you're here," whispered Freya. "You forgot didn't you?" I looked around and noticed how clean and orderly the coffee shop looked, almost as neat as if it had just opened. But, as this was the afternoon shift, just after the lunchtime crowd, I expected there to be a few gaps in the shelves, the odd ring of spilt coffee on the high-traffic tables, an air of malaise over the staff, but then it hit me.

"The big cheese!"

"Yes! He will be here in less than an hour and you need to change and get tidying up." I didn't wait to find out what exactly needed tidying up, not that I could immediately notice, but I went straight to the disabled toilet to change, hoping that one of the usual characters wouldn't be found in there. "Don't forget your new badge!"

Moments later I was pushing the broom around unoccupied tables, loading the dishwasher, and serving

163

drinks like it was a normal day. Perhaps the normalcy made the entrance of the Democracy Coffee CEO all the more memorable.

There was no entourage, no paparazzi, as I had imagined. There were three older men, two in non-descript grey suits with appropriately forgettable ties and haircuts. The other man had dishevelled hair and wore a collarless sweatshirt and fashionably tight-legged jeans. My suspicions were confirmed when Freya stepped forward and introduced herself forcibly upon him. Between them, there seemed a real spark of authentic energy; I paused to watch and his colleagues, flanking him, smiled politely, dutifully, but he beamed. He seemed to be taking in everything she was saying whilst simultaneously soaking up every minute detail about the store itself. An overwhelming urge to be a part of that conversation took me. I replaced my broom in the rack, dusted down my apron, and stepped forward.

"Mr. Wright, this is Francesco, one of our staff members."

"Great to meet you!" Wright clasped my hand and met my stare with piercing, bright eyes. "Thank you for your service. I hope I'm not inconveniencing you too much – I literally had to come and see what a fantastic job you guys were doing here."

"Nice to meet you," I said, "Thank you."

"Francesco, I want to catch up with you later, if you're cool with that. Freya, why don't you talk to me about how I can help you do your job even better?" With his attention turning to Freya, I stepped back and went behind the counter. The other two executives engaged in a private conversation of their own.

I found it hard to keep my eyes off of Wright as he walked around with a confidence that never veered into superiority. His gestures were decisive and clear. I couldn't place him in the company of my parents' opinions of businesspeople – they saw them as single-minded, selfish, willing to crawl and fight over others to get what they wanted. He seemed warm, charming, and, I don't know, could I call him 'genuine'? He carried on about the store for a few minutes as I continued serving a gentle trickle of customers.

After the store closed, Noah Wright held court with all of us. He briefly talked about the corporate vision but, perhaps sensing a lack of interest amongst the part-time staff, he changed tack and told us about his philanthropy, building wells in Sierra Leone over last summer.

"It truly is inspiring to see these people, who have none of the comforts we take for granted, dancing for joy. Once we broke through to the subterranean aquifer and the fresh water could be brought to the surface, wow, it was just so great. Many of them had not washed that week and the village we were in had been burning whatever they could lay their hands on so that they could boil water to make it safe to drink." Lucy and Freya were enraptured. Rob cut a typically sullen figure. I felt something in between disbelief and veneration.

"One kid, I think his name was Boba or Booboo, or something, he came up to me, he was only this high," Wright waved a tanned hand, his wrist enclosed by several bracelets of beads or red string, to show us how small this child was. "He grabbed my hand so tight and said, and I'll never forget it, he said 'Mr. Wright, thank you.' It just… it meant so much, to me, those few words that made all of the back-breaking work and travelling so far and seeing such deprivation, what he said made it all worthwhile." He rubbed at his eye with the knuckle of his thumb as Lucy gasped an 'awww' sound.

"I'm sorry, guys, I've taken so much of your time. I promise I won't hang around for too much longer. Listen, why don't you ask me some questions and I'll see if I can answer them, yeah?"

Lucy's hand shot up. "Mr. Wright…"

"Please, Noah."

"Okay, um, Noah, would you say that building that well in Sierra Leone was your biggest achievement?"

"Oh wow, what a toughie to start with!" He chuckled and the two executives who had patiently waited with him smiled and nodded in assent. "Gosh, well, it really was something I am personally very proud of but, no, I think the biggest achievement in my life was… hmm… which do I go for…? Oh, I've got it. The biggest achievement must be the award I received from the Hands of Light Institution for funding a concert for victims of Hurricane Katrina with Reese Witherspoon and Lil Wayne where we raised nearly $20 million to house the cats and dogs that had been made homeless. It was so humbling to get recognition for what we did."

I thought about asking a follow up question but Rob beat me to it.

"How much is Democracy Coffee worth?"

"Ha ha! There's always someone with real business smarts. Good question, man. Last time I checked, we were doing around fifty million dollars in annual revenue and, thanks to you guys, that continues to show market-beating growth year-on-year."

"And how much are *you* worth?" Rob called out.

"Wow, okay, well, I've made some pretty smart investments and, you know what, you can look this all up online, right? It's public knowledge," He chuckled sharply. "I won't make the cover of Forbes, right? I've been told I'm worth roughly thirty million dollars. That's not really that much if you compare me to some of the guys on that list – Zuckerberg, Gates, you know, billionaires." One of the suited executives muttered something and Wright clapped his hands together.

"Okay, it's been great to see everyone but I need to have a few more minutes with your manager and then I'll have to say goodbye." He walked towards the back office, with Freya following close behind. Lucy remained beatific, Rob sneered and rolled his eyes, and I went back to my broom.

"Can I grab a moment with you, Francesco?"

"Of course, Mr. Wright. How can I help?" His skin was remarkably smooth, like a perma-tanned snooker ball, and his smile was genuine yet his teeth were unnaturally white. I was fascinated by his appearance, which entranced me. It was as if he had taken a stride off of the front of a magazine.

"How are you finding it here?"

"Good, yeah, great, I'm enjoying it."

"That's great, I'm really pleased to hear that, Francesco," he replied. His eyes were locked on mine and the rest of the store seemed to fade away. I remember now a sensation that Noah Wright had nothing else on his mind but talking to me. "What can I do to make it even more delightful for you?"

The question really made me think; what can *he* do that would make *my life* better. It was no different to Ernesto's question in that it made me stop and think but, in this context, I felt like there might be a more specific answer. I thought about practicalities but nothing particularly revolutionary came to mind. He must have had to deal with plenty of hesitating employees as he calmly waited and watched me think.

"I think it would be good... if... So, we only have one big pocket on these aprons. What about a smaller pocket? For pens and keys?" Wright put his hand to the side of his face, emphasising that he was really taking in what it was I was saying, but did not appear exactly moved by the idea. In fact, it was hard to read from his expression exactly what he thought, so I persevered.

"Um, why do we print our logo on the serviettes? They just get thrown away anyway so what if we just went with plain serviettes instead and saved money on the printing? We must print millions, so that could add up to... a lot..." I couldn't tell whether he was impressed but he continued to look to me in silence, shifting his posture.

The only thing I could think of was what Chelsea had been protesting about; the absence of Fair Trade coffee in the store. I had told her I had spoken to Freya about it, even though I hadn't and had just told her that for the sake of a quiet life. I also felt guilty about how quickly I had found forgiveness for Ollie but had been harsh on her. Maybe now was a chance to make it up to her.

"I mean, it's really important to me, us, that we change our coffee supplier. All of our coffee beans should be Fair Trade, not just the seasonal blends, and should come from ethically sourced suppliers." Wright nodded and frowned simultaneously, giving me the impression of consideration. I carried on, hoping that I wasn't rambling. "We need to make sure that our supply of coffee is sustainable and that would benefit the growers, we could get more customers, who would be in favour of buying products they knew were ethically right, and you could get some additional publicity if you moved to Fair Trade."

Why did I suddenly feel uneasy by saying all this, as though it would make Chelsea proud of me, as if that was what I wanted? What a fraud I must seem.

Wright gesticulated towards one of his companions and, before he reached us, whispered to me, "Let me take care of that."

"Hi."

"Eric, can you take a note? Remind me we need to look into our suppliers. I want to know how quickly we can get them all Fair Trade accredited or switch to accredited growers. Thanks." The grey-suited man tapped on his tablet and scampered away.

"You know, I've been meaning to do that for some time but the board wanted to keep our overheads down. Perhaps it's time we finally did what our competitors have been doing for some time. It's great to hear that you share the same vision as me, Francesco." A small, dirty lightbulb of warming troubled pride glowed into life inside me. "I see you're from Val Verde." I nodded and felt my chest swell further; he recognised the flag, which was more than could be said for most people. "Have you been here long?"

"I was born here – my parents are from Val Verde."

"Fantastic. Have you been over there?"

I wanted to say 'No, not that I can remember', which was the truth, but I didn't want to let him down so I just said "Yes, yeah, really beautiful country."

"Beautiful country! It's distressing to hear what's going on there, politically speaking, of course. The regime is crippling us with export taxes. I could really do with someone like you who knows the country and who could help us work with them… I'm sure you wouldn't be interested in that kind of thing. It could be a kind of boring job. Anyway, listen, Democracy is sponsoring an exhibition that's opening at the Birmingham Museum in a couple of weeks, the Central American Cultural Artefacts exhibition. It's touring of course but I couldn't ignore Birmingham when it's the home of my favourite Scintilla. Why don't you join me when we raise the curtain on it?"

"That's very kind, Mr. Wright, but don't you think you should be inviting Freya or the rest of the staff." I didn't want to mention the fact that I might be making my first, compulsory visit to Val Verde very soon.

"It's Noah, seriously. Francesco, I can see you're someone with some great ideas. I really think you would enjoy it too – and who else would get the most out of the exhibit but you?" From his wallet, he pulled out a black, card rectangle with gold writing and a strange tribal emblem pressed into it. "Here. Show this at the door and you'll get straight in."

"Thank you."

"In fact," He took his wallet out again and pulled out another card. I wondered how many he had in there; it seemed as if there might be an unlimited supply. "Why not have two and you can bring someone special, if you like."

"That's very kind, thank you."

"No, thank *you* Francesco – it was great to hear your ideas and I look forward to seeing you again very soon." He beamed once more and turned away, he shook Freya's hand and passed her some more compliments, before sweeping through the door with his two assistants and, with his absence, the store seemed emptier.

Chapter 14 – Tuesday 7th June
(16 days to go)

The meeting that evening was in the softly lit back room of a small Latin American restaurant I'd never heard of before. The heat from the kitchen seeped into the close space and the sound of cooking mingled with the beat of a radio, turned down so the staff might hear one another over it. In one corner were small barrels of olive oil, beside a stuffed steel shelving unit that ran along one wall. In the middle, beneath a neon strip light, was a table, dressed with tablecloth and napkins, where Ernesto and Marcos sat.

"Hi guys," I said.

"Francesco! *Buena noches*, come and sit," replied Ernesto.

"What happened to the hotel?"

"Ah, this is better, isn't it? We don't have the distractions that threaten to tear us from our task." A waiter, I guessed, arrived and gave the two men an opened bottle of beer and an empty glass each before disappearing from where he had come from. The ashtray in the middle of the table was already full and it looked to me as if they had been there for some time.

"Where's Eva tonight?" Marcos snorted.

"She's coming, running late maybe," stated Ernesto. "But how are you? How's work going?"

"Good thanks, yeah, it was busy this week…"

"And your studies?"

"Oh, yeah, fine, I suppose…"

"*Chido*! I love to hear you're making something of yourself. Education *es mas importante,* don't let anyone tell you otherwise." They both took a drink and I wondered whether I could expect one too or if I'd have to ask the waiter myself. "You hungry? We can get you something… *¡Luis! ¡Nuestro amigo quiere comer algo!*" The waiter came back and looked at me, Ernesto nodded at him, and off he went again without taking my order or even bringing a menu, which I thought was pretty odd but then maybe Ernesto knew him well enough for that not to be weird, although I didn't even know what they served so I assumed it must be somewhat limited if was to have no choice in the matter. It struck me that I was focusing on the wrong thing.

"What's this meeting about, Ernesto? Eva gave me the impression that it was important. More important."

"It is, it is, but we'll get to that. You should eat first. *¡Luis! ¡Dale una chela también, zoquete!* You look like you need it. Work getting to you?"

"No, no, it was a good day but, you know, tiring."

Marcos sighed and leaned back on the two back legs of his wooden chair.

"Nothing interesting happened since the last time we met?"

"Not really, but we did have the CEO of the company stop by."

"Sounds serious – you're not in trouble, are you?" He chuckled and Marcos laughed along.

"Of course not, I think he visits all the stores." Luis arrived with a beer – no glass – and a small plate of *empanadas*, that always made me think of little Cornish pasties, like I used to have when we visited the Jurassic Coast in the south-west.

"*Ese plato es para lamer los bigotes – ¡si pudiera dejarse uno!*" Marcos said, pulling himself upright and letting out a deep, throaty laugh, which Luis accompanied with a shorter, quieter giggle.

"Marcos!" barked Ernesto.

I took a bite and followed it up with a slug of beer as it was surprisingly hot and a little spicy too. At that moment, when my face was flushed, and with the condensation from the beer bottle dripping down my jumper, Eva walked in.

"Eva! I thought you had forgotten…" Ernesto put on a clownishly sad expression.

"It was work, I had some stuff to do in the office – one of the clerks was off."

"*Trabajas más duro que un camello…*" spat Marcos. That I sort of understood; something about working like a camel, whatever that meant. "*Grandes jorobas también…*" He cackled in that guttural way again and swigged on his beer.

"*Ladilla.*" She glared at him and it was the first time I noticed anyone stand up to Marcos, at least, in a pretty modest way. Marcos didn't respond; he slugged back another mouthful and the sneer scorned the opportunity to clear from his expression. "Hi, Frankie, you okay?"

"Yeah, good, you?"

"Tired. After you left, I had to sort a few things out at the law firm."

"'Frankie' was telling us about how the CEO paid him a visit," Ernesto interjected.

"Wow, did you manage to impress him?" Eva was mocking in her tone but I was sure she was undeniably interested.

"Yes, actually," and I thought I would try and impress her here myself, "I came up with some suggestions to improve the company and I think he really took them on board. He seemed interested and told me he would be changing the coffee suppliers to Fair Trade and he invited me to the opening of an exhibit he's sponsoring at the museum."

Ernesto and Marcos turned in unison to glare at me. "What exhibit?"

"Umm.." I dug out the two card tickets from my coat pocket and read out the title. "Central American Cultural Artefacts exhibition, Friday 17th of June, Birmingham Museum and Art Gallery. VIP tickets too, pretty sweet, right?" Eva responded with a 'Very impressive' but what I noticed was how Marcos and Ernesto leaned in to one another and whispered in Spanish as soon as I had told them about the tickets.

"Can I see?" Eva held out her hand and I passed her one of the tickets. She flipped it over and felt it between her fingertips, apparently contemplating the thickness and gold leaf. "Do you know what that is?" She held up the back of it, which had a t-shaped symbol on it that looked vaguely ethnic in design, to my eyes at least. I shook my head.

"Not a clue. Is it symbolic?" The two men's hushed conversation continued, cloaked by cooking noise, repeated drumbeats from the radio, and distance.

"Very much so, yes, it's a *tumi*. A sacrificial knife from one of the ancient nations that flourished in pre-Columbian central and south America. You see the little guy on the handle?" I looked at her ticket, held out by her slender fingers, forgetting I had one of my own in my hand. "That's *Maximón*. Have you heard of him?" I shook my head again, feeling a little embarrassed. "The legend of *Maximón* tells a story of a deity, like a demi-god, who loved playing tricks on people."

"Like Loki in *Thor*," I suggested.

"Exactly. He was said to represent both dark and light, you know, how the Norse gods, Greek gods, and so on each represented different things. Well, *Maximón* was summoned by fishermen who were heading out for a fishing trip to look after their wives and make sure they were faithful. But *Maximón* is the god of both fidelity and adultery so whilst they wanted him to do one thing, he ended up doing the other, right? He could change his appearance so he transformed each evening and every night he went into one of the fisherman's homes and seduced and slept with his wife until he had slept with each and every one of the fishermen's wives. It's been interpreted as a morality tale to both be careful what you

176

wish for and not to trust people who seem to offer help whilst wearing a mask, or something like that."

"How do you know all that?"

"My family. On those trips on the boat out on Lake Maracaibo, we might be there for hours so we had to tell stories and there are no better stories than those that only exist because people had to share them through word of mouth. You can't watch a repeat or rewind the tape so you need to memorise those fables or they disappear."

"What did the fishermen do?"

"You know it's just a story, it's not real, right?" She smirked but continued anyway. "*Maximón* was gone by the time they came back. If I was writing the story now, I'd say something clever like" and here she put on a dramatic narrator's voice; "'their nets were full but their hearts were empty'." We both laughed. The memory of that shared laugh is still as fresh in my mind as anything else I recalled from my childhood.

"And this *Maximón tumi* – is it going to be at the exhibit?" I turned the card over between my fingertips. The neon strip light that buzzed above us made the gold ink on the card glitter. The drumbeats that concealed Ernesto and Marcos' murmured discussion grew faster.

"I don't know for sure, but I think so. I saw some posters for the event with a load of different artefacts on it around the city centre and the *tumi* was one of them."

"You know what that is, don't you, Francesco?" Ernesto turned his attention to us now. I didn't have a chance to reply before he spat out his judgement. "Cultural terrorism! These exhibits, they are celebratory

177

carnivals for Imperialism. A festival of appropriation of our history. How do you think all of these incredible objects got there? The kindness of other nations to donate their people's treasures? Trade for goods and services? Conquest. War. Murder. Slavery. Rape. Theft. It's disgraceful."

"*El cuchillo es nuestro*." Marcos scowled, all of the ribald humour gone from his demeanour. "Knife. Is ours."

"He's right," said Eva. "That *tumi* isn't some old dusty piece of rubbish. It has a power, just like *Maximón*'s magic." I nervously ate a little more *empanada* and drank a few sips of beer. The tension in the room was more like a passion. The way they spoke and behaved hinted at the way my parents had changed from my mother and father into *mi papá y mamá* in all their dissenting fervour. Whilst I was once strongly against their activism, especially after what happened to my Dad, this was different: Ernesto had invited me into the circle and had inspired me with how he led them. Eva was smart, beautiful, and, well, with the benefit of hindsight, I realise I was attracted to her and she could have convinced me to do anything. As for Marcos, I felt sorry for the *policia* who raised a truncheon to him – only one of them would be going to hospital with a cracked skull. Right now, I had to listen to Eva's explanation.

"The *tumi* has held a sacred position in the culture of the Yarina people. Have you heard of them?" I shook my head. "They were one of most widespread civilisations throughout south and central America, like the Incas, Aztecs, Mayans, Olmecs, Muisca, and so on. The Yarina have a nomadic impulse and over the years have spread through most of the countries across the region. Their temples might no longer exist but there is still a strong sense of belonging amongst them, even though they must remain hidden."

"How come I've never heard of them before?" I felt as if I had heard of the Yarina, but I couldn't recall where. If I guessed or said something wrong, I thought Eva might think I was an idiot so I feigned ignorance to protect myself. Childish perhaps, but it seemed like the right thing to do at the time.

"Most people lumped them in with the other civilisations. Remember I told you about the *Marabinos* in Zulia and how they often stood up to a Government that was unjust? The Yarina were the forefathers of the Zulians, they fought the Conquistadors but, when they knew they would be defeated, they scattered, keeping their culture alive in secret."

"It all seems a bit far-fetched…"

"Ha! You haven't heard Ernesto's theory yet, have you? Go on, *cuadillo*, tell him." Ernesto pointed to the kitchen and Marcos sprung up, peered inside, barked an order, and closed the door, dampening the sounds from within. When he had sat down, Ernesto scooched forward in his chair.

"Listen," he began. "The Yarina people are in trouble. President Calderon sees threats from every direction and the indigenous people are an easy target; the descendants of all those civilizations that Eva mentioned. They have been persecuted for as long as I can remember, are, in most cases, easily identifiable by their appearance, and have lived in poverty for decades. They may be weak but they are many. Yet the Yarina, as Eva said, they are preserving their culture in secret. There are thousands of them hiding, watching their brothers and sisters cower beneath the boot of Calderon's thugs. They are outsiders in their own country, Francesco. Can you imagine how that might feel?" A distant ringing bell of recognition began to peal deep inside my psyche.

I hadn't talked to anyone about the row between Ollie and Chelsea and how it had boiled over onto me but I imagined that Ernesto would understand more than anyone. My forgiveness, which I had given to both of them in different ways, might have been gracious and given me a short-lived sense of superiority but it would only put a plaster over the wound, which still stung and, I feared, would never truly heal. I imagined carrying that feeling of being an outsider like a scar that you covered up, with a scarf or hat, and, whilst nobody else could see it, you knew it was there, aching.

"They were forced from their land, forced underground, and, now, if they were to reveal themselves or share their identity publicly, it could mean further reprisals."

"Have they never come out of hiding?"

"No hiding," grunted Marcos.

"But how does that link to the knife and the exhibit?"

"People will unite around symbols," Ernesto continued. "You see it with the Brexit vote, don't you? A word – leave or remain; an idea – unity or independence; a flag. The Yarina need a symbol, something to unite around that will show them it is safe to come out of hiding and to fight against oppression once more. Imagine the potential for change if ten thousand, thirty thousand people, could step forward and challenge the tyranny of Calderon's regime?"

"See, his idea is crazy, Frankie," interjected Eva. "As if thousands of people will undo years of hiding, protecting themselves, just for one symbolic moment. It seems very far-fetched to me." Marcos growled at her - literally. It was a slow, reverberating noise that seemed to come from his Adam's apple. Eva ignored him.

"You can think what you like, but I know that this *tumi* represents the match that could set our homelands ablaze with the fire of liberation. And that is one fire that, when it is ignited, never goes out."

The nagging feeling I had felt about the word 'outsider' increased as our conversation about the Yarina progressed. The knowledge that the Yarina led a secret existence seemed implausible yet their story echoed with recognition.

"The time is right to tell you, Francesco, that I am more than I appear to be," proclaimed Ernesto. "This organisation is my project, my legacy, but I am in charge of another organisation that is just as important to me, and our people, but cannot be made public." My eyes widened, and this time it wasn't because of the empanadas; was he a spy?

"Far from the reaches of Calderon and his secret police, I have been leading the *Partido Acción Revolucionara de Todos Yarina*, *el PARTY*, a political movement that will unite the Yarina once more and we can challenge the Val Verdean regime, we can overthrow the dictators that have oppressed the Yarina people for too long. I have been looking for the right opportunity to lead the *Partido* out of the shadows and onto the global political arena." I was a little disappointed that he wasn't a spy but his grand words sounded impressive. I worried that his rhetoric would not seem to resonate with the enthusiasm and power that they had when I first saw him speak at the hotel but the energy he had demonstrated did not waver now.

"And the Yarina can't do this all by themselves? They need you to do it for them?"

"Yes, yes, they are clever and discreet, but they lack the ambition and organisation to act for themselves. Imagine how powerful they might be if we could unite them as one?" Marcos grinned. Eva shrugged. Ernesto looked at each one of us. I listened intently. "They are like computers - smart and ready to respond - but the *Partido* is the network, the Internet. If we can connect the individuals together, the collective will be a true force to be reckoned with."

"And the *tumi* is the key?"

"*¡Exactamente!* Yes, the *tumi* is absolutely the key. The British stole it from us many years ago and for us to steal it back would be the ultimate revenge." He nearly leapt from his seat, leering forward, punctuating his words with urgent thrusts of his fists and jerks of his head. "Once we have it, and the Yarina see what we have done in their name, they will unite under our banner and we can claim victory at the polls. Once the Val Verdeans see that they can get the better of those imperial nations that once subjugated their people, they will turn to us as we are an organisation that has their freedom at the heart of everything it does. This *tumi* is a sign of their identity and a symbol of their unity and a beacon for their emancipation."

An electric current ran through us, charged by Ernesto's ardour and the vision he portrayed; an oppressed nation rising up to regain what was rightfully theirs after centuries of persecution. I might have felt uninspired initially, doubtful even, but now I was empowered by what this seemingly uninteresting artefact might do for the Yarina.

"Wait, wait, wait," Eva urged. "Did you say you're going to *steal* it?"

"No, no, that's my fault. I should not have said 'steal'." Marcos laughed and Ernesto, smiled. "I should have said 'repatriate'. It is ours after all."

"How are you going to 'repatriate' it?" I asked. Eva snorted.

"That's where you come in, Francesco. After all, your parents would be proud of your eagerness to find out about your heritage."

"Wait, what? You knew my parents?"

"Knew them? *¡Por supuesto!* We fought the police in the streets of London outside of the Val Verdean embassy when you were a *niño*, your *mamá* had you strapped to her chest the first time we linked arms. I'm surprised you don't remember more about the Yarina; your *papá* and me, we spoke about them often."

I struggled to recall the memory that contained those conversations or a younger looking Ernesto crowded into our small kitchen-diner. But I continued;

"Hold on, how does this involve me?"

"It's simple. You will take Eva to this gala opening and find a way to liberate the *tumi*. Marcos and I will take possession of the artefact a couple of days later and, then, we will return to Val Verde and reveal to the world that the symbol of Yarina unity is back on home soil."

"You want us to break into a museum? That's madness - think about it. There will be CCTV, security guards, all of the guests. What experience do you think Frankie or I have with burglary?"

Marcos thrust his chair back with his thighs and stood up, leering over us, jabbing one meaty forefinger out repeatedly towards Eva and I. The vein bulged in his neck and his eyes were like boiled eggs, his pupils broad as yolks. "*¡Coños patéticos y cobardes! ¿Crees que tengo estas cicatrices por firmar peticiones? ¡Cobardes!*"

"*¡Tranquilo! ¡Siéntate, Marcos!* Okay, no problem, we have already thought about this. Firstly, Birmingham Museum will not be as well protected as you might think. These institutions survive only on donations from the public so they won't have the high-tech surveillance that would make it difficult for us. CCTV yes but none of that *Mission; Impossible* stuff, you know, like laser beams or heat sensors. Secondly, Frankie and Eva," he waved the side of his hand in our direction, "will be there as guests, so nobody will suspect them of being there for anything other than a good time. Thirdly, we have some experience at this sort of thing and can help. Marcos will be going to the museum as a tourist and will conceal some tools for you to use. Once he has done this, I will tell you where you can find them on the night of the opening. All you need to do is stay hidden until all the guests have left, open the case, take out the *tumi*, and get out of the building. I'm sure two young, educated people like you can manage that."

"Ernesto, wait a minute." I had to speak up. "I have to tell you something. The Home Office are deporting me. Or at least trying to. I was going to mention it to you later but… well, I can't do this. Imagine how bad it would look for me if I got caught? There would be no appealing it!"

"Don't worry. Seriously, don't worry. I know people who can sort out these kind of problems. I've dealt with situations like this before." Just as Eva promised, Ernesto told me he could handle it. Perhaps my worries about remaining in the country might be over. I was enraptured by his words and it made logical sense to me then that he must have the power to persuade anyone to do anything - fuck, we were about to become international art thieves off of the back of one of his speeches, imagine what a jobsworth on minimum wage at the Home Office would be swayed to do?

"So, you think you can help. I mean, help me not to get kicked out?" He nodded slowly, deliberately. In the pit of my stomach was a lurch, an ache, a realisation. The drumbeats from the kitchen stopped.

"It would be my pleasure. So long as you help me with my situation first."

"Listen, I want to help the Yarina as much as anyone but this plan sounds crazy," interjected Eva. "You want us, with no criminal experience, to steal a sacred *tumi* from a museum filled with security during a party full of guests? Ernesto, *eso suena a locura*!"

"*¡Basta de quejas!* Eva Estrellas, you want to help these people? You have always told me you want to make a difference in your life, you say you have the Zulian spirit, you are a *Marabino*, this is what you were born to do." She lowered her chin, frowned, but was silent. "Francesco Cualquiera, you have nothing to lose, you have told me you might be deported, you lack a purpose, don't you? You want to do something that helps people too, I see that in you. Even your name - did you know? - even your name tells of you achieving great things." Now it was my turn to frown.

"Cualquiera comes from the Yarina language - *Kalguasiza* - the image of all that existed and will exist, the oracle, as the Ancient Greeks might have called you. Oracles were destined to predict and, therefore, influence the future. Great leaders put a lot of faith in their oracles and I put a lot of faith in you, Francesco, a lot of faith. I have already given you my prophecy of what can happen once the *tumi* is liberated. The both of you will make that prophecy come true."

The two of us knew that there was no talking our way out of this. Ernesto's words and Marcos' leaden glare made sure of that.

Chapter 15 – Wednesday 8th June (15 days to go)

The bluntness and simplicity of Ernesto's questions was both dangerous and inspiring.

"What have you really got to look forward to?" he had asked, in what seemed like an entire life ago, when we met in the Galloping Gendarme. Only now were answers beginning to form before me.

Street lamps flickered off. Momentary shadows on the cobbles glistened with sunrise. I wandered towards home, but my mind was drawn back to the hotel conference room and the first-floor bar and now the seedy restaurant. What had I truly got to look forward to?

The words had been spoken slowly and insistently by Ernesto when I first got to see his persuasive powers at their most potent but I could not shake the impression that this mentor, of sorts, could have ruined the impact the more he spoke. Yet, he persisted, pressing his message further.

"No, no, not the weekend, not your next payslip. Not a holiday. What is it that makes you jump out of bed in the morning?"

The ache I felt was not caused by the answers but a lack of them. I felt the corners of my mouth turn down in a sneer, disappointed in myself, almost disgusted, and shook my head. I was born here, or so I thought. That fact, the uncontemplated cornerstone of my being, was now in question, thanks to... Thanks to who? The Home Office? They were just doing what they were told to do by the Students' Loans Company. But the Students' Loans Company were led by the University. But the

University's out-dated systems relied on the Students' Loans Company. And it seemed as if both of them were reliant on the Post Office. Could it be that one postman, rather than simply put the letter in a neighbour's letterbox or leave it at a sorting office for collection, had caused all of this trouble for me?

I was educated, my family didn't seem to be poor, I had none of the disadvantages that might have excused any lack of... lack of what precisely? Lack of wealth? Lack of success? It was something less precise than that.

"Exactly. So, you see, you must find what it is that makes you feel alive. That makes you go the extra mile."

Ernesto's skill was not in giving solutions but leading you to work them out for yourself. I knew just what I lacked now. Power over something. Control. Purpose.

What did I stand for? What did I want to achieve? If I was a meteor, how big would the crater be that I left behind? Pond-sized, a puddle perhaps? God, that was depressing. I looked back and thought about what things I had accomplished - my GCSEs, my A-Levels, the first of my family to go to University, my model railway village that had taken months, if not years, of secretive construction, my new job, my flatmates - they all felt insignificant now. I used to laugh at those students who mucked about and didn't take their education seriously, and still do, but, yet, here I was dismissing all I felt I had achieved off the back of a rousing speech from a Central American politician-in-exile, if that's really what he was, who he claimed to be, in the back room of a restaurant. It was so hard to fathom.

What made me feel alive? Not Ollie and Chelsea, not Philosophy, not Scintilla, that much I knew. If I was having doubts about the qualifications I already had, how sure could I be that I knew what to do with the qualifications I would earn when I'd graduated? When I was a kid, at least in the first few years before I became a teenager, I had wanted to get into politics, to make a difference to people's lives up and down the country, internationally even, to change things for the better. I was inspired a little by mum and dad. As I got older, I only saw more and more of the side they had tried to conceal from me; the rejection, the scorn, the brutality.

But what did that mean for me? Should I go back to my first stirrings of direction, before I became lost in the immediacy of the life I was living now, or should I stick to what I can be sure of and what I've already got? This was too hard to think about.

Maybe Ernesto could help lead me to the answers to all of these questions. Questions I didn't know needed answering until tonight. He had stirred up these doubts and so he might be able to provide the solution.

"What are you thinking about?" Eva held my hand and I started.

"All sorts," my gaze drifted away from the starlit puddles and followed the line of the pavement, where the road ended and Chamberlain Square opened out. "What time is it?"

"Four."

"My shift starts in four hours." I nodded towards Scintilla as it came into view. Eva tensed. Opposite the coffee shop was the Museum and they had put up a huge

189

banner, twenty feet by forty feet, I'd guess, across the front, advertising the Central American Cultural Artefacts exhibit and, among the antiques on the black, looming sheet, centred between four other lesser objects, was a graphical rendering of the golden *tumi*.

"You're still not doing it?" I asked, with an unnecessary inflection.

"No way."

"What about the Yarina?"

"They've kept themselves a secret for hundreds of years. I'm sure they can stay that way as long as they want. We've already talked about it." She was right; we had. From the walk from the restaurant to her place and in her kitchen when she demanded that I listen to reason - her choice of words - and forget this ludicrous plan. I couldn't tell her whether I was committed to do it or not. If I had been asked on any other day, one, two months earlier, I would have flat out said no, just like she did. It was hard to express to Eva exactly what it was that made me hesitate. I didn't know for sure myself.

She was so decisive, so sure about everything. Even when she kissed me it was what she wanted, so she did it. I was not expecting it at all, as much as I wanted her, and it came at me so out of the blue that I immediately wanted to take it back and try it again properly. Perhaps she didn't notice or didn't have high expectations of me; the kiss lasts and I feel it still, so I felt like I must have gotten away with it.

The second time came just as suddenly a few minutes later, a soft, ticklish kiss that smothered me with feelings of comfort, when we were sat on her sofa. That first kiss still pulsing in my mind, Eva turned and walked into the kitchen, continuing our conversation without a beat, returning with two cans of Coke and a bag of nachos. She sat first, I followed, recoiling, wondering if another kiss or something else might be forthcoming, God, that first kiss, but she carried on talking. I must have participated in the conversation but it felt like I was outside of my own skin, a feeling I could only draw parallels with when I had flu or was really hungover and felt my, I don't know, 'soul', or something, sort of floating above my head, like I could see the world from the perspective of someone who was four, five inches taller than me, then she kissed me the second time in the middle of a sentence, when I was in the middle of a thought, and I felt at home.

She carried on talking, I could not. The impact of those kisses she gave me halted me, stunned me, just as sharply and as brutally as Chelsea's words had and the emotions I felt were so similar I was disorientated. I felt anger. I felt love, if anyone can ever define exactly what that feels like. I felt shock.

Hours later we are here, in the middle of the city, with street lights buzzing from colour into neutral and irregular sounds of shop shutters clattering up, dust bin lorries reversing streets away, and the soft breathing of her exhalations over her lips. My lips now, no, still hers, possibly ours, I squeezed her hand to see if she was really here and she squeezed back. This was something real. Ernesto may have kindled some unanswered questions in me but it could be Eva who was the answer.

"You're right," Be decisive, I told myself. "We won't do it."

At the flat, I found Ollie and Chelsea sitting in the living room in complete silence. Eva had chivalrously walked me home before going back to hers for some sleep and I needed to take a shower and eat something before my shift started. If I could, I would get an hour or two of sleep, but I doubted that would be possible.

"What are you two up to?"

"*Hola Francesco*, I'm organising the mail outs for the Remain campaign." She swept her hand artfully across a series of piles of paperwork that looked like six games of Solitaire all being played at once. "Two from these three flyers needs to go into one envelope, depending on whether the recipient is a supporter, undecided, or unknown, and then I have to drop them around Fiona's flat as she's getting the team to put them through letterboxes." Ollie grunted.

"Much too complicated."

"What about you, Ollie?"

"I've got a stack of beer mats, some flyers, badges, these little furry dudes with googly eyes, and fridge magnets. I'm chucking them in carrier bags and dropping them off at a few pubs and bars and public places." They glanced at one another and I could tell from the atmosphere that they'd recently finished up an argument about something.

"Where have you been?" Chelsea wouldn't have asked unless she was interested and I knew that there might still be a small part of her that was protective of me.

"I had a meeting," I knew if I told the truth, I could relax about forgetting what lies I had told to whom.

"All night?" she probed, with an air of suspicion.

"Yep." I decided that I need not tell her any more than she needed to know for now. I was not yet ready to trust either of them again, especially considering the subject of the conversation with Ernesto, Eva, and Marcos.

"Any chance I can get some help, mate?" I looked at Ollie and then at Chelsea. She shrugged and turned away.

"Er…"

"Could do with a spare pair of hands. Just for an hour or so."

"I can't, I've got to get ready for work…"

"Oh, right, okay," he said. "Do you reckon you could help me out afterward though as I've got loads to get out there. I'd really appreciate it and I know the guys would be grateful."

"Sure," I was too tired to protest. "Yeah, no worries. I'll be home about lunchtime." Chelsea tutted and muttered something under her breath. Ollie pretended to ignore her. "Do you need any help too, Chels?"

They both turned to look at me.

"Yes, thanks, that would be great. I'm sure we can count on your support too when it comes to the voting too, right?"

"Woah, woah, hold on, you can't support both sides. You're either for independence from bureaucracy or you're not."

"Oliver, he can do what he likes."

"No, you have to pick a side, and you can either fill my carrier bags for freedom or stuff her envelopes for an end to British democracy. That's your choice."

"Don't be so simplistic. Your bags of tat are spreading lies about immigration and 'destiny'" - she did the air speech marks gesture - "whilst my literature explains the benefits of being part of something bigger than ourselves."

"You're so full of shit!"

"How dare you! You've fallen for the propaganda, Oliver, you need to get rid of those old ways of thinking and look to the future."

"Why are you so keen to forget tradition and where you're from?" They stood facing each other now. I watched and felt the fog clear. I could support both sides of the argument. It just wouldn't be their argument.

"I'm having a shower. I'll be back later." Through the door and under the hum of the extractor fan, their bickering continued and I simply tuned them out. In the steam, I was free to think for myself. If I wanted to support Ollie's campaign for tradition, what could be better than helping a centuries old people? As for his desire for 'independence' - no air quotation marks from me, I was in the shower, but they existed in my head - then independence from oppression was what the Yarina needed. Chelsea's desire to contribute to a bigger cause resonated with me and taking one small action to help free the Yarina made a lot of sense, even if that one small action might be inherently risky for me.

As I cogitated on my situation, I came to the realisation that any decision would be based on risk versus reward. What was the best outcome possible? What was the worst that could happen? The worst was obviously deportation - but that might happen even if I didn't help Ernesto. I supposed that I might get imprisoned but, from what I'd seen recently on the news, anyone convicted of a crime who was considered to be a foreign national would end up getting deported rather than imprisoned in the UK, so there were not two separate potential risks but one. The best outcome, for me, would be to *not* be caught and for Ernesto to help me stave off the deportation. But was that really it?

Sure, the next step might be that the Yarina may unite around this symbol and this might prevent them from being eradicated by Calderon's death squads. But, selfish I knew, that didn't make a difference to me as I'd not even heard about them until a few days ago. I mean, it didn't matter to me whether they were Yarina, or French, or gay, or human-sized squirrels, or gay, French, human-sized squirrels... What mattered to me was that I mattered to them, or at least if they never knew who I was, my actions would impact them. If I could do something, anything, that improved the lives of hundreds or thousands of people, surely that would mean something. It might be the one thing I did in my life I could actually be proud of having accomplished, more impressive than any degree. After all, thousands of people get a degree every year in the UK alone but how many people around the world can say they've done something to liberate an entire race of people? I hoped they would find out who had done it for them though, that would make it all a bit more worthwhile, but then it would make it easy for me to be caught and, if Ernesto came through with his side of the bargain, I could end up in prison in this country anyway... Man, this was giving me brain freeze...

So by being selfish about my reasons for stealing the *tumi*, I could be doing the most generous act possible. In doing so, I might be deported or not deported but imprisoned, but only imprisoned if I was identified, and if I was identified, I might become a hero to these people, and even if I wasn't successful, knowing that someone was acting for them, maybe that might give the Yarina the courage to rise up against the Government. And what were the chances I would actually get convicted? I'd never committed a crime before so maybe there would be mitigating circumstances that would mean I got off with just a slap on the wrist, a charge or something, from the police.

At this point, I knew that I had convinced myself that I was going to go through with it. With or without the blessing of Eva. And if I had thought a little more about that crucial part of this hare-brained scheme, I might not be in the situation I find myself in today.

Chapter 16 – Friday 10th June (13 days to go)

Scintilla seemed like a sanctuary. I could avoid the rows between Chelsea and Ollie that were now an almost daily occurrence. I had distance from Ernesto, preventing my mind from dwelling on the crime I had been volunteered for. Within those four walls, everything was predictable and mundane, which was just what I needed for the time being.

Eva and I had spoken on the phone but it was one of those new romance 'check-ins', where neither of you is confident enough to make a real conversation but you want to make sure that the other is okay and, without being obvious, still willing to give the relationship a chance. I couldn't face the thought of her ghosting me or either one of us simply drifting away from the other.

On Wednesday afternoon, I had sat cross-legged at the coffee table, a buffer between the uncharacteristically silent Chelsea and the unusually seething Ollie as they both folded flyers and stuffed envelopes. Neither seemed ready to try again to convince me, or one another, who to support. I think my preceding years of indecision and lack of direction had finally been understood. Able to help both, I chose neither, folding one Leave flyer then stuffing one Remain envelope and so on, consciously trying to help in an entirely even-handed way so as not to show any kind of favouritism.

The day of the referendum seemed like it would never arrive and all I desired at that point was for the whole affair to be over with and everyone's lives to go back to normal. Although there would be no more normal for me, thanks to the Home Office. My mind was consumed with thoughts of becoming a cat burglar - why are there no *dog* burglars...? - and if I didn't distract myself with the mundane, repetitive actions I was carrying out for my flatmates' benefit, I worried that I might blurt out the entire scheme to them. My preference had always been keeping things to myself; ensuring personal matters remained personal. Lately, I felt the exciting urge to gossip, titillating perhaps because of what the ramifications would be and how much trouble I might get into.

Ollie snorted as a Remain pamphlet encroached on his half of the coffee table. Chelsea hummed as she tickled it back with her fingertips. I coughed, softly, like a librarian in a library sensing impending disorder. He glared at her. She sneered at him. I kept my eyes down and kept on folding, and stuffing, and sticking.

"Tea?" growled Ollie.

"Sure," grumbled Chelsea.

"Love one, thanks," I giggled.

It was funny how roles could be reversed like this. My parents were the upbeat ones, bustling and harrying, in preparation for the impending deadline of their mostly peaceful protests. I was the one grimacing and moaning in the corner, reluctant to help them get into more trouble for a cause that did not affect me at all. Or so I thought then. Now, I was the cheery one - even if it was exaggerated for their benefit - whilst the two with most to gain, if you can put a price on pride, were the ones coming across as churlish and sullen.

"Where are you at with this deportation nonsense?" asked Chelsea

"They told me to speak to the Citizens' Advice Bureau."

"And they can help?"

"No." Fold. Stuff. Stick.

"Are you going to go and see them?" She leaned her head to one side, dispensing wisdom.

"No. What's the point?"

"So what's your next move?" enquired Ollie, juggling mugs back from the kitchen.

"I don't know. I'm working on it." The impulse to open up like a blossom in a shaft of sunlight rose again but I kept it inside once more. "I'll keep you posted." I waved a batch of envelopes in the air and they both groaned. Even if they were at loggerheads, the least I could do would be to try and bring them together. I couldn't hold a grudge over what they had said, as ignorant and thoughtless as it was, because I didn't want to lose them as friends or at least confidantes. Who else could I share things with when I wanted to? I didn't see the point in getting so animated about politics, certainly not so much so that you drive your mates away - or, in their case, girlfriend or boyfriend. After all, as far as I could tell, in British politics nothing ever changes for the better so why get so annoyed by it? At least with Val Verdean politics, it was so volatile that change happened frequently and at pace - you could almost see evidence of evolution through revolution happen before your eyes. The glacial pace of change here, and the lack of genuine drama and controversy, meant that most MPs could be replaced by their counterparts from one or two decades ago and most of the population would be none the wiser.

By Friday, Chelsea and her cronies had returned to the square, protesting something or other, which surprised me, considering how much effort she had been putting into the anti-Brexit work. I assumed that would be her focus for the next few weeks but then she was always someone who had lots of interests and a range of activities at any one time. Although, come to think of it, all she was doing when I was there helping her get ready for her demonstration was sorting papers into piles and putting them into envelopes for other people to distribute. Maybe that's what she thought campaigning was.

Lucy and Rob and Freya and the rest of the staff carried on, ignorant of the clandestine operation I had been asked to carry out. There was no way I could risk giving away any clue of the scheme as there would, at this point, only be one outcome. So long as I was getting paid, I was happy to stay there and keep up the innocent pretence.

It was after the lunchtime rush that Eva arrived. I had no idea she would be coming to visit me and she caught me on the back foot. I didn't expect her to be popping in already - that's a much later stage in our relationship that I wasn't totally convinced we would get to, and definitely not so soon. But here she was and I had to act natural if I was going to come across as the chilled out guys I thought that she was attracted to.

"Hey, what's up?"

"Hey, no, nothing, I wanted to see you."

"Cool, cool," Yes, I was playing it *very* cool, wasn't I? "Do you want some lunch… or something?"

"Sure. Let's go somewhere else though. Can you take a break?"

"Yeah, no worries." I stepped into the back room, where Freya was reading through some emails and begged her to let me go on my lunch break, even though Rob had only just gone, and I would totally pay her back if she could just cover me this one time.

"So, what do you want to eat?" I asked.

"I like Italian. You?"

"Sounds... cool..." She reached for my hand and led me across the street. We went to an Italian restaurant around the corner, which had the usual trappings. The oversized pepper grinders like Cluedo candlesticks, gingham check tablecloths - famously Italian, of course - and green bottles of chilli oil, next to balsamic vinegar, olive oil, salt, vinegar, and tomato ketchup on each table. I was reminded how I was torn between who I felt I was and who I was being told I was by those around me and how, if I wanted to keep others happy, how I would have to adapt and become someone that was a pastiche of those two identities. Neither one nor the other.

"We have to talk." Four words nobody wants to hear from a current or potential partner.

"Okay," I responded, accentuating my reply with an overly casual shrug and then droop of the shoulders. Very Italian, I thought.

"I don't want you to get involved with Ernesto's plan," she whispered. "It's dangerous." Menus were slid onto the table but, at a glance from her, Eva spooked the waiter off temporarily.

"But don't you think it could be the start of something really important?"

"I do. And I agree with his ambition. I don't think this is the right way to go about it. The *Partido* are still small and I'm not convinced that the *tumi* and the Yarina, will be enough to give them the votes to topple Calderon." She picked up a menu, holding it between us, her dark eyes flitting across it with the top half of her head the only thing I could see. That was the end of that conversation then.

I remembered a poster that Chelsea had stuck up in her bedroom; 'Well-behaved women seldom make history.' I wondered if Eva had heard that quote before. I remembered it so vividly because it was something my Mamá had said when getting ready to leave with Papá during the G20 riots, I think. Their depth of knowledge and ability to recall succinct and impactful quotations always impressed me. It was a talent that had not taken root in me, despite my desire to be seen as intelligent. All I had was the ability to think philosophically, I supposed. That and my skill at making miniature models of the architecture of the English countryside but that was not something I really felt comfortable sharing with Eva yet. Our feelings for each other were still new and fresh and revealing a hobby that was insanely nerdy and specific - I know, I can admit it - like that could only jeopardise what we might have. Perhaps I might have a hidden talent for cat-burglary? There would be only one way to find out.

"What are you having?"

"Probably just a pizza. I'm trying to save some money." The hint that she would be paying for her own food was welcome but I couldn't resist making a proposal.

"I can get it."

"You sure?"

"Yeah," I paused. "Imagine how much money Ernesto would pay for the *tumi*? I could buy the whole restaurant!"

Eva didn't laugh. "I'm not kidding. I don't want you getting involved."

"I know, I won't." I changed the subject and we talked about her job in the law office and how her day was going. She talked to me about philosophy, Scintilla, and anything else that would take my mind off of the impending deportation or the *tumi*. I liked listening to her more than speaking about my own dramas so when she began recounting anecdotes from her childhood, I was all ears. It sounded like her parents were not quite shady but definitely not wholly law-abiding citizens. Her dad, it seemed, was a fisherman by trade but a fence at night, with all kinds of contraband being ferried across Lake Maracaibo. Mostly homemade booze, knock-off fashion, and pirated videos; nothing especially criminal but a handy side gig to put his daughter through college and then send her to University in England. She seemed embarrassed but not ashamed to tell me about him. I need not have wondered why.

"It's important to me that you don't become like him - he was always having to look over his shoulder and hide things, or get me to hide things for him. And you do one person a favour and you end up doing favours for everyone and some of the people he dealt with did him a favour but kept that against him for a long time... I needed to share that with you because I don't want you becoming like him."

"That makes two dads I don't want to be like."

"Yours sounds like someone with strong principles. There's nothing wrong with that."

"I meant because he abandoned me here." That was a real conversation killer and we both took a mouthful of food - her pepperoni and peppers pizza, my carbonara. It felt like an opportune moment to salvage what risked becoming a very negative lunch break. "Do you still want to come to the opening night though?"

"Mm, yeah, it should be nice. Do we need to dress up?"

I fished the invitation out of my wallet and took a look. "It looks like. Maybe a dress and shoes?"

"And what will *I* wear?" she joked.

"You can wear what you want - I'm sure you'll look amazing."

"Do you even own a suit?"

"Yeah, of course. I've got a grey two-piece from River Island. Perfect for my court appearance." We both smiled a connection, a moment where I knew we were going to be together, at least a while longer.

"I'm serious, though. I don't trust Ernesto and I don't like his plan."

"I... Okay, look, if Ernesto could guarantee that I wouldn't get deported, like 100% not going to happen, don't you think it's worth the risk?" Sometimes, you say something and you see from the other person's expression, maybe before you've even finished what you're saying, that what you've said has been as well received as a slug in a sandal.

"Why would you come up with hypotheticals like that? You'll get your hopes up that he will help you or, I don't know, hold up his side of the deal, and you'll only get let down. Worst of all, if you did this, I would never be able to trust you. You've told me that you would not go through with it so why keep talking about it?" The wind went out of my sails and I nodded, eating a mouthful of pasta just to give us both time to step back from the edge.

"Can we change the subject?"

"Yeah, of course." We ate and she measured the pause. "Look, I came to see you because I need to talk to you about something."

"Not just Ernesto's plan?"

"I thought you said you wanted to change the subject? Listen, I spoke to one of the guys I work with in the law office. He said he would help if he could and he did a little bit of investigation work, to try and see if you have good grounds for fighting the Home Office."

"Oh, wow, and what did he say?"

"Oh, nothing firm yet but he does think he could speak to someone at the British Consulate in Escalón to see if your parents have been registered or, um, incarcerated there…"

"What have they got to do with anything?"

Eva hesitated. "Frankie, if they had proof that you were born here, a birth certificate, a photograph, something, then maybe we can find an angle."

"Do we have to bring them into it?"

"Can they help you to stay in the country? Yes, we do have to bring them into it." I wasn't ready for a fight and I couldn't risk saying something I would regret and she might throw back at me. What was the problem? So they left me to fend for myself and put me into care, I was okay now, wasn't I?

There was nothing I felt like I could add so that line of discussion was quickly cut short and I had to come up with something else to distract from my reluctance to involve my parents in this at all, so I talked a bit about Chelsea and Oliver's new rivalry and that seemed to smooth over the disagreement.

We ended up in better moods than we might have and whilst I went back to work, Eva had to go to a class. But I was still indecisive about what to do; there was a chance of staying in the UK, there was the sense of doing something significant, but there was still the risk of deportation and now the threat of letting down Eva, who I would really, really prefer to impress. Okay, I said to myself, time to be decisive again. I was growing to like this new proactive me - the old me would have found someone else to decide for me but there was no possibility of talking to Chels and Ollie about this over a pint. The old me might have procrastinated until everything had either resolved itself or been forgotten; there was no chance of that happening now.

In just a few days' time, the opening of the exhibition would take place and that was my hard deadline. It would only be a week or so after that before, I imagined, the blacked out Transit would pull up with a screech and balaclavaed ex-squaddies would jump out before bundling me in the back and driving me to some RAF airfield, where a hollowed out old Hercules would fly me and a handful of confused, scared, tan-coloured people off to Val Verde, or a neighbouring country, without time to pack our bags, say goodbye, or cancel the Sky Sports subscription.

I had seen enough documentaries to know that's what it was like for people back home - if I could call it home - and countless other nations in the region. Not paying your parking fine? Disappeared. Speaking up against the local mayor? Vanished. I heard it was worse in Brazil and Mexico with the death squads and narco gangs but I was more worried about the countries you *didn't* hear about. They must have some really scary shit going on there when journalists are too scared to visit or nobody is willing to reveal what's really happening. I wondered what Eva's family would have experienced in Venezuela. Her dad sounded like someone who would know how to avoid detection - or perhaps he knew who to persuade and how.

Right, back to work, and then I'd talk to Ernesto.

"Hello?"

"Is that Mr. Cal… Kwal…"

"Cualquiera."

"Yes, that's right. Mr. Cal-key-error?"

"Yeah, who's calling?"

"Good afternoon, it's Paul Holding from the University." Six months ago, I would have been curious. Now I was concerned.

"Hi Paul. What's up?" Play it cool...

"Mr... er, Francesco we have some bad news, I'm afraid." I tugged the sleeve of my coat up and, looking around, spotted a bus stop. I sat down on the grey metal ledge, unsure if I could take more bad news. "The University has determined that we can no longer consider you as an undergraduate at this time. They will be unenrolling you from your Philosophy Bachelor of Arts course this month. I am sorry to be telling you, of course."

"Why?" I quavered.

"As we understand it, you are in the country without a visa. We cannot allow you to continue your studies if you are here illegally."

"I see," I replied. "There's probably been some kind of mistake. I am here legally and I don't require a visa. There has been an error at the Home Office. I'm getting it sorted... right now..."

"Ah, of course, yes, well, you see, we can keep your place open for you so that you can resume your studies next academic year."

"Wait, I have a class on Monday - are you telling me I can't go?"

"That's right, unfortunately. But if you could come into the office with a valid visa or passport, then we can see what we can do. We might be able to keep your place open if you could do it within the next month."

"I don't have a passport and I don't need a visa."

"Oh, well... I don't understand. You don't have a passport?"

"No," I felt sure I had already had this conversation numerous times before. "I never got round to getting one."

"You could apply for one."

"Yes but that takes four to six weeks. I don't have that kind of time." I wasn't in the mood to explain why to him.

"Oh, right... I see." He didn't, obviously.

"And you can't apply for a visa... Sorry, you said you don't need one... Is there any other way you could get a proof of British nationality? Perhaps from the Home Office?"

I exhaled. "I don't think so."

"I'm sorry then, it seems like there's nothing else you can do. But don't worry, I'll make a note on your file that if you do come in with a visa or a passport then we will keep your place open for the next 12 months. I'm sorry... sir."

He hung up and I sat looking for buses but with no desire to catch one. I tugged my phone out of my jacket pocket and texted Ernesto. I had to see him and there was no time to waste.

It was the early evening when I saw him striding across the square in a navy roll neck, slim dark jeans, and a camel suede bomber jacket. His face was framed by a sleek pair of Ray-Bans. He reminded me of a Silicon Valley entrepreneur, one of those start-up guys who makes a quick million, sells stock for a billion, and looks for his next project. Just before the bubble bursts.

"Francesco!" He was all warm smiles and handshakes, resting his left hand on my bicep as he squeezed firmly. "I was so pleased to get your message."

"Thanks for coming, I…"

"Let's get a bite to eat, yes?" He led me to Bouji's, a newish little brasserie that was less corporate than Scintilla. They put their cakes on wooden tiles because they were cheap; we did it to look down to earth. "You'll love their fougasse!"

It was mild weather so we sat outside, not too far from a heat lamp, at a high table on the square. I didn't feel particularly hungry but Ernesto had ordered and I now had in front of me a 'French bowl', which, from what I could tell, was a bucket of thin coffee served in a soup tureen, along with a Danish pastry. He had a large filter coffee and a fougasse, which appeared to be some kind of savoury bread with goats' cheese, walnuts, and garlic baked into it.

"What did you want to talk to me about?"

"How likely is it that you could help me to stay?"

He nodded. "*Si, claro*, pretty likely I would say. You have a home address here, yes? You're studying here, you have a job, should be no problem." It felt like the wrong time to mention the phone call.

"I don't have a passport or my birth certificate. Would that be a problem?"

"A little, but we can work around it."

"How much will it cost?"

"Francesco, no, for you, nothing." His broad grin was infectious.

"How long would it take?"

"You're full of questions today, aren't you?" As I did not respond, he answered. "One week, maybe two. Give or take a day for administrative delays." I began calculating and bit a corner off of my pastry.

"I'm having second thoughts." It was an odd thing to say, for me anyway. Recollecting that final conversation with Ernesto before the opening night of the exhibition, it struck me that I only said it because I must have been asking to be convinced.

"Okay," he replied. He sipped his coffee and, with his other hand, sliced it through the air in front of him as if drawing attention to the entirety of the square. I followed the arc of his gesture but it wasn't immediately clear what he was suggesting.

"Take a real look at what you see. Don't just gaze at our surroundings but think how everything got here." I was still none the wiser. I think he could tell from my expression. "The columns that hold up the balcony on the front of the museum. You see those? They're Corinthian style – from the ancient Greek city state of Corinth. How about the ones on the front of that restaurant?" I shrugged. "Ionic, from Ionia, also from ancient Greece, but now part of Turkey." I failed to see his point and, regardless, he carried on.

"Those concrete sphinx sculptures? Egyptian. Where do you think the inspiration for these designs came from?"

"I've no idea."

"Would you imagine that the designers simply found inspiration from, huh, I don't know, the rain fell from the sky or they had a dream? Like a lit match bursts to life, there must be roughness first, you know? *Fricción*?"

I looked blankly back at him.

His eyes roamed the square, probing and squinting. "Ah, okay, maybe I should explain a different way. You see the statue?"

"Queen Victoria," I notified him.

"She holds the crown jewels – a crown, sceptre and orb. You know what they are, yes?" I nodded. "Where did they come from?" He picked up his fougasse, a cue for me to answer but I waited and thought about it first. What did he *want* me to say? What would be a correct answer?

"Inside the crown is the Koh-i-Noor diamond, one of the world's most famous diamonds. Absolutely priceless. Where do you think that came from? The

British Empire's rule over India. Did they buy the diamond from the Indian people or did they just take it? The Indian workers who dug the mine, who risked their lives, whose fingers bled from the effort, what do they have to show for their discovery? Now think about the sceptre – at the top is another diamond, the Great Star of Africa. It was mined by slave labour in South Africa in appalling conditions. And what did these South Africans get for their labours? Nothing." I didn't immediately make the connection between what he was saying about the crown jewels and the architecture of the city I lived in.

"Britain did not buy or earn these things; they took them by force or threats of violence. They are the spoils of war, the loot of a robbery on a grand scale."

Deep down, I felt like I always knew this but that that knowledge had never been scrutinised before. He was right, of course, about what the Victorians did and how for every school opened or cricket pitch laid in one country, in another the army looted from royal palaces or destroyed entire cities with naval bombardments. Some information I knew, but didn't know how I knew or remembered where I learned about it. But so what? This was the 21st century in a modern British city and what they did in the past to other countries couldn't be my burden.

"I know that but what's your point?"

"It isn't just India and South Africa; it is Val Verde and Venezuela and Honduras and Chile and all nations of the Americas. If you look inside that Museum, you will see items from all over the world. In the past, the British Empire was too powerful for people to fight back but, now, it has all changed. We have a right, a duty even, to repatriate those items that they stole."

213

I shook my head. "It's the duty of governments to negotiate their return. Philosophically speaking, it's the duty of the citizens that want their historic artefacts returned to elect politicians to negotiate on their behalf. It's called a social contract…"

"And if the politicians do not do what their electorate wants?"

"They get voted out…"

"And if the elections are rigged?"

"Then…"

"Then what, huh? So, I know what you were going to say. You were going to say the people can protest. I would reply with 'What if the politicians used the army to suppress the protesters?' You see? However you decide to view the situation, the democracy we have does not work and we will never get back what is rightfully our nations unless we act."

"Can't you speak to politicians here, in the UK? Surely they can decide to give it back."

"You think I haven't already thought of that? They do not care. *Ellos viven en una nube hecha de pedos.* They live on a cloud made of farts, Frankie, they are out of touch with reality. You read the newspapers, right?" I nodded, lying. "These *capullos* are stealing the electorate's money for... for what? Chocolate bars? Taxi rides? A castle for ducks! And what do the great British public do? Do they throw off their chains and overthrow their oppressors? Do they take to the streets demanding retribution? No, they vote them back in - you watch and see. There's an election next year. You'll see. The only change we can be assured of is in our homeland. The *Partido* will be victorious - *if* you are successful."

Rain fell suddenly but lightly and a waiter came out and erected a canopy over us as we finished up our drinks and snacks. I could argue with him but it would be fruitless; he was right, and he knew it. I knew it too.

"Why was Eva so eager to persuade you not to steal the *tumi*?"

"She is worried. About me." She wasn't the only one but, aside from looking after my own back, who else was there to worry about me? Perhaps Ernesto – I wasn't convinced fully on that front. Not Chelsea or Ollie. Not my parents. "About me becoming like her dad. She told me he was a kind of criminal. Not a bad one, but he did some shady stuff, you know. Moving things for shady people across the lake." Ernesto smirked and nodded, respecting the graft or the spirit of the man but wary of the dishonesty influencing me in some way, almost fatherly himself.

"I understand. There is risk of course. You're not an idiot, you can see that there is a danger if you get caught." He contemplated. "On the other hand, you must consider what we can achieve if you do not get caught. What other nation can say they stood up to an imperialist country, a nation with billions and trillions of resources and military power, and gave them a black eye?"

If I wasn't careful, he would get on to one of his speeches again.

"I think I know you, Francesco, at least a little. You are worried and I understand. If this plan fails, you will get deported, or, if I am successful in helping you stay, put in prison. But if it succeeds, would it not feel good to get one over on the country that has disowned you?"

"And what do I need to do to help me stay?"

"*Sencillo*, I need something with your home address on, some ID, maybe a driving licence, and a portrait photograph of you from a photo booth. You got my message, right? Did you bring them with you?"

I nodded. From my jacket, I passed him a mobile phone bill, my drivers' licence, and a 1" square head shot photo. "But I don't have long. Less than two weeks, I think."

"This is all I need to get you a passport. Trust me, it is not so difficult when you know the right people in the right places."

I felt a sense of relief about the passport but also what he said about the added feeling of outfoxing the authorities. This wasn't just some grand cause, that was, admittedly, very tempting for my own sense of accomplishment, but this was something more personal too and Ernesto had worked out how to sway me with this concept. I pictured myself sitting in front of the Home Office agents again, unable to tell them what I had done and just what it meant for the great country whose work they were carrying out. I would have that twitching, itching feeling spreading across my top lip, urging me to laugh hyena-like, a cackling, guilt-free, guffaw that would provoke curious stares and demands for an explanation, demands which would have to go unanswered. What a feeling that would be.

And the alternative? Sat in a six-foot square lockup with my cellmate prying with the stereotypical 'What're you in for?' line. I would answer with the truth about not having indefinite leave to remain but would hold back on the reality until I could trust him and, only then, would I reveal that I was the very person to have stolen the sacred South American curio that had sparked wild celebrations in a little-known nation and a bloodless coup against the regime there. Perhaps, with my fellow cons enamoured by my Robin Hood-style cunning, we might free ourselves from the surly bonds of concrete and steel just as the Yarina would do thousands of miles away. Yes, my fantasies were fuelled by episodes of *Prison Break* but that didn't mean they were any less possible.

There was just one remaining hurdle. "What about Eva?"

"What about Eva?"

"If I do this, you cannot tell her. I promised I wouldn't do it and, if she finds out I've lied to her, she'll break up with me." He smiled again, that transmittable, creeping grin that made you feel like the only person in the world at that moment.

"You have nothing to worry about. I will not speak of our plan to her again and, if she asks, I will tell her that Marcos talked me out of it. Maybe he saw one too many security guards, yes? But let us be clear – can I count on you?"

I spoke decisively. "Yes." It was the single most costly word I have ever uttered.

Chapter 17 – Tuesday 14th June (9 days to go…)

There was no time to lose, according to Ernesto. It was imperative that we met to discuss exactly how I would be repatriating the *tumi* from the museum. Whilst I knew cat burgling would never be my specialist subject on Pointless, I hoped there would be some expertise in the room with me.

"Why are we meeting here?" I had envisaged that we would be having this discussion in a far more insalubrious setting.

"Why not? It is perfect for what we need." It might be Ernesto's idea of perfection but, to me, it was the dusty back room of a church. Not a grand gothic construction of flying buttresses and stained glass, with Catholic red and gold adorning every level surface. This was, simply put, bland and soulless.

Laid out on a foldable table were several A3 sheets, covered with pen lines and pencil sketches, with patches rubbed out beyond legibility. On top of them was placed a couple of half-empty coffee mugs, a ring of fire keys, a selection of small hand tools, and pens and pencils and other bits of stationery.

"Marcos has already paid a visit to the museum and taken a look at what we may need to know, such as where the entrances and exits are, how many security guards there are, where the cameras are pointed, and so on."

"Cased the joint," I murmured.

"What?"

"Nothing, carry on."

"Have you been to the museum before, Francesco?"

I shook my head. "No, never had the time." I said it with some shame, as it was an outright lie. I had plenty of time and ample opportunity to visit and to learn about all of the people and places and times represented within the ever-changing exhibits within. But, somehow, I had never gotten around to it. It was one of those places that lingered in my mind, as if I was neglecting myself by not going there, like an old friend I really should have called but, somehow, had not and the time between our conversations was now uncomfortably long. Had it announced a museum equivalent of a closing down sale, no doubt I would have ensured that I was first in line to snatch a last-minute glimpse of all of the things that had remained unseen. It's existence - nay, persistence - was an unacknowledged touchstone in my life, like traffic lights or skimmed milk.

Only now did I look quickly at Ernesto, who leaned against a steel-barred window, next to the table that bore a selection of hot drinks and biscuits, laid on by the church. His ambivalence towards me was wholly acknowledged. There was no way to mistake his dislike for me so I turned away from him, making the sketches my focus.

"Here," Ernesto prodded, "Is the main entrance. We can expect guests to come in here and make their way up the stairs to where the main reception will be held." He drew his index fingers across the map, curving sharply following the line of the staircase.

"Where will the objective be secured?" I asked.

"Objective? You mean the *tumi*, yes?" I nodded. "Just here, in this large hall. Marcos saw that it had been temporarily closed and workmen were constructing a case. We can assume that, as it is a temporary display, the case itself should not be too complex."

"Suficientemente complicado para él..."

"The case cannot be too large, or else it will prevent people from moving around it, so we estimate that it has to be no bigger than 1.3 metres wide by the same length. In fact, it is most likely that they will use one of their existing display cabinets, which are of that size."

I nodded.

"You should be able to pick the lock to gain access to the case. The glass side panels may be removed." Ernesto swept away the top sheets to show a sketch, like that of an architect, of what was clearly the display case they expected to be used.

"And how exactly do I pick a lock?"

"Don't worry, we have time for that later." Ernesto proceeded to talk me through where the lock would be in relation to the cabinet; how I should tilt the glass panel, not push it, in case it crashed into the opposite pane; how to replace the panel without being too rough, again, in case it broke and gave us - me - away.

"But what about the lock?"

Ernesto made a eureka-like sound before lifting a small tool bag onto the table. "The bump gun."

"The what?"

"The bump gun. It really is incredible what you can buy on Amazon these days." He pulled out a silver pistol that looked like the kind of thing fair dames of the Wild West kept stuffed in their hosiery. Pulling on the trigger sent a vibration down the 'barrel', a sort of needle-nosed plier thing that, according to Ernesto, would help shake the lock open. I was unconvinced but he invited me to try it out on a small padlock.

I inserted the barrel into the keyhole and clicked the trigger. Nothing happened but a short pop sound. I tried the clasp but it was still locked shut. I tried again with the same result.

"Am I doing this right?"

"How should I know? It only arrived this morning. Hold on." He took out his phone and found an instructional video on YouTube. We watched it a couple of times before I thought I could figure it out on my own. Bored, Marcos had gone for a walk - or '*Preferiría lastimarme los pies*' as he put it.

When I tried it myself, it only took a handful of goes before I could pop the clasp out from the padlock.

"Do you have anything bigger? How big will the lock on the case be anyway?"

Ernesto shrugged. "Probably no bigger than that. They can't be too big or they obstruct the view of the artefacts." I wasn't wholly persuaded but I was mildly encouraged by our - my - success with the bump gun.

"What kind of manpower can I expect to encounter? Will they be carrying much heat?"

Ernesto looked blankly at me.

"Security guards. How many will there be and will they be armed?"

"Francesco, I wonder if you have watched too many movies. This is England. There will be no more than four security guards, more for the duration of the event, but possibly as few as two by the time you need to open the case. And, no, no, they will not be armed. Unless you are afraid of a walkie-talkie and an extendable baton?" From his tone, I took the question to be moot.

I returned to the maps, if you could call them that, and the guidebooks that Marcos had picked up. It was not clear from them what the situation was with regard to cameras, guard dogs, security guards, and so on. Any early confidence I had waned when I noticed the lack of detail in their research. Was there any window of opportunity to back out of this caper or, now, at the planning meeting, was I already in too deep?

"And what about an extraction point?"

Ernesto cocked his head. "You are wondering how you are getting out, aren't you?"

"Affirmative, I mean, yeah. Yes."

"We have planned this through too. You see here," He pointed at one of two large staircases that ran from the ground level up to a balcony that surrounded the exhibition hall. "Inside this staircase is a storage cupboard, plenty big enough for you to hide in, but too big for Marcos and too cramped for me."

I looked up at him, examining him for something.

"I have osteoarthritis." He carried on. "During the evening, you will need to find a way to hide in this cupboard. Marcos will unlock it during the day - it is a simple Allen key lock - and you need to stay there overnight. In the morning, the back door is opened for staff to come in after 7 o'clock. It is just through this door at the rear of the tearoom. You will put this on and walk out without anyone taking a second look at you." He picked up a hi-viz vest in fluorescent yellow. "If you wear this, you become invisible, even though it was designed for you to be seen. Ironic, no?"

Examining the map, I saw the route from the cupboard through the Industrial Gallery and into the tearoom, before a ninety degree right turn through a fire exit, along a short corridor, and out of another fire exit into a courtyard. It was surprisingly simple; no acrobatic Chinese contortionists, no high-tech pressure sensitive floors.

"What's this?"

"This is called a *blueprint*."

"No, this. On the blueprint."

"That's a space enclosed by the museum and art gallery and council buildings for staff parking and deliveries, so the hi-viz will make you look like you are dropping something off or picking something up."

"What should I say if I'm challenged by someone?"

"Make it up, it doesn't matter. It's going to be seven in the morning. You can say whatever you like, so long as it is not too memorable. Most people will not listen to anything too complicated." I nodded, empathising.

"What about these?" I indicated two semi-circles drawn on the wall dividing the tearoom from the exhibition hall.

"Cameras."

"Right. And how exactly do I avoid these?"

It seemed whenever I posed a question or hinted at my doubts, Ernesto would smirk knowingly before presenting the most simple of solutions. Even now, he was no different.

"You see these cases here? The cameras are trained on them, not the wall that runs along the side of the room. After all," He paused expectantly. "Who wants to steal a wall?"

I took a moment more to trace the escape route which seemed so direct and straightforward that I had to run through it two or three times; not so I could remember it but so I could justify the simplicity to myself.

"And this camera?"

"Pointed at the cashier, not the room."

"This one?"

"At this door, but not this one, so go that way."

"And Marcos is going to leave the tools and a hi-viz for me where?"

"Men's toilets, end cubicle, in the cistern, in a waterproof bag. The hi-viz you need to pick up from the cloakroom. It will be in the pocket of another coat that you can wear until you need to put on the hi-viz."

"Why can't I just carry them in a bag and drop them into the cloakroom?"

"What if someone gives another guest your bag by mistake?"

"Why can't we snatch it after the event?"

"Isn't the fact it will be so busy going to make it easier for you to hide?"

"What do I do with the *tumi* itself?"

"What do you think you do with the *tumi* itself?" I paused. "It is always people who doubt the simplest thing that ask the most questions. We hardly ever question the existence of the universe, dark matter, or black holes, but we always sniff the milk in the fridge." He chuckled but I could only force a slim grin.

"Sorry but I do have a lot riding on this plan going to... plan..."

"The *tumi* goes with you in the cupboard, in the bag, and you can put it amongst the tools. After all, it is metal so the sound and weight would be consistent with an adjustable spanner or a hammer."

He appeared to have an answer for any question or at least another question for every question. Maybe I should be more trusting; they seemed to have done their homework.

"I know you are nervous and I understand. I would be too if I was in your position. But I think that your nerves do not just come from your fears of being caught, no." He stepped towards me, his palm placed firmly on my chest. "No, you are anxious because there is such heavy responsibility on your shoulders. You finally know what is truly at stake here. Not the *tumi*, not your own innocence, but the opportunity to free thousands of oppressed individuals for the first time in living memory. A chance to do something truly amazing with your life that is both selfless and inspiring. Now you know, you can feel it, can't you? Yes?"

It would have been odd had I not nodded right then. And in that instinctive agreement, he nodded in response and turned back to the table, rolling up the plans and sliding them into a cardboard tube. Our preparations for the most dangerous thing I've ever done were concluded.

Chapter 18 – Friday 17th June (6 days to go...)

An extra fifteen minutes in the bathroom is really noticeable in a flat shared by three people. Ollie banged on the door and yelled 'Hurry up!' I sensed Chelsea wanted to moan to Ollie rather than risk a tongue-lashing from me again.

"What took you so long?"

"I had to have a shave and try to look a bit more presentable."

"Got yourself a date finally?" He didn't wait for an answer before locking the door behind him.

"Yes... Actually..."

"Morning, Francesco. You look nice."

"Thanks." I went into my bathroom and dressed whilst trying to examine how Lyonesse-on-Lethe was progressing. With so much else going on, I hadn't given much more time over to it, aside from painting up a couple of wooden slat benches when procrastinating to avoid doing my wider reading on Rawls and Estlund's works on contemporary political philosophy, which threatened to be as engaging as it sounded. My Brawa miniature telephone box had been added to the embankment, close by to the two benches that were positioned outside of the train station, which had taken me two weeks to construct and paint. I had based it with two fine grey coats, then added a brown ink wash to create a wooden appearance to the canopy. I then used hair spray, which was a technique I learned from one of the many YouTube channels I got tips from, and then layered it up with a white paint. With a bit of trickery using Chelsea's hair dryer – don't tell her I used it – and a toothpick, I created a brilliant peeled paint effect. I couldn't help but keep looking at my handiwork. Any further developments would have to wait. I had to get ready for a lecture, which I hoped would get me up to speed on the current topic, a shift at Scintilla just after lunch until mid-afternoon as Rob had called in sick, leaving me with just enough time to dash home, spruce myself up, change, and meet Eva outside the museum. I couldn't have wished the day to have gone any faster, I was so excited about the opening of the exhibition. Obviously, I wanted to enjoy a night with Eva but I would also have one eye on the *tumi* and the lie of the land inside. I couldn't let on what I had agreed with Ernesto and, somehow, I would need her to make herself scarce when I was supposed to hide in the toilets. He had called to talk me through the plan once again on Thursday morning, with the addition of one or two minor additions, and whilst he intended to calm my nerves, it actually made me excited to be doing it at all.

I hadn't forgotten about all the threats to my liberty and happiness but, as I sped closer to the task itself, they were suppressed and dreams of success took their place in my consciousness. A little what I imagine it's like when you buy a lottery ticket. Nobody thinks 'Damn, what could I have done with two pounds?' The only thing on their mind is deciding what colour to paint their yacht.

Chelsea was glued to the breakfast news on TV but smiled when I returned to the living room.

"Watching anything interesting?"

"A gorilla has been shot in America. So senseless. Why must we keep these poor animals in cages like that?"

"Oh wow. That's awful. What's happening now?"

"There is a candlelight vigil at the zoo. The parents might be prosecuted. It's so sad, isn't it?"

"Yeah, I guess people need to do something about zoos, don't they? They're just there to make money anyway."

"It's all so terrible, isn't it? We have to play our part to try and bring about positive change, don't we?" She had adopted the pleading sort of face that you often saw on charity adverts around Christmas time.

"It's always the same people behind the bad news, isn't it."

"You are so right. It *is* the same people; the selfish, the powerful, the rich, oh Francesco, it's simply awful. How can they sleep at night when their actions hurt so many of us?" My stomach reminded me of the need to eat something.

"Have you heard that Noah Wright is in town tonight?"

"What? Who told you that?" She stood and I could see I had grabbed her attention.

"He did. He came to the shop a few weeks ago. I'm sure I told you…" Maybe some cereal.

"Did you ask him about Fair Trade coffee? You know they get most of their beans from intensive farming practices in Central America."

"Yes, I did actually. He seemed interested in it, to be fair, but I could be wrong." Across the kitchen counter, I continued. "He gave me an invite to the opening of an exhibit at the museum tonight."

"The Meso-American culture exhibit?"

"Yeah, he sponsored it so will be there. A few celebrities too, I would imagine. Should be interesting. I'm taking Eva."

"Oh my God, I need to... I have to make some calls."

"What for?" Toast. That's what I fancied. I popped two slices into the toaster.

"You know what for. We have to make sure he makes all Democracy Coffee Fair Trade and adds more vegan milk substitutes. Francesco, did you know that drinking milk can cause allergic reactions in up to twenty percent of people? Lactose intolerance is a growing issue and Democracy is not taking this seriously."

"And tonight's the night when you should be telling him this?"

"Absolutely! I'm sure there will be plenty of press there and Noah Wright needs to understand how these major issues are not just affecting people here but throughout the developing world too, where their *un*fair trade coffee and cow milk is ruining lives."

"Maybe you're right. It starts at 7 o'clock, just so you know." Ping! It was done.

"I need to ring around but, um, yeah, have a nice time..." Chelsea dashed to her bedroom with the television remote in her hand and a head full of schemes. Scooping up my phone, wallet, and keys with one hand, sliding them into my satchel as I walked through the door, with my toast in the other, I headed towards the bus stop to go to the main campus. All pretty seamless.

Ollie and I hadn't spoken at length for a while now. I'd mentioned Eva to him, which was met with a fist bump and a knowing wink. That was typical of him. We had said we would go for a beer when we were both next free but his shifts at the museum had clashed with mine, or I'd been at a WMSCACE meeting, or he already had plans. We'd get around to it but, at this point, our mutual social life and, therefore, our relationship, had taken a back seat.

As for Chelsea, this morning had been one of the longest chats we had since our confrontation in the city centre – or, perhaps it would be better to categorise it as a 'telling off', as confrontation suggests an equal power status between the two antagonists. This morning served to demonstrate that I now had the advantage over her. The conversation had gone precisely as Ernesto had said. Just as we discussed, it didn't matter what the issue was; as long as I could tell her that Noah Wright was going to be in town, it wouldn't have taken much to prompt her into reacting. All that was left was for her to lurch into action, rallying her followers, and to cause a real scene outside the museum before tonight's gathering.

By the time I came back home, sweaty and tired, Ollie had already left and Chelsea was corralling three of her friends around our coffee table. Between them they had a couple of placards, a borrowed megaphone, and some blown-up stock photographs of Central American farmers that were suitably pitiable looking. She was directing, her friends were doing, but together they appeared to be making swift progress on the tools for their demonstration.

Neither of us paid each other a great deal of attention, both of us were mentally preoccupied. I had to freshen up, change into my suit, and meet Eva in about an hour. I could make out Chelsea's shrill urging, hassling her cronies to leave with as much as they could carry whilst simultaneously ringing anyone she could who might be willing to attend in support of their cause.

Her urgency and insistence, as well as the belief that what she was doing was undeniably right raised the hackles on the back of my neck. Just like my parents, everything else was blocked out, except for the one, myopic goal of kicking sand into the eyes of the powerful. God! What would she be like if her desperate pleas *actually* did some good?

Had I been able to view the square from the elevated position above those great, stone, Corinthian columns, I would have seen the cobbles shaped like vast cockleshell arcs of sugar cubes. Circular contours overlapping and spreading out from the Museum entrance as if it was a stone thrown into a still and stagnant pond. Half hidden by the shadows cast by the dazzling spotlights that swept through their cycles, probing and cold, the square would have seemed ethereal and otherworldly. The lizard's tongue of red darting from the brightly illuminated mouth with black clad flies buzzing within reach. From that perch, safe from the chattering crowds and glad-handing dignitaries, a calmness could have enveloped me.

Instead, like the few others that had arrived on foot, I lugubriously strode up the stone flags at an

unnecessary speed as they were too deep to walk up
without lunging and not deep enough to complete an
evenly paced walk at each ascending level. The tightness
of the trouser against the backs of my thighs when I
reached out my leg slowed me further. I couldn't afford to
buy another pair if I tore them.

From a loftier position, I might have been able to
avoid witnessing the agitated figures haranguing the
guests as they arrived. Peering down over a weathered
chunk of granite, I would have recognised the instigator
of this maelstrom of action, as her long-limbed body
gesticulated flamboyantly skyward and another clinger-on
would spring into action to lend their support. The well-
turned-out guests hurried past, glancing up at the last
moment, deaf to the chants and cries of the small group of
partisans. The scrawled messages on their placards,
proclaiming that Democracy Coffee were heartless
dictators, with graphic claims that would be a on a par
with anything Pinochet, Armas, Stroessner, or Banzer or
any of the other despots I could recall from my sketchy
recollections of my parents' left-wing parenting might
have done during their reigns.

A trio of put-upon security guards, their ties
uncomfortably tight, their jackets now unbuttoned and
flailing behind them, rushed to step in, now that the
invitees' cars were pulling up in front of the museum. The
first held his palms out, pleading, but, based on his facial
expression, with little success. The second had one hand
on a radio, plucked from his belt clip, and the other hand
thrust out like a karate chop, waving it wildly before him
in exaggerated and aggressive motions; he, also, was
mostly ignored by Chelsea's cadre of followers. The last
man had his hands stuffed deep into his pockets and was
failing to conceal the mischievous smirk that spread
across his face.

I saw her before she saw me. Petite, I thought, no, something else. Demure maybe, I don't know, but she didn't carry herself as she had before, with that assuredness and defiance. She tucked her hair behind her ear and, catching my eye, waved unsteadily. Saving my trousers integrity, I slowed and regained my breath.

"Hi."

"Hi," she replied. "I didn't expect it to be quite this fancy." I followed her glance and saw another sleek, black car pull to a halt and eject another well-heeled couple, him in a black tuxedo, her in a green silk gown, both suddenly caught unawares that they arrived amidst a full-blown riot that, if you asked their opinion, should be quashed at the soonest opportunity by the police or, if not them, then the home guard. At least, from their limited experiences of a genuine protest, they expected to be separated from the mob by the security of a flat screen TV and several acres of English countryside; this seemed to be the sort of thing that should result in an urgent reappraisal of capital punishment.

"Yeah, me either." Her eyes flicked from my suede shoes to my midnight blue tie for confirmation. I reached for her hand but she had taken a sudden step towards the red carpet.

"Let's get inside. I'm freezing."

I followed, catching up, and was bolstered to walk up the carpeted steps beside her. Cautiously though.

Through the tall wooden doors was a modest entrance hall expertly decorated to suggest a Central American theme. That expert, however, appeared to have never left Bromsgrove.

Issuing drinks upon arrival were two pairs of scantily clad models, both crowned with feather and patterned textiles. Around their waists were what appeared like palm leaves in a skirt style and each had daubed white lines on top of their spray tans across their cheeks. It was an unexpected clash with the traditional Victorian tile floor decorated with pastel, floral patterns and the marble wall panelling. Eva and I both took a glass of wine and sniggered as we ascended the dog-leg staircase.

In the foyer above, there was a similar scene; inflatable parrots peeked out from behind oversized plastic palm trees, prop hessian bags of coffee beans. Pan pipe music crackled from the speakers and nylon flags of every nation hung from sagging bunting overhead. The space was busy with the well-dressed guests and waiting staff gliding between them. Amidst the glad-handing and back-slapping, we sought out a quieter oasis and held back, whilst the crowd progressed into the Round Room.

"It's not what I was expecting," Eva said.

"Can I get you a drink?"

"Let's do it." She strode forward just as a parting in the crowd opened up and I scampered to follow her. The end of the bar, or this one at least, was moderately clearer, perhaps due to the proximity from the archway that joined the red, circular gallery with the Bridge Gallery and Bridge Café, from where waiting staff exited with full trays of cold canapés but had barely taken ten paces before they had to turn on their heels and return to the hectic traffic of the pop-up serving area. Seeing the temporary plastic doors flung open and swing forward and back, I was stung by the reminder of why I was here tonight.

"Frankie?"

"What? Oh, er, just a beer thanks." I needed that distraction. Eva dazzled and, at least for the next hour or two, I could try to get to know her better. But that time flew past before I could get my mind into the right place to savour it or think enough about the stories she told and the questions she asked. In an instant, almost everyone was congregating in to the long, glass-ceilinged Industrial Gallery, via the gift shop, whose wares and display units had been manoeuvred to the edges, forming a corridor of space, through which everyone was ushered in by half-hearted waiting staff. Upon seeing the two of us deep in conversation, they opted not to interrupt us but wrangle the other guests into the vaulted hall so that they could start clearing up as much as they could, before the same crowd would hurry back to the bars and canapés.

"Is something on your mind?" Eva enquired. There was so much, too much, that I froze between my instinct to say nothing and shrug off my distractedness as being down to the occasion and a compunction to share everything that was racing through my mind with her. The tilt of her head, the cute furrowing of her eyebrows, they urged me to overshare but I knew, if I did, then this night would be over too soon, like Cinderella at the Prince's ball.

"I'm just surprised at how good you look…"

Her frown deepened. "Surprised?"

"No, no, I mean, uh, I mean… not shocked, uh…" Every word that came to mind sounded like a tolling bell, off key somehow, and not conveying my true meaning - which was to say that she looking incredible and I felt blessed to be able to have her at my side but even that, written some months later, feels inadequate and unable to fairly explain how impressed I was by her, regardless of her costume and make-up, and that such as serious and remarkable woman could also be so attractive.

The upturned corner of her lip and raised cheek told me I hadn't got into trouble for offending her. "It's okay! I think I know what you're getting at so - thank you - kind of. You look surprisingly handsome too. Much better than your Scintilla apron."

"Thanks. Sorry. That's exactly what I meant."

"What? That you think I'm handsome?"

"Yes, for a woman, whatever handsome is for a woman."

"Pretty?"

"No, pretty sounds so… like tissue paper flowers. Kind of fragile and pointless, you're not fragile, you're strong - or you seem that way to me. Handsome suggests some kind of gravitas, you know? Like a building or a statue."

"I'll take handsome. I like it. It works for me." Her understanding saved my embarrassment. "To gravitas." She raised her glass.

We were almost alone now; waiting staff either tidying around us or ferrying drinks to the crowd, who were milling together in the vast spaces beyond the round room, pointing at unseen observations, talking loudly so they could be heard, and over-exaggerating their emotions, as strangers do.

"Listen, Frankie. I need to talk to you about something serious. About Ernesto and his schemes."

"What do you mean?" A felt heat behind my cheeks.

"He wants to help, I'm sure he does, he wants to do what he thinks is right, for the *gaitanos*, the *Marabinos*, the Yarina, all indigenous peoples, but his methods are not always so benevolent."

"What do you mean?"

"Well, this idea of his is crazier than a goat with chicks. I get that the *tumi* can be a powerful symbol to unite the Yarina but *stealing* it from a museum is madness. He can't start at eleven, you know, he should speak to the Val Verdean embassy first, get them to petition the Foreign Office, lobby some MPs, raise awareness that the UK has taken possession of a valuable, sacred artefact that they do not own. I'm sure loads of people would sign a petition to get it repatriated. Please, just for my sake, tell me again that you're not going through with it?"

"No, no, definitely not. It's crazy, right?" I sipped at my beer, nearly empty. "Do you want another?"

"Sure." Placated, she put her glass on the bar, an ending to her plea clearly punctuated.

"How did you meet Ernesto anyway?"

"You know that old man's pub, the Head In Clouds, with the curry club on Tuesdays? I was working there for a while and he came in, after I'd emailed the group. I served him something and he started chatting to me. I think he could tell I wasn't local. He spoke Spanish to me before he said a word in English. He seemed kind-hearted, sort of funny, you know? So, we spoke a bit and I told him I was training to be a solicitor. He got me my job in the clerk's office, so I said I would repay him and, you know him, he said 'No, no, *con mucho gusto*' and then, after I started at the firm, he asked me to help him more with WMSCACE. Obviously, I couldn't say no, could I?"

"Sounds sort of familiar. He found me in Scintilla. I thought he was kind of odd to begin with, like those elderly customers who are overly friendly because they don't have that many people to talk to anymore," She nodded. "But then I saw him speak and I was captivated. He was inspiring and I felt as if I had to be a part of whatever it was he was doing."

"Even the shady stuff?"

"What..? No, not like that… I wanted to make a difference, I've always wanted to make a difference, but now it seems like there's someone or some people that are like me and want to make things better too." I noticed her smirk and that showed me she knew what I meant; I was sure that she felt the same as me, at that moment. "What shady stuff are you referring to? We know about his plot to snatch the *tumi*, but what else is there?"

The smirk faded. "I don't really want to talk about it."

"Why not? How bad could it be?"

"You really don't want to know."

"Illegal…?"

"You don't... not really, no, but immoral, yes."
She paused at the same moment as it seemed a hush fell
over the party. "I really don't want to talk about it. I
wouldn't want to ruin our night."

"Don't you think I ought to know if I've already
told you I want to help the cause?"

"No, not right now. You've got other things to
worry about. What are you doing about the Home Office?
Can't you contact your parents at all? Can they not help
clear things up?"

"I wouldn't know how to get hold of them, even if
I wanted to."

"You don't want to?"

"Your parents were close to the Yarina cause,
remember, just like the *Marabinos*, so I would imagine
that they..." She was cut off by the arrival of a small
entourage, led by a mid-sized man in a very well-fitted
suit over his cashmere roll neck and extremely large silver
watch.

"Francesco, isn't it?" He thrust out a fist, rather
than a hand, and I bumped it as he hoped I would. "So
great you could come - and who's your plus one?"

"Eva Estrella, Mr. Wright, she's..." Oh no, what
came next? What should I say?

"We're seeing each other. Pleased to make your
acquaintance." She extended a hand and he hesitatingly
shook it.

"Nice to meet you too, Miss Estrella. That's quite
a grip - do you row?" She let go of his hand but did not

reply. "Francesco, why don't you join us? I was about to make a little entrance in front of all of my guests and I wouldn't want you two feeling left out. Come on." He turned and swaggered through the arch, precisely through the gift shop, flanked by his executives, followed instinctively by us, and watched by everyone else.

"You imagine what?" I whispered to Eva.

"Later, Frankie, I'll tell you later." Her eyes remained focused on the room before us and on the man fist-bumping his path up to the steel-bannistered stairs that led from the floor of the Industrial Gallery up to the balcony that ran around its perimeter. His lackeys, in the same grey suits as they had been in when they accompanied Wright's visit to Scintilla, halted abruptly at the foot of the steps and we slammed on the proverbial brakes behind them. Noah hopped up the stairs, two at a time, until he reached the top. The crowd applauded, a couple even whooped, which was most unlike anything I'd expected his reception to be like in the heart of a city renowned for sarcasm and cynicism.

"Thank you so much, each and every one of you!" The applause that had died down returned, more fervent than before. "Thank you all! Wow!" He gazed around the room, pointing at a specific person, who we couldn't make out from our vantage point, and tossing affectionate gestures towards them, before repeating the process to another, and another. "God, it is a privilege to be here tonight." He had no use for a microphone or PA system as his words carried confidently around the hall. "And, of course, to see so many of you, dressed up so sharp too. Wow, man, amazing. I want to thank Edward for organising tonight - where are you, man? - Oh, there he is! Say 'Hi' to everyone Edward," Gazes turned and a sheepish man, wearing iron-striped, pleated trousers and a stiff, blue blazer with a name badge on it, raised his hand to waist height. "He's awesome. But we gotta remember why we're here. We're here to raise money for the people that, over the years, have made my companies, and yours, incredibly successful. They don't get the credit they deserve and often work in extreme circumstances for a tiny wage. Can you all see the screens, down here, yeah?" Large, flat-screen TVs mounted on wheeled podia were situated evenly around the hall, two at the foot of the stairs and six more along the same side of the room. The blank white rectangles faded to black and the Democracy Coffee Limited logo, in glistening gold, morphed into solidity. The logo and black background disappeared together to be replaced with Noah Wright in full wide-angle shot, staring thoughtfully across a dusty strip of land, book-ended by single-storey, squat, yellow, adobe buildings, where outside one a dog lay in the narrow strip of shadow and a washing line, full with clothes in pinks and greens, lightly swayed.

"Val Verde," began the voiceover, recognisably Noah Wright himself. "A land of simple beauty and complex coffee. A land of contrasts, challenges, opportunities, but, most of all, hope." The shot changed to Wright, sat on a pile of rock, playing with a stone between his fingers. A rich, orange sunset cast a late afternoon glow across his face, which was shielded by a khaki baseball cap, perfectly accompanied by his rough cotton shirt, with the sleeves rolled up, and forest green combat trousers. "I've been coming here for many years," he continued, picking up from where the voiceover left off. "I've met some incredible, humble folks, who work hard, raise their families, and want nothing more than the freedoms they deserve and to feel the satisfaction of a long day's work well done." He tossed the stone, casually, and began walking, the scene unravelled behind him as the camera panned back with him. "We take things

242

for granted, don't we? Clean water, a good education, our health, our homes. The people of Val Verde deserve to take those things for granted too, don't they?" The town, wind-beaten, bleached, and disorganised, painted a picture of the country that I could not totally recognise. "Democracy Coffee provides jobs for these folks so they can put food on their tables, a roof over their heads, and clothes on their backs. We've worked hand-in-hand with the people of this nation for over a decade and we've seen the towns we work in prosper."

Now, the camera cut to a close-up of a farmer, I guessed, in a straw hat and patchworked shirt, hunched over a table. He spooned a meagre amount of fried beans into his mouth without making any expression of satisfaction. The voice over began again, as the scene was replaced by that of a child and a dog scrabbling over a mountainous pile of rubbish. "But the lives they have worked so hard to make are at risk." Now it was a fishing boat, small, alone on the vast lake, its crew dragging in almost empty netting. Now it was a line of cars queueing along the roadside leading to a petrol station, where an attendant, perhaps, waved his arms above his head wildly. "The Government of Val Verde is proposing to introduce new tariffs on exports, risking everything Democracy Coffee has done to create communities, opportunities, and livelihoods, all across this wonderful land." The scene on the screens was now the interior of a parliament building, with suited, sweaty-faced men, mouthing aggressive silences to one another. "Their actions jeopardise all we have built and all we hope to achieve."

I looked at Eva for a sign of what she made of all this. Her stern expression gave little away and she was transfixed not on the screens but on Noah Wright, who was surveilling the hallful of guests who, in turn, were hanging on every word his disembodied voice spoke.

243

"But there is always hope." A gentle, classical backing music increased in volume beneath the words. The scene changed once more to a vast plantation of green. Cut to a group of farmers, under their straw, wide-brimmed hats and with rolled-up shirt sleeves, smiling, and picking beans from the leaves and depositing them into oval baskets bound to their waists. "With your help, Democracy Coffee can bring about positive change in Val Verde. Your generous donations to the DC Foundation build village schools to educate all children," The screen cut to the interior of a busy but spacious classroom. "Fund lobbyists, provide much-needed healthcare for all, provide defence contractors," The images scrolled through white-shirted women shaking hands, a doctor holding a chart above a bed, bearing an elderly man, smiling and looking anything but sick, another man, this time in a black baseball cap, wrap-around shades, Kevlar body armour, and with an assault rifle slung under his arm but crouching down and handing the long stem of a yellow flower to a boy with a football. "Generating clean electricity, and ensuring a wealth of employment opportunities." The final scenes were of a wind-turbine mounted upon a wooden derrick, hard-hatted men comparing clipboards, and then a girl, no older than seven or eight, running through long grass, blowing the pappi from a dandelion, whilst the generic classical music, reached its crescendo. "The DC Foundation and I thank you for your generosity but, most importantly of all, the people of Val Verde thank you." The final scene began with a tight shot of Wright, with two Val Verdeans, one man and one woman, either side of him, their arms draped over one another's shoulders, before panning out to reveal Wright in the centre of a vast crowd of a hundred of so who, right on cue, called out '*Gracias!*'

The assembled notaries erupted into applause, turning their gaze - and affections - back to Wright who put one hand on his chest, where he assumed his heart might be, and blew kisses with the other. Then he put his hands together, as if pleading for silence or perhaps something else.

"Thank you all, so, so much. Thank you. Oh wow, okay, *thank* you. Those people you saw on that video really do mean a lot to me. They want to get the most out of their lives, almost like you or I do. It's up to us to help them do that. Please get your wallets and your purses out and donate generously tonight so we can protect them and help them all. Thank you." Another ripple of applause occurred whilst four of Wright's grey-suited associates with short haircuts and broad, ceramic smiles circulated with silver salvers, inviting contributions from the congregation.

As gymnastically as he had skipped up the stairs, he descended, making a beeline for Eva and I.

"That was incredible, wasn't it? You really get to see the true people behind the coffee, don't you? I'm so glad we can help your people, Frankie, I truly am. You can see what we're doing is improving their poor lives so drastically, can't you?" I didn't know what to say, so I just smiled and nodded. Eva's jaw tenderised the words stewing within her throat. Behind him, past his bodyguards - as I now assumed they must be, rather than simply 'executives' - I saw the platters piled higher and higher with cheques of all pastel colours scattered with fifty-pound notes in a tempting, flamingo pink. The associates ferried the money from the donors back to a table behind the stairway, where everything was deposited into a large, black safe, that almost resembled a ballot box.

"All this money is going to help build schools and provide clean water?"

"Every penny of it," Noah replied. "The DC Foundation is a charity that will help improve the lives of Val Verdeans like you all across your country." He placed his hand upon my shoulder, munificent and authoritative, but tanned and hairless, like a bald tiger's paw. "I'm serious about what I said, Frankie. I do need someone who can help the Foundation do the most good. I'd love you to meet some people who are working with me in Val Verde to improve those folks' lives and help us to secure a regular supply of fair trade coffee. They'd love to meet you too."

He gently guided me towards the middle of the room, followed by Eva and his entourage, and into the orbit of a group of middle-aged men and women who, up until we intervened, were talking softly and closely.

"I'd like you all to meet Francesco Cuelaquiara, he's a genuine Val Verdean who is studying here in Birmingham."

"Nice to meet you, Francesco."

"Pleasure."

The group all, in their own way, were welcoming and polite, turning their attention fully to me. I looked back at their expectant faces, imploring me to respond somehow.

"Good evening." I stammered.

"Francesco is an example of someone with the graft and moxy to make something of his life without any

246

help." I remained outwardly emotionless at this new narrative of my existence thus far. "I can't tell you how helpful he has been to me at our Birmingham Scintilla branch." Eva stifled a chuckle, I supposed at the way his American accent drawled out every letter of my home town.

"Isn't it great to have someone here who knows about the heritage of the Yarina and the lost culture of Val Verde."

"Absolutely." I listened but did not speak a word to dent their enthusiasm. In fact, it was surprising to me to hear people - English people - so pleased at the idea of seeing the *tumi* on display. They were grateful, it seemed, perhaps towards me, as if I had anything to do with the damned thing up to this point.

"It's wonderful to meet you," spoke a white-haired woman in pearls. "You must be delighted to see a traditional Yarinan sacrificial blade on display to the public for the first time." The others nodded in agreement.

"Yes," I hadn't thought about it in this way before at all. "It's... delightful... that so many people can see a traditional artefact." They beamed beatifically towards me, as though I was a sort of cultural envoy, extolling all of the values they associated with the Yarina or the Val Verdean people. I felt uncomfortably honoured.

"The Yarinan culture was heavily influenced by the Mayans, and their frequent bloodletting and barbaric ritual sacrifices." She continued and, from her demeanour, she appeared to know a little about the Yarina, which put me at a disadvantage having only heard about them a matter of days ago. "It is incredibly difficult to acquire any Yarina subject matter as they are all but

247

extinct, due to the Spanish conquests of the 16th Century, European imperial ambitions, and subsequent, shall we say, *colonial* practices."

"Which European empires might you be referring to? Specifically." asked Eva, her phrasing carefully chosen. The woman caught Eva's meaning and halted, saved by her partner's intervention.

"Like many items on display in this museum, it is absolutely imperative that we protect this cultural capital for future generations. Imagine if institutions like this did not exist? How many marvels of the ancient worlds might be lost to treasure hunters and grave robbers? We promote the protection and conservation of the world's finest works."

"For sure," chimed in Wright. "Look at the British Museum, with the Rosetta Stone and the Elgin Marbles, they're under lock and key for their own protection. Or the Dendera zodiac at the Louvre…"

"Absolutely right, without the protection of the laws of those nations, anyone might get their hands on such invaluable treasures and sell them on to the highest bidder. They are better off where they are, aren't they?" The guests smiled with satisfaction at such an obvious notion being concisely explained so well.

"Or the Leyden plaque at the National Museum of Ethnology in the Netherlands? Or the Eberswalde hoard in Moscow's Pushkin Museum?" The guests stared at Eva. "There are numerous examples of looted art, like the ones on display here, aren't there? But those laws don't prosecute *all* thieves, do they?"

I didn't know what to do. The gathered faces hardened. Noah looked into the middle distance. His men stared at their feet, understanding the mood if not the details. Not for the first time, an intervention by my flatmates salvaged the moment.

One of the associates had left the task of raking in alms and approached Noah. He whispered something into his employer's ear, received a tersely spoken directive, and scampered away again. Noah turned to face me, with a boyish grin, and mercifully changed the subject.

"Francesco, can I borrow you and your girlfriend for a moment? Thanks so much." As a group, we marched in time with Wright to the Round Room, across the Bridge Gallery and into a smaller room filled with plates, bowls, and other bits of crockery, according to my untrained eye. I didn't wonder for too long about why we had been escorted out of the main event.

Chelsea stood there, looking proudly defiant - or at least doing her best to look utterly miffed.

"I understand you know Miss Couzen-Weekes?" Next to her stood two security guards, which, including the other one that I had seen with his colleagues out in front of the museum, appeared to make up the entire security detail. That meant that there was likely to be one more monitoring the CCTV, and, perhaps, two more in the Industrial Gallery, so six or seven in total. Not a great deal and certainly almost as small a team as Ernesto had suggested. His ploy to flush them out and observe their relative numbers seemed to have worked. Now I felt a little more confident that, within such a large space, I could avoid discovery - a couple would probably go home after the party so if I had to avoid the cameras and around three or four guards, I thought that was manageable. For now though, I had to handle Chelsea.

"Hola Frankie." And then, turning her attention to Noah Wright, with her expression turning from condescending superiority to burning rage, or a semblance of that feeling; "You can't fight the truth! We have a right to protest!" Her chest burst forth and her arms swung back behind her, but neither of the guards were restraining her. She reminded me of the playground fights in primary school where, somehow, two unlikely champions were corralled into a face off and one would yell 'Hold me back!' to nobody in particular and, when they discovered that nobody was going to hold them back and staggered to the realisation that they would actually have to fight the boy standing in front of them, they became sullen and nervous, empowering their adversary. A bout of windmilling later and the first child would be crying, sniffing back a mix of snot and blood.

"What spirit and passion! Wow, she's like a force of nature, isn't she?"

"You can hide behind your fancy parties but we know what's happening to the poor farmers in Val Verde."

"Oh really? What is that exactly?" He crossed his arms and stood before her.

"You're oppressing them with your cruel and excessive demands for more and more coffee! They're not cheap labour, yeah - they're people too, you know." With a nod from Wright, the security guards returned to other duties. Chelsea's aggression faded to be replaced with confusion.

"Miss Couzen-Weekes, may I call you Chelsea? Chelsea, I hear what you are saying and I understand. I really do. But I think you may not be aware of what we're doing for those very farmers in Val Verde through the Democracy Coffee Foundation." It was Chelsea's turn to fold her arms.

"Francesco and, um, Eva, right, were both here when I showed both of them, our guests, our funders, everyone, exactly what we are doing to help the farmers of Val Verde, and other countries in the region, to be safe, secure, educated, healthy, and wealthy."

"Have you ever heard of 'greenwashing', Mister Wright?"

"I have, of course I have, and I find it distasteful…"

"How is what you are saying any different? These fine words are just words; you cannot expect me to believe you without proof, can you?" Noah turned to Eva and I.

"Of course not, but you can trust the word of your friend, can't you?" He urged me to step forward and intercede with a tilt of the head and a wave of his left hand. I looked at Eva, who seemed to be on the verge of growling. "They watched the whole video and met with the generous backers of the projects in Escalón, Belmonte and Port Rivington."

"…"

"Francesco, go ahead, tell Chelsea what you saw and what you heard."

"..."

"Tell her."

"From what we saw on the video," I turned to Eva, hoping to gain her involvement and endorse what I was about to say, "It seemed like the farmers in Val Verde were being looked after. You know, with schools, doctors, that kind of thing." Eva didn't look at me whilst I spoke.

"Thank you. You see, Chelsea, I want to do right by the people who work for me. I have no desire to take advantage of them. Imagine how that would appear to our customers or reflect on my public image, to say nothing about our share price." Eva groaned.

"Well," Chelsea began, hesitantly, "I do feel a bit of a fool now. Perhaps I should have done some deeper research..."

"No, no, it's not a problem. I'm glad we could have this conversation."

"I should go and speak to my followers outside."

"That's okay, I can ask security to take care of them. Why don't you stay here and we can talk more about what we're doing at the DC Foundation?" Eva snorted. I looked from her to Chelsea and then back again. Noah languidly reached out, plucked a flute of champagne from a passing waiter's tray, and passed it to Chelsea.

"I shouldn't. I should go and be with them." I knew she didn't mean us.

"Please. It would be an honour."

They left together, without a word to either Eva or I, and we stood in the crockery exhibition.

"I should go."

"Huh? Why?" I replied.

"I've got a bad feeling about tonight. Noah, those people, Chelsea, the whole thing." I felt like I should reach for her hand, but I didn't.

"I think Noah means well, he's just a bit, you know, *American*..."

"And those people were a bit *British*."

"Yeah, yeah, I know what you mean..."

"And you were a bit spineless." My eyes locked with hers. I halted. She meant it. Come to think of it, I think she *meant* everything she said, so perhaps I shouldn't have been so surprised.

"What do you mean?" I now know what she meant and why she said it.

"You really think that *our* history, *our* legacy is better protected here than in our own lands? You *really* think that those people are so generous and kind as to take care of antiques like the *tumi* out of the goodness of their heart? You must be from another planet."

"I never said that," I muttered. "I don't agree with them, I don't."

"Then you should have done something. You should have said something."

"I didn't want to offend Noah; it's his party and they are donating money to his Foundation…"

"…Because they think we can't take care of ourselves? That those farmers need the kindly Western corporation to feed them, to heal them, to protect them? *Corto de luces*, come on, you know better than that."

"You're starting to sound like Ernesto…"

"…And with Chelsea? She's a real piece of work, isn't she? One compliment and a glass of champagne and she's best friends with her sworn enemy."

"…"

"*No te vayas a morder la lengua, que te puedes envenenar!*" She spat the words like a curse. "Listen, you need to speak up. Not just for yourself, but for *us* - your people."

"I am, I mean, I will…"

She turned towards the archway. "I hope so. I really do." I began to follow. "No, you stay. I'm going home." My heart sank; I'd blown it with another woman. But this time, rather than simply leaving it to them to call me back or follow up from a date, I couldn't let Eva slip away. I took another step and opened my mouth but she cut me off. "No, it's okay, I need to cool off. I'll call you tomorrow. Good night."

Chapter 19 – Friday 17th June
(6 days to go...)

I stood for a moment before remembering that I was alone now. I had to think about what to do with my hands so I stuffed them in my jacket pockets and then thought I might look weird so I plunged them into my trouser pockets instead and tried to look casual. At the bar, I had a beer - as an accessory - and walked back into the Industrial Gallery.

How could I have pissed off Eva? Of all the people I wanted to keep close to me, she was number one in a short list. In doing the right thing, what I thought was right, she was mad at me. She was right, of course, about me being weak in situations when I should have been stronger, and that I should act rather than do nothing. But what she was advocating, albeit inadvertently, led me to the plan she demanded that I reject. If I was to take action and speak up for our people, in a way, then stealing the *tumi* would fit the bill. Ernesto's promises to one side, Eva was who had to be impressed, she was too good for me, too decisive, dynamic, dazzlingly gorgeous, but maybe this would be the grand gesture that would win her over.

She had said she'd call me but other than an autopsy of tonight's unimpressive date, we would have nothing to talk about. Unless I had secured a prize, of sorts, a prize for my lady, like the Arthurian knights, questing for the Holy Grail. I, Lancelot, her, Guinevere, or maybe I was Arthur, I can't remember, but I'm sure they all ended up fine in the end.

With my beer bottle, casually held between relaxed finger tips, I strolled around the perimeter of the gallery, beneath the stairs and under the surrounding balcony. I made sure to smile when guests looked my way but to appear as if on my way to meet someone or wandering, examining the exhibits whilst my companion was elsewhere - in the bathroom, I would say, if pressed, as the location was already on my mind.

I had noticed the security camera hanging from a long, white pendulum, which covered the archway from the Round Room into the gift shop, so going through there would be tricky - I had to find the tools Marcos had squirrelled away in the toilets as the guests were starting to leave, so that there were people coming and going, in and out of the exhibit, to keep the security guards distracted. Then when I returned from the toilet, I would have to go through to the Industrial Gallery, without being seen acting in any way suspicious. From the long hall, the other exit led to the Mini Museum; I couldn't really tell what that was but it was where a temporary cloakroom had been established. There was one camera fixed to the right of the arch and pointing into the long gallery, so the left side of the arch was not covered. That was a weakness I might need to utilise. Another nod and a smile to the lady in the pearls who had offended Eva.

Through to the Mini Museum and there were spotlights - perhaps motion activated - over the soft play area and the cloakroom but no cameras. Beyond that was another high-ceilinged gallery with a balcony running around the roof. Tables and chairs were grouped throughout the ground floor and it was an ornately decorated cafe called the Edwardian Tearoom. Spotlights again but no cameras. Wait, not quite true. There was one camera that didn't look like it could be remotely moved to scan the whole room. It was pointing at only one thing and one thing only; the cash register behind the counter.

I turned, looked as nonchalant as possible, observing the presence of fire exits on the floor I was standing on and, directly above it, on the balcony floor. Then I walked back where I came from, seeing how the balconies were connected through the Mini Museum, where there were no further cameras, and that there was one camera I had not previously spotted above me, on the balcony level of the Industrial Gallery diligently guarding a selection of ceramics from the Staffordshire Potteries. On my route back through the main gallery, I pretended to examine some of the existing exhibits, which were scattered along the side of the room beside the staircase, facing a range of ornate stained-glass windows, presumably rescued from various churches rather than stolen like some of the more exotic items.

The cavity beneath the stairs was walled up with wood panels, which initially caused me some consternation, as I thought that it might make an excellent temporary screen under which to hide as I passed through the room. But I then spotted the bold yellow and black sign discouraging entry from any unauthorised persons. Then, I saw that the wooden panels had two narrow vents like letterboxes embedded in them. You wouldn't need to circulate air unless it was a room or a storage space. Just as I thought, there was the door painted and decorated in such a way as to be quite inconspicuous, except for two brass handles. If it wasn't for the sign, I might not have believed that there was a room there at all.

As I sidled casually past, I let my elbow nudge the metal handle gently. It gave way enough for me to know it was unlocked. Most importantly, there were no alarms, no sirens, no guards scrambled to my location like you'd expect from one of those crime caper movies. I carried on walking, taking in the cut glass crystal decanters and the red-cheeked Toby jugs, and looped back, around the foot of the stairs, where a dense throng of people gathered around the one display case that looked most out of place.

By the time I had got to the front, as I couldn't afford to be too pushy, I could take in exactly what was on show. The cardboard panel explained how this was merely a sample of the priceless ephemera that would be taken around the country by the DC Foundation to raise awareness of the issues facing the crop growers and how Democracy Coffee were providing the solution. What intrigued me was what was inside, as it wasn't solely the *tumi* as I had expected.

The display case was 1.8 metres wide by 1.2 metres deep by 2.2 metres high; significantly larger than I had expected. It was equipped with a light-activated motion sensor in the base that sent a beam of light from the ground-mounted unit to a reflector at the top of the glass half of the case which, if broken, would set off a silent alarm and initiate lockdown protocols throughout the building, preventing the would-be thief from escaping through any of the external doors or windows. The security guards - a detail of just five, it transpired, so I wasn't too far off - would congregate at the location where the alarm was triggered, taking the burglar into custody until they could be charged by the West Midlands Police Force. I found all of this out by reading the newspapers afterwards.

Inside the case were five items; the first, a modest-looking, clay sculpture that reminded me of Dustin Hoffman reciting a piece of Shakespeare. It was pre-Colombian, which meant before the Conquistadors and Christopher Colombus, and it was called a Quimbayan sculpture, was about 30 centimetres high, and was very likely to be shattered into thousands of pieces if dropped by a would-be criminal evading capture. The next pieces were a tall, thin vase, with a painting of a naked man on it, poised dynamically as if ready to pounce, and two jaguar-type sculptures, that looked quite docile, with sad eyes, almost like depressed sabre-toothed tigers, but were beautifully coloured. The man would call out if picked up, alerting the appropriate authorities to his kidnapping. The jaguars would spring to life, pinning the assailant by his hands, until the appropriate authorities could be summoned to deal with the cat-napper...

The most impressive was a Moche headdress, almost a mask, that was horned by two dragon-like creatures with jagged teeth and curved tongues. The centre, the crown of the mask, bore an emotionless face with oversized eyes and teeth placed upon a chiselled torso, with both arms extended above the forehead of the mask; one held a dagger, the other a severed head. It was originally from Peru, from roughly 500 AD, and may have been used for sacrifices, worn by the priest or priestess that carried out the grisly act or for re-enactments of great battles that the Mochica culture revered. Damn, they were a violent lot, I thought. Would fit in well down Broad Street on a Friday night. Pressed flat, in bright, yellow gold, with jade eyes and a stern, serious expression, it appeared to have presence, like Eva did, and her eyes followed me as I stepped around the unit, to get a better look at the *tumi*. Those eyes were accusing me, judging me, and I wondered if the priestess who wore the mask might disapprove of what I was doing and slice me open as a tribute for their pagan gods or encourage me on this endeavour - and sacrifice someone else to ask the gods to grant me good luck.

The *tumi* itself was not large, not as large as the mask or the vase, which drew some attention from the guests, notably from the female ones, curious about the vase's provenance as much as the exaggerated penis painted on the leaping man. The *tumi* was made from the same material as the mask but did not shine so bright, as if it did not need to attract anyone's attention. The *tumi* was mislabelled as being from Peru and from the Yarinian civilisation, although I could not debate the date it was said to have originated from - 750-1100 CE - as I hadn't a clue about that sort of thing and had only known about the *tumi* a few days ago. I may have said that before. The nerves were beginning to get to me.

Its blade was wide, curved, and full; it looked like an elaborate pizza cutter. There was the face of a serious looking man, I guessed, checking for genitalia, wait, no, there was a hint of a penis. These ancient South Americans loved to put faces and dicks on stuff. Above the head was an elaborate headdress, fanning across the skull, with intricately detailed metalwork, twisting and bending the slender strips of gold into rolling waves and jagged mountain peaks. Within the pierced ears of it were set large blue jewels that seemed dull but occasionally twinkled when the light found them at just the right angle. For a handle, it looked uncomfortable, but the blade looked as sharp as it ever had been. I continued my circuit around the unit, looking at the *tumi* with one eye and considering how I was going to get it out of there with the other. On the back of the *tumi*, I could see with more detail that this was indeed the deity Maxímon; the penis was absent but breasts adorned the chest and the expression altered from firm and judgemental to smiling, not happy, but mischievous. Long braids of hair, twined from gold strips, fell down the sides of the face, between the cheeks and the bejewelled ears. Below the legs and feet, which were the same on either side, the blade - undecorated, with the odd dent or smudge on it, it contrasted the image of the god of chance or luck or fidelity or adultery or whatever he or she chose to represent. I wondered how much blood had been spilt with that incisive edge.

Worrying that staying here too long might draw attention to me, I backed away, a plan formed in my head, and aimed straight for the toilets in the corner of the gift shop. Passing attendees, I remembered to slow it down to an insouciant loafing pace, tried to look like I was trying to decide where to place my empty bottle, and padded out of the gallery and into the men's toilets.

Avoiding eye contact, I slipped into the cubicle furthest from the door. Logically, that made sense to me as that would be where I would put them, if I was planning on committing a felony. Which, I realised, I was.

In the end cubicle, I sat on the lid of the toilet for a few minutes whilst other people left and it sounded as if there wasn't anyone else present. I looked around me for some kind of clue. Nothing on or in the toilet roll holder. The latch seemed ordinary. I stood and peered under the lid of the toilet - there was a snaking arrow scrawled on it in black Sharpie pointing upwards.

Instinctively, I looked up, following where the arrow pointed and there, on the ceiling, was written a short, graffitied message; '*Que se joda todo, pendejo*'.

I knew what *pendejo* meant and it would be characteristic of Marcos to get an insult or two into his instructions. The rest I had to piece together with my GCSE Spanish from eight years ago. *Todo* means everything. *Que* means what. *Se* could mean me, myself, I know, I am... I didn't realise this would be like an escape room.

Google Translate would help so I tapped the phrase in and waited a moment for the answer. Classic Marcos… I looked around and saw that the cistern of the toilet was concealed behind a panel. There were two screws in the top corners, protruding just enough to get my fingernails behind the head. I twisted gently, but holding on firmly, and palmed the first screw. The second came away just as easily and I could get my fingers into the space behind the panel and slide it up and out of the wall. Behind it was the white cistern, coated with plaster dust and abandoned cobwebs. The lip of the lid showed signs that the dust had recently been disturbed; a narrow band of white plastic revealed by the wriggling motion required to remove the top.

Removing the lid was easy but I couldn't see inside. I placed the lid at the base of the toilet, trying not to make a sound. The creak of the bathroom door. I waited; the lid poised between my fingertips. There was no talking my way out of this if I was discovered now. The tell-tale signs of someone using a urinal. Smart shoes clacked away as it flushed. No tap water sound. Disgusting.

I leant the lid against the toilet and dipped my left hand into the top of the cistern. Immediately, I felt wetness and revulsion. Who knew what I might find in here. I groped sightlessly and felt the plastic flush mechanism. There was a gap between the back side of the cistern and the slender arm and I plunged my hand further in. I was up to my elbow now, groping and probing. Then I felt something out of place. Something thin, plasticky, a bag. I gripped it, not wanting to lose it and have to squirm around the wet interior more than once. It caught briefly against the internal apparatus but squirted out with a splash. I shook off the toilet water and saw that it was a large sandwich bag with a seal that ran along the top.

Opening it, inside I found all of the tools and implements Ernesto, Marcos and I had gone through earlier that week.

There was a small, thumb-length screwdriver, with a removable bottom, that twisted off to reveal four different heads, which could be swapped out for the Phillips head that was in the drive tip. There was the steel bump gun, looking to the untrained eye like a starting gun for an athletics event, but without the barrel. Sellotaped to the pistol was a smaller plastic bag containing the flexible steel rod that tapered to a flat point and an Allen key with bladed ends rather than hexagonal tips. I would need to put this together so that the bump gun could be used properly. Two round, orange handles with black rubber suction cups that could fit in the palm of my hand. These were connected with a black plastic chain that linked the handles together. The final items were a packet of chewing gum and a folded up piece of paper, which I opened, to read;

1.   Block sensor with this
2.   Open panel
3.   Secure panel
4.   Open base
5.   GET TUMI!
6.   Hide
7.   Go before people come

Trust Marcos to doubt my ability to remember the plan in detail. The time was only nine o'clock and I needed to move quickly, before everyone should have left so that I could get into the cupboard under the stairs; the advertised end of the soiree was 22:30 but some might hang around a little longer, finishing drinks, finding their coats, waiting for taxis, that kind of thing. I didn't have long to make my move.

I listened intently as other men came in and out of the bathroom. The frequency at which they entered subsided and I sat still, the damp plastic bag, dried somewhat with toilet tissue, on my lap and cradled between my crossed arms. What was I doing? How had I ended up here?

Was it a fear of failure that made me freeze or the uncertainty of success? Up to this point, I considered, I could be proud of myself; composed, analytical, I was like a fucking spy. Now that I had the equipment I needed to actually go through with this damned scheme, I was impotent once more. Every inch I crept towards my goal also increased my anxiety. What to do, what to do, what to do. Go ahead and gamble it all. Put the tools back, forget about this shit, forget about Ernesto and Marcos and WMSCACE and Val Verde and everything else. I just needed a few minutes to get my nerves back.

If I waited too long, I would be swimming against the tide and would make myself too noticeable. I had to go now and try not to let my growing anxiety show.

Chapter 20 – Friday 17th to Saturday 18th June
(5 days to go...)

I heard the gentle noise of casual conversation outside of the bathroom so I knew people would be outside in the foyer and bar area. The plastic bag, dried under the hand dryer for ten furtive seconds, was pressed beneath my armpit and inside my suit jacket. I stepped confidently out of the bathroom, my right arm unnaturally stiff, but with both hands in my trouser pockets, I didn't look any more rigid than the majority of the aristocratic guests.

From the bathroom, I walked along the back of the racks in the gift shop, which partly blocked my view of the static camera leering over the till and, I guessed, their view of me. Heads turned my way briefly but were dismissed with a curt nod or lazy smile. I walked into the Industrial Gallery and intended to make a circuitous beeline for the cupboard. However, I noticed one hurried couple moving in the opposite direction, the husband clutching a raffle ticket, not too dissimilar to the one left for me.

I followed back through the gift shop, ambivalent of the camera this time, through the Round Room and to the cloakroom in the foyer. Through a stable door-like hatch, stood a disinterested Lucy, demonstrating significantly less enthusiasm than she did at Scintilla. Oh no, this I did not need. Noah and Eva and Chelsea and Ollie all knew I was here, as well as Ernesto and Marcos of course. If anything went missing, I would be as likely to be accused as anyone. Now another acquaintance would be able to place me at the scene. It was too late now, I was in the queue, and there were already several other character witnesses so I would just have to hope that everything in Ernesto's plan ran as smoothly as he had convinced me it would.

"Frankie!" she beamed. "What are you doing here?"

"Hey, Lucy. Noah invited me, Noah Wright."

"No way! Oh my God, you are so lucky."

"I didn't know you worked here?" I tried to change the subject to prevent her from doting on him again.

"You know how it is - got to pay to put a roof over my head." I nodded and fished into my pocket for my ticket.

"It's number 13."

"Unlucky for some!" she chirped. "Oh wait, this isn't right. Did you get this tonight?" I calculated what she could mean - why would I *not* have got the ticket tonight? Of course, Marcos must have left something in the cloakroom previously. So, something about the ticket was wrong. It couldn't be the number so it must be the colour. Different coloured tickets for different days, I guessed.

"No, no, I came here a few days ago and left my coat, so I thought I'd come pick it up while I'm here. Today. Tonight, I mean." She smiled and turned to rifle through the racks of left items.

"Here you go." She brought back a thick, black, donkey jacket with pleather patches on the front and back shoulders and both elbows. Absolutely not my style and more suited to the guys who collected our bins on Tuesdays. "Is it this one?"

266

"Um, yeah, yes, definitely."

"Are you going home then?"

"Yes, sure," I replied, folding the jacket over my arm, allowing me to relax my elbow grip on the bag, whilst keeping it concealed behind the bulky outerwear item. "Oh yeah, but first, I need to say goodbye to some people."

"So... see you tomorrow then?"

"Yes, sure, sure. See you tomorrow." Without waiting for further salutations, I turned away and half walked, half scampered to my next location. Around the racks and displays of the gift shop, into the Industrial Gallery, making sure I went through the crowds, so they might make it more difficult to spot me amidst their throng, and popping out, like a cork, beside the stairwell. There were still too many people to be brazen so I slowed my pace and followed a group of four who were examining a marble sculpture of a nude couple and a porcelain greyhound. They had halted but, as I neared, turned and went to the painted tiles that hung from the wall on the other side of the back of the stairs. I followed closely, but not too closely. When I felt safe to do so, I unfurled the jacket, whipped it over my shoulders, looking every bit - from the neck to the thigh - the working-class labourer doing some overtime, and slipped into the cupboard without catching anyone's attention.

I was immediately plunged into darkness and a musty odour. The door threatened to swing back out, like the saloon doors in a Western, but I held it firm. Having not encountered anything to bang into or knock over, I felt for the wall; it was bare and cold. I leaned one arm against it and lowered myself down, clenching the bag between my bicep and ribs. Slowly, steadily, I met the ground, sat with my knees pulled up in as small a spot as I could, and breathed out. I fairly thumped my head on the wall when I tried to lean back but was discreetly sequestered in my hiding place. All I had to do now was wait - what I should have been doing was reconsidering my disastrous series of decisions.

At around quarter to eleven, the sounds of the party died away, voices, indistinct of one another, lowered before a handful of clarion-like calls by those who had overdone it. The clatter of folding tables and cleaning up formed a foundation of noise for no more than twenty minutes. I did my best not to fall into a slumber and forced myself to sit uncomfortably.

After one, the light seeping into the edge of the room through the air vents and the cracks between the doors and the architrave, was cut off. I closed my eyes for a second before biting my cheek to fend off the temptation.

The silence and the darkness pervaded my entire existence. The nothingness beyond the cupboard swallowed all thoughts and actions, replacing them with dreams or nightmares. The former, containing blurred images of waving emerald green banners, glistening gold knives raised skyward, and the primal feeling of climbing up and up and up. I remember being flanked by people - unclear beyond that - with wide, proud smiles, commending me and firing out compliments like confetti. The people then became a crowd, encircling me. Their smiles broadened to sharp-fanged maws lined with diamond-shaped teeth. They had hoisted me above their heads now, propelling me forwards and further upwards. The steep ascent ended with the hands with fingers splayed out like palm fronds lowering me on to a stone bed. The banners fell and the knives seemed tipped with ruby blood. Leering over me was Eva, her long dark hair cascading over her bare shoulders and her dress, as sheer as dragonfly wings, hypnotically swayed in a calming *pampero* breeze. Above her head, she lifted the gold *tumi*, its blade hanging like a pendulum above my chest. At three thirty, I planned to make my move, and with a jolt I awoke from my dark fantasy with only minutes to spare.

I tested the door with a toe and relief filled me with hope as it gave and let in a slim gleam of grey through the breach. I was unprepared for trying to stand now. My legs were overcooked spaghetti, flopping, lolling, impossible to twirl on a fork, and I stumbled out of the doors, both flung wide behind me, and thumped into the wall opposite, narrowly avoiding destroying the 19th Century panel of wall tiles by English potter William de Morgan bearing a selection of fantastically blue animals. I returned to a seated position just below them and caught my breath. A quick check of the bag confirmed that everything was still there and a further examination of the coat led to the retrieval of a hi-viz tabard in an outer pocket with the word 'Security' emblazoned on the rear. I was reassured at just how prepared we really were, closely followed by the realisation that perhaps *he* would have been best placed to do this instead of me.

From my vantage point, I knew that there were no cameras or lights activated or likely to catch me in the act. To be on the safe side, I crawled to the left of the cupboard under the stairs, the opposite side to the fixed

CCTV camera that monitored the arch through to the Mini Museum. The ceiling mounted cameras were too far away to be a concern - one spying on anyone exiting the gift shop without having paid in full and the other more concerned with 16th Century earthenware.

On hands and knees still, I moved to the display unit where I could closely examine what I was up against. Marcos' note said to start with the sensor. I hunkered down along the narrow end of the rectangle of wood and glass. Getting up to my knees, and feeling the stabbing sensation of pins and needles down my legs, I looked for a sensor in the upper cabinet. There was nothing given away by running my eyes around the top, then where the sides met one another, and then the edge, until I saw a small black lens, only two centimetres across and reflective like glass. I saw a red LED glow inside and followed an imaginary line to the top of the case, where I noticed a silver rectangle, the same size as the glass lens. Now, I am definitely not qualified to be considered an expert but I recognised this as being the sensor because Scintilla had one very similar running across the front door. If you go to most shops, you will see one too; it's a beam of light that counts the number of people that go in or out of the venue, simply speaking. It also acts as a security system, when set by Freya, for instance, so should anyone attempt to break in through the front door, they would set off an alarm that would either scare them off or alert the local constabulary. I knew that it should be relatively simple to render it inactive using the chewing gum wrapper.

I didn't normally go for chewing gum as I always assumed anyone masticating on something containing similar ingredients to condoms was inherently stupid, either because they did it with their mouth open, suggested a poor upbringing, or that the repetitive action of their jaw reminded me of cows, which are not renowned for their witty conversational skills or deft problem-solving abilities. As I chewed, I uncreased the wrapper, trying to keep it as clean and reflective as possible.

Three more sticks went in and I chewed relentlessly, for what else was I going to do with them? The four wrappers were folded together, shiny sides out, into a semi-stiff ice lolly stick shape about an inch long. The glass case was sat on top of the wooden base, forming a butted join around the edges, with the surface on which the artefacts were displayed enclosed within the wooden base and resting on top of a wood batten running around the edge. That meant I had to create a gap between the glass and the base, slide the wrappers in and try to push it up and over the edge of the display surface so that it would cover the sensor and, hopefully, present a reflection of the light and fool it into thinking that everything was absolutely fine.

Taking the Phillips blade head out of the base of the screwdriver, I swapped it in for the flat head, and used it as a sort of chisel to wedge a slight gap between the two, heavy parts of the unit. The folded wrappers slid in but if I tried to get them to bend up the batten and over the top of the sensor, they crumpled easily. I tried again but this still bent under any pressure.

I checked the bag again looking for anything that might help me to overcome this problem. I thought about using the thin metal shaft that came with the bump gun, but I couldn't risk using it in case it broke or could not be removed. That was what I needed though; some thin, flexible but not too flexible piece of metal, maybe two to three centimetres long, just to stiffen the wrappers.

Maybe a paper clip? There would be plenty in the gift shop but then I'd definitely be caught on camera. How about part of a hanger? No, too wide and too stiff. Then I had it. The cloakroom ticket. I pulled my coat off and looked in the collar. Sure enough, there was a corresponding ticket bearing the number 13 affixed to the label in the jacket by a safety pin!

Removing it, I released the pin from the clasp and rocked it backwards and forwards, slowly stretching the whole thing out into one right-angled arm, with the clasp at one end and the spring in the middle like an elbow. It slipped into the middle of the wrappers and I got the needle of it into the gap and up the side of the thin piece of timber.

That was when I heard footsteps.

Like a dizzy rabbit, my hind legs not yet functioning properly, I scooted myself around the back of the stairs without a sound, taking the bag with me. The doors would open for me but I held off, fearing the motion or an unexpected sound could give me away.

I craned my ears, waiting for a sign to reveal where the feet were falling.

The awful calm continued.

Clap. Clap. Clap. Clap.

To my right, somewhere. The Mini Museum?

Clap. Clap. Clap. Clap.

A monotonous march so orderly and patient. It felt like the steady clang of a bell.

Clap. Clap. Clap. Clap.

No, wait, above me, above and to the right. On the balcony, by the camera and the Jacobean ceramic crockery. Crockery. Jugs. The jug, the case, my silver wrapper! Damn, I'd left it hanging there, poking out like a pube in a smile.

Clap. Clap. Clap.

Now coming towards the top of the stairs. Was it time to make a run for it?

Clap. Clap.

Was he already suspicious? If he wasn't before, seeing the unexpected glint of silver sticking out of the display surely would raise alarm.

Clap. Clap.

Please don't look, please don't look.

He turned. Clap. Clap. Clap.

Moving away now, away from the stairs and my hiding place.

The solid footsteps rang through the hallway. What if he circled round the other side of the balcony? He'd get the perfect view of my handiwork over the stained glass window exhibition.

I could only wait, again, wait until I was reasonably sure that I could return to the case to try again. I knew I had to act fast but I couldn't be hasty. The silver tipped pin popped out over the batten. I couldn't risk gradually breaking the beam of light and triggering the alarm; I had to do it quickly and in one go. My fingers itched and I envisioned the swift swing across of the reflective material. I pinched the soft end of the chewing gum wrapper that still stuck out of the bottom of the case, the hinge of it pivoted on the corner of the wooden batten. My other hand rested on the outside of the base, my shoulder too, grasping the whole slab to gain any extra ounce of control over my actions. Three, two, one, go.

In a flash, the silver sheet, swung over the sensor in a smooth, accurate motion. Silence. No sirens. But I paused. I strained to hear any clapping sound of boots on vinyl flooring. Still nothing.

Step one done and I was already sweating. I looked for a panel and realised that I had been hugging it all this time. The base was made of four rectangular panes of wood that were sealed up tight with mastic, with the exception of the slimmer end closest to me. That was attached with four screws, one in each corner, covered with a plastic cap, and a keyhole in the top right, presumably locked. It was simple enough to take off the caps and put them in my bag. Then I unscrewed the screws, putting them with the caps, but the panel, unsurprisingly considering this was meant to protect some pretty valuable bric-a-brac, didn't come away.

I looked at the lock and took out the bump gun. I clicked the metal tongue into place and slid it into the lock. But when I pulled the trigger, the short snap that had barely registered inside the church hall sounded like a whip crack.

I paused again. Holding my breath and craning my ears. A moment later, convinced I was still alone, I pulled the trigger again. And again. And again. The device sent a kinetic jolt along the barrel and into the lock and I noticed the lock turn a little. I tried to pull the panel again but there was no give. Each crack of the gun raised the hairs on the back of my neck.

The Allen key went in and I turned it but, I reasoned, I could try leaving it in. The metal taper then went in without resistance. I cracked the trigger again, and again, and again, watching the balcony as I did. Inside the lock, the light feedback of pins stopped and I was able to turn the Allen key a little more. As I did, the heavy panel juddered loose, slipping out of the housing and crunching on to my toes. The shriek was muffled into my elbow before I wept a tear away. With my bruised foot as the fulcrum, I twisted the panel away and put it against the corner of the base. Behind it was a great chamber, empty and dark, revealing the four stout legs upon which each side panel was attached and above which resided the floor of the display itself, made from Perspex and covered with a silky material that was clipped to the underside of the board.

The space was large enough for me to crawl into and I soon realised that the suction cups now had to come into play. I attached one to the Perspex and one to the panel and it held the panel in place whilst the screws could be removed. I considered how much time, and luck, I had left but hoped I could be done in a few minutes and then I could retire to the cupboard instead.

Whilst the sensor was disabled, there was no way to remove the glass top as it was simply too heavy; I could tell that from looking at it regardless of the instructions given to me by Ernesto. The only option, as Marcos had correctly recognised, was to get at the display from underneath. Using my phone light, I got out the screwdriver and removed the screws that held the wooden batten in place along two sides of the base. With them removed, I could tilt the Perspex enough to reach my hand in and, with a little bit more luck, take what I needed.

The battens came away easily enough and I felt the Perspex move above me. I had to shuffle into the far corner and tilt it but, when I moved back to where I hoped to reach up and grab the *tumi*, it slumped back into place, closing up the gap. I tried again. And again. I needed to move the weight above it to one corner so it might balance open.

I removed a couple of the clips holding the fabric in place and gave it a heave, cinching it into the corner, pulling the items with it.

The jug clinked against the jaguars and I froze.

Above me, one hand grasping the white silk, the other flat against the Perspex, I heard the ancient jug wobble, topple, and then right itself again.

Gentler, I tugged the material again, sliding the mask forward until I could see its jagged corona over the edge of the white sheet. Scooching forward, with my flat palm holding everything steady - the Perspex, the sheet, the artefacts, the future of the Yarina, my liberty - I reached my other hand up and around, feeling for something recognisable.

I dragged the mask out of the way, laying it shining on the floor, and fingered for the blade. I had to nudge aside the clay jaguars but the textured hilt of the knife was within reach. Ouch!

I scraped the cutting edge of the *tumi* and felt blood on my index and middle fingers. Rushing and panicked, I swung myself around, switching position, and swapping one hand for the other. The cut fingers splayed out above me, holding the wobbling Perspex, whilst my uninjured hand burst through the gap and prevented the vase from falling once more. Equilibrium restored, I more gingerly wrapped my hand around the handle and pulled the *tumi* free from its stand. It came through the gap with ease and, placing it on top of the mask, I pushed the Perspex panel back into place with both hands. The mask! Oh crap, how was I going to put that back now?

I took stock. I was concealed, aside from the wooden side panel I had removed. I had the *tumi*. I wasn't too badly hurt, only tired. I also had the Moche mask. So far as I knew, nobody had any suspicion I was still here. Right then.

It took me a few moments to reattach the battens, screwing the securely back into place, keeping the Perspex level. I stuffed all of the items back into the plastic bag, save for the screwdriver. Then I backed myself out of the open end and hoisted the panel back into the housing. I couldn't lock the bolt but I put the screws and caps back on. With seemingly so much accomplished so quickly, I looked around desperately, expecting my unanticipated success to come undone, but there were no clues that anyone else was even in the museum besides me.

I swept the silver wrapper off of the sensor and tugged the safety pin and foil out. I didn't want to risk any evidence being left behind. With a rapid backward glance, I confirmed that none of my blood had been left on the scrunched up white sheet. Aside from the absence of the mask and the *tumi*, the material was less bunched than I thought it would be and the other items were all close to their original positions.

On my hands and knees, I slithered back to the stairs and the cupboard hiding place. It felt like the cupboard had protected me well and I owed it something so I stuck to the plan and stayed low and quiet as I slipped back inside. I knew that there was an exit at the back, through the Edwardian Tearooms, so I could have made a break for it. It occurred to me that if I deviated from the plan, any failure would be all my fault. If I stuck to what had been planned out, success might be mine but failure would be all on Ernesto.

The first dull rays of light were intruding through leaded windows and I could see that inside the closet were tools and liquids for cleaning, so I pulled a bucket-sized tub of paint and sat on top of it. I set my phone alarm to vibrate me awake at 5am. That would give me, I guessed, an hour to leave before the cleaning or security staff arrived. Balling up the jacket, I rested it between my shoulder and the wall and drifted into a shallow sleep.

Chapter 21 – Saturday 18th June (5 days to go...)

The buzz in my pocket grew more violent and I awoke just after five. In a daze, I unravelled the jacket and pulled it on, followed by the hi-viz tabard. I took the items out of the bag and wedged them deep into the outer pockets, spreading them out as evenly as I could. I screwed up the carrier bag and put that in the inner pocket with the chewing gum. One more stick went in my mouth - not because I wanted to carry anything less - after all, what difference would it have made? - but because I thought people who chewed gum came across as more casual, and that would fit with my disguise as a low-paid keyworker patrolling the museum with a chip on his shoulder, an ungrateful cow for a wife, and two sprogs that don't know when to bleedin' shush... I was really getting into character.

The *tumi* was in an inside poacher's pocket all of its own and the Moche mask lined an outer pocket, that was further covered by my hand and the wide cuff of the sleeve.

I sloped out of the cupboard, holding the door with care, eyeing the room from both directions. No bodies, no sound. I returned to the crouching position and trotted to the side of the stairs closest to the gift shop. I looked around again. I hurried to the display cabinet, outwardly undisturbed. Then I cantered to the other side of the chamber, concealed behind the stained-glass window exhibit and shielded by other display cases. Hugging the wall, I sidestepped to the corner, meaning the fixed CCTV camera on the far side of the archway into the Mini Museum had no chance of spotting me.

Through the arch, the security lights might have been a worry but, with the dawn rising, they were disabled. Into the Edwardian Tearooms, there were no customers nor staff just yet so the potent hustle and bustle was unrealised. I saw the camera, hawk-like, watching for any mistake made by a staff member, any light-fingered employee. With it firmly in my view, I strafed through the groups of tables and comfortable armchairs, weaving patiently towards the door at the back of the counter. The camera remained concentrated on the fear that someone might pinch a fiver at the end of their shift, whilst I made my way through the door with a gold sacrificial knife and a two-thousand-year-old Moche mask.

Through the double fire doors, was a narrow corridor, and I nearly tripped over a fire extinguisher. The pale green walls and laminate floor were a stark contrast to what I had woken up to. The doors had opened up into a corridor running to the left and to the right; I had expected some kind of quick getaway into the square or a useful side street. Indecision halted my progress.

I decided to carry on to the right. The more doors I found, leading back into the museum itself, the more concerned I got. Distant sounds and slippery glimmers of the changing light put the scares into me so I turned about and went back the way I came, past the fortunately empty staff room and, two doors later, across from the disabled toilets, the fire exit.

I ducked into the toilet to catch my breath and, I reasoned, because if I was intercepted coming out of the toilet, I would be far less likely to be asked about my reasons for being there than if I came out of some other door. Three minutes later, I counted, I walked out, attempting self-assurance. There it was - a relatively unexciting wooden door, this time with four frosted glass panels inlaid at eye level, a clearly marked fire exit sign, and a modern, metal push bar. With as much bravado as I could muster, the *tumi* fairly rattling in my jacket, I shoved the bar and burst out into the dingy sunlight.

Around me towered the entirety of the museum and art gallery building and the council head offices. Before me spread a tarmac square, sliced by painted parking bays, and bare but for two cars, several stairwells, a ramp and short flight of steps running down from the door I had just thrust open, and a scattering of stubbed cigarette butts. One fizzed through the air and struck me on the side of the head.

"What the fuck are you doing out here?" I spun towards the direction from which the filter had flown. My eyes met a black donkey jacket with leatherette shoulders and elbow patches covered with a Hi-Viz tabard which, probably, had 'Security' stencilled on the back just like mine.

"Oh!" I reacted.

"Frankie?"

"Ollie?" His eyes froze and I could tell the explanations for my appearance were sparking and extinguishing as soon as he worked logically through them. I half expected him to ask if I'd got a job there, but he would have known. Perhaps he would make some quip about going to a fancy-dress party, but what we were wearing wasn't fancy by anyone's definition and certainly not suitable for any party within our limited social circles. Well, perhaps some of his Territorial Army friends but then they were the sort that thought blacking up for Hallowe'en was absolutely acceptable.

"What are you doing here, Frankie?" He'd put his phone away now and was striding towards me. "How did you get in here?" The way he brushed away the tobacco from his jacket and faultlessly tossed a mint into his mouth, suggested he wasn't supposed to be smoking or on a break.

"I… I…" I had thought about what to say, if I encountered security or a member of staff but I was dumbstruck by meeting my own flatmate. "I… I was at the party… and… I, ah, I fell asleep…"

"In a security vest? Do you think I'm an idiot?"

"…got a job… at the museum…" He frowned. "…fancy dress…?" I muttered in close to a whisper.

"You need to tell me now before you get in serious trouble." He was close-up and, despite not being particularly tall or broad, he had a threatening menace to him.

"I can't tell you."

"You'd better fucking tell me."

"I can't - it's personal."

"If you don't fucking tell me, I'm going to radio my fucking super and he's going to be here in two fucking minutes so you'd better tell me now or have a pretty fucking spectacular answer for him." I looked him square in the face and then tilted my head down to my chest, where the jacket was held slightly open, and I slid out the handle of the *tumi*. Even in the grim surrounding of the municipal buildings' courtyard, the precious metal shone with a lustre that was out of place.

"Mother fucker!" Spontaneously, Ollie spun his head on a swivel, scanning the courtyard. "Holy shit, Frankie, holy shit. What have you done?"

"I stole it, Ollie, what does it bloody look like?"

"Do you know how much shit you are in right now?" With a slipped jerk, he wrapped his right arm around my shoulder, blocking my bounty from sight, and turning me back towards the door. "I don't know if I can help you but I can put a good word in maybe but you are in so much fucking trouble that you are definitely going to prison or maybe you will get deported now because of this shit shit shit..." He had the door open with one hand and his grip still firmly around me, his weight moving forward to heft me through the space and back inside and, I imagined, towards whatever doom the supervisor would dispense upon me.

"Woah, wait," I barked, jerking my shoulders backwards like a dog who has just realised that this isn't the park, this is the vet... "Wait a minute." A shrugged him off me, leaving him blocking up the door and me backing away down the ramp. "Wait a minute, are you clocking off right now?"

"Yes, so get inside and stop wasting my bloody time," he growled.

"You were on night shift, weren't you?"

"What the fuck's that got to do with the price of milk?" Then he clocked. The door thudded shut behind him. "Now, you wait a minute... You... Hold on, now..."

It was my turn to issue orders. "Ollie, you need to come with me. This is important."

"Too right it is! It's my job if this gets out - and worse for you. You've got to get inside and put it back." He reached for the door again but I pushed his arm down.

"No, Ollie, no, you need to get your shit together and come back to the flat with me." I stepped back down the ramp, letting his arm fall limp to his side. Just as he had run through the possibilities for my appearance in such unusual attire, he worked through what choice he might have.

"I'm not taking it up the arse because my flat mate's a thief. Forget that."

"Just clock off and come with me. Everything's going to be alright. I know it is." I didn't and it wasn't, but I had come this far now, had changed so much, that I couldn't let him get in my way, our way, and prevent what might happen next. He looked about, kicked his shoes against the base of the handrail, patted his pockets, and followed.

"Fine. But as soon as we get in, you had better have some unbelievably good explanation for what you're doing."

"I can make it unbelievable." He noticed my smirk.

"You know what I mean - logical, realistic, whatever - just good or else we're both fucked."

"So, if it's logical and realistic, we're not fucked?" He stopped.

"No, no. Hold it, don't try that shit with me. It's funny when I do it to Chels."

"Does she think so?"

"Don't try to change the subject. What's got into you?"

Ollie heaved open the kind of unlocked door and whumped into his armchair. I made sure it was kind of locked behind us and emptied my pockets on to the kitchen counter.

"Right, I'm all ears." I ignored Ollie's impatience and tried to get composed. I had a lot to explain and I didn't want to give him too many opportunities to twist my words around or pick holes in what I knew was a pretty shaky scheme.

"Tea?"

"Fuck off."

"Coffee it is then…" I didn't put any pressure on him by watching but when I returned with two steaming mugs, he had the *tumi* in his hand, held up like a new-born. He nodded and I set the coffees down, mirroring his cautious delight.

"Wow… it's not light but it's so... so *balanced*, it's kind of… magical…"

"Spiritual?"

"Yeah, yeah, maybe. What is it?"

"A knife. Yarinan priestesses used it for blood-letting and ritual sacrifices about fifteen hundred years ago."

He barely flinched. "No way." He had no idea what I was on about. "Why do you have it?" On top of my discarded wool jacket, he deftly lay the blade down with both hands.

"You don't have any idea who the Yarina are, do you?"

"Not the foggiest." Ollie sat on the stool and clasped his coffee. "But it must be worth something to someone if you're breaking into the biggest museum in Birmingham to nick it. Are you a fence?"

"A what?"

"Someone who sells stuff someone else has pinched. But, no, if you were you wouldn't pinch it yourself - you'd get someone on the inside to do it." I raised my eyebrows. "Alright, calm down. So, you're a professional cat burglar, or an art thief, or maybe you're like Indiana Jones." He looked me up and down, then snorted.

"Nothing like that, I promise. This is the first time I've done anything like this."

"But why?"

I explained to him who the Yarina were, and why they were in hiding, and how that the *tumi* had significant cultural meaning to them, and how it had been stolen by the British hundreds of years ago, and if one of their own - sort of - could repatriate it, it would give their diaspora a unifying symbol, an act of rebellion against colonial oppressors and slave traders, that could bring them all together from across Central and South America, to overthrow the tyranny of President Calderon, and restore their rights and status in their homeland, perhaps close to what they had before the Spanish Conquistadors forced them into hiding.

"What a load of old bollocks." I had expected that kind of response. "Why do they need an old knife to overthrow Calderon? Can't they just decide amongst themselves that they've had enough and kick him out? They don't need a sacrificial blade; they need a WhatsApp group."

It was my turn to snort at his comments. "What are you campaigning for? All those leaflets going through all those letterboxes - they carry nothing but a word. And that word has meaning, right?, for you, and the other guys you're meeting with, and some of the people you're giving the flyers to. It's just a word."

"Brexit isn't just a word - it's an idea, a promise - that if we get our country out of Europe, we can take back control. We decide what laws to pass. Well, our MPs. But then we get to vote for the MPs and they are gifted power by the people. And then we can control who comes in, what rights our citizens have, where we spend our money. Do you want your taxes to be spent on some Eastern Europeans to get jobs that could be done by people in this country?"

"The *tumi* is no different. You feel like the UK has had its rights stolen by the EU. The *tumi* was *actually* stolen. You want to have freedom because you have had laws imposed on you that aren't your laws. The Yarina have been victimised by the governments of Val Verde for *centuries*."

"But you've broken the law. The Government sets the law and, like it or not, you have to follow the rules, or else there would be chaos." Ollie sipped his coffee, attempting to draw a line under his words - or perhaps put some distance between us.

"The British stole this knife. I've stolen it back. I know that two wrongs don't make a right," I saw him thinking it. "but my wrong puts it right."

"It's my duty to report this."

"If you do, you're fired anyway. The *tumi* was stolen on *your* shift." Had we lived in a quieter neighbourhood, I might have heard his molars grinding. "You consider yourself British, right?"

"Yes, of course."

"What did the British do when they were faced by the Germans in World War Two?"

"We fought them and won."

"But they were stronger, and more powerful. You know how close the country was to starving because of the blockades in the North Sea." He nodded, proudly. "What if the British had said 'Oh well, I suppose we should let them win, they are stronger after all'?"

"Not bloody likely!"

"That's the British spirit, isn't it? Never quit when you're down, never be dismayed by the odds, fight until the end. You want to fight the EU; they're bigger, richer, more powerful than Britain but you don't let that stop you campaigning for independence. The Yarina are different but the same."

"Yes, but who even are they?"

I frowned, both for not knowing a succinct answer but also for his ignorant way of asking the question. "They were people my parents fought for, before they were extradited. For me, the Yarina might be my only connection to my parents. If I can do something to help the Yarina, it's like I'm putting right all of the things I did to hurt my parents." I hoped he wouldn't ask what they were too.

"And what's in it for you?"

"For me..?"

"Everyone is motivated by personal gain, even a little bit. Money? Power? Influence?" He was drifting towards his *Scarface* impression but I interjected before he butchered Al Pacino.

"I only want to say that I've done something strangers will know me for." I raised my mug and drank. We were silent for a moment, not long. The outside world turned around us, shifting and shaping lives beyond the double-glazing of our little flat. A marvel of interacting relationships that juddered from chaos and imminent disaster to peaceful order and clockwork precision. Ollie lifted his giant Sports Direct mug and I mirrored him with my blue one; we clinked them together and the astonishing world beyond our windows moved once more, nudged by our interaction within that flat.

Chapter 22 – Sunday 19th June
(4 days to go...)

My initial satisfaction at persuading Ollie to if not support
my cause then at least not to grass me up to the
authorities, was short lived. To be honest, he didn't seem
to need all that much persuading. But for an hour or two
that morning, whilst we ate toast and drank tea in front of
the telly, I felt more like my old self. That is to say I was
happily oblivious to the dramas and machinations that
went on outside of my bubble. We loafed on the sofa and
played FIFA for a bit. Neither of us said much but we
joked about and teased each other when the moment
called for it. Ollie even wished me a happy birthday and
offered to cook me breakfast. I declined as I didn't have
much of an appetite.

It must have been mid-morning by the time we
stopped and I felt like I needed to have a shower. I was
barely dry when I heard Ollie scream my name. I rushed
out of the bathroom, the towel tied around my waist, and
saw a look of anguish on his face.

"...the theft of a high-value piece of South
American art from a museum in Birmingham has resulted
in a police appeal. The theft took place yesterday evening
at Birmingham Museum and Art Gallery, where the
opening night of a new exhibition of South and Central
American art was being held.

The unknown thief entered the venue and stole a
gold mask and a gold sacrificial knife from a display
cabinet."

The image on the television changed from the crisp
studio to an uncomfortable looking man in a suit too big

for him and a stiff white shirt with a collar too small for him.

"The West Midlands Police are examining the CCTV footage from the Museum and working with the Museum to identify any possible suspects from the list of guests at the opening gala. We are appealing for any witnesses who may have seen the suspect leaving the museum with the stolen items, or putting them into a bag. Alternatively, we are keen to hear from anyone who may have seen the item being offered for sale or noticed it within someone's home. Anyone with information that could assist our investigation should call 101 quoting crime reference number 765423-626."

I gawped at the screen whilst Ollie did the same.

"We are joined by the CEO of Democracy Coffee, Noah Wright, whose foundation sponsors the exhibition. Good morning, Mister Wright. What can you tell us about the stolen items?" The screen in the studio was suddenly filled to the edge with a close-up of Wright, before he tapped the screen with his finger and moved back, revealing his head and shoulders and a background composed of a bookcase empty of literature but full of *objets d'art*.

"Good morning. Yes, so the stolen items are absolutely priceless and extremely old."

"And what might members of the public notice about these items?" He proceeded to describe the knife and the mask, giving real emphasis to the fact that they were made from gold and were both over a thousand years old. Not knowing much of this, I watched on, feeling the cold as the water dried on my skin.

"I would like to add," he continued, "that I am willing to offer a generous reward for information leading to the recovery of these sacred items. If anyone provides the Police with a credible lead, I am willing to offer £10,000 of my own money."

"That's an incredibly generous offer but do you not think the Police should be given time to follow their own lines of enquiry first?"

"I have complete faith in the abilities of the West Midlands Police Force. I would just like to recover my, these, objects as soon as possible." Ollie clicked the television off before the presenter could lead into the next news item. I shivered and ducked back into the bathroom.

When I re-emerged a moment later, he was sitting in his comfy armchair again, staring into space.

"What are you going to do?" he asked when I sat close by on the settee.

"What do you mean?"

He jerked an arm out towards the black rectangle that dominated the living area. "Mate, you could get ten grand in your back pocket for those things. And nobody needs to know it was you who took them. Just drop them in a bin down a back street, make a note of the location, and call in and say 'Er, yeah, I've seen them in a dustbin.' Tell them where they are and your account details and, boom, you've got ten Gs."

"No! No way. I didn't take them to hand them back. And what use is ten grand when I'm in Val Verde?"

"I bet it could go a lot further than it could here. Have you seen the price of a pint nowadays?" I didn't want to mention that I could remember a time before he had been quite so comfortable in his job when he used to steal them from the pub by using the old library card trick.

"No," I stated resolutely, getting to my feet. "No, I've made a promise. I'm going to help get them to the Yarina. And then I'm going to stay here. To hell with the Home Office - *esos asquerosos hijos de puta!*"

"I haven't heard you speak Spanish for a while. What does that mean?"

"You don't want to know but it's not nice. I remember my *Mamá* used to say it when they had run-ins with the police." He frowned then wiggled his mug at me. I nodded, then took a seat at the kitchen table as I realised that I had to put my socks on, and he started making a round of teas.

"What sort of run-ins?" His question should have been anticipated. After all, I had kept my parents lives so secret these past few years that, now, when I had discovered more about their involvement in the very movement I had tied my colours to, I felt torn. There was pride at sharing what they had stood for and what they had risked for the good of their own country, or so they believed, and how they had wanted me to be safe in England, even though they knew they could not be with me. There was anger too but that was less precise; I was both angry at being abandoned, regardless of their intentions, and at the last four years of my life during which they had vanished and, so far as I knew, not once tried to get in touch with me. Our last communication was a postcard with no return address. And I was angry that they had kept the passion they had and the urgency they felt for taking action and affecting change to themselves - yes, I was young, but age is no barrier to standing for what you believe in. Maybe I was even a little angry at myself for having taken so long to realise that and for pushing them away.

"They were…" I halted on 'protestors', as it felt so pitiful. Dishevelled masses, squawking into a void, thousands taking to the streets but the only evidence they were there was the rubbish swept to the kerbside once they had dispersed. "Radicals. They believed in fairness and, to them, it didn't matter who was in charge - left, right, whatever. They always stood up for the oppressed. The police don't like that - the oppressed don't pay their wages."

Ollie grunted assent and came back with the teas. "Right on, brother. Smash the patriarchy!" We laughed loudly. Too loudly.

"Ahoy there, flatmates. What are you two laughing about?" Chelsea strode in, ignoring the fact that she wore the same outfit as she had the night before.

"Nothing," said Ollie, too quickly.

"Come on now, I like a laugh too you know, I'm not always super serious." Neither of us volunteered a comment. "Come on." We sipped our tea and sniggered to each other. "Fine. I'm going to put the telly on."

"No!" yelped Ollie. "Don't!"

"What's wrong with you?" Chelsea planted her feet and put a hand on one hip, toying with the remote with her other hand.

"Nothing!" I might have been able to manage the urge to tell them every little detail of what I had planned and what I had done but Ollie was on the verge of giving away our secret to the first person he saw. Chelsea looked at him inquisitively and then looked at me.

I tried to change the subject. "What's with the outfit?"

"What do you mean?"

"You wore it last night at the exhibition." She flushed and realised the hand on her hip held the straps of her shoes and she wore discoloured stockings, picking up the dirt and filth of the city.

"Oh, I... went to a party afterwards."

"Who with?" asked Ollie.

"No-one, it was just a party. But don't change the subject - what are you two up to? You don't normally act like this, like you've got something to hide." Ollie went and sat on the sofa, stretching his legs out in front of him. I followed, sitting beside him, and leaning forward, my elbows on my knees. Unable to sit down, except in Ollie's comfy chair, which would make any conversation feel like an interview, Chelsea huffed and went to their bedroom.

"We can't tell her about last night," Ollie spat, as soon as he thought she was out of earshot.

"Shh, don't even talk about it in the flat," I said. "It's too risky - she might come out at any time."

"Okay, fine. What about your room?"

I hesitated. "My room? Why?"

"Well she's not exactly going to just walk in on us in there, is she?"

"I never let anyone in my room."

"Listen," Ollie turned towards me and I felt as I had once before that he was a friend. Perhaps he could be trusted, but did I trust him enough to let him into my personal space and reveal the secrets that lay behind my closed door? It was hard to say and trust was earned not claimed. The only way to trust someone was to give them an opportunity to betray you. He had already been given one opportunity but had decided to give me the benefit of the doubt. Maybe I could do the same. "Listen, I know you've got your secrets - we all have skeletons in our closet - but if we are going to do something that will make us infamous, then we have to share those secrets. I can't help you if I can't trust you."

"What's this 'we' business?"

He smirked. "In for a penny, in for a pound, right? I get why you're doing this, I do - your parents, the Yarina, your legacy - but if you want me to keep this all hushed up, I need something out of it too."

"What?"

"Not here." He nodded towards my closed door.

"Fine, but only because I need your help." Assenting to his demands would have given me greater pause for thought two months ago but, with all that had happened, my hesitancy and isolation seemed to be fading. He followed me to the door and through, mirroring my careful steps and precise movement to avoid my creation.

I advanced to the window sill on the far side of the small room and Ollie stood in his grubby tracksuit bottoms and scruffy rugby shirt with the mystery stain down the middle, looking back from where we had entered. and took in what was drawn out before him.

All along the right-hand wall was my bed, a small, pine bedside chest of drawers, and a cupboard with my minimal wardrobe hung within it or stuffed into the wide drawers at the bottom. I leaned against the radiator beneath the window, which looked out upon the car park and garages at the back of our block. Jutting out into the room and extending along the left-hand wall, running from where I stood almost all the way to the door - which would not have opened if I hadn't bought a variable-speed, cordless jigsaw from the Homebase up the road - was my creation. Lyonesse-on-Lethe.

Made from MDF boards attached to fold out pasting tables, the model village covered a footprint 350cm by 110cm, plus the 60cm by 60cm peninsula which Ollie now examined.

"It didn't start out like this. It was only a three-foot square sheet in the beginning." He didn't reply. His attention was drawn to the door end, where the diagonal edge formed my harbour, containing a small leisure craft, moored on wood-slatted docks. Beside it, on top of a gently raised piece of land built using high density pink modelling foam, was a small shelter containing a small boy in a yellow mac, looking out to the sea.

A rail line ran along the back of the hillock to a small station closest to the door but the track continued all along the length of the room, splitting to pass through a tunnel made of Noch Terra-Form wire and crepe paper shaped to create a hill in the centre of my model and a branch line that went up and down an incline, wrapped around the tunnel and the hill the main line dissected, and led to a terminus in a town constructed of a handful of key buildings arranged around a grey, flagstone town square; a church with a square steeple and masonry spire on top, with accompanying graveyard behind it; a factory with its own siding and goods shed; a parcel office close to the station with a road running onto a high street; a parade of shop fronts, including a butchers, pet shop, bakers, cafe - with al fresco seating - and convenience store on the corner. I'd left some space at the end farthest from the door, at the 'southern' end of the town for a school, possibly. I wasn't sure yet but I had my eye on a Metcalfe Manor Farm House set that might look the part. My Brawa 5437 phone box was positioned on the pavement that ran in front of the shelter beside the wharf but I hadn't wired it up yet.

Ollie gingerly reached for the control panel - I wanted a Hornby Elite but could only afford a second-hand Gaugemaster for now - but held back.

"This is insane." I couldn't be sure if he meant that as a compliment. "How come you didn't tell us about this?"

"What? That I'm a model railway nerd?"

"Ha, yeah you are. But this is quality, I mean, the details are amazing." He strode towards me. "Look at that. That's like a mini Scintilla. And is that an Italian restaurant?" He placed his hands on his knees and leant forward, peering through the window at what the people of Lyonesse-on-Lethe might be up to. "How did you make this river? The water is so blue and looks real." He gave it a curious prod.

"There's a model shop up the road, really well stocked. You can get this Vallejo Pacific Blue water effects stuff. It's amazing."

"It's like the kind of blue sea you see on those holiday programmes…"

"Alright, don't get too excited." He grinned at me and backed up. "A guy's got to have a hobby."

"Did you make all this?"

"Yeah, most of it. All the terrain, the electrics, the shops. I painted everything and flocked the grass bits."

"You did what?"

"Flock. It's… never mind. I couldn't afford to buy everything I wanted to get so I worked out how to make the more detailed stuff and anything that didn't need any wiring." What took his fancy was the cul-de-sac of houses on the headland that protruded into the room, separating the wharf at the 'northern' end from the town at the other. They were typically British with red-tiled roofs, terraced, save for the end semis, and with mostly immaculate front lawns.

"You should have told me sooner. You know I'm good with my hands - I would love to help you with all this." That was one way of putting the fact that he was a petty thief. Not that I could talk.

"This must have cost a fortune!"

"Not really. Most of it I picked up second hand, cheap bits and bobs off eBay, the occasional car boot sale. It's just grown a bit more than I planned."

"You should show those idiots from the Home Office."

"Why?"

"There's nothing more British than a model railway nerd, is there? Next thing, you'll be taking up Morris dancing…" As he chuckled, his eyes ran along the part-painted street. "What's with this house?" His finger jabbed at one building I hadn't quite finished, one that stood out amongst the uniformity of the rest.

"That's my house. My parents' house. The one in Digbeth. I haven't had a chance to finish it yet."

"What do you mean? Everything else looks like it's perfect. Why's this one so incomplete?"

I shook my head. "The *tumi* - we need to keep it here until the Police have given up looking. There's no way they will know I did it."

"Why not? You were at the party. And what about me? I was on duty so I'll definitely be a suspect."

"What's my motive? And why would you jeopardise a job you've only recently started?"

"Maybe I got the job so I could steal priceless art?"

"Do you have a track record of breaking the law? I don't."

"Where is it anyway?" He looked around the room but, aside from the craft materials blocking my wardrobe, a pile of unread philosophy textbooks by my bed, and a dirty laundry basket, there was little on show. I stepped around him towards the door, which remained ajar, and lifted up the model phone box. The red metal skeleton, its plastic glass panels dull and opaque, concealed the handle of the *tumi*.

"I had to press the blade into the foam to get it to go in." I pulled the handle and the sheer gold plate followed with little resistance. I felt like Arthur Pendragon.

With extraordinarily impeccable timing, that was precisely when Chelsea took the opportunity to walk into my room for the first time.

Chapter 23 – Sunday 19th June
(4 days to go...)

"What's tha...? Wait..." She froze, framed by the doorway, confused by what she saw, and transfixed by the glistening sun that wobbled from the golden blade.

"Chels, you need to leave." Ollie tried to order her from my room. She stood as still as one of my models.

"I can explain," I replied. It was instinctive and potentially untrue. Both Ollie and Chelsea looked at me. Their expressions conveyed very different expectations. The realisation that there would be no hiding, no secrecy now, made it easier to be bold. We walked into the living room and stood in the space between the kitchen counter, dining table, and sofa. "I took the *tumi*. From the museum."

"*You* did?" gasped Chelsea.

"Yes, and I had to because it's for a very good cause." With Chelsea, I had to choose my words carefully. It was fine to blurt out the truth with Ollie and he had a knack of being able to cut to the most vital business at hand. "A very, very important cause that most people," I nodded towards the window, "don't even know about."

"But you stole something that doesn't belong to you, Francesco, you can't do that."

"But, C, what if I took it because the cause was more important than the law?" Ollie nodded solemnly.

"It doesn't matter. You cannot break the law and expect everything to be okay. That's why it's the law."

"And if the law is wrong, shouldn't we do something about it? Shouldn't we take action if something is unjust?"

"No, no, not like this." She began to pace in what limited space she could. "This is all wrong. How could you do this?"

"With a crowbar and a balaclava, probably..."

"It will free thousands of people from... from... "

"Injustice?" Ollie contributed.

"Yes, and persecution and torture." Chelsea was staring at the floor as she walked up one way and down the next, turning on the heel of her filthy socks. "I didn't steal it anyway; I am repatriating it. For the Yarina people."

She stopped. "Who?" Her lip curled. "You did steal it and it doesn't matter who or what for. You have to give it back."

"Chels, listen, I thought you would be supportive of Frankie, you understand what it means to make a stand for something you believe in and that's all he's done."

"No, Oliver, no, it's nothing like what I do, nothing at all like it. I raise awareness of serious issues that affect people all over the world, I petition governments and politicians, I bring together like minded people to speak truth to power, I campaign for things that matter to me, and you, and Francesco. I don't steal, I don't break things, I don't hurt anyone. By stealing those artefacts, he is hurting the people that are trying to make the world a better place, he is risking your livelihood, he is jeopardising his own life, and he is ruining our friendship. Yes, Frankie, our friendship." She turned to face me now. "I thought we were friends and if you are bringing stolen goods into my flat then, I'm sorry, but you are risking that relationship because I don't want to be accused of harbouring a criminal or handling stolen goods and thrown into prison, even one of the nice, open ones, and I don't want a criminal record, all because you did something stupid for something you believe in. I don't want any of it." If I remember rightly, she even stamped her foot at this point.

With all of the potency taken out of the air and Chelsea's tirade seemingly over, the noticeable silence was all consuming.

"What about this party then, eh?" ventured Ollie.

"... Oh yes! The party. It was just some of the guys I went to the exhibition with."

"Didn't you speak to Noah Wright?" I shouldn't have asked - or perhaps I should, it's difficult to say what actions you take that you later regret because sometimes they turn out to reveal a lot about people based on what they do next. Maybe I knew what I was doing. After all, we both knew the answer to the question.

"Who? Oh, you mean the Democracy Coffee guy, yes, yeah, we spoke. Anyway, I have to get changed and then I have work to do." She pranced straight to her bedroom and closed the door behind her.

"What's got into her?" I didn't want to offer my guess. "Right. Now she knows so we have to be more careful about who knows about all this. Who else knows?" Now he knew enough to get him into trouble, it didn't make sense to withhold anything else from him.

"The guys that planned it all out."

"Guys? How many guys?"

"Two. I assume. Ernesto and Marcos from the group I've been going to." I thought for a moment and realised that although I knew they knew about the theft, there were no assurances that they had kept it to themselves.

"And do you have any evidence tying them to this?"

"No."

"Do they have any evidence tying you to this?"

"No. I don't know. Like what?"

"Any record of the conversations that took place, any personal items, anything that connects you to them." Wracking my brains, I couldn't think of anything specific. I was in the clear when it came to embroiling WMSCACE into it. That is, assuming Ernesto had given my driving licence, photo, and household bill to someone already so that they could sort out my British passport. What if he hadn't? What if he still had them? The clock wasn't just ticking - the alarm was ringing. I needed to see him and fast.

"Shit."

"No, no, no, don't say 'shit', don't say that. I don't want to have the fuzz kicking down our door. You need to sort this mess out - now!"

I pulled out my phone and looked for Ernesto's number. He needed to know that I had secured the *tumi* - and the mask, but purely by accident - and I wanted to know how he was getting on with helping me to get indefinite leave to remain.

"Hold on…" Ollie furrowed his brow and walked to their bedroom as I listened to the dial tone. He banged on the door. "Chels. Chels. Come here a sec." Voicemail.

"Hey, it's Frankie. I've got the… things you wanted. Let me know when you want me to get it to you. I'm home all day today so call me or drop me a text. Bye."

"Yes?"

"Chels, you said something and it stuck with me."

"Good! I am pleased you are seeing my side of things. We can't get involved in…"

"No," he held up a finger. "You said 'those artefacts'. You said 'stealing those artefacts, he is hurting people'." I hung up, craning to hear what was being said. "You only saw the knife that Frankie showed me."

She halted; an expression developed that suggested she had been quite offended. "Whatever do you mean?"

"You only saw one artefact so why did you say 'those artefacts'?"

I was interested too now. "Yeah."

"Nothing, I mean, no, I didn't."

"You did," I said. "Who was at the party?"

306

"Look, I had a couple of drinks, that's all. Maybe I'm not thinking straight this morning."

"You were thinking straight enough to decide that Frankie had broken the law and you wanted no part of it. Why did you say 'those' and who was at the party?" It occurred to me that Ollie may have been wasted as a security guard and he might be better off as a private investigator. When he had to get to the answer, he pushed all the necessary buttons. At his insisting tone, Chelsea's throat turned red.

"I'm too tired to talk right now."

"Someone told you about the other item, didn't they? But there was no way you could have found out on the news because we only saw it just before you came home."

"Babes, can we not do this here." Then I was convinced that this was bigger than a late night out, sure, I had my suspicions but now they were confirmed. Even Ollie took a step back as he realised what had happened. He clammed up, turned about, grabbed his coat, and slammed the door kind-of-shut as he left the flat. Chelsea turned to me. "Thanks for your help, Frankie. It's all fucked up now because of you." She disappeared back into her room and whatever she did next was muffled by her turning her radio up and my phone ringing.

Carrying a millennium old relic is tricky at the best of times, I'm sure, but two at the same time must be absolutely terrifying. Every step I took was punctuated by the backpack thumping against me, every rattle gave me palpitations about whether I was damaging what I had concealed within. What would be worse - desecrating a sacred, irreplaceable relic but at least it could have the opportunity to fulfil its new purpose or keeping it in pristine condition but having it taken from me and imprisoned without it ever seeing it propel the Yarina into action.

Getting on the bus was another leg of the journey which filled me with trepidation. I eyed the other passengers suspiciously, wondering if they knew what I had in my possession or if they somehow knew who I was and what I was up to. I looked at the man in the lumberjack shirt and puffer jacket a little too long, considering whether or not he was an undercover police officer, until he stared back at me and frowned. The girl with the buggy and hooped earrings shot out a 'What?' at me and my eyes flitted to the sky beyond the bus's mud-spattered windows.

I had to hop off the X21 and walk through the courtyard of the University. From ground level, it was a vast lawn sliced into triangles by concrete and stone upon which students and staff, and even visitors, would meander, congregating in small groups, sitting on spaces of grass where they could. A food market had been erected and the sizzling sound and smell of pork cobs with apple sauce triggered that hunger I had been suppressing for the past eighteen hours or so. From the top of the Joseph Chamberlain Memorial Clock Tower - which everyone called 'Old Joe' - the courtyard resembles a Trivial Pursuit counter.

Dominating one corner was the grey steel block, decorated with an off-gold colour zig-zagging through it, made up of panels and beams, which housed the library. I recalled bumping into Eva, before even the idea of the predicament I now found myself in had been a possibility.

Now I returned to the same location to try and resolve everything that had been set in motion since then. I cut through the lawns, sticking to the stone paving, and weaving between dawdling students.

I felt like a trespasser after the call from Paul Holding. According to the University, I shouldn't be there and I was convinced that my pass card would not let me through the security gates at the Main Library but that was where he wanted to meet and, in my nervousness, I agreed without thinking about the hurdles. Every glance felt like accusatory glares. Private conversations were knowing whispers. I held a hand over my eyes to shield it from the sun but it might well have been an interrogation lamp in a police interview room.

In front of the library, along a dissecting stone path, ran a raised stone wall with a wooden, slatted bench topped along it. It provided the user with a view of some of the quad and a grove of tall elms. The bench, several metres long, ran beside a main pedestrian thoroughfare so it was regularly busy and tricky to get a perch at times. Yet, with the positioning of the trees, nobody would be able to easily watch what two people said if they sat talking there.

"Do you have it?" I noted the grey in Ernesto's eyebrows twitch.

"Nice to see you too," I ventured.

"You have it?" His voice was low and I strained to hear over the sounds of passing conversation and late Spring jollity. It was an ideal spot for couples with their young children and several times the flow of traffic was upset by two buggies pushed wheel to wheel so the parents could spark up a chat. He glanced around furtively whilst I took my backpack off and placed it between my feet. Between the open zip, a curved tip of gold glinted skyward. "Don't." He growled. Getting it out was a thought that had most definitely not crossed my mind.

"And…" I tilted the bag so he could see further inside and his eyes narrowed at the sight of the Moche mask.

"Well, you are quite the rogue, aren't you? Where exactly is the *tumi*?"

"It's safe but I want my passport before I give it to you. You promised that you could help and I agreed to help you back. Now it's time to honour that promise."

"So, what is this then, huh?"

"Proof. I took them. I have them. And you can get them both, just as soon as I get my passport." He crossed his arms, leaning back to rest on the bench. His eyes turned from me and out, through the tall, aged trunks, below which there were two Asian women laughing and smiling whilst their sons, perhaps no older than three or four, tumbled and rolled in the warmth of the sunlit lawn. Ernesto exhaled and the bell in the clock tower rung twelve. I watched him, at first, then, after just a moment or so, I zipped the bag up and swung it on to my back.

A taught palm gripped the top of the bag, pushing it down, and I felt the fingers, thick as rope, close around the handle, bunching the material together and holding firm.

"Does Marcos need to look after this, Francesco?" Twisting my neck around, the thug leered over me, so close I could see the odd patch in his close-cropped stubble. "Or should I just take it now and you can go home?" I considered writhing loose but I could only do that by releasing myself from the backpack straps, and that would mean losing the mask. It was also likely that Marcos' other hand might spring to life for some other purpose.

"As soon as you give me my passport, I will give you the *tumi* and the mask."

"Listen here, *gusano*, I want my *tumi* and you are going to give it to me." All the control, the calmness, all of his power that I had been so entranced by dissipated. There was anger in his words and his top lip curled in a snarl. It might have been because I was unable to do so, but I didn't shift back or cower. His face shifted back to the controlled dignity with which he had addressed his followers and he returned to his original pose. "You are smart, Francesco, I know I made the right choice in choosing you. I admire smart people and, you know, if you do ever come to Val Verde when the *Partido* take power, I am sure I can find a position that would stimulate you intellectually. For now though, I will keep your paperwork and your ID and your passport and you will give me the mask. But I will make sure you have your passport in your hands just as soon as I have the *tumi* in mine."

"And I will give you the *tumi*."

"I know." He ran a hand through his hair. "*¿Qué marca es esa mochila?*"

Marcos grunted in reply; "Eastpak."

311

"When we next meet, bring that same rucksack with the *tumi* in it. I will take the mask now, for safekeeping of course." At his nod, Marcos roughly unzipped the bag and slid the mask out, concealing it inside his puffer jacket. "But I want something else too."

"You will have everything. I don't have anything else." Marcos shook me once, vigorously, and I stopped speaking.

"You will give me Eva." Ernesto crossed his legs. I felt a chill as the morning turned to afternoon. "She likes you, doesn't she? And you like her, of course. She is very beautiful and loyal too. I should say she was loyal - to me, to our cause - but now she turns to…" The pause and the vertical flick of his pupils hurt. "…you. I want her loyalty again but this time I want more than only loyalty." As he spoke, he leered closer, the sweet aftershave smell piercing through the lawn trimmings and heather.

"I'm sorry but I don't know what you mean…" He raised a hand like a conductor and I stopped talking.

"Okay, enough. You don't have the *tumi*, so we are going to end this meeting now. When you are ready to bring me the knife, we can meet again, but I suggest you think quickly because your days in this country are numbered, are they not?"

Chapter 24 – Sunday 19th June (4 days to go...)

Without my backpack or the mask or my paperwork, my ID, or my passport, I felt like I'd been mugged. I was an idiot to have thought I might have outwitted Ernesto, or at least negotiated with him more successfully. I had gotten away from them as quickly as I could without looking like I was afraid or panicking. They moved off in unison and I watched from my vantage point fifty metres or so away. In lock step, Marcos followed Ernesto, scanning the surroundings as they progressed, Ernesto walking with purpose out of the quad and towards the city centre. I turned and slumped against the brickwork of the building, letting my shoulders droop, free of the backpack but not the memory of Marcos' grip.

The uncertainty I thought I had overcome returned. What could I do? What power did I have? I gripped my palms together and pressed. Thoughts of calling the police and getting them to sort all this out crossed my mind; after all, the most prison time I would serve was ten years, wasn't it? No, no, I couldn't do that to myself. Who else could help? Eva? I'd managed to piss her off already so if she knew I'd stolen the knife, despite me promising to her that I wouldn't, there would be no winning her back.

Ernesto was right; my days were numbered and there were only a handful left before the Home Office would be coming for me. Rubbing my temples provided no relief for the situation. I needed that passport and the only course of action seemed to me to go back to the flat, get the *tumi*, and get it to Ernesto as quickly as possible. This provided some sense of certainty but did not provide me with any comfort that what I needed to do would be the right course of action or would be easy. Perhaps Ollie or Chelsea would try and stop me but there was no way either of them could hold me back.

"Do you want to tell me what the hell's going on?" I half-jumped, half-stood, staggering away from my brick barricade.

"Ollie! What are you doing here?"

"I followed you," he said, with poorly concealed pride in his voice. "I was worried about you…" he continued, "…and I don't want the only person that knows I aided and abetted a criminal going and telling the cops."

I shook my head. "No sense in doing that or we're both in the shit."

"So, who were those two?"

"You saw that? They're the guys that set up the… I hate the word theft; can we call it 'extraction'? You know, like they say about hostages in those SAS books you read."

He shrugged. "You stole it, but whatever helps you sleep at night."

"So, they wanted me to give them the *tumi* but I wasn't sure if he would come through on his side of the deal." As clouds gathered and the sky dimmed, we both recognised it and started the walk to the bus stop.

"What deal?"

"It's complicated." As I should have known, as anyone reading this will know, I assume, saying 'It's complicated' never placates the listener. It merely stokes an interest that might have been simply simmering away on the stove to the point where it bubbles over.

"Are you saying I'm too stupid to understand?" Ollie turned to face me. "Listen, I get enough of that shit from Chels, she always saying how Leave voters are imbeciles, well, I'm not and I don't expect that kind of thing from you!"

"No, no, that's not what I meant - I meant that it's *actually* complicated, like it's a long, long story."

"Twenty minutes long or 'Lord of The Rings' long?"

It took up most of the bus ride to explain exactly why Ernesto was so desperate for this knife and our conversation - although I was the one doing much of the talking - covered who the Yarina are (from 'never heard of them? Did they play against Celtic in the Europa League last year?' to 'wow, that's actually proper crazy'), a rough overview of the politics of Val Verde ('General Arius, communist, then Velazquez, fascist, then Esperanza, fascist, San Marcos, communist, now Calderon, fascist. Have I got that right?'), explained what WMSCACE did, why the *tumi* was so important to the Yarina - and to Ernesto -, and then who Ernesto was and what he hoped he could achieve by repatriating the knife to Val Verde.

"So is Ernesto fascist or communist?"

"Neither, he's more centre-ground, I think. He wants the Yarina to be free and neither the fascists nor the communists improved rights for indigenous people. If either a fascist or a communist takes over from Calderon, then the situation for the Yarina will never improve."

"When are the elections?"

"Next year. Ernesto is like the head of a government-in-waiting-in-exile, he thinks."

"And what do you think, about all this?"

"I don't know. I've lived here my whole life but, at the moment, it seems like I'm being asked to speak for a whole nation I've never even met." He nodded but he wouldn't be able to empathise. The razor-sharp sound escaping from the headphones on the teenager two rows behind us told me that I did not have to worry about him overhearing us. The top deck was always a place safe from intruding eyes and inquisitive ears. That said, it did attract its fair share of drunks, thugs, and tramps, so intrigued nostrils often discovered more than they expected.

"Look, I don't know everything you know and I'm only one person but if you need any help, you only have to ask."

"Thanks, but I'm not sure what to do next, so I wouldn't know how you could help, unless you could magic up a visa, another *tumi*, or a shitload of money, I don't know what to ask of you."

He sucked through his teeth. "Listen, you're a good guy and I'm happy to help but, my God, you can't make a decision. What do you need right now? You need a solution, don't you?" I nodded. "All of those things are just parts of a problem and maybe we need them, maybe we don't, but the way I see it we need you to be able to stay in the UK and we need the Yarina to be free. Let's tackle one thing at a time. The visa - how do we get you one of those?"

"We can't. I'm being deported so I can't apply for one."

"Okay," he knotted his fingers together. "Who says?"

"The Home Office."

"Ri-i-ight... After you've been deported, can you apply for one and come straight back?"

"Not for two years."

"I see...," his fingers, meeting at the tips like a church spire, tapped his pursed lips. "I see. Two years... What if you had a passport?"

"Same. I need a birth certificate and I think my parents have the only copy. And it gets worse. If I get arrested and charged with having stolen the *tumi*, then I might not be allowed to apply for a visa for ten years."

"Damn! How do you know so much about this?"

"Eva's working in a law firm that specialises in immigration."

"And she knows all about that?"

"Not the *tumi* thing, not the 'extraction', no, I've kept that to myself - and you can't tell her either. She made me promise I wouldn't do it and now I have, and I think I pissed her off too, so, yeah, that's going really well, thanks for asking." If it wasn't one problem it was another.

"Why do you think I'd tell her? I've not even met the bird. Are you going to invite her over one day?" I

317

smiled and he jabbed an elbow into my ribs. I didn't mind the discomfort. Nodding, I let my gaze drift and stare out of the window, away from the musty smell of the bus, and out to the tall grey and red buildings that were both recognisable and indistinct. Ollie joined me in easy silence, the journey bobbing and lurching to our destination.

"I don't mean to pry but she doesn't want you to be a thief, does she?"

"No way, no, she warned me off it. Said she didn't trust Ernesto and didn't like his plan."

"And you ignored her?"

"Yeah," I laughed. "Stupid, right?"

"We all do crap like that, though. You must have seen that Chels and I aren't exactly Jay-Z and Beyoncé!" He jangled his door keys, as if calculating how heavy they were and feeling for the comfort in that weight, that was regular and consistent and never changed regardless of the number of doors open or locked. "You know we fight." He looked sharply for a denial or an expression of surprise, which I couldn't give him. "I think it's too much."

"I'm nobody to talk to about relationship advice."

"Maybe not but you used to date her, you know what she can be like when she's fixated on something." Dragging up the dirty laundry from old relationships was never my style but Ollie had no problem with it, happily telling Chelsea about old girlfriends or flings. He could swat away the griping with an easily spoken phrase such as 'Yes, but I'm with *you* now so you're an upgrade'. It was glib but C seemed to warm like the centre of a soft-boiled egg. "And stop putting yourself down, man! Fake it, till you make it. I'm sure your relationship with Eva is going better than mine."

We paused at the door but Chelsea was either out or in her room.

"We'll see. I should call her, shouldn't I?"

"I've told you, be more decisive. And, anyway, you know the answer to that, don't you?" I nodded and started to text her. "No, women love it when you ring them. It shows you're making more of an effort than sending a text - and they can tell you're not with anyone else when you're doing it…"

"What are you going to say to Chelsea?"

"I don't know. I.. I don't know. Maybe I was jumping to conclusions. I was thinking about it earlier, when I was following you, and I've got to change too. We can't keep arguing and I know some of it is my fault and that. You know what mate, I'm going out again. I'm going to go and buy something nice to make for dinner. You want anything?" I shook my head and he ducked out of the front door, that shuddered ajar, before he gave it a heave to clunk it sort of shut. I looked at my phone, opened the Phonebook app, scrolled to Eva's name, hovered my thumb over the telephone symbol, and then selected 'Compose Message' instead.

As it was a Sunday, Eva was free to come over. I couldn't tell from the tone of her reply whether she would be happy to see more or not after the way we left it before.

Ominously, her reply included the words 'We need to talk'. If ever there was a phrase to instil a primeval fear and existential dread in a person it was those four words. I was at a loss as to how I should reply so I didn't and I left the conversation resolved with her agreeing to drop by in the next hour or so. That left me with plenty of time to chew my nails, pace the kitchen floor level, and fret about what it was we needed to talk about and if that involved ending our very brief relationship before it had truly flourished.

When she knocked on the door, it was like a starting pistol. I leapt up and yanked the door almost off its hinges.

"Hi," I panted.

"Hi."

"Come in, come in."

"What's up with you?"

"Nothing, just happy to see you." We looked at each other in a sheepish manner, holding back. She pecked me on the cheek and I was still none the wiser.

Can I get you two a drink?" Ollie mooned from over the kitchen counter, the grin on his face more of a lecherous leer than a welcoming beam.

"Eva, Ollie, Ollie, Eva," I mumbled.

"No, I'm alright. Thank you." Ollie gave me a curt nod before going back to his cooking. Come and sit down - I've got some news." She was pregnant. She was leaving me. She was running away to the circus. I stopped myself, gained some composure and sat on the sofa next

320

to her. "It's only early days but I might have found a solution to your problem."

"Which problem?"

"The deportation. Is there anything else?"

"No, no, go on."

"I can't, I mean, not yet at least. I had to come over to tell you that I'm sort of making progress in one direction that could mean you won't get deported but it's still too soon to confirm anything and, I, I'm sorry, I'm really not sure how much I can really tell you yet... One of the partners I work with has found something. A paper trail. Uh, I don't know what I can say... It could be nothing, it could be something, it all depends on what he can dig up and, and, so on... Maybe I will have a drink. What have you got?"

I sprung up again, a gunshot victim in reverse, blood pumping back into me. "Coke? Beer? Tea?"

"Yeah, can I have a tea?"

The distraction of that gave my heart to resume its normal pace and, I assumed, Eva to put her thoughts into words again. So far, all she had said was vague and noncommittal and, whilst I had no problem seeing her and gauging from her tone that we - our relationship - were fine, I wanted to know more.

"Can you tell me anything about what you've found?"

"What *he's* found, the guy at my office, he... never mind... I can't say much more than I've said..." Which wasn't a great deal. "Let me just say that if what

321

he's found pays off, you've got nothing to worry about with regard to living, working, studying, whatever, in the UK."

"Good, good, I'll keep my fingers crossed." Not just for her own investigation but also for Ernesto's attempts at getting me a passport. I knew it would be shady so I didn't want to jeopardise anything by telling Eva all about it yet. She didn't trust Ernesto and telling her I was relying on him to get me out of this dilemma, would put me firmly in his camp, which, despite it being a turn of phrase, might have been in a completely different campsite, in another county, a long, long way from her campsite and, right now, I wanted to be curling up under the stars, watching the embers of the fire smoulder, our legs sweaty and intertwined inside a sleeping bag...

"About the other night…" I handed her a mug and she waited until I was sat and looking dead at her again to continue. "I feel really bad about having a go at that woman in front of you. It was your night too and I can't help but feel I upset you."

"Me? No, no…"

"I couldn't listen to what she said and not speak up, but that's me. You didn't want to say anything and that's fine, it's not your fight, it's mine, and you were there to enjoy yourself and have a nice night. I'm sorry if I made you feel uncomfortable."

"Oh. Okay."

She sipped her tea and let me think about what she had said. When she put the mug down, I remembered what Ollie had said about needing to be more decisive so I leant forward and kissed her. Properly. On the lips. I

322

almost didn't think about Ollie, beavering away on make-up dinner in the kitchen.

"I forgive you."

"What?"

"I forgive you..."

"No, Frankie, I'm not asking you to forgive me. That's not what I'm saying." I waited, hoping for an explanation as I tried to figure out where I'd got this wrong. "I'm not asking for you to accept an apology from me. There's nothing I said to that woman I would not say again if she was standing right here. I'm just sorry that you were uncomfortable because of what I said. So, there, *¿Lo entiendes?*" I nodded but then shook my head.

"So why did you say 'sorry'?"

"I'm sorry that you were uncomfortable. I really am. These people are always talking like they know best, like they have all the answers, but they don't. They don't know the first thing about Val Verde, or Venezuela, or Chile, or Brazil, or anything. You are better qualified to be a museum curator or archaeologist than those idiots."

"So you're not sorry to me, you're sorry *for* me...?"

"Exactly. I am sympathising with you because you must have felt really awkward. That your date was having a go at one of the people who thinks they're protecting your cultural heritage when all they are doing is profiteering from it. I'm glad someone broke in and stole that stuff, I really am." I noticed that the slurping way she drank her tea did not bother me in the slightest.

323

"Right, well, I'm over it now, yeah. I agree with you. Someone had to do something, didn't they? To liberate the, the stolen artefacts, and relics, and stuff, to repatriate them for the good of the… thu… the Yarina and the Zuni and the Val Verdean people…" 'Stop, stop, stop!' called the voice in my head.

"Damn right," she said. "I have to go but I will call you again. Soon. With news, I hope. I have a really important meeting down in London on Wednesday morning so I will have to update you on Thursday, yeah?"

"Thursday? That's the deadline from the Home Office."

"I know." She stood, planting her feet and putting her right hand on her hip, kicking it out with a flourish as she did. "I will do everything I can to make sure you are not getting blindfolded and forced on some RAF Hercules on a runway in Leicestershire or somewhere. You are staying here." Had I been from the Home Office, she would have had no arguments from me. Then she kissed me properly, on the lips. "With me."

There wasn't a single place I would rather be at that moment. Despite the mess, typical of a student flat, the enclosed spaces, and the catastrophic events I had got myself into, Eva's kiss and fresh dressing gown after a hot shower embrace made all of those worries evaporate. I looked at her, deeply, hoping that this would be one of the new memories I might create and that it wouldn't be only me thinking about moments that have happened in the past and will never be experienced in the same way again but perhaps both of us will have shared memories that endure.

"Oh, so you've told her, have you?" squawked Chelsea, striding out of her room. "Or are you in on this stupid heist as well?"

"What..?"

"I don't want that thing in my flat so you two need to get rid of it. Pronto!" Chelsea lunged at us as she spoke, jabbing her bony fingers and appearing like an anaemic Barbie doll.

"Frankie, what is she talking about?" Her hands slid down my arms to fall by her side. Her face bore the serious look I had seen before, her nostrils flared and eyebrows tightened. "Francesco." I couldn't help it; I glanced at my bedroom. She looked first at Chelsea who had abruptly receded into silence. Then the bedroom door.

"Eva." I didn't know what I was planning to say after that. "It's not what you think…" Oh, no, it was *exactly* what she was thinking and I was too naïve to realise that there was nothing I could say that would prevent her from striding over the short distance to my bedroom door, flinging it open, adopting a bewildered expression when presented with my elaborate pet project, before almost immediately spying the glistening gold handle peering from its hiding place inside the foam terrain under the recently detached model phone box.

I awaited the lambasting that I expected would issue forth from her at any moment but she prised the *tumi* out by the pommel, turned and walked to the kitchen table, and slapped it down with an almighty clang that I thought wouldn't just startle anyone in the block but rouse their ancestors from the grave.

Without a word, she extended a soft, caramel palm and gesticulated firmly at the knife.

I stood and gawped, unsure whether to try a 'How on earth did that get there?' or to try and take charge of this disaster. Not only had I seemed weak for not having a pop at the old lady at the gala for her bigoted views but now I had broken my promise to her that I would have nothing to do with Ernesto's scheme.

"I had to," I ventured. "Ernesto promised that he would get me a passport if I could get him the *tumi*. I know I promised I wouldn't but that was before." I tried to fend off the impending insults and accusations. "These are the lengths I would go to to be able to stay here. With you."

Her deep coal eyes bored into me like my lecturers reading an essay that had been typed up in Comic Sans. "With me. With me?" Her voice was level and steady. I thought she was about to hit me but she leaned on the table. God, I loved her like this. All simmering rage and potent destruction. "What makes you think you ever *had* me?"

"...We kissed... and..."

She grasped the handle off the knife and hoisted it above her head; the Sword of Damocles held by a lithe wrist rather than a horsehair. In a flash, she brought it down as hard as she could, pizza-cutter blade first, and smashed our kitchen table into two, the *tumi* clattering to the floor, and the halves of the table crashing into each other with a bang that deafened the first.

"You made a promise to me that you would not do anything so stupid as to go along with that idiot's insane scheme and instead you lie to my face, take me to that party, steal this damn knife, try to hide it here where nobody will find it but I find it, don't I?, and then try to tell me that you did it for *me*? Are you as *insane* as Ernesto or as *stupid* as Marcos?" She didn't waver and neither did her tone. Before I could give her an answer, neither of which would have painted me in the best of lights, she snatched up her coat and bag and stormed out. Or rather, she would have stormed out and, no doubt, slammed the door for dramatic effect but the lock was stuck and I had to jerk it up and wiggle it to open the door, shepherding her back a step so that she wasn't hit by the corner of it and then, after she had walked through the threshold without a word, I had to force it to close with a shoulder.

"She's fucked our table!" shrieked Chelsea. Her colourless cheeks were pulled open in shock, her demeanour like that of the village priest's wife at her first post-match rugby club social.

"You've fucked more than that," laughed Ollie over the kitchen counter, before stopping short, realising that his pun had back-fired. Chelsea's expression changed faster than he could crack the ring pull on his second 'Chef's cooking lager'. Chelsea wasn't in the mood for it and it became apparent that there would be no make-up anything tonight and she huffed into her bedroom. Ollie went back to the hob with a pall-bearer's look on his face and I surveyed the damage.

327

Chapter 25 – Monday 20th June (3 days to go...)

I wonder whether highly charged moments in life have a knock-on effect when it comes to dreams. Some say that it's eating cheese late at night that causes vivid dreams. Others say it is something traumatic that can bring a long-forgotten moment to the front of your mind. I'm no expert but it felt as if anything particularly emotionally volatile in my waking life unleashed the past whilst I slept. It had been hard enough to get to sleep with everything racing through my mind.

The clock was ticking on a final decision from the Home Office. In less than one hundred hours, I would be informed whether I was going to be deported or not. It seemed to me like a sure thing that my life in Britain was about to end - twenty years of obliviously going through my life as if I had nothing to worry about. I almost pined for the ignorance again. I stared up at the ceiling and images faded in and vanished. Would they kick the front door in like Papá's stories, with no regard for the calm they would be destroying?

Now that the University had suspended me, I had no grounds to argue that I had to stay for my education and there did not seem to be any reason for them to reverse their decision. What weighed on my mind wasn't anything like disappointment at not getting to finish what I had started or missing out on learning something that would give me a better chance of a career or a better life ahead of me. What I was thinking about was that because they had kicked me out, the decision about what to do with my life could be put off no longer. Going from school, to college, to University seemed a normal route down which to go. What I realised was that by following the well-trodden path that others who had walked it before me swore was the best - and only - option for me, I was simply delaying the vital choice I had to make. What was I going to do with my life? Ernesto's razor-sharp questions that had drawn me deeper into his orbit still stung. 'What have you really got to look forward to? What is it that makes you jump out of bed in the morning?' I was no closer to answering either of those. Visualising Ernesto, I clenched my jaw and tensed my shoulders.

Most of all, thinking of him only made it easier to picture Eva. I had fucked that up, hadn't I? It would take something special to mend the bridges in that relationship. If she was still mad at me for not defending her, our, cultural heritage, I could do nothing more honourable than repatriate not just one but two valuable antiquities. Obviously, it would not be sensible to bring that up as a defence plea. Now I had broken my promise to her, could I make it up by returning the knife and the mask? Maybe, but then if I had nothing to give to Ernesto, there was no way I could avoid extradition. Eva had hinted at something, vaguely possible that might help, but without more information, I couldn't hang my hopes on that - and there was no guarantee she would even choose to help me now that she had discovered the *tumi*.

After hours of tossing these thoughts around inside my head, I finally got to sleep. I wished I had never closed my eyes.

I was back in our old house Digbeth. It seemed so much smaller in this memory than most recent dreams. It began in my bedroom, where the winter sun fell between the plastic slats of the blind, creating the effect of prison bars over my bed, desk, and bookcase, then dog-legging at the foot of the wall.

On my bedside table, I took in the lamp with the ceramic body that I was sure had broken when I moved into my current flat, my old Nokia, some college textbook, and an empty can of Coke.

The me inside the old me's head felt my body heave itself out of bed and lurch unsteadily towards the door. A warm dressing gown shrugged on around my shoulders and the handle of the bedroom door turned.

On the upstairs landing, I heard raised voices echo through the ground floor. That wasn't unusual so it did not appear to be anything more than part of this long lost memory; or a version of the past that was recreated with common experiences all mashed together. Perhaps in the real experience, I had not worn a dressing gown. Yet I felt an undeniable familiarity. Compelled, my recollection moved me forward, the blue carpet poking between my bare toes like hot sand, and onward to the top of the stairs, where I continued down, towards the front door, my hands on the balustrades. At the foot, my view swung round to the right, along the hallway, past the lounge on my left, and on to the dining room and kitchenette.

A nauseous sensation flooded through me, like staring over the edge of a cliff at the moment that the wind really picks up and the waves crash against the jagged boulders at the bottom that await a misstep. Mamá and Papá were stood, their backs to me, and hunched over the dining table. Between them there was an electricity - I think it was love and now, as someone who can empathise, I am sure. Their gestures to one another were unconscious - her hand glancing his, his shoulder bumping against hers, her fingers untangling her long, dark hair, his fist tapping the tabletop as he spoke.

"*Buenos dias, cariño*," spoke Mamá first, looking at me from over her shoulder. "You're going to be late. Don't you have a class first thing?"

"No, second period," came the mumbled and alien reply. This old me, the avatar my sleeping mind inhabited, trudged towards sustenance.

"Are you going to join us again?" asked Papá. I vicariously experienced the motion of my heavy head turning to look at him and shrug. "Ah! *Perezoso…*" Mamá tutted at him. I could see the cornflakes poured into a bowl, hear the milk splash over them, and salivate at the spoonful of sugar sprinkled over them but none of that alleviated the disquiet that made my stomach feel empty when it was full.

"It won't be like last time," she said.

"Huh?"

"In London, you remember? We've told you about this already." My frown was replaced with a steeled glare. "What? It will be fine." They both carried on with their planning; lists of people with phone numbers and emails to go through, stacks of flyers to be thrown on the floor or handed back to them by disinterested passers-by, three or four folded fabric banners bearing their demands in Latin American Spanish, a loud-speaker, which was not something I had noticed that they had ever brought out before, and, leaning against the far side of the table, a forest of wooden handles sticking up, attached to reinforced plastic signs, seemingly made for purposefully for this occasion.

"It's a bit much, isn't it?" I commented. Dad grunted.

"You don't have to come if you don't want to," said Mamá. "Nobody is going to force you."

"You're wasting your time," interjected Papá. "Francesco has never supported what we do. He doesn't understand what it means to us, let him stay here, he can watch his TV shows and play his computer games."

"Sounds fine to me."

"*Ciertamente*, your majesty," he snorted. His fist pumped against the table again. Mamá pulled out a chair for me and I sat, cornflakes and orange juice carefully balanced in one hand.

"I don't know why you bother with all this," I vented, between mouthfuls. "Nothing ever changes." They both looked at me. The space between us hung heavy like steam.

"All that education and what does he know…" Mamá tutted again.

"He thinks he knows everything, is what he knows!"

"Tell me then, what has changed? What have all your protests accomplished? You phone people to get them to donate, you give out flyers in the city centre, you have market stalls now, and you're going down to the embassy again to do what? Get your heads kicked in by the police?"

"*¿Y que?* What do you want us to do?"

"Just stop it. Just stop, that's it."

"And what should we do if we're not trying to change things for the better? Huh?"

"I didn't say that. I don't want you getting hurt."

"But it's okay for other people to get hurt. People we grew up with. People like us. That's what you think?" Mamá leaned over me, her throat turning red.

"*Querida, cálmate por favor.*" Papá put his hand on her shoulder and she huffed and turned away, striding into the kitchen. "I know you worry about us, *hijo*, but we're okay. We know the risks in doing what we do, but we do it anyway. If we can bring freedom to our people, then it's worth it."

The spoon clattered on the side of the bowl. Mamá looked across to me again, a dark volatility in her glower. "And what about me, huh? I was all alone while you two were off chanting and fighting and whatever! You abandoned me!" I remember vividly speaking very slowly, in the Spanish that had earned me another GCSE, that they were so keen to ridicule. "*¡Me abandonaste! ¡Me dejaste!* Do you understand? *¿Entiendes lo que te estoy diciendo?* Either of you?" I leapt up enraged; the fire in my chest searing open a barrel of pent-up anger that spewed out uncontrollably, taking over my words and actions. But it was a dream; yes, I felt let down but not like this, not at the time. The dream was a jumble of graphic memories reignited by my present state of high emotion. The way alcohol cracked open the secrets that I hoped were mine to conceal.

The orange juice surged forward, toppling over and flooding the table.

"Look what you've done!" Papá yelled.

"*¡Maldita sea!*" Mamá scrambled forward with a dish cloth in her hand.

"I don't care about all this… stuff, I don't. And you two have to stop or you'll get hurt!" I turned to address Dad. "Again!"

As my suddenly small, industrious mother extracted the hand-written lists, shook them, and draped those that had been caught in the tide on the back of the dining chairs, Papá stepped to me, chest square and chin out. I took a half step back.

"*Si lo entendi*, I understand just fine. You are too afraid to stand up to bullies. You don't want to roll your sleeves up when things aren't going your way, don't you?" Just as Mamá, in her faded home dress seemed smaller as she mopped up the mess I had made, Papá grew and loomed, filling my field of vision. "Then maybe you are not tough enough to be one of us. Maybe you are too scared to be a Cualquiera. Maybe you want to live with some other family." My heel felt the closeness of the imagined kitchen doorway. "Fine." He never took his eyes from me as he moved back to Mamá and the table. "But we're going without you and, even though you won't be there, you should know that we are campaigning for you, for us, and for people like us, even if you can't bring yourself to do it. And if you can't stand up to bullies, then maybe you deserve whatever you get from life."

I waited. Papá turned to Mamá and helped her arrange the papers, moving the electric megaphone away from the remaining liquid. She kept her eyes on the task at hand. I waited for one of them to look my way. Mamá went to the sink and wrung out the dish cloth, giving it a long rinse in hot water. Papá opened a pad and took out his pen and began trying to copy down the information that had been erased. I recall the feeling of fury at my father, the words that cut me the deepest, then the sense of disappointment and frustration that they would not reconsider what I felt was a fruitless and dangerous journey. I waited for those feelings to abate but they did not.

The alarm didn't ring and the sun did not glare through the window in my bedroom. I didn't need either of those things to sit bolt upright, catapulted forward from my slumber like a mouse trap. The time that has passed since then means I feel okay in admitting that I cried as soon as I awoke; not a soft sob, but a ghoulish wail that came from the darkness parts of me, the inside of a man - or, perhaps, a boy - that waits patiently for the moment when it breaks open, as if like a kraken breaching the surface of the ocean to strangle a vessel and drag it back down with it. After what seemed like an eternity, I had howled so long and so deeply that my body ached - across my shoulders, through my chest and back, and my eyes and nose stang with redness. It was nothing like I had experienced before or since and I don't long to repeat it. The feeling of anguish will never truly go, only subside at times, before reappearing like grief at unexpected moments. But the final vision within my dream was what launched me out of bed.

I had waited. The front door closed softly behind them, replacing one sort of silence for another. I listened for the ignition to turn in the second-hand hatchback. The wheels turned across the gravel in the driveway and the sound changed to smooth tarmac acceleration. I waited until I could be sure they had not forgotten anything and would turn the steering wheel back to the house. My feet felt cold on the blue carpet up the stairs. I searched it up on my computer. The mattress below me felt thinner, as if the slats beneath it were reaching up to shake hands with the grey bars of shadow and press me within their grip. I waited to hear a voice.

"Immigration Enforcement hotline, how can I help?"

Chapter 26 – Tuesday 21st June
(2 days to go...)

"Ollie," I said, giving away nothing about the previous night's awful recollection.

"What's up with you?"

"Forget all that, I need your help." At that, his ears seemed to prick up, keen to be useful and active and not simply annoying and active like he could often be.

"Sure."

"I, I mean, we, we need to get rid of that knife. The sooner it's gone the better. I think we should give it to Ernesto as soon as possible." He stroked his chin at this. "Yes, we should definitely give it to Ernesto because, firstly, perhaps he can do some good with it, and, secondly, with things being back to normal, or as much as possible, I might be able to make it up to Eva."

"Hmm," was his considered response. "I see what you mean and, don't get me wrong, I like this new decisive you. You've got a smile on your face for a change. But," and no great plan of action was ever met with a but, "doesn't that still mean you will get deported?"

"Not if Ernesto comes through with my passport - and that's where you come in." He crossed his arms but I was not to be deterred by defensive body language. "Can you get your mate, Mayhew, and the guys from the TA? I reckon if we go to meet Ernesto mob-handed, we can try and stop him from pulling a fast one." I waited to hear his acceptance of my plan.

"Didn't he tell you he wanted you to break up with Eva?"

"Yes, but that's the smart thing - *she's* already broken up with me! So now, technically, we're not together so I don't need to break up with her. If that works for Ernesto, I can try and win her back *after* he's got the *tumi*. You see?" I tapped the side of my head with my index finger. He shook his head in reply.

"No, it won't work. You need to think like him, don't you. Yes, you've got something he wants but he has something you want too. And he's got your home address too. If you're out of the country, what's stopping him coming over here and taking the knife?"

Maybe this wasn't the great or decisive plan I thought it might be. The wind was taken out of my sails and I slumped on a dining chair but found I was unable to rest my elbows and hold my head in my hands like some forlorn traveller who had missed their flight home because the dining table was in pieces on the floor in front of me. I'd put the *tumi* back in its hiding place - which, I realised, almost everybody who mattered now knew about. I was still energised though, despite the tepid reaction to my action plan. The horrible realisation that I was in this situation because of my own selfish response to disappointment had charged me with a voltage of urgency that hummed through my body. People talk about being in the flow and I had experienced that but this was more than that.

"Right, right, okay… mkay..." I had adopted the pose of Rodin's The Thinker. Ollie watched me without saying a word. My toe tapped an irregular rhythm. "What about if we hide it completely?"

He shook his head.

"Can we just give it back and say 'Sorry'?"

"Can we just hand ourselves in to the Police?"

After a few minutes, I was resigned to the fact that I didn't have a plan and I needed help. "Can you come up with anything?"

"Not this second but I will have a think. I mean, what are mates for?"

"So we're mates now?"

"Yeah," he affirmed. "We were flatmates but now we're mates mates."

Ollie's pleasant and convivial demeanour did not last long although, it must be said, he never treated me with anything less than a fresh form of friendship, a kind of new relationship bromance but without all the soppy outward expressions of emotion or oversharing, which he still thought was a bit 'gay', despite Chelsea and I protesting that he couldn't really still say that in the 21st Century, or in fact, at all.

I had to be happy with small victories for now and so his puppy-like eagerness to help and to be a mate remained unchanged. However, it was now out in the open that he and Chelsea were not getting on anywhere near like as well as he and I, and our collective flatfriendship was on very thin ice after everything that had happened most recently. Even if I managed to stay in the country, staying in the flat might not be possible.

Her xenophobic outburst, her sleeping with Noah - which I had inferred even though she had not yet admitted it - and, bizarrely, I didn't feel particularly aggrieved by that as I'm not her boyfriend any more. Perhaps I never truly was. Yet I still felt a strange pang of anger towards her, perhaps vicariously how I thought Ollie should have reacted, if he could have been sure at that point of what she had done - but, most of all, I was simmering with resentment that it was her who had told Eva about my theft of the knife.

When they entered into one another's orbit that morning, the mood was clear.

"Morning Francesco," Chelsea smiled. "Oliver."

"Hey, Frankie," Ollie smirked. "Chelsea."

I don't recall the last time we greeted one another with more than nods or grunts on weekdays, but I also didn't think that I was the real object of those greetings. By the afternoon, the poorly-concealed animosity was now exposed.

"Will you be coming to the rally on Thursday?" Chelsea asked.

"Huh?"

"The vote? The Brexit referendum? On Thursday?" She looked at me and me alone.

"Er, yeah, maybe, I haven't really thought about it." To say I had other things on my mind would have been a serious understatement.

"You must come, Francesco, we could really do with your support. It should be a real carnival atmosphere too. I've coordinated with the girls and they will be bringing balloons, champers, and even a bunch of European flag sunglasses. It will be epic."

"No invite for me then," grumbled Ollie.

"You want to go?" I queried.

"I am going but don't expect me to be there with her. I'm going with a few of the lads from work. We'll have a few pints in the Head In Clouds, then on to the Dog's Bollocks, and then we'll join in a singsong with a few cans in the square. Stick with her dull lot of smug... smug... smugfaces if you want or come and have a laugh with us."

It was Chelsea's turn to smirk.

"What? You think it's funny?"

"No, no, I think it's actually a bit sad." Chelsea thumbed through her contacts. Without waiting for any further confirmation or denial of my presence at said epic jamboree, Chelsea hurried off to pester some of her other acquaintances.

"God, she's... gah!" Ollie rubbed his forehead.

"I think it sounds alright, actually. Maybe I will join you." Was it possible that our newly solidified friendship might actually lead to other friends? I had hoped that WMSCACE would be where I would find like-minded people to develop, over time, into mates. Look how that had turned out.

"Great! They're a good bunch of lads, once you get to know them."

With her coat on and bag collected, Chelsea ambled back into the living room, glued to her phone. As she neared, Ollie gestured wildly, pointing at me and then himself, mouthing what looked like 'He's picked me, he's picked me'. Chelsea brushed a manicured hand towards him before stopping dead.

"I'll call you back. Yeah, ciao."

"He's coming with me. On Thursday. Not you."

She let out a huge lungful of air. "Francesco. I like you, I do, and you are a free man, you can do whatever you like. Go with Ollie, don't go, I honestly don't care." I'd never heard C say she didn't care about *anything* before. This seemed unlike her. "Oliver. You are a grade-A prick. You only want Francesco to join your stupid group of drunken buddies and your pathetic lost cause to get at me, don't you? All you try and do is wind me up with your ridiculous ideas and sad, little comments. I assume it's because the sex is so much better when we've had an argument but it's not worth the hassle anymore. We're over, Oliver."

He wore an odd expression, as if he had been told he'd got a terminal disease just after winning the lottery. I honestly thought he might cry laugh.

"You're breaking up with me? Don't bother, Chels, I'm out of here. You can go back to your stupid bedroom and ring all your acquaintances - because they're not friends, not like us," Woah, don't bring me into this, I thought. "They're just hangers-on who think you're some kind of queen bee who they can follow around for a bit until they find some other cause to support. It's fucking embarrassing, I'm embarrassed *for* you." He grabbed his jacket but I noticed it was Chelsea's turn to look horrified - well, a better description might be aghast because it conveys that haughty vibe she radiated. Rather than respond, and I think we both thought her instinct would be to say something else, to get the last word, she nodded, turned, and retreated into her bedroom.

"I'm sorry, mate, but I need to clear my head."

"Wait, wait, hold up. Hold up…" I followed him out into the hallway, where he stopped at the top of the stairs. I checked that the front door was closed behind us; I knew it would be easy to get back in, even if my keys were in my bedroom. Ollie stood, waiting. "Listen, just take a minute. Think about this. You two have been together for over a year, you shouldn't throw it all away, especially not over me!"

He stuffed his hands in his pockets. "It's been like this for a while though, hasn't it? We fight, she's right about that, and we don't see eye to eye on pretty much anything, you know."

He had a point but something told me that there was a relationship worth keeping together. It had nothing to do about us living together; it was all about them. This was the right thing to do. "I know, I know. But, can I be honest with you?" He shrugged. "Do you want to be together?" He shrugged again but, from the way he tilted his head, it felt like a grudging 'Yes'. "You have a laugh, don't you?" This time he did nod, discreetly. "Well, I'm sorry but you are going to need to make a change then. You always row, but it's because you're provoking her."

"This isn't much of a confidence booster, mate…"

"No, seriously, you do though. You enjoy a good debate but it goes too far. Sometimes, you've got to let her have the final word - even if you totally disagree with her. Give it a try."

"I can't," he started. "I.. uh.. fine, okay, yes, I know you're right…"

"When's the last time you said that to her?"

"Shut up, very funny, listen, okay, I don't always let things slide and I do, sometimes, say things that I know wind her up. But what she doesn't get is that it's because I love her. I want her to feel something for me too. You know?"

"You don't think she feels anything?"

"I dunno, it's hard to tell sometimes. She can be… aloof, at times." He wafted his hand in the air for effect, which made me think he might be staying. "You think I should try talking to her?" I nodded. "Should I let her cool off for a minute?"

"Her or you?"

"Both, I s'pose."

"Just try to be calm and composed, let her speak and you listen."

"Fine, come on then." I jiggled the handle and gave the door a forceful boot. Chelsea had now taken her coat off and slippers on and was perched on the sofa. The two of us came in looking like we had just been caught doing something we shouldn't. Chelsea looked us both over and then deliberately turned to the television. Ollie looked at me, a want in his eye, but I nudged him with my elbow instead.

"Chelsea, Chels. Can I talk to you? Please?" After a pause, she tapped the mute button and turned to face him square on.

"What is it, Oliver?"

"Chelsea, I want to say…" He looked at me but it was my turn to give him the cold shoulder. I pulled up a dining chair and kept out of it. "I want to say, I'm sorry. You're right. I do say things because I know they will upset you." Ollie clasped his hands in front of him. He was kind of hunched, unsure whether to sit, stand, run, stay. He looked like he was talking to someone in a wheelchair - not wanting them to have to crane their neck to have a conversation but not wanting to be condescending by squatting down. "I don't want us to break up, Chels. I know we fight but that's mostly my fault and I can try to be more supportive and less…" He mined for a word that wouldn't come; argumentative, belligerent, polemic, confrontational, bellicose. She waited for him stoically. "Less of a dick."

"Oliver," she began. "We are two different souls. You have your way of thinking and I have mine. Yes, we have had good times together and we do have a laugh, don't we? But we've grown apart."

"Have we? Haven't we just grown? I love that you're passionate about issues that matter. I appreciate that you are always there for me. Frankie thinks we're good together, don't you?" They both faced me and I could do nothing but nod. "Can we not give it a go and if I don't change, then we agree to put it behind us?"

Chelsea squirmed.

"We might have different views but we're stronger together, aren't we, like Yin and Yang, Ozzy and Sharon, Big Mac and pickles. If I promise to do better, will you give us another chance?"

Chelsea smiled.

"I can't. I'm sorry, Ollie. Everything you said was amazing and I am so glad that you're thinking about us and not yourself. Hearing you appreciate that you know you're overly argumentative makes me feel like we can have a second chance together." She stood, tossing the remote on the sofa behind her. "But it's my turn to be honest with you. At the exhibition, I met someone, and I've asked him to come over. Now. I'm sorry, Ollie, but we slept together. I was feeling very upset towards you and I know it wasn't the right thing to do but it happened and I think we might be a good match, not that we aren't, but a better match. Thank you though for everything you said. It was very brave of you." I was agog. Ollie looked like he had been kicked between the legs. He had put on such an effort and been very persuasive - hell, if I was Chelsea, I would have at least given him a chance to do better. But she was cold, putting him out of his misery like George did for Lenny in 'Of Mice and Men'.

"What? You fucked someone else?"

"Ollie, I said I'm sorry. You were being so honest, it felt like a good time to share that with you. I didn't intend it to be any more than a fling - one which I would have liked to have protected you from - but we found that we had a lot in common."

"Who is he?"

Chelsea looked at me, I wasn't sure why. Perhaps seeking reassurance or validation? "It's Noah Wright," she said. To me.

"The coffee douche?"

"Yes," she sighed. "We connected and he is very kind and sweet, so I think I'm going to give it a chance to develop into something more." As if, with everything else that was going on, this wasn't enough to drive me crazy. My ex-girlfriend and, now, mate's ex-girlfriend, and flatmate, was going to try to build a relationship with the CEO of the company I was working for. It was insanity - until it occurred to me that this odd state of affairs would be rendered irrelevant if I ended up being sent to Val Verde anyway. I wouldn't have to worry about her twisting his ear about changing all the travel mugs for phthalate- and chlorine-free reusable cardboard cups made by vegans and swapping the chairs for beanbags... I was starting to think more like Ollie, which, whilst not completely unpleasant, was certainly unexpected. Thinking of Ollie, I was expecting him to flip, from the calm and composed version who had walked back through the front door to give his relationship another go, to his pugnacious, laddish, normal self.

Instead, he nodded slowly and listened. His gaze didn't leave the toes of his shoes. Chelsea expanded on what she was attracted to and why Ollie and her could not continue, and he actually listened for a change. He did seem a bit like a kid stood in front of the principal, scolded for smoking behind the bike sheds, but he didn't appear weak or frightened to me. The longer she spoke, the more he grew into his old self. His shoulders rolled back and he extended his neck. His hands went from defensively gripped in front of his belt buckle to stuck into his jean pockets.

347

After a few moments, he nodded firmly and raised his left hand. "Okay, I hear what you're saying. Look, C, I can tell that we've run out of road and as much as I don't want to admit it, I can understand how some of it was my fault," Chelsea punctuated his admission with a mouthed 'thank you', as if that was the intended message. "and you no longer want us to be together. I'm not happy about it but I've known we've not been in a great place for a while so this could all be inevitable. I only want to say two things and you might not want to hear either of them."

"It's okay, I think we can be honest with each other, can't we?" She smiled and gave herself a little air handshake. I felt my stomach take a lurch for the worst.

"Thank you. So, the first thing is," and it's important to note that he paused here and gained his self-assurance, and then did not once raise his voice above a typical, room-temperature, conversational volume, "fuck you, you fucking bitch, I cannot believe you slept with someone whilst we were still going out, that is fucking out of order and I will never fully forgive you for that." She attempted to speak but he would not cede the floor and let out a cathartic sigh. "Secondly, I really do think you owe me a favour for having done such a shitty thing." I half expected him to continue but he stopped dead, as if all he had said would be self-explanatory.

"Oliver, I deserve your anger, I'm sorry I upset you...

"...I'm not upset - I'm disappointed..."

"...but I don't see why I owe you anything. I know, and you know, that I've been paying for you to live here for all the time you've been here and for the bills, and the food, and everything, and, if anything, you owe me, but I would never stoop to the level where I would beg for a favour…"

"No, Chelsea, no, you don't get what I'm asking - I don't want you to do *me* a favour; I want you to do Frankie a favour." My ears pricked up and they both faced me, sat, as I was, like an umpire at Wimbledon, on my own, on the frail looking dining chair that accented the shattered dining room table.

"Francesco? What does he mean?"

"Chels, it was Frankie that told you Noah was going to the exhibit. He got you there and now you've got what you wanted - he was your matchmaker. Didn't he do you a favour too in talking to Noah about fair trade coffee? Really, you owe him a hell of a lot but *I'm* asking you to grant him one favour." Her focus shifted back to Ollie, who still stood with his jacket on, beside the front door.

"Frankie's too smart to be working shifts at Scintilla all his life. But he's not decisive enough to ask for what he deserves." I wouldn't say I was indecisive, but perhaps I was too cautious or maybe hesitant… "If you're banging his boss," she blushed at Ollie's bluntness, "then you should ask him - no, tell him - to give Frankie a promotion. Or a new job. Yeah, how about an advisor, an *executive* advisor for Val Verde. That sounds pretty sweet, doesn't it?" She rolled her eyes.

"And what exactly makes you think I would ask him that after one night together and, even if I did, why would he give it to Frankie?"

"Are you saying Frankie's not smart enough to do that job?"

"No, no, of course not, no, but what if there isn't an advisory - sorry, *executive* advisory - position available for someone with Frankie's experience?"

"You know what these American CEOs are like - they can hire and fire people at a heartbeat. He can create that position for him." Despite nobody asking my opinion on this, I was thrilled by the idea of a promotion but wary about the chances of this ever happening. Although, at Scintilla, he had suggested that he was looking for someone to give him some insight on the country and, at the exhibition, he did say a lot about Val Verde so perhaps I could help in some way - not that I knew anything about the country, but I had a feeling that I could work out how to be useful. "Frankie, what do you reckon? Fancy being Noah Wright's right-hand man?"

Weighing it up was what I would have ordinarily done but Ollie's criticism of me seemed a little harsh. And the fact that Chelsea seemed to think I wasn't capable of doing the job - the fictional job that may not even exist - stung too.

"Sounds great! Thanks C, it would really mean a lot to me if you could sort it."

"*No hay problemo*, Francesco…" Her words drifted and she looked at her phone, as if seeking something, but she didn't unlock it. Ollie clapped his hands together and shrugged off his coat. There was something odd going on; he turned to go to the bedroom, seemed to think better of it, picked his coat up, put it down again, and then walked into the kitchen and opened the fridge. She went quiet and not just stopped talking but as if her heart stopped beating and all you could see and hear of her was through the depths of an ocean, her moves laborious and hesitant.

"I've got one more thing I need to tell you though. Both of you." A bedside consolatory expression, like that which matrons and headmistresses have trained out of them, formed on Chelsea's face and she suddenly couldn't make eye contact with either of us. "So, I might have been a little angry with you earlier... A-a-and, I sent a text that I can't unsend... I told Noah that you know something about the break-in at the museum..."

"What the fuck!" yelled Ollie. "How could you?"

"I'm sorry, I'm really sorry, I was angry at you for being mad at me and I was angry at you," she looked at me now, "for choosing Ollie's side over mine for the protest and I needed to do something about it..." A string of dribble hung from her bottom lip. "I'm so sorry." She found the words easy to say now.

"We've got to get out of here with that knife or we're all screwed." I thought that sounded more decisive, didn't it?

"When will he get here?"

"I don't know, um, maybe ten, fifteen minutes."

"Okay, let me think." Ollie paced and Chelsea watched as I stuffed my fingers into my mouth and hopped from one foot to the other.

"Make it quick," I garbled through knuckles.

"Okay, hold on, hold on. Right, Frankie, you need to stay in your room and guard the knife. He doesn't know anything except that we know something about the theft, right?" Chelsea nodded eagerly, sniffing back a bubble of snot. "Okay... okay. Frankie, you sit tight, Chelsea, try and be nice to him but do not tell him anything more. I'll handle it."

"You're not going to hurt him, are you?"

"No, no, of course not. Listen, Chels, I'm not even going to tell him I'm, I mean, I was, your boyfriend, I'm going to talk to him, nice and friendly."

"Calm and composed," I reminded him.

There was a cheery knock at the door.

Chapter 27 – Tuesday 21st June (still) (2 days to go...)

"You must be Noah."

"Yeah, hey man, how's it going?" Noah didn't pause to wait for an answer before striding into the flat. "Hey, Chelsea, nice place you got." She hugged him and, under Ollie's glare, they shared an urgent, deep kiss. He looked for all the world like Michael McConaughey in 'Wolf of Wall Street', if the Texan actor had left his tie at home, swapped his pleated, pinstripe trousers for board shorts, and traded his suit blazer for a linen sports jacket instead.

"Oh ah, yes, this is my flatmate, Oliver, Ollie - Ollie, this is Noah."

"Nice to meet you. Oh wow, what happened to your table?"

"Don't ask. I need to quickly change so, um, grab a pew here and I'll be back in a jiff." Chelsea scampered and looked right at me. Our eyes met through the crack in the door and she seemed to speak with that look, as if to say, what the hell is Ollie doing or get back inside your room or relating to any of the other twenty-five things I was worrying about at that moment.

"You run Democracy Coffee, yeah? And Scintilla's in town?"

"That's right, guilty as charged!" He chuckled, alone. "So, listen buddy, you might have seen me on the news today, after an ancient artefact - priceless artefact - was stolen by someone at the museum, stolen from me, right in the middle of an exhibition. Chelsea tells me that you might know something about the person that stole that artefact. Is that right?" Ollie had to take a half-step back as Noah towered above him. He raised his left leg and his foot met the coffee table with a thump.

"Yeah, yeah, I, I do know something, yeah."

"Uh-huh, so you'd better speak up." Wright leered forward.

"Yeah, yes, of course... Can I get you a drink?"

"I'm not thirsty."

"Right, um, look... have a seat..."

"I'm good."

"Okay, well, I know who *arranged* to have it stolen but I don't know who actually took it." Noah seemed unmoved. "I can tell you he's someone really important."

"I'm listening."

Ollie shifted on his feet again. "Good, but I need to know that you're a man of your word, Mr. Wright. I saw the news." Noah smiled, slowly nodding.

"Yup, I'm sure you did. It's the only story in this shithole town. I assume you're asking whether I'm good for the ten-grand reward? You don't need to worry about that, my man." Ollie breathed and I craned for a better listen to what they were saying. "If you can tell me who orchestrated this little heist, I'll wire you the cash right now." To illustrate his point, Wright pulled out his phone from his jacket pocket. He flipped open the top half of the handset and, putting his foot up on our coffee table - a risky manoeuvre - waggled it in front of Ollie. "I can put it right into your account, if you want to give me a name."

"It's a very generous reward for information, Mr. Wright."

"Don't look a gift horse in the mouth, man. Anyway, why do you think I pay for insurance if I can't make a claim sometime? And this claim, I don't mind tellin' you, was a biggie." He chuckled to himself, his flip phone wavering.

"Why didn't you get a fake one made and display that? You know that ninety-nine percent of all of the photographs tourists take of the Mona Lisa are with the fake one, right?"

"Is that so? You're a smart kid," Neither of them knew that they were actually born only two years apart from one another. "I do have a fake one, as it is, that I've got back at my hotel. If I don't get the original back in the next few days, we'll put the fake on show and *tell* everyone we recovered it anyway. Then, if the original ever comes up on the art black market, we'll tell everyone *that's* the fake and buy it back on the cheap."

"Very clever," Ollie retorted. "I've got an idea, if you, you know, don't mind listening?"

"I love good ideas but I'd love to hear a name…"

"So, my mate, he knows someone who is a real big deal. The guy he knows is running for President."

"In America?"

"No, no, some central American country, you've probably never heard of it, and I reckon he'd love to get his hands on your knife. My mate told me that he's trying to swing the vote and this candidate told him that if he could get hold of that knife, he was absolutely positive that the ethnic vote, the people that worship the idol on the knife, would push him over the edge."

"Which country did he say he was from?"

"Um, Valle Verd, you heard of it?"

"Val Verde? Sure." His leg must have started to ache now, I thought, but Noah didn't move.

"If you wanted to have the ear of someone in power in… Val Verde? Right? Well, I could get the fake knife to him and my friend could tell him it's the real one."

"So, what you're saying is, I give *you* my fake knife, your buddy will give it to this El Presidente guy, tell him it's the real deal, he can win the election, and how do I get something out of this? I lose both my knives and end up with my dick in my hand." I had so many jokes and I'm sure Ollie did too, but he resisted the urge to make an uncalled-for innuendo.

"No, he can tell the president-elect that it was a donation - from you - but you don't want to make it public. Maybe… maybe, we can say that the theft was faked because you needed a cover to get him the *real* knife..." Noah was nodding along as Ollie spoke. Either through discomfort or something else, Wright stood upright now, none of that California start-up intensity. He was as stock still as I'd ever seen him, and I'd seen him twice.

"You know, I do a lot of business in that country. Speaking to their President, instead of their shit for brains farmers, they keep trying to put the price of coffee up and up, would make my life a lot easier - and my shareholders pretty damned happy too. But what about the real knife? Who the hell's got that?" I watched, expecting Ollie's charade to collapse, for Noah to do something, say something, that would mean Ollie had to betray me. I looked about me, what for I don't know, as if I was going to be the one attacked or my room invaded. All I could see that might serve as a deterrent was my hot wire cutters and a hardback copy of 'Freedom In Exile'.

"Does it matter? If you get an insurance pay out and the chance to influence the Government of Val Verde, do you even *need* the real knife?" I froze. All I could do was watch.

Noah considered. "Maybe not, The damned thing's not priceless, like I said, it's worthless. You can't sell it or Interpol will come for you. You can't melt it down or the liberals will get you. Fuck it. Alrighty then, I'll bring you that phoney knife but I still want a name."

"And what about the reward?"

"You're pushing your luck, man. You said you would tell me who organised to have the museum burglarized and here I am with no information."

"It's one of the president-in-waiting's advisors. Guy named Marcos. He wanted to steal it to get into his boss' good books but he has to wait for the heat to die down to give it to him. If we can get your fake knife to the candidate first, this advisor will have to get rid of the real knife."

"And you want to tell me this advisor's name?"

"I can't, he made me promise not to. If anyone else found out, he would lose the trust of the politician and the whole plan might fail." I wasn't convinced, but Ollie made it sound more important through the way he spoke. Wright didn't seem convinced either until a flicker of deceit lit up his face.

"Hey, your buddy could tell him that the fake one was on display and that was the one that got stolen!"

"Perfect, yeah, exactly." They grinned and nodded. Noah looked at Ollie with admiration. I couldn't see what expression Ollie was putting on. "So, I've given you the name of the guy that stole the knife and come up with a plan that gives you a direct line to the future President of Val Verde. That's got to be worth ten grand, hasn't it?"

I didn't come out of my room until the door had closed properly behind Noah and Chelsea. It had taken about half an hour but Noah had left Chelsea putting make-up on, had dashed back to his hotel, returned and gave Ollie the fake *tumi* in a bum bag (or 'fanny pack' as Noah called it), and then gone to see Chelsea, without her even realising he had gone and come back. Ollie had retreated into the kitchen when Chelsea came out and was all sweetness and light as they reached for each other, feeling their way through the early days of their infatuation.

"Wow, that was, I don't know what that was, but wow." He threw me a can of beer from the fridge and we dropped into the sofa. "That was some good going. I saw it but I don't know how you managed it."

"What do you think I did?"

"Fleeced him - he's shagged your girl so you've shagged his bank account..." Ollie shook his head and scoffed.

"No, not quite but I like the way you're thinking." He then did something I never expected him to do, not because of who he was, then, but because I didn't let myself believe that we had become friends. "The money is yours. I don't deserve it."

"What do you mean?" Ollie unlocked his phone and, with a silence broken by digital clicks, tapped on the screen before putting it on the coffee table. My phone pinged and I clicked the notification that opened my banking app.

I'd never seen such a lot of money in one place before, even if it was only a series of numbers on a screen, rather than a suitcase full of unused notes or a pallet piled high with gold bars, like in the movies. The fragility of the device belied the value displayed on it - enough for me, Ollie, or Chelsea, to practically start a new life. Or, more realistically, pay off a sizeable chunk of our student loans in one go.

"You broke into the museum and nicked the knife. All I did was turn a blind eye and spin Noah a yarn, so you should have it."

I couldn't bring myself to take it. "I don't deserve it. I broke the law."

"You think the law matters? It doesn't apply to people like Wright, does it? How much tax has Democracy Coffee paid last year?"

"It's still the law."

"Sometimes you need to break the law, if you want to make a significant change," he said. "You 'repatriated' the *tumi* because you think giving it to Ernesto will help you stay in the UK - isn't that breaking the law too? The law says you're out, even though you know the law is wrong. If you didn't break the law, you'd be kicked out of uni and the UK with nothing to show for your life." He made a persuasive point but I was still hesitant to pile on further criminal activities that might prejudice any case I might have had for staying in the country. He could easily sense my reluctance and he tried to hammer home his point.

"Take Chelsea. How many causes has she championed since you've known her? What impact has it had? None. Not a thing. Why? Because she won't do what is necessary to get the job done."

"And you would?" My defences were falling but I still had the resistance to lash out with a needless barb.

"Yeah, I would, I think. Only, I haven't found my cause yet. But I'd rather you had this anyway. I still feel guilty about what Chelsea and I said and I didn't exactly stand up for you when I should have." It felt like the right thing to do to accept the money now and I looked back at the black and white digits displayed on my screen, examining it, like an art dealer making sure what she's got in front of her isn't a fake.

"I can at least buy you a pint then!"

"A bloody big one!" He grinned and we fist-bumped before I felt secure enough to close the app and put my phone inside my chest pocket, as close to my chest as it could be. "There's one more thing though and you have to trust me."

"Sure."

"In fact, you might say that you owe me a favour." He had a point. He'd cashed one favour in on my behalf with Chelsea which may or may not go anywhere, but that was a discussion to be had at another time. I couldn't argue that I owed him something. "You need to speak to Ernesto. Tell him that you know someone who is an advisor to the CEO of Democracy Coffee, who can convince him to invest in Val Verde or Ernesto's political party, whatever you think will get him interested. Tell Ernesto that you'll give him the knife but you want the mask, to give to this 'advisor', as a payment to make sure Noah Wright does what Ernesto wants."

"That all sounds a bit complicated," I said.

"There you go being indecisive again. Trust me, I've got a plan. I came up with it last night and just needed the added pressure from Chelsea's bloody text message for it to come together." I attempted to get him to explain more but he cut me off. "All will be revealed. Trust me." Whenever someone has to say - and repeat - the phrase 'Trust me', it often means that, whatever the circumstances, you should absolutely not trust that person whatsoever. I had already seen Ollie in action; the shoplifting and the card trick in the pub, so he was not someone I could put a great deal of faith in. However, I had to accept that he was my only friend and, considering he had just handed me enough money to buy a car, now seemed the most apt time to put that faith to the test.

"Okay, fine. He is expecting me to call him."

I had never enjoyed making phone calls. For one thing, you can't see the facial expressions on the other end so it's hard to tell if the person at the other end is being sarcastic, if they're gesticulating to someone else in the room, and even speaking out loud made me feel self-conscious. I'd once recorded myself on a tape deck as a kid, when I had some short-lived fantasy of being a radio presenter. In between songs taped off of the chart show, with the beginnings and end cut off to avoid another presenter's voice appearing in my rehearsal, I would introduce the songs with a little fact I had heard someone else say on TV. I thought it was brilliant but as soon as I played it back to myself, I knew I could never be a presenter. My voice sounded so weirdly alien, yet undeniably mine. That recognition that it was my voice and, therefore, clumsy and immature, along with the jarringly obvious audible quirks I had somehow never heard before meant that I put the plug-in microphone under my bed and it never saw the light of day again.

At least with text messages I had the time to think about what I wanted to say to someone, to compose it, read it back for mistakes, and then, when I was satisfied with it, then I could send it, confident that it fairly represented me and my opinions. If you're caught off guard answering a phone call, you feel somehow out of control. That's how salespeople get you; if they email you, you can just delete it or mark it as spam, but if one of them calls you, and you answer, they think they have a better chance of getting you to part with your cash.

"*Hola, Francesco. ¿Cómo estás?*"

"Listen, Ernesto, I have what you want." I listened for any sign of what state of mind he was in, or whether Marcos was there too. "But things have changed. I have something more to offer."

There was silence for a short while.

"What I want is the *tumi*, so whatever you have to offer had better come with the knife."

I tried to say nothing, to see if he would say something next to give away what he was thinking. The lack of dialogue felt uncomfortable.

"One of my friends is an advisor to the CEO of Democracy Coffee and I know they are big investors in Val Verde, right?" The disquieting silence continued. "Well, he thinks he could get the CEO to lend his support to the *Partido* but he needs to see that you're serious first." I felt Ernesto's mood change but couldn't see anything to tell me which way he was leaning.

"Your friend?" he spat. "Your friend is worthless to me." I hoped he wouldn't think that but for Ollie's plan to work, whatever it might be, I had to press home the issue.

"But Democracy Coffee isn't, is it? How much do they invest in Val Verde per year? Five million dollars? Ten million? How many seats might that swing for you in the elections?" I found out later that I was miles off; it was twenty-five million dollars.

Ernesto said nothing. I heard shuffling which sounded further away from the phone; I assumed it was Marcos. There was whispering, before he replied.

"This friend - why won't you give me their name?"

"You know why."

"Why doesn't he come to me? Why do we need you?"

"It was my idea." I was improvising but I had no other choice.

"What does he want?" I know from my two days of training at the call centre two summers ago that this is what they called 'a bite'. I didn't take the job though - too much time on phone calls.

"If you give him the mask, then he'll know you're serious about the election and he can persuade the CEO to invest in the *Partido*."

"And you're his... *¿Cómo lo llaman los estadounidenses?* His 'gopher', yes? You give me the *tumi*, I give you the *la máscara*, then what? I receive a million American dollars in my account? Come on, Francesco, what do you take me for? An idiot?"

I had to use my Hail Mary pass to get this done. I hoped it would work but, more than that, I hoped that whatever Ollie had planned would ensure I was in less trouble than I was already in.

"Okay, have it your way. I can always tell him you're not interested and they can find another political party to support. They don't care who wins, so long as Calderon is out..."

"Ha ha, I said it before, didn't I Marcos? Huh? *Si*, I said it before - this one is very smart. Very clever. *Vale*, let us make the exchange. You give me the *tumi*, I give you *la máscara*, yes? So simple." I'd got him - now it was up to Ollie. "But you are forgetting something, aren't you? Maybe you thought I would have forgotten too. Eva."

"About that. You see, we had a bit of a row and… now I don't think we're going out, so, yeah."

He gave a throaty chuckle that brought my arms out in goosebumps. "Oh no, Francesco and Eva had their hearts broken? *¿Y qué?* That's just your word and I don't think I can trust you. I think you're smart, *verdad*, but I don't trust you. So, we will make the exchange in a *very* public place and you will bring Eva and, in front of me, you will *tell* her it is over. I don't want any funny business, you see?"

"Where and when? Let's get this over with." That wasn't what I really hoped for; I hoped that I could make it up to Eva somehow, that she would forgive me and we could start over again, so perhaps 'get this over with' was a poorly chosen phrase.

"Thursday morning, 10am, Victoria Square. The Brexit vote. There will be plenty of people there to see you break her sweet heart!" The click on his line ended the call and my hopes of getting back with Eva.

Chapter 28 – Tuesday 21st June (still) (2 days to go...)

Eva was at the forefront of my thoughts. I had managed to get by without thinking about her for the past few hours, as the whole Noah and Ollie scheme began and progressed, but now she was being drawn back into this disaster, she was visualised and remembered as if she was in the room with me. This time I couldn't just try and distract myself by doing something unrelated, like taking myself away to the best bits of my childhood by working on the model village. I had to call her to arrange for her to be there on Thursday. If she wasn't there - or didn't want to come with me - there was no telling what Ernesto might do, or what he might get Marcos to do for him.

She didn't answer the first couple of times I rang and I didn't really give her much time to listen to the voicemails I left her before redialling. Eventually, she picked up.

"What do you want, Frankie? I'm in the middle of something."

"I'm sorry, I have to talk to you."

"You're talking now so spit it out."

"I need to see you."

"I'm busy. What did you want?"

There was so much I wanted to say. "I wanted to apologise - for breaking my promise. I…" Saying everything I wanted to say meant it all spraying out like a post-sex piss. I held back and focused on what I needed her to agree to. "Can we meet? Thursday at 10 o'clock? It's really important."

"Just so you can say sorry again? No. But I was about to call you myself anyway. We might have something that can help with the visa."

"No, no, it's… more than that, I can't tell you right now but I need you to meet me." The line went quiet for a while. I heard rustling paper and fidgeting down the line. There was the indistinct chatter of a busy office shrouding her. The soft noises altered and it sounded as if Eva was on the move - a squeak of a chair, a distant spoken excuse, the thud of fire doors colliding. "Wait, what do you mean 'something that can help' anyway?"

"Frankie, I meant to call you later on, it's really important. But you have to tell me what's going on."

"If you agree to meet me, I can tell you, but I need you to come - it's my only chance at staying in the UK. Everything else has... ugh, there's no other option for me."

"You don't know that. Wait, it's Ernesto isn't it? He's got you a passport?"

"He'll give it to me on Thursday morning but he needs you to be there too." The background noises were no longer those of an office but of the outside world - traffic, people, the city.

"I have to talk to you."

"Oh, okay, but are you going to be there on Thursday?" She hesitated.

"What I have to tell you might mean that whatever you and Ernesto have cooked up for Thursday is totally irrelevant." There was a screech of brakes and competing horns parping through the tiny speaker. Then traffic pulling away and chatter and commotion continued. "I'm coming over. I'll be there in half an hour. Don't go anywhere."

"What? Here? The flat?" She had hung up. I looked about the living room and shepherded the empty mugs and bowls into the kitchen sink, dashing water into them. I went back and rearranged the cushions by size, then colour, then shape, then back to size. The sudden stop to our conversation filled me with apprehension. What did she have to say to me? Why did it seem so urgent? I supposed that I would just have to wait and find out, so I went to brush my hair and teeth once again.

"You need to sit down."

There was no affection in her arrival. The coldness I first noticed in her had returned, her jawline as prominent and intractable as when I had met her at the hotel and her eyes dark and predatory.

"I'm serious, sit down." She took a seat too and put her briefcase on the floor and folded her jacket over it. Her hands crossed in her lap and she exhaled. I jumped when she reached out to me and clasped my hands in hers.

"What is it?"

"Tell me why Ernesto wants me to go with you to meet him on Thursday morning?" She wasn't simply attractive - or 'handsome' as I had clumsily called her - but compelling. I might have once dwelt on whether or not to tell her, what the repercussions might be for me, what the impact might be on my chances of avoiding extradition, and so on and so on, but not now.

"He wants me to break up with you." She scoffed. "In public, in front of him, because he thinks he can, I don't know, have you for himself. He wants you to want him too."

"That guy can't take a hint. I let him down gently, before... before us, but he - and Marcos - are still... *¡Maldito sea!* They can be so annoying." She still had a hold of my hands. Her grip was firm.

"I told him that we had... had a fight... broken up," I let the last words hang in the air with the hope that it would leave open a window of opportunity for her to deny what I feared was true.

"And what did he say?"

"He said it didn't matter, he wanted me to end it with you. When we make the exchange." She couldn't help but roll her eyes. "I have to give him the *tumi* for my passport. It's the only way..."

"You said. The only way you can stay here. With me." That felt like the moment she hinted that there was hope for us. Until she pulled her hands away, and I stared down at my empty grip, palms heavenward and fingers curling back into fists.

She continued; "Why do you think I didn't answer your calls? It wasn't because I didn't want to speak to you; I'm not that petty. We had a fight, maybe two if you want to keep thinking about the stupid *bruja* at the museum - which I don't think about at all, by the way - but that does not mean we are over. If you finish something you haven't even really started over something so little, you'll never make anything from your life, right?" I nodded, thinking that, in fact, she had given me a moment in which to salvage our relationship. It didn't seem completely secure so there was no need to get overconfident. Not that overconfidence had ever been one of my failings, of course.

"I wanted to speak to you, I needed to, and it's not about us," she explained. "It's bigger than that."

"What is it?"

"Frankie, it's your parents."

I stared at her. My loosely clenched fists grew damp and a shiver ran down my back. What was it? Instinctively, I feared the worst. There would be no chance to apologise for what I had done, for how selfishly I had behaved. In pure clarity, I saw their faces smiling at me in happier times. My shoulders flexed with the memory of playful hugs and being protectively enfolded by their arms.

"They're alive."

A thousand questions exploded like fireworks but I could only say one at a time. "How do you know?"

"You know I said I'd see if anyone at the office could look into your case? It turns out your parents were not the only ones who got deported, there were a few at the time, but James, my mentor, he found them."

"Where are they?"

"The Val Verdean Embassy in London. They had friends on the inside, it seems, that took the two of them in and kept them safe. They've been stashed away in a couple of rooms on Belgrave Square, doing odd jobs on the quiet for the staff there."

The carnival of questions was so great that I found it hard to pin down any one question. There were so many things I wanted to ask her but, more so, to say to them. The shivers and sweats did not subside. I got up and paced, turning to ask more questions before stopping, pacing, and then coming to sit back down but found that I couldn't sit in one place for more than a moment. Eva remained still, although she had to keep turning her head to follow me around the room.

"Can I see them?"

"Yes. I've spoken to James. He and I were supposed to go down to London on Wednesday but something else came up and he has had to rearrange, but he has two return train tickets. I was trying to find a way to tell you, but I only found out a couple of days ago, I should have said something but there was never the right moment."

How had it come to this that she felt like she should apologise to me? She had just changed my life - although whether it was for better or worse, we would soon see - but she had nothing to say sorry for. Had I been a different person, I would have kissed her there and then or carried her into my bedroom. Instead, I worried and pondered.

"This week? We're going to see them tomorrow?" This had to be a fantasy.

"Yes." It had not fully sunk in but I might actually have the chance to see them after so long apart. And apologise for what I did, if they would accept it. In fact, and the idea embedded itself in my mind right up until we were stood outside the Embassy, what if they flat out refused to see me at all?

Chapter 29 – Wednesday 22nd June (1 day to go...)

When we met at New Street, neither of us reached for the other, or leant in for a kiss, as much as that small action would have sparked my hopes into life again. She gave me a punch on the shoulder, turned towards the ticket barriers, and I followed. Few words were spoken either; Eva passed over the long, pink tickets to the attendant, who let us through. We boarded halfway along the Virgin Pendolino, or British Rail Class 390, if I'm being specific, but that's hardly relevant is it. I had hoped that working in a law office might mean that they would have sprung for first class tickets but I supposed that standard class was a sacrifice so that they could spend more money on their clients, who were mostly asylum seekers and immigrants and were not renowned for their easy and steady supplies of disposable cash to cover the extensive costs of fighting a court case.

Eva got out some paperwork at the table and made annotations and wrote copious additional observations in her notebook. On the other hand, sitting across from her, all I could do was try to find distraction. The on-board magazine was consumed in minutes. I scrolled through all of the new Facebook posts within another ten or so minutes. I wasn't in the mood to have anything from the snack trolley but I found a space for a Kit Kat and a coffee - not that I was hungry but that I sought out some kind of distraction.

Grey shadows were replaced by brown suburbs and then verdant plateaus interspersed with ponds and trees that gradually filled out and fattened with thick green leaves. The transition was little different to the childhood memories I clung on to and I tried to emulate with my model railway. The time I spent designing and shaping the landscape and precisely arranging the buildings and environment would add up to hours upon hours, days upon days, months of painstaking construction. Others could not understand it, had I given them a chance to, and only Ollie had truly taken an interest. The ordered - by my eyes, at least - layout and system was one of the few things I could rely on; the lights turned on at the flick of a switch, the trains ran on time to my own schedule of fleeting whims, buildings were erected according to my grand plan, and none of the real-world problems for town planners, architects, councils and mayors mattered to me. There was only one person in charge and the King of the entire realm was me. How it clashed with my life past the bedroom door. Even on this train, which ran to a clearly defined timetable on keenly engineered rails and was operated by a trained crew, the journey we had embarked on was totally out of my control. I was neither a monarch nor even a Fat Controller in this world. At least my overthinking kept me occupied for the journey to Milton Keynes Central.

"Can we talk?" I knew I would be interrupting Eva's work but what I had to say could not be said later on. She looked up, tilting her papers down to meet my look. "Why didn't you tell me the truth?"

"What do you mean?"

"About my parents. How long had you known about them?"

"Not long, I promise. Since Friday. I wanted to tell you but I didn't know how much I was allowed to share and what if you got your hopes up and it all turned out to be a waste of time? What if they weren't really there? James and I were going to check it out but we got confirmation sooner than we expected." She was holding back but if I was patient, I felt sure that she would lay everything on the table. Outside the greenery burst into bleak, squat office blocks, like a rockery of urban vandalism. This must be Watford.

"I tried to tell you on Sunday. I really wanted to but I couldn't find the words."

"I suppose that's the difference between us."

"What do you mean?"

"You tell me you can't find the words - I'm lost for words so I end up not saying anything." She smiled.

"And the other thing got in the way so we need to talk about that." She tidied her documents like a croupier shuffling the pack and posted them into her briefcase. The other thing. For me, it had been the only thing, up until twenty-four hours ago. The Home Office, the University, everything, was tied together by the knife. Rather than separating, it was going to bring everything together for me. As soon as I gave it to Ernesto, I would have my passport, I could get Ali at the Students' Loan Company to update their records, I would take it to the University offices and Paul Holder and they would reinstate me into my course and I could actually graduate with a degree that I could be proud of having accomplished, and I would have the ability to live in the UK and come and go as I please and all because I took a relic which, by any definition, actually *belonged* to the Yarina and Ernesto would be the one to wield it and bring them together, out of hiding, once and for all. With everything weighing on that one object, it was as important to me as the golden ticket to Charlie Bucket, the feather to Dumbo, or Moby Dick to Captain Ahab.

"What is there to talk about? I have it, I need to give it to Ernesto, that's it, right?"

"Frankie, you *stole* it," she dropped her voice to a whisper, "and I know about it. How do you think that makes me look? I work in a law office, for Christ's sake."

"They don't have to know about it."

"No, but if you get caught with it, obviously I'll be questioned by the police and they could accuse me of being your accomplice or an accessory to the crime. That's the end of my legal career, isn't it?"

"You yourself said it was stolen, so I just stole it back."

"I know what I said but what I said and what happens in the real world are not always compatible." Her stubbornness was almost admirable. What she prompted me to realise was that I had thought about the benefits of my actions but not the negative implications. Sure, I worried more than anyone before hiding in the museum and breaking into the display case, and I fought every urge to panic whilst I was doing it, but once it was done, I thought about how I might get arrested or deported but I didn't give any thought to the repercussions of my success on other people.

"I thought you would be happier that I was returning the *tumi* to its rightful owners and doing something meaningful for someone else. That's what you want to do too, isn't it?"

She shook her head. "Yes and no. Not like this." We would be in London soon and there was more to discuss, but I could tell we were at an impasse.

It was a taxi ride to Belgrave Square from Euston Station. Eva walked with purpose to the taxi rank and climbed into the cab at the head of the queue. I scampered after her and hopped in, sitting beside her on the rear bench. We lurched away, racing north up Eversholt Street, past pubs - Prince this, Royal that - and looped around Mornington Crescent. Soon we were heading south again, towards the BT Tower. Then it was down side streets, threading between glistening tower blocks and grubby council flats. It was nothing like my last time in London - or at least the view or the route was completely different. Walking and driving through the city were incomparable. So much of it was nondescript; brick walls and windows may change in shape and colour but they held no deeper meaning for me. There was only one thing that was preoccupying my thoughts.

We passed along limestone terraces and I briefly thought we might already have arrived. I looked up, drawing Eva's attention, but both of us soon reverted to our silent, morose demeanours. The tension was only briefly broken when the cabbie swore loudly as we ran into traffic on Great Portland Street, forgetting that he had left the microphone on.

"Sorry." Click. I thought I saw a smile from Eva.

The lack of progress on Marylebone Road exacerbated the awkwardness between us. One of us would have to cut through it but I wasn't sure what she wanted to hear so I held my tongue. At least the changing scenery on the train had alleviated the mood, or served as a distraction. Staring at the fluorescent back end of a bike courier wasn't quite the same experience that inspired Theroux or Zola to pick up their pens.

"What are you expecting?"

"Not Lance Armstrong's arse, that's for sure…"

"No!" she laughed. "What are you expecting it to be like, when you see them?"

"I don't know…" Of course, we had spoken about my parents but mainly it had been their absence or their activism rather than their personalities. There had been no time to explain to her my nightmarish realisation. "I'm sure they will have plenty to say. So do I. I'm just not sure how I'm going to say it yet."

Sunlight broke through the grey sky, illuminating subterranean windows through heavily painted, black ironwork. Seeing it wash up the white stone slabs that skirted around the red brick buildings, stained like smoker's teeth, lifted my spirits. One moment we were crawling past limestone exteriors, punctuated with broad-shouldered, unwelcome doorways, then we were hurtling past rows of glass, showing off sleek furniture and sparse interiors. Candles and coffees, clothes and cards, beggars and banks, sunglasses and suits, burgers and books. The hotels changed from those with a neon 'Vacancy' sign in their front windows to those which hung enormous Union flags over the entrance.

By the time we reached the back of Selfridges, on James Street, I thought I had seen every type of restaurant I might ever want. Yet I wasn't hungry. The matt terracottas and ivory creams which paraded above the

limit of our windows flashed by and we were making
progress again.

At Park Lane it was gridlock. Tour buses and
flatbed scaffolding trucks and buzzing mopeds and other
black cabs and a kaleidoscope of cars all funnelled into
the flowing artery. Grosvenor, BMW, Harrods Estates,
The Dorchester with a fleet of sports cars lined up in front
of it, Hilton, all raced by me, without giving them a
second thought.

We turned off of the route as we got to Wellington
Arch but it was only when I saw a vast flag hanging over
a building which wasn't a hotel that I started to really feel
nervous. Belgium, Argentina, Malaysia, Turkey. We must
be close now. Eva knew too; she smoothed down her seal
grey blazer lapels and flicked hair away from her
shoulders. A police van was parked on the square and I
instinctively bristled.

"Here alright, love?" Eva slid folded notes through
the gap in the plastic divider and stepped down from the
taxi. We looked up at the Val Verdean Embassy.
Ordinarily, an imposing and impressive building but here,
in diplomatic London, it was unremarkable and ordinary.

Beneath the still pennant, the black, green, and red
tricolour, which would have filled our field of vision had
we looked up, the two of us took hesitant steps up to the
mahogany and glass front door. Both doors swung lightly
inward and we were ensconced within a majestic foyer of
traditional wainscoting and plaster cornices. Daylight
filled the room, despite there being just four windows
looking out on the square from the ground floor. One wall
was dominated by a vast, unused fireplace, with a
surround made of green marble. There was a bold smell
of aloe vera and apricot which dissipated as we moved

379

through, towards two absolute specimens in close-cut, single-breasted jackets that looked tight on the bicep and trousers that looked loose below the knee. They watched us as we went towards the broad desk that commanded a view of the whole room from our right. Behind a gigantic bouquet of Chilean jasmine in an artfully-battered copper vase, sat two receptionists.

"Good afternoon," Eva took charge. "Señorita Estrellas y Señor Cualquiera to see Ambassador Provechoso."

"Good afternoon, Señorita Estrellas. The ambassador is not going to be able to attend your meeting today but his aide, Señor Suplente has offered to assist you. Please take a seat and he will be right out."

We accepted the invitation to sit, perching on firm, cubular, single-seat settees that lacked the homeliness of a cushion but had unique, hand-woven throws draped over the backs of each of them. Eva reached for a magazine from the glass coffee table which seemed to wobble rhythmically. I gazed out towards the square, through the vast portrait windows. Birds sped across the sky and my eyes followed them without thinking, wondering about their origin and destination. I felt the hairs on my arms rub against my shirt for the first time. Eva reached out and put her hand on my knee, stopping my leg from bouncing up and down. The rattle of the coffee table stopped too.

"It's going to be okay." I pursed my lips in a semi-smile and hoped she was right.

A short, dark-haired man descended the staircase that ran up in front of the empty fireplace. He extended his hand half several paces before he reached us, revealing a gold-faced watch.

"*Buenos dias. Mi nombre es Señor Suplente. Es un placer conocerlos a ambos.*"

"*Disculpas, mi colega, señor Cualquiera, no habla mucho español.*"

"Of course, no problem at all. Miss Estrella, I was sorry to hear that your partner was unable to join us today but I can assure you that we remain very happy to help you with this delicate matter." He turned to me and tilted his head. "*Señor Cualquiera*, it is a pleasure to meet you. I have heard a great deal about you and it is a great shame that we have not had a chance to meet one another sooner."

"Thank you." We shook hands and he indicated that we should proceed across the foyer and ascend the substantial, L-shaped stairs.

"Miss Estrellas and her colleague, Mister Baxter-Evans, have informed me of the difficult situation you have been put in, Señor Cualquiera. We have a great deal of information to share with you, of course, and I hope that this will be of assistance." He stopped speaking with decisiveness and, at the head of the stairs, we came to a second reception, which had an open plan of desks laid out behind it - the modern Formica and metal clashing with the formal, classical decoration, which continued the plasterwork, flocked wallpaper, and large, ornate paintings from the ground floor. The one centred between two identical, tall windows was a painted sketch of flowers.

Either side of the office area were temporary-looking offices, constructed from glass and plastic, and containing little in the way of furniture. Through frosted panels, I watched someone stand from their chair and stretch, cradling a telephone handset to their shoulder. Lowered conversations continued, regardless of our arrival.

"We are in here." Suplente led us towards one of the offices. We passed a group of people standing around a table, talking over one another, and jabbing their fingers at papers splashed across the surface. Behind them, back towards the entrance, was a small kitchenette, where a coffee grinder whirred and two colleagues spoke, and flirted. We moved further into the embassy, leaving the box-like offices behind and heading towards a tall, gilded set of double doors. Either side of it were more paintings in a similar style to the flowers - one, a steam locomotive winding through mountains, on which the railway line seemed precariously perched. The other was a windswept coastal scene, portraying a bay pinned in by sheer bluffs, and cresting hills. A lone explorer stood on the headland, staring across the churning waves.

He held open one of the doors, allowing Eva and I to pass in to the salon. The carpet dramatically improved in quality. Rather than desks and office chairs, there were coral-coloured sofas, more white, sash box windows that offered impressive views of Belgrave Square and the street below, and two early-Twentieth century portraits on the walls - both men - the one on the left was depicted standing on crop bags, handing what appeared to be fruit to a crowd of people with their hands reaching up for him. The one on the right was a smartly-dressed man, stood on the back of a wagon or truck, grasping a piece of paper in his hand, held aloft, mid-flow of a speech, which clearly entranced the audience gathered around him. But there was another man in the room, sitting, facing away from us, towards the wide varnished desk that took up most of the space to the rear of the salon.

From only the back of his head, I knew who it was. My feet would not do what my head wanted. Eva looked over her shoulder and stopped. Suplente paused too, caught between two duties. The seated man, and the shorter woman sat beside him, who I had not noticed beneath the horizon of the sofa back, stood. As they turned, I considered doing the same.

"*Señor y Señora Cualquiera - Señor Cualquiera... Júnior...*"

It was unmistakably them. Both they and I stood and stared. Neither seemed able to speak. It took Eva's intervention to interrupt the paralysis.

"Mister Cualquiera, Missus Cualquiera, my name is Eva Estrella and I am working with James Baxter-Evans on Francesco's residency case."

Papá was the first to approach and, as he stepped forward, so did I, but with a tentativeness I had thought I had overcome. His tan was long faded and he had failed to prevent the annexation of his youth by grey hairs. The vision of my guilt-ridden, secretive phone call was scratched into my inner eye. I didn't know whether he was going to punch me or hug me. If he chose the former course of action, I feared he still had the raw power of his younger days. The scars he bore appeared clearer and more well defined than I remember and it was apparent that the stories he told of violent incursions by the police were not tall tales. I didn't flinch, I am proud to say. His arms wrapped around mine and he dragged me close in a clutch I had no intention of leaving. His chest throbbed against mine, the heartbeat as powerful as ever.

Mamá clucked, the tears welling as she embraced us both, her sobs infectious. Her shoulders heaved once and she cried, not loudly but distinctly. She gripped us so tight it felt like she would never let go, forever in her protection. I felt so many emotions at once - relief, anger, grief, delight - that I had to turn to look away from them both surreptitiously. Suplente passed Eva a box of tissues and she took one, before holding it out to Mamá. That was her cue to relinquish us and grab a handful to press against her eyes. Her knuckles whitened and she might have crushed a more brittle substance.

"Francesco," Papá said, and we both started sobbing uncontrollably again. Then we laughed. He planted his hands on my shoulders and looked at me properly for the first time in over four years. "Oh shit, sorry." He leaned away, dabbed at his eyes with a handkerchief, and then and reached out, making a formal handshake seem more. Suplente went to the low table and poured out five glasses of water, so we took the hint to sit.

"You must have many questions for one another but may I first say that it has been an honour to have your parents working with us at the embassy. They are not here as prisoners or anything of that nature."

"Why *are* you here?" I asked.

"For our protection," Mamá answered. "We could not stay in Val Verde under San Marcos and could not go back under Calderon."

"You've been here for four years?"

"Yes." It was Papá's turn to speak as Mamá held the bunched tissues close to her chest. "The embassy has been very good to us, they've kept us hidden here for all this time, and we could not have asked for more of them." Suplente nodded a discreet, modest gratitude.

"But... how? I…"

"We have friends here. We have had friends here for a while. After the protest we came down for - you remember that? My God, you were so scared when the fighting started - they looked out for us. When they heard we were being deported, they stepped in."

"If it wasn't for them, I don't want to think what would have happened to us." Eva looked at me as I took all of this in. My parents seemed so calm, as if this was normal for them, but then, I suppose, living in the Embassy for four years meant that these surroundings had become normal to them. I had barely time to process an answer before another question was desperate to be asked.

"There are good people here, no matter who is in power, who are committed to protecting Val Verdeans of any political opinion. Isn't that right?" asked Eva.

"Of course. We have to be the… permanence that our people can rely on." Suplente added.

"Can't you live anywhere else?"

"No, the Embassy is a haven where British laws do not apply. If we leave the building, the police can arrest us because of the extradition treaty."

"But they've done nothing wrong here," I protested.

"No, not here in the UK." Suplente clarified. "And the treaty was agreed years ago. Anyone committing a crime in Val Verde that comes to the UK must be extradited for trial in Escalón. The opposite is true also; anyone committing a crime in the UK who flees to Val Verde must be brought back to the UK for trial."

From nowhere, I lunged and hugged my mother. It was impossible to consider stopping it. It had been so long since I was able to feel so close to my parents that I did not want it to end. When I felt the hug reach a natural end, I retook my seat.

"And you couldn't contact me? A phone call? Anything?"

Mamá and Papá exchanged a look and pleaded with their eyes to the Ambassador's aide to intervene.

"No, I'm sorry, it would have been too dangerous. If they had spoken with you, the Government in Val Verde would have known they were here. It could have resulted in any number of staff being sent home or imprisoned."

"Whenever some dignitary or politician would visit, we would have to hide in the cloakroom, didn't we?" It was charming to see Papá laugh and Mamá smile like she used too. But her face had new lines too. There was no way to conceal it.

I took a drink of water, to give myself a moment of composure. It had all been so shocking and so thrilling but I had to face up to what I had done. It was best done like my Papá told me I should take off plasters; in one confident go rather than drawing out the torture.

"I have to tell you something," I began, my throat already feeling dry again. None of the people in the room were anticipating what I had to say. The words I needed to use would not come. I had another sip of water. What would Eva think of me? I assumed that she had already decided that we had no future together but this might be the stake in the heart of that dream. I might get kicked out of the embassy for bringing shame to my people. My imagination struggled to create a model of what the conversation would be like but had no problem coming up with reasons why it would all end in tears. Yet, I persevered. "It was me who called the immigration hotline."

Perhaps I wanted to wallow in my deeds or maybe I wanted the drama to enhance an already spectacularly unusual day. I could not say now, or then.

"We know." Mamá spoke first with a calm assurance. "We assumed that it must have been you, we were too careful."

"It probably helped us, honestly," added Papá. "We were angry with you to begin with, you did it because you were young, or upset, I get it, but by being here we have not had to live checking our shoulders, you know. "

"But I was mad at you, for putting your protests ahead of me, for abandoning me in London, for everything…"

"We never abandoned you! We were *looking* for you. Everything was for you. Even organising the demonstrations were because we wanted you to have a better life if you ever wanted to go back to Val Verde." The rosy-cheeked picture of his mother, hair tied back, sunglasses on, as an infant Frankie sat on his father's shoulders made sense now. The music and the boisterous atmosphere, bobbing along like a kite, tethered to his parents, striding and singing as they washed along with waves of brightly coloured compatriots.

"We're not angry anymore, now we've had time to figure it out."

"But don't you want to leave here, to be free? I put you in here because I was selfish."

"Of course, yes, we want our liberty but we are also patient."

"And good at hiding!" Mamá added.

"Yes, yes, and they have put us to work too - we insisted! Your mother and I help with liaising with other Val Verdeans in the UK, we meet them here, listen to them, try to do what we can to ensure that they are okay. It puts a roof over our heads!" He was so buoyant; I swore that he actually enjoyed being incarcerated like this. "But we have it on good authority that all this will change with the upcoming elections, so... And the staff here are working on retracting the extradition treaty too. We see ourselves as two of the luckier ones. Others were not so fortunate and were taken back."

"What have you been doing though? We have only been able to find out small things, here and there." Mamá attempted to lighten the mood, and Papá's face changed from a scowl to a beam.

"Yes! We know you were placed with a family but what now?"

"Um, well, I'm studying Philosophy at the University of Birmingham." A lie but I knew they would be proud that I had advanced my academic career. Don't tell them about the knife. "I'm living in a flat with a couple of, uh, friends - Chelsea and Ollie." Do not tell them about the knife. "I've been busy with reading and, oh yes, I got a job in a coffee shop," Knife. "which is in the middle of the, uh, city centre, so...." Knifey knifey. "uh, yes, that's, that's about it, I guess..." Knife? I turned to Eva. "Is that... ah... is that right?" Her eyes appeared to be almost completely white.

"Yes, yes, I think that about covers it."

"I'd ask you the same," I ventured, "but..." Fortunately, we could all muster a small laugh.

"We're just happy to see you, both of you, because we want to help if we can."

"Yes, sorry, Frank... Francesco, there is a legal matter I have to explain to all of you and I wanted, needed, you all here together so that you can decide, together, how you would like us to proceed."

Eva pulled up an upholstered stool that matched the sofa's dusky pink colour and sat at the head of the table. Señor Suplente plonked himself down next to me, with my parents on the opposite side of the glass-topped furniture. She spread out documentation in front of us, so thick with printed text that it looked like Marmite on white toast.

"There is a small opportunity for Francesco to be able to remain in the country. The only way he can stay in the UK is if he can prove that he has family living here already." They all leaned forward as we looked intently at the pages in front of us but, it turned out to be so indecipherable that we all looked at Eva for answers instead. "This would be fine if your parents were living on British soil without risk of their own deportation, but they are not. The decision you all have to reach is whether Frankie is deported by the Home Office or the Cualquieras relocate to a residency in the UK to ensure that Frankie stays here." Eva must have thought nobody would notice but I did. Her right hand pressed my left knee and then she withdrew it without hurrying or making eye contact.

"Hold on though, I thought we were speaking to my parents to try and get a copy of my birth certificate. I'm a British citizen, I was born in Druids Heath, wasn't I?"

It was at that point I knew something wasn't right. My parents shared a knowing glance. Their answer did not come quickly.

"We had to run," Papá explained. "There was no time to go to a hospital."

At first it didn't register what he was saying. But, when I didn't respond, he must have taken my blank stare for an expectation that he would continue. "We crossed the border at Mentira. The border is only patrolled where there are roads or railways, nothing like that there. We had to stay off of the roads. There was a shallow river, but the bridge had guard posts on either end so we had to hide in the bushes until the tide was low. We nearly got stuck in the wet sand but we kept running, through the night, as best we could. I had a friend in El Escondido who could help us for a day or two, so we went there but it took all night and through until morning until we got there and your Mamá, she was pretty far along. We had to get to

Maiquetía, in Caracas, to make a flight to Madrid and then on to London. Spain had an extradition treaty then but England did not so we had to use fake passports. We picked them up on the drive east, and we had to swing south to make the lake crossing. My friend knew a guy who knew a guy from south of the big lake who helped. You remember?" Mamá nodded and hmm-ed. "I had to tell the driver to stop at a petrol station about six times until we found one with a photobooth. I don't think the glue was even dry when we got to the airport."

"Your father loves a good story."

"Anyway, on the road, your contractions started, didn't they? We didn't want to risk a hospital because they would take details that might lead the police to us and they might have kept us in for a few days."

"It was my choice. There was no way I wanted to risk being separated from my first-born child. So, I told Gervaso to stop the car and I had you in the back seat. I had to lie about your age to get on the flight."

The feeling that I had been lied to and the truth concealed from me would ordinarily be more profound. However, the way they told the story and the fact that I had not quite yet gotten over my own guilt about what I had done, meant I listened intensely without judgement.

"We lied to you because it was the only option we had. You were a child and did not need to know the truth. And we did not want you to go back to what we left behind; we were poor, we lived in fear, all for being members of a union and speaking up when things happened that hurt others."

"What if you had been asked? You might have given away that we were from Val Verde and then we would all have been in trouble?"

Eva intervened, sensing that we might continue on a tangent without resolving the key issue of my residential status. "I'm afraid the choice you have is between a skinny dog or it's fleas." Papá snorted and Mamá tutted at Eva's clever idiom. "Either Francesco gets to stay but the two of you will need to come out of hiding and, in all likelihood, be deported as there is an outstanding order on your deportation that has to be served. Or, the two of you can stay safe here but Francesco will be taken by the Home Office to a detention area and then sent back to Val Verde."

In contrast to his upbeat mood whilst retelling his anecdote, Papá exhaled and slumped. Whatever was decided, someone would lose.

Chapter 30 – Wednesday 22nd June (1 day to go...)

Despite Eva's well intentioned desire for an urgent decision to be made, neither my parents nor I could bring ourselves to make that choice. We spoke more about what life was like inside the embassy and, whilst they spent their whole lives in a confined space, even though it was spread over several floors, the accommodation they showed me was very comfortable, albeit not as luxurious as the rest of the diplomatic space. It became clear I had little more to tell them about what I had done with my late teenage years and, under my own scrutiny, my lack of activity beyond lectures and work bored even me. I couldn't tell them about Ernesto, the *tumi*, or any of that; it was bad enough that I was a criminal, but making them an accessory would have only made things worse.

We parted with hugs as needful as when we met. Knowing that they were safe - alive, even - and somewhere I had every right to visit unaccompanied, now that I knew I was Val Verdean, meant I could leave with a newly discovered peace of mind. *Jus sanguinis*, as Eva explained, meant that if both of my parents were Val Verdean, then the law should consider me to be the same. That would change when I got my passport from Ernesto but that would not prevent me from seeing my parents. In fact, it would mean that because I could stay in the country, I could see them more often.

There was more to say between Eva and I but we couldn't have our conversation at the embassy. Suplente escorted us through the building and was keen to show his willingness to help, if he could. He reassured me that my parents would be kept safe and, if we agreed that they would leave, he would help with finding a place to live. It was a nice gesture but we knew that there was a high likelihood that they would not be able to stay at any new found accommodation for very long before being deported.

"There is one other thing you should think about," said Eva. This time, there were no documents between us on the train table to take her focus. "If you get caught with the you know what…" she looked down the carriage aisle, "then there's no coming back. There's a chance you could get charged here and, if found guilty, you will definitely get deported. Then you would not have any right to return. If you are not convicted, you could come back in two years, possibly, but probably not at all."

The threat of actually being caught had dissipated whilst we were at the embassy but it had never truly left. Now it returned like the smell of cooked fish in a microwave.

"There are other considerations too, of course. If you were to leave voluntarily, and if you could buy your own ticket to Val Verde, then you could come back within 12 months."

I caught my reflection in the window and, for the first time, noticed how red and puffy my eyes were. Was it emotion or tiredness?

"You can appeal whilst you are detained. If we can build a case that you've been in the UK for your whole life, are integrated in the UK, and it would be difficult for you to integrate into life in Val Verde, then there's a chance that you would not be deported. There's no guarantee it would succeed and, if you did choose to appeal and lose, you can't come back for two years. That doesn't take into account any criminal charges."

"If you had told me all this a few months ago, I don't know if I could have made a decision." I thought I looked pensive staring out of the window, as London disappeared from view, but she might have interpreted me as being simply gormless. I jumped in to prevent that idea crossing her mind. "And if I was convicted, how long would I have to serve?"

"Definitely longer…"

"If my parents can spend four years in isolation, then I'm sure I could get by for one in Val Verde..." I thought I sounded noble, but who was I to judge? I didn't want to seem resigned to my fate because there was still the passport to get from Ernesto. If I could trust him and if he did let me down, then I still had a decision to make with my parents; I couldn't talk for them but the choice was obvious to me. "But it won't matter when I get my passport so there's no use worrying about it." She smiled.

There was still another problem to overcome though before I would need to decide on what to do next and there was so little time to come up with any kind of scheme to avoid having to give Ernesto the *tumi*, even if it was going to be a facsimile of the original. I had to hope that Ollie's plan paid off and Ernesto didn't smell a rat.

"Are you worried about tomorrow?"

"Yes." I hesitated. "But let's not talk about it. I've got plenty to be grateful for today and I don't want to ruin it. Thank you, I don't think I ever said it to you, but thank you for tracking down my parents. And arranging all this. It's too much to ever be able to repay you for." It was my turn to reach for her, and I held her hand. She did not pull away.

"It's easy for me to isolate different things. Trying to help you to stay in the country is not connected to you stea... to the knife. You might have done something incredibly stupid that I told you not to and totally disagree with and am very angry with you for doing because you promised to me that you wouldn't, but," she finally took a breath. "That doesn't mean you deserve to be deported or for me to keep your parents' safety to myself."

"But they are connected. If I give it to Ernesto, I get a passport, everything will be fine." She shook her head but didn't need to say anything she hadn't said before. "Okay, maybe not everything but, in general, I will have a British passport and the Home Office won't be able to deport me."

New Street had never seemed welcoming; in fact, large parts of Birmingham had a downright antagonistic feel to them, but I was relieved to be home. What was strange was that it *was* my home right up until I was told it wasn't. The magic of Druid's Heath was gone because now I knew the truth that I was born somewhere between Escalón, Val Verde, and Caracas, Venezuela. Maybe nobody knew exactly where I was born and, for the first time in my life, that eternal, permanent touchstone of my birthplace was removed. There was no existential dread, no confusion about my identity, it was only a small fact about me that was now no longer known. Bitten by curiosity, I had Googled several questions about identity and nationality on the train home and fallen into a rabbit hole of different terms and websites. Interestingly, I discovered, there were such things as Skyborns - people born in mid-air - who, technically, were born in a part of the world that had no international borders. They were stateless. Whilst the same law applied to me also applied to them, *jus sanguinis*, I was intrigued by the concept of being defined no longer by my nationality, or heritage, or race. I could be just me without the baggage that came from being all of that.

I invited Eva over, despite her previous eventful visits being fresh in our minds. She decided against it, saying that she was tired out from the long day. Had I had things go my way, perhaps I would have missed the exchange in the morning, but Eva's decision not to follow me upstairs put paid to those fantasies.

Chapter 31 – Thursday 23rd June (Brexit Referendum Day)

"You ready?" Ollie called through the door. "You up?" He didn't know that I had been awake since three and then half four and then from six. I swung my feet on to the floor and took stock of my room. Eight plastic tubs, stuffed to their limit and stacked on top of one another, stood in place of my model village. The pasting tables were collapsed and leant against the wall. An expanding tool box protected the brushes, hand drills, hot wire cutter, pliers, and so on. The vast, complex world I had built painstakingly over the past few years had been reduced to no more than a square foot or so of floor space. It reminded me of a funeral - the cremated remains sloshing around inside an urn are all that's left of the years and months and weeks and days of lived experience. So much can become so little so quickly.

Aside from all that stuff, I had a double-wardrobe full of clothes and a stack of books and that was all I possessed. If what I owned reflected the life I'd lived, it was a pretty empty existence.

But I didn't intend to spend Noah's cash on more stuff just for the sake of it. I didn't have any ambition to become like the Pharaohs; untold ill-gotten wealth and surrounded by it for their journey into the afterlife. I came to realise that it wasn't the contents of my urn that defined me but the people I had around me. And I was far from dead yet.

Upon entering the living room, I was met with the sort of a sense of animosity you might have encountered walking into 1990s Sarajevo; Chelsea was metaphorically draped in a Serbian flag although literally draped in an

EU flag, which matched her blue gym leggings, blue and yellow hooped leg warmers, and gold star deely-boppers. Ollie - metaphorically in a Bosnian flag - had chosen nothing quite so eye-catching as Chelsea but did opted for a Union Flag t-shirt under his Harrington jacket, which was adorned with a spattering of patriotic pin badges. One could quite reasonably infer from this that their relationship was beyond saving. I donned my invisible blue helmet and tried to avoid the crossfire en route to the kitchenette. It wasn't worth getting drawn into the conflict for tea and toast.

"What are your plans, mate? Only me, Mayhew and the lads are thinking of having a few beers this afternoon. You know, to celebrate." Chelsea rolled her eyes at his clumsy emphasis.

"Don't know. Make the swap and play it by ear from there." Ollie pulled out a bundle from behind his back. It looked like a particularly uncomfortable cardboard dildo.

"Here you go," he enthused. "I wrapped it up - bubble-wrap, sellotape, brown paper, the lot, as you would do if it was real." I offered my thanks and returned to the toaster.

"Uh, Francesco, you know you are welcome to come and have a few glasses of bubbly with the girls and I once we have finished at the vote. It'll be a lot of fun." Ollie glared at her but she ignored him and smiled as wide as she could.

"I'll let you know - I'll let you both know."

Ollie left first, with fewer accessories to carry. Chelsea followed soon after with a loud hailer, a rolled-up vinyl banner, a placard made out of card, a broom handle, a long vine of tinsel, and a hamper with snacks in. It might only have been nine o'clock but I was as sure there was wine in the hamper as I was sure that Ollie, Mayhew, and 'the lads' would be congregating at the Head In Clouds for a few cheeky pints, as it was the only watering hole open this early. Considering my somewhat uninspiring breakfast, I felt as if I could do with a stiff drink, but those momentary thoughts were quickly overwhelmed by concern for what I had to do next.

Knife? Check. Mask? Check. Eastpak backpack? Check. I had everything I might need for this morning. Once I had gotten dressed, I would leave. I checked everything again. What about the weather? Would it rain? Would I need an umbrella? No, no, come on Frankie, just go. With a shaking hand, I jerked open the front door.

New Street was noisy. All along the side where Scintilla fronted out towards the crossroad with Lower Temple Street were several groups of people. A retinue of Chelsea's hangers-on were in the midst of them. Almost without exception, they wore various combinations of gold and navy clothing, or had hair dyed blue - or sea green in the case of some who had peaked too soon and ended up showering some of the colour out. Spirited chants broke out arhythmically and died down soon after. Flags were worn like capes and soft drink bottles were surreptitiously passed along for a concealed swig, under the watchful eye of the police. The Remainers, with their doe-eyed hopefulness, were treating the day like a music festival. Such was their confidence and their conviction that their cause was the logical one and, therefore, the only one anyone could support, that they wandered in and out of their fiefdom without concern. A few strolled up the street and on to the Victoria Square, where the polling station was situated, or into the supermarket, ambling back with some baguettes, soft cheese, and a family-sized bag of Kettle chips.

A row of fluorescent jackets banked the blue river, strung out all along the length of the main shopping street, like they were morse code on a plain sheet of paper; dot, dot, dot, dash, dash, dash, dot, dot, dot. Yet there was so little activity to draw the attention of any of the officers, they seemed almost out of place. They bore the look of teachers on a Year 8 day trip - put upon expressions, eagle-eyed and short-tempered, but actually just glad for a change in their normal routine.

Behind the cordon, across the crossroads was the Head In Clouds. Outside that, huddled in their own group, around tall tables and bar stools, were the other side, the Leavers, the patriots. From a distance, they appeared not too dissimilar to the Remain group - apart from the flags. They too were eating and drinking; pints and chips, in their case. Rather than dyed hair, there was a smattering of bald heads, like an open egg carton. The atmosphere there was jolly too; they had their own police officers who were keeping an eye on them, but rather than attempt to ignore the thin blue line, they were engaged in harmless banter. The gulf between the two groups was not so large that songs from the pub could not be heard. The Leavers started heroically with 'Jerusalem' but it got garbled the longer they went and everyone was confused by the third stanza so it morphed into 'Land of Hope and Glory' for some and 'Vindaloo' for others.

Navigating their way around or through the boisterous cliques was everybody else. Some who may have cared, many who didn't, but all, it seemed, simply trying to do a bit of shopping in peace or get to somewhere more tranquil.

I looked carefully at both sets of congregated groups but could not make out Ernesto. I wasn't sure which decision he would lean towards, if he was able to vote. I checked my watch. The shoulder strap tugged, reminding me of how important my cargo was. My arm straightened to my side. Oh God, a tan-skinned man with a rucksack, checking his watch, in a public space, surrounded by police. That was a recipe for application of lethal force if ever there was one.

I could appear nonchalant, couldn't I? You don't want to be especially conspicuous in these situations. I tried whistling, and I never whistle normally. There I stood, frozen to the spot, whistling out of tune. A police woman in a thick black jacket and a small bowler hat turned and frowned at me. Damn. What if I walked whilst I whistled? Scintilla looked like a safe space, so I very casually strolled in that direction, trying to land on a recognisably off-hand tune. There we are, all good, nothing to see here, officer.

I had to check my watch again. This time, clever me, I looked at my phone instead. Throw them off the scent, and all that. I was early. There was still half an hour to wait. My feet tingled and my legs jangled. I needed to sit to keep still. Or maybe if I kept moving that would be less suspicious?

"You alright, mate? Oh! Sorry, didn't mean to startle you." It was only Rob.

"Hey! Hey, Rob, yeah, good thanks, yeah, good to see you. What are you up to?" He looked blankly at me. I realised he was holding his motorbike jacket under his arm and he wore the brown Scintilla polo. "Ah, right! Work. Of course."

"Yes. And you?"

"Me? Ah, I thought I'd come out and see what all the fuss was about with this Brexit thing."

Rob snorted. "Load of rubbish, mate. Doesn't matter what happens - nothing will change for us, eh? See you later." I smiled as he went inside and took a seat in the al fresco area outside the coffee shop. There was no way of knowing how long Ernesto might be. I told myself that there was nothing to be nervous about. Except whether or not he would figure out that the *tumi* was a fake. Whether or not he would come through with my passport. Whether or not Marcos would grab me by the nape of the neck and turn me inside out, like a giant banana. And it wasn't nerves; it was excitement, it was anticipation. I texted Eva. She still needed to be here, that was why.

Killing time was easy for me, ordinarily. This was an unordinary day though. By the time it was ten to ten, I was already out of my seat and walking up to the square. The polling station was opening and the two sets of groups were gradually making their way in the same direction as me. Bags and placards banged against my legs and shoulders but I could not let them distract me. Voices were raised and the songs from the Remainers got louder and more urgent. If I drifted too close to them, the Leavers would eye-ball me. If I got too near to the Leavers, I worried one would bear hug me and cajole me into their football chants. Plastic pint glasses cracked underfoot and shoppers darted into shops to clear a path.

It was hard to tell if anyone was the instigator but the procession surged ahead now. The mobs of red and blue and blue and gold bled into one another so that it was hard to tell who was who. I clutched my backpack, which I chose to wear across my chest. The two- or three-minute walking time doubled towards the bottleneck of Greggs and Nando's. Check-shirted, red-faced men forged a bow wave that others followed through. Pale and lean Remainers recoiled in the wake, righted, and then shadowed.

An enthusiastically shaken can of flat lager, the ring pull yanked off, but the foamy head dribbling weakly out. Hitting the square, the groups - perhaps upon remembering that there was a lack of a decent pub - scattered and coagulated and scattered again, all at a loss of what to do and where to go. The police officers, buffeted along like bobbing apples, attached themselves to likely looking contingents, hoping to quash any potential unrest with their mere presence.

Ernesto was not wrong when he said there would be plenty of people. The Remainers, seemingly more easily persuaded by one vocal leader, orbited close to Nando's and then made their way along the right-hand side of the square. It seemed as though someone had spotted a wine bar that would sell take out. The Leavers, far louder but with less consensus, scattered to the left, until some realised that they could hang around the Greggs, the Eat, and a small bar that would serve pints in plastic bottles. I didn't need to have a particularly vivid imagination to sense what might happen to them once their contents had been seen off. As the Europhiles squeezed through the ever-decreasing exit from New Street, their political rivals started up braying and jeering.

Extensive fencing blocked off any chance of a serious crowd forming. Those who had registered to vote walked up the steps, past the female statue in the fountain - 'the floozie in the jacuzzi', I heard someone call it - and towards the city council building.

From the same direction, I saw Ernesto and Marcos walk towards me. Ernesto held a blue Eastpak rucksack tightly in one hand. The pantomime booing got louder and I was compelled to advance towards them, to avoid being caught up in anything. Where was Eva? With a jerk of his head towards me, he veered off following a group of Remainers who were dancing up the steps and towards the town hall. They may have been happy to be there or relieved to be escaping the attention of a few of the tougher-looking Leavers. After all, they had rolled their checked sleeves up so, you know, read into that what you will...

I had to scamper to avoid losing them within the crowd. They were in amongst it now; the back of Marcos' leather jacket shrouded by arms waved in the air, flags swirled around, and golden deely-boppers doing exactly what they were designed to do. With a hop, I darted up the first few steps - moving more freely than in the smart trousers I had worn at the exhibition - and swerved between the demonstrators who were mid-conversation. I was too quick to hear any criticism and I ducked under a placard and was down a side street, out of the main body. It seemed just as busy at first but, after a minute or two, the mass of bodies cleared away and I could see Marcos and Ernesto up ahead. The latter turned, looked at me, smiled, and carried on ahead.

Was I being led on a wild goose chase, I wondered? No, surely not. Ernesto must still believe that I have the *tumi*; there would be no benefit to him in keeping me moving around like this.

The crowd of protestors and students and other people with seemingly very little to do in the middle of a Thursday, hove into view again at the end of the street. How had they managed to get ahead of me? But, no, there was the cathedral and an oasis of green around it. This must have been a different group, I reasoned, and I soon realised that they were taking advantage of the warmth and picnicking in the church grounds, rather than get into any kind of confrontation on the square. Ernesto jinked left across the road, not quickly, but with purpose. I almost lost them as my phone rang.

"Eva?"

"I'm at the square. Where are you?"

"Erm..." I searched for a street sign. "Waterloo Street. I'm heading towards the cathedral."

"Why? You said meet me here?"

"I know, but Ernesto wants me to meet him up here." As someone came out from an office, I lurched into the road to evade them.

"I'm going to wait for you here. This is stupid."

"No, come on, please. Just come and do this break up for me and I can get my stuff and then we can go. I'm sure it won't take long." She hung up. I prayed that that was a good sign. I darted between parked cars to cross the road then swung round the corner and nearly ran straight into the two of them. Or rather, in the case of Marcos, bounced off.

"Francesco. You made the right decision." I think I will be the judge of that, I thought. "Where is your girlfriend?"

I snorted. "She's not my girlfriend." That showed him. "And she's coming. She'll be here soon." The flow of demonstrators wavered, with many distracted by the appeal of the peaceful oasis of greenery that encircled the church almost as much as the hordes of people spilling out onto the pavement from the pub we stood outside. That was just typical, wasn't it? Anything significant in my life had to involve alcohol.

"You have the *tumi*?" I watched Marcos as I slipped off the rucksack. Ernesto could not break his gaze from it.

"It's in here. Don't you worry." I waited for a pedestrian to pass. "Have you got my documents and my passport?" Ernesto nodded. "Then let's get on with it."

"Not so fast. I want Eva to be here first. Marcos, *tomar algunas bebidas*."

"*Si - ¿una servir, señor?*" Marcos rocked his granite like skull back, let out a single chesty guffaw, and went inside.

"*Cerveza...zoguete...*" I mumbled. Ernesto, arms crossed, sat upright on the high chair, surveying me. He still possessed that aura of composure and regal poise that had instantly impressed.

"How are you going to get the *tumi* to Val Verde? I suppose you want to take all the glory and lead the new government?" I rubbed the palms of my hands together, gripping the thumb intermittently.

"I can explain my plans to you once Eva is here. I don't want to have to repeat myself for her benefit."

Neither of us had too long to wait. Eva came from the same direction I had and Marcos had taken no time at all to get a round of drinks. He thumped all four of them down on a high table. Eva squinted her eyes and marched towards us. I swallowed a mouthful of lager to steady myself.

"Welcome! *Señora Estrellas, ¿cómo está?*"

"Fine. What did you want to see me for?"

"Miss Estrellas, Mister Cualquiera would like to show you something. What's in the bag, Francesco?" I frowned and glanced towards the road. I looked past Marcos, through the gloom of the towering window pane. Then I hoisted my backpack onto my lap. Ernesto shuffled closer, barring any view of the contents to passing pedestrians.

The brown paper package made a full-bodied thud on the table top, despite the thickness of the wrapping Ollie had done. I didn't let go.

"Now, where's my passport?"

Marcos grabbed the *tumi* and, without any obvious exertion, yanked it out of my grip.

"Don't worry, Francesco, I have it all here. But let us see what a wonderful present you have brought to us first."

Marcos stripped the tape back from one end and slid the sharp side of his hand under the flap of brown paper. The glittering blade nicked his thumb. He barely reacted, sneering with disdain at the weakness of his own injury.

Satisfied, Ernesto lifted his matching backpack up and opened the main compartment. "But first, don't you have something you need to say to Miss Estrellas?"

I couldn't believe he was going to make me go through with it. He knew we weren't together. It was just demeaning or maybe he got some grim satisfaction out of this whole business.

"Do I really have to?" His silent sneer told me the answer. "Okay. Eva, listen." I put my right hand under her left elbow. "I'm sorry but…" I turned back to Ernesto and saw his scowling face. Marcos had a mischievous smirk too as he quaffed a pint of whatever it was he was drinking. The *tumi* was on top of another table but, this time, I was sure it would not break anything apart any more. It had bisected our dining room table as well as Eva and I, not to mention the fact it had made a criminal of me and my flatmates. In the past eight weeks, a rift had been created between the life I had made and my new reality. There was no way back to University, as far as I could see, and my own sense of self was revealed to be a fantasy. I was sick of division, whether it was Ollie and Chelsea, me and my parents, Leavers and Remainers, enough was enough.

"No. I'm not doing it. Eva, I love you. I don't care what these two muppets do. I'm sorry I lied to you and I'm sorry if I've disappointed you but I want us to be together."

Marcos choked. Ernesto sniffed. But the only response that mattered was Eva.

"Ha, you've got to do better than that if you want me back but it's a start." She pecked me on the cheek. "Now what, *Señor* Benemerito?"

"You're not as intelligent as I thought, Francesco. You don't want to upset me, do you?"

"Does it matter? You can take your *tumi* - all it's done is bring me problems. I'll take that passport now." I held out my hand.

"Not so fast." Ernesto picked up the package and I felt my neck rise in temperature. "Let's just see what you have for me. If I can't have Eva, I will have this *tumi* and I think I'll keep the mask too. I need both for the reward, don't I?"

"What do you mean?" queried Eva.

Ernesto peeled away the rest of the packing tape from the other end and the top layer of wrapping paper, smeared with Marcos' blood. He laid it all flat on the table and began unpicking the bubble wrap with far more care than his compatriot. The glisten of metal reflected through the lens of the curved pint glass, augmenting the glow of the lager inside it.

"Perfect." Having removed the wrapping entirely, Ernesto examined the pommel and the carvings of *Maximón*. "Absolutely perfect."

"You really think it's smart to wave that around here? In public?"

"Ha, come along now, Francesco. Do you really think these people know anything about South American art?"

410

"No, but they might know about the reward on offer."

"What do you mean 'reward'?" insisted Eva.

"You must have seen the news, no?" Ernesto intervened. "That American imbecile, Noah Wright, he is offering ten thousand pounds for information leading to the return of these stolen items. He can keep his filthy money. What is it worth to someone who has the destiny of a nation in the palm of his hand? We can leave *este maldito país* with its awful weather, boring food, and constant complaining behind."

"What about the Yarina?" demanded Eva.

"I have not forgotten about them, Francesco, they are your parents' people. They've spent the last few hundred years in hiding, one more Presidential cycle won't make a difference, will it?"

"But you said you wanted to make a difference? To overthrow Calderon?" She turned to Marcos. "*¿Y ese cabrón de Calderon?*"

"He knows as well as me that change does not come solely through symbols, like this *tumi*. Change needs money and a bit of madness. I don't need *el Partido* to become the next President, with their democracy, meetings, votes, and nonsense. The solution is so simple; I return the *tumi* as a hero - after all, it was I who liberated it from the colonial oppressors. We unite the Yarina around the symbol, the freedom it represents, give them something to hope for. And then? Then we destroy it."

"What? Destroy the *tumi*?" I couldn't understand what he meant at first.

Tears welled in Eva's eyes. "*¡Maldito gilipollas!*
You promised us that you were going to fight *for* the
Yarina not use them for anarchy! What about
WMSCACE, huh?"

"Hah, of course you are angry, you are proving my
point. The Yarina do not simply flock to the polling
stations - they get ma*d, enfadado*, *enfurecido*! So long as
I make myself the saviour to them, then the victim, they
won't cast their vote but tear down the polling stations."
Eva's words stalled in her throat as Ernesto continued.
"Where's the harm in telling you? We have already got
our plans in motion. All I must do is appeal to the Yarina
for calm, whilst blaming Calderon's men for the
destruction of the *tumi*. At the same time, I know enough
of the older, traditional elites to convince them that I am
the only one who can assure peace and stability as a
leader who puts law and order to the forefront of their
campaign. With the Yarina beside me and the wealthy
upper-classes shifting their support, Calderon will have to
step aside."

"What about all the donations we gave you? The
money we raised?" She gripped the edge of the table,
turning her knuckles white.

"Seed money. To get us started. We needed money
to show the old industrialists that we mean business. You
keep your stupid ideals, your dreams. What are they
worth? *¡Nada!* You can't change the world, Eva Estrellas,
with dreams and wishes. You need money and you need
power."

"What power do you have?" I asked. "You'll be in
charge of a divided nation."

"So what? You think politicians make money from keeping everyone happy? They make it from conflict. Conflict creates business opportunities - and what better business than coffee. I give the *máscara* back to Mister Wright and he will have to show me some gratitude." He flattened the lapels of his blazer and smoothed down his roll neck. Marcos pulled their bag up onto the table and swapped it for mine.

"Democracy Coffee won't work with you, not if I have anything to say about it."

That caught Ernesto's attention. "What are you talking about?"

"Oh, did I forget to mention? I've got a new job. It's really very exciting. Noah Wright has appointed me as his personal advisor on Val Verde. What his Foundation can do to help the poor farmers. What suppliers they should work with. Where they should invest. Everything." Marcos had stopped drinking his beer.

"Ah, so *you're* this advisor friend you mentioned? Ah, *vale*. And you think I won't have his attention when I bring him the artefacts myself? Please, you are nothing to him - or to me."

"I told him I could get him in front of the President-elect of Val Verde. That's going to be you, right? But if you're not serious, I'm sure Eva and I can discuss moving Democracy Coffee's multi-million-dollar investments into Zulia instead." I looked at her and she looked back, with a devilish wink. "I understand that the area is trying to move away from oil money, right."

She nodded. "Absolutely."

He thought he had the artefacts which might have made him think he was temporarily well off, but he would not get rich without external investment. "What use would the *tumi* and the mask be if I was the first person to give Noah information that led to their discovery?"

Now he was pissed. "Very clever. Very clever. Okay, *hijo*, okay. Let me make you an offer. You tell him to back me and I'll give him the relics. Both of them. You do that, and I'll make sure Marcos here doesn't mess with your girlfriend. *Su novia*. Fair?"

Eva recoiled. Marcos leered and, for the first time, I could see that there wasn't only one knife at this meeting.

"Okay, deal. And I get my passport?"

"Of course," he grinned. "What would I want it for anyway?" Marcos shoved the bag towards me. I grabbed it, before he changed his mind or made some other threat. I practically tore open the top and looked inside. The documents were thrown onto the table - my driving licence, a phone bill, and so on - and I yanked out a palm-sized, thin, maroon booklet. The feel was new and firm, it was solid, real. I flipped it over and saw the gold lettering and instantly recognisable coat of arms. A circular shield, with the unmistakable outline of Mount Belmonte in the centre.

"What the fuck?"

"You wanted a passport. I got you a passport!" Marcos cackled and Ernesto quickly joined in. "You can go home now!"

Eva reacted fastest, tossing the contents of my drink all down Ernesto, yelling a curt obscenity at him. Ernesto simply reached out to Marcos and put his palm on the big guy's arm, which had snapped inside his jacket. The pommel of the stiletto poked through the flesh of his fist.

"I think that just about brings our meeting to an end, doesn't it?" He dabbed at his cashmere sweater with a napkin. "I won't lie by saying it has been pleasurable…"

"…That would be a first…"

"…But I will say that it has been memorable. Now, make sure to have that conversation with Mister Wright or it won't be beer that is thrown in someone's face next. *Adiós. Siempre.*" As they walked away, I held Eva's wrist but I felt the same rage as her. I wasn't ready yet to act on it.

"*Ese hijo de puta*, Frankie, we have to do something."

"I know, we will. Let me just get my head around this." The burgundy card-bound document had thrown me. I looked inside and, sure enough, there was my photograph, my name, my date of birth, and a place of birth. It said Mentira; where my parents said they had crossed the border into Venezuela. How appropriate that it was both somewhere I had no recollection of ever being and somewhere that straddled two nations.

"I'm sorry." Eva had realised what I had not comprehended yet but I was soon to realise what it meant.

"There's something you don't know," I admitted, now that we were alone. "The *tumi*. The one Ernesto has is fake. Noah had a facsimile made for the exhibition and Ollie got it and gave it to me."

"What? So he thinks he's got the real one?"

"Yes, incredible, right? If they're smart, the Yarina will spot it's a fake as soon as he tries to destroy it - and he can't even melt it down for money."

"This might seem a little crazy but, if you have the real one, and now you've got a passport, you could always go and inspire the Yarina yourself. There's nothing stopping you from copying Ernesto's plan yourself, except for the lunatic power grab, of course. There could be enough of them willing to come out of hiding for you to have your own political party. You heard what Ernesto said. It could be a nice life for you."

I would have been lying to her and myself if I had not fleetingly thought of that outcome but I felt the same as I had before I'd broken in to the museum; as if the thing I was thinking might happen was only a fantasy and there would be some inevitable intervention to prevent it from ever happening. When what you've experienced most recently is disappointment and rejection, you don't suddenly expect a miraculous moment of serendipity. I felt like I'd used up all my good fortune getting the *tumi* and then getting this far without being arrested. After, seemingly, getting Eva back, any more would be pushing my luck too far.

"No, I couldn't do that. I had better get home." Eva held my hand and I felt lifted. The pub was now overflowing with Leave voters, finishing off their dregs as the party atmosphere cooled. The churchyard remained

416

full of Remain voters, enjoying the sunshine, tossing a frisbee, and drinking rosé.

Both groups had their own vision of what the future would hold but delusions about how much power they had to influence it. Ollie stood on one side of the argument, with unwavering confidence in himself, and Chelsea on the other, with her unshakeable belief that whatever she was doing was morally right, and me, in between the two extremes, with no sense of power and no vision, but also having to accept decisions made by people I would never meet. Perhaps we were all the same after all. I looked one more time at my passport before stashing it in the rucksack with all of the paperwork. "This bloody country."

Chapter 32 – Friday 24th June

Eva helped me pack my things. She didn't ask about the plastic tubs stacked up already and I didn't tell her that I was going to throw them all away. I was putting my old life behind me. Tomorrow was supposed to be the day that I was going to be collected, for want of a better word, by the Home Office. That meant saying goodbye to my flatmates, my studies, my parents but also the sense of abandonment, my loneliness, even, to a lesser extent, the overwhelming feeling of powerlessness. Yes, I was going to be deported because of circumstances out of my control but I had gone past the confusion, denial and anger and on to acceptance. I had to hope that I had more control of what came next as it had to be possible to have more of a say about my future than I had of my present.

She threw me my shirts from the wardrobe and I folded them. When she could tell I was getting particular about how I organised the contents of my suitcase, she went and cracked open one of Chelsea's bottles of wine. We nestled together on the sofa.

It was the early evening when Ollie and Chelsea returned. Both were tipsy but they entered together, with a warm glow about them.

"Oh, hello you two," said Chelsea.

"You look like you've been having a good time," replied Eva.

"Well, we had a few drinks after the polls closed. There didn't seem any sense in being angry at each other now that the campaigning is all over." She looked briefly at Ollie and then slumped next to Eva - before spotting the bottle of wine and, rather than complain, went to the kitchen to fetch herself an empty glass. Ollie sat in his chair, a smirk etched across his face.

"What's up with you?" I asked.

"Nothing…" he said. "Just feeling good about life again." He glanced up at Chelsea, who was rinsing out a flute at the sink, and then leaned forward. "How did your meeting go?"

"Mission accomplished," I replied, keeping my voice to a whisper. "But there was one fly in the ointment. Ernesto pulled a fast one."

"What? How?"

"You want a beer, Ollie?" asked Chelsea.

"Yes - cheers, C."

"He gave me a passport alright but it's not a British one - it's a Val Verdean passport." The pale look of shock was abruptly replaced by a wave of pink as his face flushed and he burst out with a nasal, snorting guffaw.

"No. Fucking. Way." He saw Eva's was implacable and I wasn't particularly amused. "Sorry, shit, what does that mean?"

"He's still getting deported. But at least he can come back in a couple of years." Eva squeezed my arm and I acknowledged it by looking into her eyes.

"What are you lot talking about?"

"Nothing, C, nothing."

"Sure," she responded. "Sounds like nothing." She sat down again after passing Ollie his beer and clinked glasses with Eva.

"Frankie," Ollie said. "I had better come clean - I told her. About the *tumi* and Ernesto and all that."

"What? When?"

"When you two were down in London." He looked at the can in his hand. "I had had a bit to drink and I was trying to rebuild some bridges."

"What do you know?" Eva demanded from Chelsea.

She shrugged offhand. "I suppose I know everything - your little criminal endeavour, this Central American would-be President who has blackmailed you but who has promised to give you a passport, the Yarina? Is that right? Yes, the Yarina, who will rise up around the symbol of the *tumi* and change the dictatorship in Val Verde. Noah's identical duplicate of the *tumi*. Am I missing anything out?"

Ollie interjected. "Not quite, I didn't tell you about one thing." He ran his forefinger around the lip of his beer bottle. We all looked at him.

"You have to know that I don't really have that many friends. Mayhew and the guys, they're not what you'd call *friends* - it's all ribbing and banter when we're together, but I don't think it's because we like each other. It's... hard... but I suppose I've always known it. They're not very nice people." He sipped from the beer, as if to stop the words rushing out uncontrollably. "Frankie, I know I can be a bit of a dick." Chelsea couldn't resist an exaggerated nod. "If C and I hadn't fought..." he paused to glance at her. "Split up, then I might never have realised that you're basically my only mate."

"Where is this going?" interjected Eva, at just the point when I was hoping to get a really emotional moment with Ollie.

"So, because you're my mate and I didn't want you to get into any trouble, I did something. I just want to say before you get upset that I really meant it, I mean it, that I really wish you didn't have to go and I want you to come back as soon as you can."

"Come on, Ollie, spit it out!" urged Chelsea.

"I swapped the *tumis*. I gave you the real one and I put the fake one in one of the plastic tubs in your bedroom." We stared blankly at him. He paused, unsure it seemed as to whether he needed to wait for our response or to explain further. "Ernesto has the real *tumi*."

"What? How did you think that was going to help?" I demanded.

"It's not a crime to have a fake Yarinan sacrificial knife. It's probably made out of aluminium or something so it probably couldn't even slice custard. If the police traced it back to you - or me - then you're in the clear. Ernesto has the real one so we can always call the tip line and get him arrested. Sounds fair now he's stitched you up."

I rubbed my forehead but it didn't relieve the headache brewing inside me. "If he's got the real *tumi*, he can carry out his plan. He'll use it to control Val Verde."

"Man, I'm confused. Do you want him to have the real *tumi* or the fake one?" Ollie asked.

"The fake one - because if I give the real one to Noah, then I can show I can be trusted and deliver on my, our, promise to get it back to him. What better way to impress your new employer? Maybe he'll give me more responsibility too. I could do more to influence their investment in Val Verde. If Ernesto's got the real one and I give Noah the fake one, he could easily just have me arrested."

Eva chimed in. "Wait, so you still want to help the Val Verdeans and the Yarina, don't you?"

"Yes. I saw how passionate you were and realised how I was only going along with the curators and party guests because I assumed they were experts but then that's not going to improve anything. They might know a bit about the history of our people but they don't have any interest in helping them now."

"People in this country have had enough of experts…" piped up Ollie.

"Shut up, Ollie!" chimed Chelsea.

"And you think Noah and Democracy Coffee can help? Aren't they just as bad? Flying in, thinking they're saints, dishing out their money like blessings on the poor impoverished, uneducated masses, and then flying out again when they get bored or they find some other noble cause to stick their noses into?" Chelsea squirmed and Ollie found something particularly engrossing on the ceiling.

"No, I mean, yes, I agree with you but no, I don't think they're as bad, I think if I have a job in Val Verde that can direct where they spend their money, that's better than them not spending their money in the country, isn't it?"

Eva conceded with a tilt of the head.

"When we met up at the University library, you told me you wished you could make a real difference. To the Zulia, to the Marabinos, to try and get the oil money out of the region. I think what I'm doing is the same. It's just a different type of black liquid."

"Um, I've also got something I need to admit," chimed Chelsea, placing her half empty glass on the table.

"What is this? A Church Confessional?" joked Ollie.

"You need to hear this too, Oliver." That silenced him quickly. "Francesco, I have something to apologise for too and I suppose it doesn't matter if you know now but it does matter that you know." She picked up her glass again and then, reconsidered whether to take a revitalising swig, put it back down. "I also swapped the *tumi*."

"Shut up!" barked Ollie.

"I'm sorry but I had to. It was silly and selfish, I know, but, Francesco, you have the real *tumi* not the fake one."

"What is with this household." Eva muttered slumping into the sofa, as if she would rather be cradling her wine someplace else.

"I've not been totally honest with you, or you Ollie. You see, I really wanted the money from the reward so after Ollie told me that he had got the fake one from Noah, I thought I could take the real one, stash it somewhere, and get one of my Remain supporters to call the tip line or the Museum or whoever and claim the reward and split it between us. I couldn't do it myself, of course. I'm so sorry."

"Sorry you did it or sorry you've had to admit it?" asked Eva.

Chelsea hesitated. "Both, I suppose. My family has always been well off but not me." Ollie and I rolled our eyes at each other. "No, I mean it. My parents wanted me to go to Oxford or Cambridge but I decided to take my own path."

"To Birmingham University. That's in the top 17 Universities in the whole country?"

"Yes, Oliver. I thought I could cope on my own, without their connections and friends. But I can't." This really had started to take on the air of a group therapy session. I slumped down further, like Eva, resting my beer bottle on my chest.

"It started last month. You remember I wanted to show my solidarity to the doctors and nurses and went to that Junior Doctors' strike at the Queen Elizabeth? Well, I thought it would be a nice gesture to raise some money for them, perhaps to buy them lunch or something. I didn't really realise how much people love the NHS and we managed to get quite a lot of donations."

"How much?" Ollie asked.

"About two thousand pounds."

"For sandwiches?"

"Yes, I know, it was quite unexpected. But, you see, nobody knew I had raised the money and if it hadn't been quite so much, perhaps I would have gone to M&S and bought a load of sandwiches. Only it was a nice amount of money so I told everyone I would bring them some lunch the next day so I could have some time to think about what to do with it. Then the strike ended and it was all forgotten about and I still had the cash. I spent it, of course and I do feel guilty about it, but then I wanted more."

"But what about the *tumi*?" I pressed.

"I didn't know what Oliver was going to do, I swear. Or else, I would not have swapped the fake one for the real one. Or the real one for the fake one. I don't know whether I did it before or after Oliver, not that it really matters does it." She emitted a nervous giggle but stopped herself short.

We all sat there in bewilderment for a moment.

"Maybe Frankie can still get another pay-out from Noah…" offered Eva. "He wouldn't miss the money, would he?"

Without saying a word, I put my beer down, stood up, and walked into my bedroom. This time, I wasn't hiding from the outside world. I came back with the *tumi*, wrapped almost identically to the one I had given to Ernesto. It was, as Ollie said, in one of the plastic tubs of model railway scenery. I unwrapped it, tossing the paper and bubble wrap behind the sofa. I laid the gold knife on

425

top of the coffee table, checking with Eva that we wouldn't have a repeat of what happened last time.

"Well, what are you going to do with it now?" Ollie enquired.

"This time, I've got the plan Ollie, so don't you worry about it." I slugged back a mouthful of beer.

Chapter 33 – Thursday 7th July
(14 days after the Referendum)

I watched Kean hold the cardboard carton out, from which Goode took a takeaway coffee cup. Kean, with the carrier in one hand and a granola bar in the other, looked about helplessly as he tried to figure out what to do. Goode was engrossed in the Departures board, blowing across the top of the cup. Kean put down the granola bar and worked out how to get rid of the cardboard carrier without dropping his coffee.

People-watching was often amusing but more so when there were more people to watch. The two passengers who simultaneously, with great physical relief, sat down back-to-back on the bench seats and clanged the backs of their heads together, causing nearby passengers to turn in surprise and wince in sympathy. The teenager slumped against the foot of the wall, who only realised that the final call for boarding was for his flight after he took his headphones off, dashing up to make it in time, and was jerked backwards by his phone charger which was not yet ready to vacate its home in the plug socket.

My own misfortune was invisible to everyone else. I had two suitcases which had been checked in. Both Kean and Goode, dressed in their civilian clothes, had watched over me as I had gone through all of the hundreds of miniscule tasks that comprise catching a flight. They stood uncomfortably close by as I checked the bags in and collected my boarding pass. No such convenience as doing it online for me. They hovered as I was searched by security and my possessions were x-rayed. They refused to allow me a moment of peace and privacy when I had to use the toilet. Kean sat in a neighbouring cubicle and broadcast intermittent coughs, so that I knew he was still there.

They didn't enquire if I wanted a drink or a snack though so there were some limits to their intervention. However, if they had asked, I would have declined as I had no need for food or drink. I was satisfied, if not quite in a state of bliss. Considering all of my rotten luck and what had happened to me over the past two months and eleven days, you would have good reason to assume I might be furious, confused, dejected, or even completely insane. Instead, I had never felt better.

I only knew the exact time I needed to be at the airport when the warden at the detainment centre told me two days before. Communication with the outside world was limited as maintaining a wide network of friends and family seemed to be incompatible with the kind of people in this situation. At least not in the eyes of the Home Office. In their view, anyone here was here for a good reason. On the night of my arrival, I was allowed to make a phone call; I wasn't in the mood to do so. I was shown to my 12 foot by 8 feet room, met my cellmates, and discovered that Morton Hall, a former women's prison and RAF base, housed around four hundred people, all men. I was given a brief induction over the next couple of days, despite knowing that my stay would be brief, compared to most. There was even the generous offer of an English as a Second Language course. I had to sit through some life skills seminars, such as budgeting, which made no sense as none of us had any money to spend, and time management, which was ironic as many of the inmates had all the time to waste they would ever need.

I was allowed to make a phone call again once I knew when, and where, my flight would be departing. All I wanted to do was say goodbye one more time. I couldn't be sure when I would come back, or if I could come back. We weren't given a lot of time to email on the communal PCs or use the payphones, so I had to decide who I needed to speak to the most. I wanted to say something to speak to my parents, Eva, Ollie, even Chelsea, but whilst I had the deep desire to speak to a familiar voice, I did not have a clue what I would say. The choice to make one call made sense to me so I rang Eva. After all, she would be able to contact my parents and knew where I lived so could pass on any message to Ollie and Chelsea.

What we said between us was for us and not for this book. Some things, especially if they are intended to be romantic, are best left unshared. As for messages to pass on, I asked her to tell my parents that I loved them dearly, was glad that they would be safe in the embassy, and I would do everything to come back and see them soon. To Ollie and Chelsea, I wanted them to know that I was glad that we had the chance to live together and grateful for their kindness, past arguments forgiven.

I wondered whether that would be that and I would not get a chance to speak to any of them again until after I had arrived in Val Verde. As you might already be able to tell, I should not make any assumptions about how things might turn out.

My two escorts had arrived at Morton Hall and picked me up that morning. We had driven the ninety minutes or so with Goode in silent concentration as she drove and Kean fiddling with the radio, until he could find a station or song he liked. I put up with this for about five minutes before deciding that I should go to sleep - or

429

at least pretend to, to avoid the risk of Kean trying to embark on a friendly conversation with me.

They parked in the short stay car park and we went into the departure lounge. I paused to look at the illuminated departures board at the entrance but the two officers did not loiter and went straight to the security office, with me in tow. They checked in with some serious looking men in police uniforms, passing on some paperwork and engaging in light chit chat. We then left the office to sit in the main departure hall. In the two weeks I had spent incarcerated, there was practically nothing for me to do. I woke, I washed, I ate, I read. There were no other Val Verdeans there, although there were a few Latinos, so I tried practicing my Spanish. This was met, at first, by derision. I was glad to have lightened their moods, even if it was at my expense. Quickly though, they thawed once the understanding that we were all in the same rotten situation progressed to a shared hatred of the place. We got on well despite knowing our destinies were inevitably heading in different directions. So I was used to sitting down and staring into space. I had learned some meditation in anger management sessions, which I had never known I had needed until I learned about breathing techniques and visualisation. I even had the chance to learn a little more about immigration law, which I thought would help me understand Eva's career a little better, and it was, surprisingly, quite interesting and very useful. That said, it was still a shit hole that I wouldn't wish anyone to spend any time in.

The reason for my greatly improved mood was the welcome arrival of Chelsea, Ollie, and Eva to the airport. I had told her of my departure details and hoped, without knowing for sure, that she would find a way to be there for our last day together.

"I'm glad you made it!"

"We couldn't let you leave without saying goodbye properly." Eva skipped the last few steps towards me and threw her arms around my neck in an embrace that pulled her off the ground and lifted me what felt like a few inches above it too. Chelsea hung back and Ollie waited his turn to steal a bear hug.

"Alright mate."

"You didn't have to come - I would have called as soon as I had landed."

The people-watching I had zoned into whilst sat waiting with the Home Office officers reversed. The airport and the perpetual motion of people within it dissolved out of focus. All that mattered at that point was Eva.

"It's great to see you all. I wasn't sure whether you would actually come. I know it's a bit weird, isn't it, all this?" I was on the verge of rambling. Chelsea bravely stepped forward and spoke.

"We're all so sorry that you're leaving and we can't wait for you to come back." I sensed Kean and Goode, who were already standing and observing us all closely, fidget at the idea that someone they had spent several months looking into, meeting, and, finally, deporting, might so easily hop on a commercial flight back to the UK. "We're staying in the flat and we'll have to rent your room out, for now, but it will still be there for you whenever you can return."

I was grateful but my attention was all on Eva. "Have you heard anything from Ernesto or Marcos?" A nagging guilt that I could not do anything to keep her safe had never truly gone away throughout my imprisonment. I hated to admit it but the powerlessness I had felt about my visa, or lack of one, and the fallout from that diminished compared to the same dread I had for her. Having had time to mull over it all, I came to the realisation that it was more keenly felt because it was one single person I wanted to protect. It wasn't a vast, disconnected, and dysfunctional set of systems which would take years to correct; I was numb to that now, as if there was no point worrying about such things because there was no hope of being able to change them. Tens if not hundreds of people just like me would suffer the same fate, for more diverse reasons and circumstances than imply logic over the coming years. Until the cold data is replaced by humans again, the separation, isolation, and frustration will continue. Or until all of the people affected by faceless administration turn on it, refusing to deal with it, to such a scale that the soulless and disembodied call centres, server farms, and officious bureaucrats become redundant. Or the people simply light their torches and hoist their pitchforks and choose revolution over renovation but that's not the British thing to do.

Chelsea, Ollie, and especially Eva had never given me the impression that they needed me but I had needed each of them in their own ways. I didn't know if I would be able to repay them or express my thanks. However, I felt like if I could be there for someone when they had been there for me, then everything would work out. Perhaps that's how the revolution really starts; when one person decides to be there for someone else, whenever they need it and for whatever reason.

I was glad when she shook her head and smiled. "I've not heard *from* them but I have heard *of* them.

Chelsea decided to tell Noah the truth - that Ernesto had stolen the mask and the knife."

"I felt bad about what I had done and whilst I couldn't pay back the money I had stolen, I could do something good instead. I told Noah that you knew Ernesto and had suspicions about him and as soon as he tried to fly to Escalón, the authorities picked him up. He is extremely grateful and looking forward to working with you." Chelsea pulled out a piece of paper bearing the Democracy Coffee Foundation letterhead. It was the job offer to be his *Executive* Advisor for Operations in Val Verde.

"This is amazing! Thank you - I can't believe you came through with this... I don't mean to say, you know, I..."

"It's okay, Francesco, I know what you mean. I've not been the best of friends to you in the past but I hope that's all it is to us now - the past - and we can start again." I hugged her and she reciprocated. There was still a spark of what might have been but that short-lived relationship was a lifetime ago now.

"What are you going to do in Val Verde? Have you got somewhere to live?" asked Ollie.

"Yes, actually. That cash you gave me covered the flight and three months' rent in an apartment in Escalón. I've got my own place now so no need to shout at me for taking too long in the shower!" He gave in to the urge to fist bump me.

Kean made his presence felt over my left shoulder.

"Ahem, *señor* Cualquiera, we need to check in and go through security in five minutes."

"Alright, I won't be long," I said, wishing for another ten minutes. Self-consciously, I patted my jacket pockets. He retired to the nearest bench, with an overtly casual gait.

Once he was out of earshot, Ollie whispered; "And what about the *tumi*?"

All three of them paused to hear what I had to reveal.

"It's somewhere safe, that's all I'm going to say for now."

"Come on," he urged. "You can tell us."

I laughed. "I'm going to go one further than that." From my inside jacket pocket, I pulled out a square, red and white, piece of thick paper. At the top, in white capitals, it read 'Sorry We Missed You'.

"What's this?"

"The *tumi*. After what happened with the Students' Loan Company, I figured that if I posted it to my parents' old address in Digbeth, it would get redirected to the sorting office like their letter and then back to the sender but I didn't put a return address so it can't be tracked back to any of us. If you take this form along with a piece of my ID in less than six months' time you can pick it up." At which, I handed him my UK Driving Licence, as I wouldn't need that where I was going. "The *tumi*'s nicely wrapped up and safe. If Noah's got the fake *tumi* back, I assume he will have to put it on display, meaning nobody will be looking for the real one."

"Holy shit!"

"That is so smart," admitted Chelsea

"What should I do with it?"

"When I know what my address is, post it to me. I think I can put it to good use in Val Verde. After all, there are elections coming up soon and one of the parties might be deserving of a boost in the polls from a sudden influx of indigenous voters."

"Typical," chuckled Eva. "The Western saviour complex strikes again. The man from Great Britain is going to the undeveloped far-off land to change things for the better. When has that ever gone wrong?" I knew she was half-joking, but that was the half that hurt most.

"I know. But I'm not getting involved - politics was not my thing, these guys know that. All I need to do is return it to its rightful owners and whatever happens, happens. It will soon be their nation again so they can make their own choices."

"Hold on," chimed Ollie. "Three months' rent ain't ten grand. What did you spend the rest of the money on? They won't let you take all that cash out of the country, will they?"

"You're right, I can't move all of that money across borders. I bought my own flight, actually. Eva told me that if I choose to go, instead of taking it through the courts, then I only need to be out of the country for a year before I'm able to apply for a visa so that I can travel back and, now I have my Val Verdean passport, I can fill in the application after twelve months and cross my fingers that I get one officially."

"That's amazing! Well done," Eva added.

"And the rest of it?"

"The rest of it I'm not taking with me. In fact, I'm leaving it here for you to look after." I turned to Eva. From my coat pocket, I pulled a padded envelope. As I dipped down before her, I pulled out a silver engagement ring.

"Eva Estrellas, will you marry me?"

Chelsea and Ollie hugged each other. Kean and Goode peered over at what I was up to.

"What?" That wasn't the answer I had expected or hoped for.

"Eva Estrellas," I repeated, with less confidence than before. "Will you…"

"Get up, you idiot!" She pulled me up by my lapel and planted a kiss full on the lips, powerful enough to knock me back down again. "What do you think you are doing?"

"Asking you to marry me. Do they not do it this way in Venezuela?"

"Don't be ridiculous. But why are you asking me now? At an airport too? No, you need to do this somewhere properly, I have standards. It has to be romantic, not like this." Chelsea turned from swooning to sniggering and Ollie made thoroughly unsupportive facial expressions.

"I know, I know, but remember when I said I had a plan? Well, this is part of it. If you agree to marry me, then there will be no issues with getting the visa as I have a family member - a partner - here in the UK."

"So, I'm your green card?" She slammed her hands on to her hips.

"Of course! But I love you too and this makes perfect sense. If you say 'yes' now, I promise I will propose properly as soon as I get back and can organise something very, *very* romantic. *Muy romántica*."

She couldn't hide her smile for long. "Close enough."

About the Author

Mark E. Wilson is a child of the 90s so fondly remembers the concept of idealism and how seemingly plausible it was.

His first published work was in a poetry anthology about sport in 1995 – it was rubbish. A lengthy period was wasted before a play was penned for a small theatre group; the title of which was determined by the fact that they had already ordered all of the t-shirts for the kids to wear.

Having written an extensively poor collection of navel-gazing poetry throughout his teens, it made perfect sense to abandon that completely and start writing novels. Early work focused on lone assassins working for secret organisations which was abandoned just as the taste for SAS-inspired novels piqued.

He gained work experience at some of the world's finest literary publishers – working on such notable titles as *When Saturday Comes* and *World Soccer*, before embarking on a financially rewarding but morally draining career in media sales. Apropos of nothing, during this time he met his wife.

A major setback was the implosion of a much-used laptop, resulting in the traumatic loss of three heavily researched but inadequately plotted novels. This novel is an attempt to overcome such a hindrance and restart a writing career that has not so much been dormant like a volcano as been in deep hibernation like a tardigrade.

He is currently an English and Media Teacher having swapped his sales career for one which is financially draining but morally rewarding.

Printed in Great Britain
by Amazon